T0039301

American
States of China

JAMES HENDERSHOT

Order this book online at www.trafford.com
or email orders@trafford.com

Most Trafford titles are also available at major online book retailers.

Printed in the United States of America.

ISBN: 978-1-4907-5278-5 (sc)
ISBN: 978-1-4907-5277-8 (e)

Trafford rev. 12/17/2014

www.trafford.com

North America & international
toll-free: 1 888 232 4444 (USA & Canada)
fax: 812 355 4082

Dedicated to page

Dedicated to my wife Younghee with special thanks,
and to my son John and daughter Nellie,
and check in coordinator Heidi Morgan.

Contents

Chapter 01

Cindy

There stood a time, and then that time fell as another time began. The foolish questions of old vanished, no longer needing an answer. Once more, I find myself sitting on our front porch while watching the sun go down, and darkness covers our small-town. The Locust Streetlights shine over our street. Swarms of insects race to enjoy this defeater of darkness. Today was fruitful for me in that I had at least two hits in each game we played in the present-day. Our baseball field is a short walk in a nearby pasture we share with the resident cattle. These animals no longer invade our playing area, finding a hit baseball delivering a sting they believe is annoying. We are fortunate to enjoy so many friends who love to play, many swinging all day such as I do. Baseball is my life, the food for my soul and definer of my world. I watch extremely little TV, which makes me an outsider with my friends while they discuss the previous night's entertainment. Everyone in our family of Johnson's watch TV except for my father and me. I read my sports magazines and small stash of library books each evening while mentally reliving my performance on our baseball field during the games. My fielding has improved, especially after my father made me field baseballs without a glove. Fortunately, we shared this experience last November, and I mean every night the earlier November in our backyard. I never realized that my father could hit so many line drives. My mother claimed the greatest miracle was that so few windows were smashed. I spent five days in December fixing windows and painting the back of our house. Luckily, our house is wooden and not vinyl siding, which would have shattered from the blistering fastballs that zipped pass me. I learned the best way to stop a baseball is with my glove, backed up with my body. The agony of not stopping a baseball is greater to me than the baseball's impact when crashing against my body. I recognize my story is not a baseball story, although much that I learned on the field saved me while hiding in the wilderness. I believed this friend one day, then enemy the next, was like a hard hit baseball going to my head. Even though, I have once held this baseball, my enemy was using it to defeat me. I did not realize how deep into overtime this game would go, and how fast my home team audience changed to support what I hoped was simply a visiting team. They apparently enjoy their easy victories. Who would not enjoy a winning season, or better yet, who is happy when that season ends especially when it ends as the champions? Lives on the playing field and in the real world, both are determined by whom is winning. When you are out on a battlefield, you not merely leave that game, but also all future games. I have discovered my life requiring much flexibility to survive; therefore, my former foundations are like quicksand currently. I find it hard to concentrate and never plan my life presently saving my energy to survive. I am wise enough to recognize I am one of the few fortunate ones.

I suppose this story should boast a beginning, and this is a good place to start. I wish my computer still worked; however, an unexpected virus turned it into a gloried black screen. I scribble notes in my diary each hot afternoon just before my nap. My sleeping habits changed for survival purposes. The dark night hours are best for moving and scavenging. Most activities happen during the afternoon, thus keeping a low profile during the afternoons just plain makes sense. Stay away when they play and creep while they sleep will add days to my lives. My story begins November 2020 in my hometown of Marked Tree, Arkansas. My name is George Johnson, the oldest son of Randy Johnson and Francis Johnson. I am fifteen years old, just two years younger than my stepsister Lisa Jones is. My mother married Randy after she divorced Lisa's father. Her father fell into the hands of the law while caught in a Poinsett County wide drug bust. His time was extended because a deputy died in a car crash while attempting to apprehend him. Apparently, the deputies cannot handle the roads as our native hillbillies can. Most of those boys begin training when they are eight years old delivering their moonshine to the elder and drugs to the younger. Fortunately, for our family, my father grew up in a grain store hauling those huge bags of grain all over Marked Tree. When our father speaks, he does not have to open his mouth. One glance in his eyes and the fear of God floods our hearts as we drop to the ground begging for forgiveness. Our father does not waste his words on his children. He tells us what to do and we do it. This is not to say that he does not talk much, because, when he invites his friends to our home, they attempt to solve every problem in the world arguing every minute detail. Most arguments find a solution within a few days, except for the great argument of 2019, which continued for two months. That one was when our county got its first wave of Asian investors. Our two large grain mills went belly-up putting most of this county's workforce in the unemployment office. With so many having most of their disposable income zapped, local families stopped shopping, especially when considering how easy it is to shift back to living off the land.

Our stores began to close, with precisely one thing saving most from total disaster. A mystery group called Building a New America purchased the stores and vacant mills for pennies on the dollar. The local banks closed their doors not able to withstand the huge debt write-offs. My father, however, found himself overburdened with much overtime. He works on a large farm and handles their delivery tasks. Because they could no longer sell their grain in the local mills, he has to drive twenty-five miles south of the mills in Memphis. No one can pinpoint the reasons our mills went out of business. Most of our grain and livestock went to Asia; however,

China acquired huge sections of Australia, converting this land into an agricultural empire logistically practically in their backyard. Our local economy could not withstand the immediate drain of their cash reserves. Questionable expansions and lack of good decisions provided the energy to burn the life from our economy. Arkansas could have rebounded within six months with a modern company owning most of our commercial establishments. Building a New America updated our technological infrastructure and established markets in Africa for themselves. Our grain and livestock went down the Mississippi River, then through the Gulf of Mexico over the Atlantic Ocean to their receiving ports in Africa. Building a New America trained their local employees, so they could produce according to their needs. For the most part, they were invisible, appearing evidently in letters, emails, and phone calls. My daddy argued with his friends, yet no one could figure out how our town fell and how it came back to life. Employees once more had paychecks, although slightly reduced and increased workloads. Everyone believed this was better than no work and a mass exodus leaving empty homes and destroyed dreams.

Jumping back and introducing my immediate family, I possess two younger brothers, Fred Johnson, who is fourteen and Don Johnson, who is thirteen. We also have our baby sister, Julia Johnson, who is twelve. She has enough tomboy in her to keep her three brothers busy and enough charm to keep Lisa, and our cousin satisfied. The final person who lives in our house is Roberta Johnson, who is sixteen. She is the daughter of an uncle who died in a car crash. He had been drinking and lost control of his vehicle. Roberta's mother died during her birth. Roberta gets along fine when all my siblings and our parents. Sometimes Roberta will spend a week with our grandparents who live in a smaller house behind ours. We call their house the little house and our home the sizable house. My father told us that our grandparents raised his younger brother and him in our large house. When our mother gave birth to Fred and Roberta joined us, our grandparents moved into the little house and gave the big house to us. Roberta is the link between Lisa and us, as they always took turns babysitting. With two extremely beautiful hens such as Roberta and Lisa protecting us at school and in our neighborhood, we had all the peace we needed. We did not bully anyone nor did anyone bully us. Lisa and Roberta were dating the two strongest football players in our school. This provided enough muscles to support us, which gave us the confidence to seek our own independence.

The summers took all our rural friends into the vast fields laboring to provide and harvest the food for our livestock. I often wonder who really has the better end of this farm deal, the animals who live safe and feed or the humans who struggle and sacrifice serving them denying they were supposed to be the masters over them. The amazement does not stop here; these animals must be fenced, and their freedom restricted as they long to escape the land of the free food and travel into a world filled with predators who do not contribute to the lives they take. Luckily, Marked Tree had plenty of children to play baseball with us. During the summers, we had to resort to charms because the muscles that worshipped Lisa and Roberta were flinging hay and harvesting grain from the fields. They noticed the number of farms decreasing while the size of the fields increases and the size of the farm equipment increase. Production numbers became the talk of the town. Our parents saw an old world fade away as fears abound from rumors that Africa was moving faster into the new modern age. We felt so lucky that big money was pouring into our community scarcely to find we were barely holding pace with the rest of the world. One peace of mind afforded us was how Building a New America was buying the aged farms and allowing the old farmers to live on these farms until they died. They even acquired their livestock. This was appealing in the old farmers could pay off their farm debts and pass a bit of cash to their children, so they can get their degrees and set up in other cities. They were wise enough to recognize rural America was dying the future would be in urban America. Strangely, their ancestors told this same thing to each new generation since the Civil War. What was also odd was this current generation was the strongest financially, yet had the least assets. Their fathers received these farms from their parents, yet this generation would not receive the sold farms. This did not create any great concerns, in that most children considered the farms as chains keeping them prisoners in a land they did not want to live. The cash to resettle and freedom from a future in Poinsett County appeared to be a winning situation when viewed from the outside our area.

We foolishly felt special that a future was evolving in Marked Tree believing the greater prospects existed in Memphis, or for that matter, anywhere but here. Our history of continual struggle, through depressions, wars, both human and livestock plagues painted a picture no one wanted to be included. The true thing that we had was certain unity, which was eroding with the new craving for privacy. Our smart phones, tablets, console games provided the shell that took us from a small town to the cradles of civilization and a false sense of security. There was no need to worry, because all answers are barely a Google and a few seconds for us. We listened to all the campaign promises from our politicians. The year 2000 saw China join the World Trade Organization, which was to bring the world closer to being one big family. No one in Marked Tree worried about Asia, especially after they stopped importing our grain and livestock. Rather than feeling inferior we secretly rejoiced that Africa needed our products. We, with Building a New America, were feasting on our lifeboat believing there would be no rough waters ahead of us. The temporary storm was gone, and the sky was sunny once more. The most practical solution was to move somewhere the waters were smoother. I believe this is what gave us peace of mind as Building a New America was going to make America strong again, and that was the important issue; we would find better jobs elsewhere and a sounder company would take our small farms and combine them using updated technology to become more productive. I developed this foundation from listening to my father and his friends debate the world's problems. We held fast to the belief in a future that was going to be great, as we would be working in new fields, fields in the service arena and not in the burning fields of a dying farm.

We did not worry all the world issues. There would be a day when we would go our separate ways, and that day was not at this moment. For now, there were greater things to be happy and thankful. I was so glad to receive two sisters and a female cousin who loved to play baseball. They helped build our confidence. These girls played hard and when we stepped on the field, it was blood and guts. I loved this, because I knew they could hit as well as their male teammates and were serious about getting to first base. I enjoyed fielding more than hitting. I was a good hitter, knowing I could hit the balls thrown by any pitcher. Fielding was the excitement I lived to discover. Each time, what looked similar produced a different result. Small, trivial variables changed the spin on the baseball heading for me. It could be something as simple as a minute pebble, which another player scooted with his foot. This time the baseball hit it requiring me to make a selection of fast adjustments. I adapted and overcame. If truly the other parts of my life were as simple as the baseball is. Despite my attempts to bury my life in baseball this year seemed to be tougher than the previous years. I was fifteen and starting to think a little harder about the big picture in life. Things were changing within me, and young women were beginning to appear so much better, almost as good as my sisters, cousin, mother, and grandmother. Female kin always set the standards; we match outsiders. No other girls even came close, but now there was one I could qualify. Cindy Moore began watching our games. Lisa invited her to play; however, she told us she did not understand how. Julia and Roberta offered to teach her how to play. I wanted to offer myself as a teacher, yet was too embarrassed and afraid everyone would laugh at me. She declined their offers and told us she simply wanted to watch us play. Cindy was in three of my classes last year, yet we never even looked at each other before. The boys stayed with boys, and girls remained with girls. We were not like the kids in the larger cities, because here, everyone knew what was happening. We dated few girls, because, before our first date, we would meet each other's family. Much talk and planning went into the first date, as, so many here married their initial date. This is not to indicate our fear of dating or desperation with the prospect of never finding a mate. The intense screening occurs before that first date.

The girls in our region usually are the predators when it comes to the serious successful first date. Cindy surprised all of us because she would stand when I was at bat, yet remained seated during the remainder of the games. Her actions caught me off guard since so many boys in our class had begged her for the magical first date. She was the single girl in our grade that had golden hair and bright blue eyes. All the boys in our class dreamed of bringing her home to meet their parents. The parents in our community were especially much aware of what potential mates were available for their sons or daughters. Nevertheless, it was important the children keep the final say in their choice of their mates. A marriage forced by the parents that when discovered, the church declared it to be disbanded and notified the community about the dissolution. We had our community rules or hillbilly code, and specific things were done a certain way and there could be no exceptions. Not all that mattered to me, since my parents obeyed the rules and totally wanted the best for us. They were afraid that many potential mates would shift to the children of the farmers who sold their farms desiring the setup cash that was expendable. We did not own a farm. Therefore, there would be no splitting a large lump sum from a farm sale. This did not mean that our parents wanted us to stay in Marked Tree, as my father planned to move us all to Memphis. He was also considering Nashville. He had a vision of us being like an adventurous family, exploring new lands and areas. Dad offered Canada as an alternative, yet we instantaneously rejected this, fearing the adjustment period would make starting new families difficult or impossible. Our father even met resistance from our mother and grandparents on this offer. Nashville was pushing the boundary and was slowly becoming the new hope of the future for all of us. We sacrificed gladly to save, or make enough money to make this happen. Our sisters would babysit and clean houses while we boys would mow grass and shovel snow in the winter. Mom would work on the farms in the summer, washed houses in the winter while my sisters and cousins were in school. Our money was building up slowly and steadily. Sacrifice and save were what built Marked Tree, nonetheless, spend, splurge, play, and feast were the premise of our many past generations.

My father would argue with his friends late into the night how that too much of today was self-centered on pleasure. His parents did not boast much money; nevertheless, they constantly found, a way to provide. Everyone in their home had what they needed. If they did not need it, they did not accept it. They were so determined they would not receive what they did not need. Many believed these unneeded things would create lust and greed for more until the weight of these items pulled them under where they belonged. They trembled at the thought of possessions owning them claiming these people could not own things unless the things first controlled them. This concept settled in my mind as I compare it as prevailing sold on something. The listener creates an overwhelming need for the unneeded object, a need so intense that all bases of logic and self-control erode. The want becomes, consequently overwhelming that no sacrifice is too small to get the unnecessary item. The elders warn that obtaining the item is but the first rung of a ladder that extends far into the firmaments. The extra weight of the added items constantly proved too much for the ladder that each rung broke. Blindness and compulsion propelled its victim to the next step. Within a few minutes, the victim existed trapped in the open sky with scarcely the weight of the constantly increasing load to guarantee a defeating demise. My father and his friends could see something such as this evolving in Marked Tree, yet with the farms were selling for sixty-five cents on the dollar, so the fall or decline was not as fast, or steep as it could have been, considering it is an American company giving those in our community a small chance once more. Rather than a swift death, a few in our community received a chance of a slow rebirth. I can sense the drama from my father's debates, even though we are not permitted to take part. I constantly opened my bedroom window and sit on the floor next to it. I had a hunger for their words. They had me cautious about the future. My eyes were starting to open. I wonder if I am ready to see all this.

My open focused eyes were getting a challenge presently. Cindy has a power over us that I had yet to experience. Why she stands when I am at bat no one can figure? She commands everyone's attention naturally. We cannot determine why she is standing for me, nevertheless, the fact that she is standing makes it honorable. Everything she does is right and everything she says is perfect. To argue otherwise would hold no merits. We desire what she wants. I behold a new power take over my body knowing her eyes were scanning me. My solitary release was through hitting the ball, and I would crack it hard. It is okay to show off if you are producing, and I was producing. Many of my hits were sailing over the fence that marked the boundary of our playing area, which scored as home runs. To understand that I had pounded the ball over the outfield fence, yet was putty in her hands. I was accordingly fortunate that she had mercy, and I believed pity on me. My mind was so confused why she was doing this to me. Naturally, when we were out of her hearing area, everyone teased me vigorously. Holding on to the slight chance that Cindy had plans for me, I took the teasing. I did not see any reason to discredit her. My mouth could not set free of any bad words about her. That would be so wrong. I had to show her I was a good man; therefore, I would need to start a conversation with her. I went to speak with her, yet froze. My body betrayed me. Fortune came my way, in that she did not notice my failed try. Nevertheless, I asked Lisa and Roberta to find out if she wanted or needed something from me. She had watched us two days now. I admired her strength and courage. She did what she wanted. My primary dream is that she was serious in being a part of my inner circle. Accordingly, I believed to older girls would give a positive impression of me, showing that my sisters and family were watching out for me and had my concerns in their hearts. This would also demonstrate that I could play as a part of a team in the real world. Likewise, I believed it would reduce a little of the anxiety she might undergo in being acquainted with my family.

When Cindy arrived early the third morning, Lisa and Roberta flanked her and began a casual conversation, continuing their campaign to recruit her as a player. This gave Julia a chance to join them. Lisa believed this would relax Cindy by having a small child in the conversation. Lisa did not worry about Julia, because we did not hide things from her. Our family tried to be open for her as an attempt to strengthen our bonding. If we were doing something that she should not know, then most likely, we were doing something, which we should not be doing. The plan was simple, yet successful. We were going to resist this new world of temptation and holdfast to our family values. We wanted each other more than we needed the modern expensive fads that everyone was compulsively overreacting. Cindy is down to Earth like we are. Cindy came home with my sisters and introduced her to our mother. They rushed to Lisa's room. A few minutes later, Lisa yells to downstairs that she wants me to come to her room. This was common in our house, as Lisa routinely would call for me to kill insects, lift heavy items and other emergencies. Mom motioned for me to attend to Lisa's calling, thus I rushed up to her room. I walked in Lisa's room and saw Lisa, Cindy, and Roberta sitting on Lisa's bed, with Julia sitting in the chair in front of Lisa's desk. I knew something was up and with Cindy among them, I suspected it was in my favor. Lisa tells me that Cindy wants to go steady with me. Cindy's face turned red in embarrassment. I felt sorry for her and did not want to leave her hanging. Therefore, I at once asked Cindy if she would please go steady with me. She smiled while answering yes. The tone of her face changed from a shy defeated dimness to be victorious. Life was exploding around her as she rushed to me and hugged me. I was shocked and paralyzed. Lisa and Roberta began laughing, finding great excitement in their brother becoming the property of a woman. The truth is, my sisters, and cousin always controlled me. They controlled me through dignity and honor. Adding Cindy to my circle was easy, especially when considering Lisa, Julia, and Roberta endorsed her.

Cindy asks me if she may tell everyone that she is my girl. With great honor, I quickly gave her the permission and told her that I would inform everyone that I was her boyfriend. The roles of boyfriend and girlfriend are serious in Marked Tree. This is almost the same as being married, with all the privileges except for sex. We do not experience sex before getting married. If the community discovers a young unmarried couple had sex found themselves immediately shunned. This was our age-old custom, in which our tradition, churches, and values demanded. We valued the virginity of our women when given in marriage. The purity of our women is important in keeping the blood in the clan. My father and his friends argue that once our community starts resettling in Memphis these values will dissolve. The ways of before will never be more, as this was the case over our crumbling nation. We always heard how great we were and how our nation was protecting and saving the world. We would later learn these various things we must not save, and that the giving heart equals a foolish mind. We were enjoying the fulfillment that comes with giving while not accepting the dismal truth that unfolded before our eyes. This created a dilemma that would not find an answer until too late. Cindy was erasing this perceived apprehension from our family, because her spirit gave our family a new hope and pride. We knew that it was not good to bear pride in the sacrifice that Cindy was making, as our father hounded us daily about being humbled. I would maintain no trouble in being unpretentious before Cindy since she was so submissive to me. We held each other's heart before ours from the beginning. Our bond did not escape the interest of any in our community, especially the small church that our family attended. Cindy's family attended the largest church in Marked Tree. My family attended the smallest church. Local custom dictates the woman will attend the church of her man. Cindy's father became extremely angry and demanded that she remained in his church or separate from his family. She packed her clothing and asked if she could live with us. My mother agreed, and Lisa shared her bed with Cindy. Lisa was hungry for love and wanted a portion in my relationship. I welcomed this as I found this relationship the same as walking barefoot over a fire.

I could not handle the mystery of Cindy's love for me. Our relationship had no basis in logic. I was low in the ranking of available boys. Cindy was the undisputed number one attainable female for all Marked Tree and Poinsett County. I confronted Cindy and asked her why she loves me. She told me her love existed based on my devoted love for her. This still did not answer my question; therefore, I asked her once more, what was the element that sparked her to root for me during our baseball games? Cindy kissed my cheek and revealed that I had appeared in her dream, declaring my eternal love for her. Naturally, I confirmed my love and joy in her special friendship. No longer would I play the final game each day. I spent this time with Cindy talking. We talked about everything. She revealed every secret she held to me. I could not believe how relaxed and open she was with me. Within a few days, I knew more about Cindy than I did any female in my life. Accordingly, I found myself sharing everything about me with Cindy. My mind was one with Cindy as I even discovered myself and reformed my relationships with everyone else. Cindy was important to Lisa, Roberta, Julia, and my mother. The women in my family gracefully shared me with Cindy, yet surprisingly felt comfortable being between Cindy and I. Cindy gave my sisters, cousin, mother, and grandmother the right to stand at my right side. She would either stand at their side, or stand on my left side.

This convinced my female clan that she respected them and wanted to be a member of our family and a part of me. Roberta spent much time talking with Cindy and did not worry about me knowing her heart. She trusted Cindy's influence over me and trusted that we had her best interests in our hearts.

I was surprised to learn so much about Roberta and what she was going through in her life. Her parents, my uncle and aunt, died in a car crash. A drunk driver hit them late at night. Unfortunately, their rescue occurred until the next morning. The killer on the wheels blood-alcohol level dropped to a legal level with the additional six hours after the accident before testing in the hospital. Roberta's parents died instantly. The drunk driver survived, even though his face ensued cut by his vehicle's glass and legs were pinned by his car. The freaky part of the accident was how his upper body spun around twisting away from his pinned legs. This damaged his spine; thereby losing control of his leg crippled for life. His face remained scarred for life. My grandparents thought that karma punished this man greater than the law could. Therefore, our family did not press any charges, especially because the man confessed the accident was his fault. Accordingly, his insurance paid all funeral costs and provided a trust for Roberta. They were under the gun by our community to right this wrong. His insurance company reduced his benefits, so they could increase what they provided for Roberta. This happened at the request of the killer. Roberta later decided that she would divide her trust fund with her new siblings. She fell in love with us, and we fell in love with her. The first few months she came to our house, we had to sleep on the living room floor because everyone, except for our parents wanted to sleep beside her. She was our sole cousin. My father merely had one brother, and my mother had no siblings. When Roberta came to live with us, our family's future generation existed now united. We felt complete with her living among us. Like the luster of all new things, our compulsion over Roberta slowly reduced itself to a normal level. Lisa and Julia naturally bonded even tighter with Roberta. My brothers and I ensured that Roberta knew in public, we would protect her and preserve her honor. Roberta and Cindy developed a special relationship. They were outsiders even though Lisa and Julia worshipped them. It was Cindy's amazing personality, which kept everyone happy. I noticed each day how hard she was joining our family. This did not seem like justice for me. Accordingly, I knew something had to change before she crumbled.

Even though my life had revolved around baseball my love for the game slipped below Cindy. I was smart enough to realize my playing skills were not qualified for the professional levels. My future was with Cindy. Even I was surprised at how fast baseball phased out, and she replaced it. Cindy worked diligently with Julia, Lisa, and Roberta to fit into our games with a few surprise performance bursts to qualify as a contributing member of her team. I valued our talking time, even though we had extremely limited time together. Under my new plan, Cindy and I would not play in the first game. We would leave our house after breakfast and walk around town until just before the second game. I ruffled selected feathers when I informed my siblings that this was Cindy and my time together. With the success, I gained in obtaining our independence for the first game; I established this as our time and added the final game as our time as well. Cindy told Lisa that she wanted this time with me; therefore, Lisa ordered we have our privacy. This made life, much better for us. Nevertheless, we had a few issues to face. I declared to Cindy that we needed to mold our souls and foundation. My loyalty was to her number one, then my family second. Even though that sounds cold, I emphasized that she would be the mother of our children, and that as the father in our family, they came first. I hated that we could not sleep together. I did not want to entertain any form of unmarried sex; I simply wanted to be with her. The few hours we remained separated each night, seemed like days for me. When we were apart, it felt as if my body did not hold a heart. I was empty inside my heart and soul. This confused me, as I have never experienced anything such as this previously. Roberta explained to us that this emptiness gave birth inside her when her parents died. No matter how deep and dedicated my family loved her, we could not replace the void left inside her.

Cindy offered the comfort of a family addition, nevertheless; she knew Cindy, and I would become united, and start our own family. Roberta understood the importance of a husband and wife relationship, as she based her foundation of life on her parent's relationship. Since Roberta was a solitary child, she enjoyed two adults just for herself. She found herself staying with our grandparents when she was craving the dedicated attention from two adults. She limited these visits because she discovered the special relationships developed among siblings as they shared parents. Roberta learned the value of being a member in a family, sharing, caring, with the available support. She initially found difficulty in joining a team, as she before enjoyed receiving all the attention. Roberta discovered the special love and comfort offered by siblings, especially the opportunity to share experiences with those who are in the first stages of life and were facing the same hurdles in their development stage of existence.

Young people had youthful ideas, and this attracted Roberta. She as well discovered adolescent people also shared the same pains she endured and that by traveling together on the road of life, overcoming many of the hurdles with help from eyes, which were looking through the corresponding window, up at the equivalent mountains, and down at the same valleys. Roberta knew this was important to identify her true self. Socialization was more significant than she originally believed. I was not as close to Roberta to the same degree previously, nonetheless; I understood this was contingent on Cindy. Therefore, I resented her hypocrisy. Sadly, she was not the lone member of my family that was using me to gain Cindy's attention. This was so confusing for me. I could not understand why they were so readily willing to use me for their individual enrichment. This was when I knew Marked Tree was not the place for our future. They were not trying to split us, but to the contrary, they were trying wiggle between us. I am not willing to share so much of Cindy. If my family gave me more space, and showed a bit of respect, my apprehension would not have developed into a slow brewing hate. Cindy was the solitary person that I could trust. I concealed my anger with everyone we knew, revealing my feelings solely to Cindy. Our summer vacation rapidly ended. My time with Cindy seemed to fly. Cindy took me to our high school the day before classes began. She spoke to the register and had our class schedules synchronized. We would be together throughout all our classes during our senior year. We were one of six committed couples. No one would spot one without their mate in these six couples. Cindy and I were no exception. We elected to avoid everyone and stay away from social functions as much as possible. We were secluded completely within ourselves. We were careful not to offend anyone responding without emotions. I responded to all males and Cindy to all women, except my sisters and cousin. Cindy was so worried that her responses could be taken the wrong way and give false hope. She had to watch each of her responses and not ignite any sparks.

The previous year, her neighbor Mitch Anderson sat beside her on the bus. Cindy's father asked him to keep an eye on her, so he could have peace of mind that she had someone to protect her. Cindy claimed that she never began a conversation with him, and merely responded to his questions with the shorted possible answers. Mitch supposedly began walking her to the bus and after school walking her home. He apparently was shocked when she moved in with my family. He decided that I needed punished for stealing what he felt belonged to him. Each time he passed us in school, we could see the hate in his eyes. I wanted to pound him with my baseball bat. Cindy recommended that we simply ignore him, thereby giving him no attention. She believed that negative attention could fuel the hope same as positive attention. By giving no form of attention, she believed the hope would slowly fade. Our problem arose when those who were around us begin responding to his actions. He would brag throughout the school how much Cindy had depended on him and even confided her secrets with him. Mitch saw this as an opportunity for him to brag about a future with Cindy. When school resumed, he was faced with shame as all his friends expected Cindy to be under his love spell. This placed Mitch against the wall with nowhere to go. In our community, bragging about such things just took place when the relationship was definite. According to the rules of our community, a battle for honor could not be avoided. The sides were aligning themselves, Mitch's friends uniting and broadcasting their version, while Cindy and my family reported the truth. We had the baseball players who witnessed our relationship develop, with Lisa and Roberta gaining the support of their friends. Each day, fights erupted as our differences intensified. The mood was rigid, and the air felt cold and heavy. Even the sun seemed to behave like the moon and hide behind the clouds. The trees wilted their leaves as if to warn us that troubled waters lay ahead on our journey.

Lisa was the first in our family to get into a fight over the Cindygate. Roberta was the initial one to label our feud as the Cindygate. One of Lisa's classmates alleged that Cindy was walking home one day with Mitch when a large dog rushed them. She claimed that Mitch grabbed a stick and swung at the dog scaring him away. The report declares Cindy was so excited that Mitch saved her; she rewarded him with a kiss. This is a serious accusation, as a kiss between the unrelated stood as a foundation for a solemn relationship and a declaration for a lifetime commitment. For Cindy not to honor such a declaration meant she dishonored herself and her family. We learned her family turned out excommunicated from their church, and their neighbors were shunning them. My family fared better in that our small church stood beside us. We never socialized that much with our neighbors; therefore, nothing changed in our neighborhood. We had too many children in our family for the senior citizens on our street to risk angering. They continued to mind their business, which was fine with us. I was surprised at the degree of variance in the response to our personal relationship. Mitch knew Cindy had kept her position above board and strived not to deceive Mitch. Every time that she said no, he would twist it a manner to provide him an open avenue. Cindy confides to me that Mitch is strange to say the least. That is all we need is a freak hounding us; nonetheless, like it or not, we had Mr. Psycho, as an enemy. Everywhere we turned; he was there. He had no pride behaving like the victim. He was a victim of his foolishness. We were the victims, as our conversation began to center on him. He would begin crying aloud in his classes. Our fortune gave us one class with him. It could have been worse; we might have had more classes. The thought about these events sent chills through my spine.

Mitch worked his way into the seat behind us in our joint class. Cindy and I sat beside each other in all our classes. One day, he stood up between Cindy and me, begging me to give the mother of his children back to him. I lost control, jumped out of my seat swinging at his face. I landed three solid hits on his face, as he offered no resistance actually playing possum. Cindy pulled me off Mitch. Our teacher took me to the principal's office. Cindy refused to stay in the class without me and demanded she accompanied us to the principal's office. The principal began by asking Mitch what happened. He testified that he simply asked us if we were happy. Cindy at once went into a rage telling the principal the horrible thing Mitch said. I verified what Cindy said. The principal asked the teacher to stay and for us to wait outside his office with Mitch. We sat beside the secretary knowing that Mitch would try to intimidate us. Strangely, he was sitting in his chair acting like an angel. We soon discovered why he was acting so innocent. His father stormed into our waiting area. Mitch told his father, we were teasing him, and that I was flaunting my conquest and brainwashing of Cindy in front of him. His father ordered the secretary to call the police, that he was pressing charges. The police arrived and arrested me. Cindy slapped one of the police officers, thereby also arrested. They put us in two separate cells in their jail, because state law forbids a female and male locked in the same cell. Marked Tree had six lawyers who practiced law in our town. Usually, they worked on divorces, contract disagreements, adoptions, wills, and other routine legal needs. This was going to be an assault case and an actual trial with a jury. This case was the event in our county, and we were fortunate enough to have three lawyers plead to represent us. The other three rushed to Mitch, who would need a lawyer because the first thing that our lawyers did was press charges for harassment definition of character. The lawyers obtained statements from many of our supporters and sent them to our town's newspaper, which published summaries of them. Once published, the police had no choice but to arrest Mitch. It was time for us to exact the revenge.

Cindy and I kissed each other through the bars that separated us. Whenever Mitch looked at us, Cindy would declare her love for me and constantly criticized Mitch as a loser who she hated. Our first night in jail, Cindy dreamed a special dream. A woman, dressed in black, came floating on a boat that quickly was beside Cindy's boat. The woman introduced herself as Saladus-naine. She warned Cindy that Mitch was unstable, and if we stayed in our town, he would kill us. Cindy asked Saladus-naine why she was telling us this. Saladus-naine told Cindy she was our guardian angel and would lead us out of Marked Tree to the ensuing stage of our life. Cindy told me about this visitation the next morning. I believed it merely to be a dream, which could also be our subconscious trying to give us a little courage and logic to the burning fire in our hearts. Naturally, I wanted to leap into the world with Cindy, nevertheless, I first wanted to set up a foundation. Our grades qualified for scholarships, and we agreed this year would be our best, as we would not simply ace every class, we took, and we would study hard for our college entrance exams. We already had the books from the library. Study time for us was time together, and justified being alone as this was required for diligent study. This developed our ability to function with each other, or as I called it our doing nothing jointly time. Cindy told me she trusted this woman because it convinced her; we should spend our lives together. I agreed with Cindy; we would not openly harass Mitch. We would respond to his attacks if he wanted to continue this charade. Mitch could not forego an opportunity to regain 'his' Cindy, therefore, continued to profess his great love for Cindy and every fault he could create about me. Cindy would not argue with Mitch. She feared this would give him hope. Cindy decided that Mitch had crossed the line, and she was going to set him in his place. She listened for our guard to open the first of two sets of doors. Cindy would then accuse Mitch of having sex with boys and animals. This puts Mitch into a violent rage.

The guard would enter our area as Mitch would be screaming at us, cursing, and hitting the bars. He even went so far once to threaten to kill us with the guard standing beside us. That was the wrong thing to do. The guard submitted a report and a complaint. Afterwards, he recommended we press more charges. Our lawyers agreed and filed the proper forms with the court. When Mitch's lawyers discovered this new charge, all three lawyers resigned. The judge had to appoint one to represent him. This lawyer explained to Mitch's father that if his son went to court, he would do time, and the lone hope was to drop the charges on us in exchange for dropping our charges. One intensive hurdle was too hard to overcome. The police department would not drop their charges on Cindy. We suspected the guards wanted to have her in their clutches. I did not want Cindy in jail alone, even though I would serve in a boy's correctional facility, and she would go to a girl's correctional facility. The main point was I did not want to be free while she was imprisoned. At least if we took our chances, Mitch would stand a chance of doing time as well. The trial date arrived as my case came first. Twelve students from our class testified what Mitch did. Mitch's witnesses played it safe by either saying they heard nothing or could not remember what they heard. The few attempts their lawyers tried to imply false claims; their witnesses became confused and tongue-tied. The judge became angry a few times when Mitch's witnesses went overboard. The judge would glance at my witnesses who would shake their heads yes or no. It was a fast glance, yet his opinions stood based on this. After three days and the lawyers rested their cases, the judge at once acquitted me. He looked at Mitch's father and told him if Mitch ever says one word to or directed at me, he would spend twenty years in the county jail. We hated the county jail, because they were rougher than the state or federal prisons. Our local jail held the philosophy that breaking the law meant a defected mind that hard work would repair the disorder.

My assault case was history, now it was time for Cindy to stand trial. The lawyers decided to base their case on her love for me and the fear of being alone. They painted it as the Romeo and Juliet story. Accordingly, they had me sit beside Cindy. The prosecuting attorney soon discovered that if Cindy went to jail, he would not be reelected. He offered a plea bargain; however, our attorney told him that they wanted to cement their victory when they ran against in the upcoming elections. This forced him to put limited effort in Cindy's prosecution. This turned out to be an effective strategy, because the judge decided in Cindy's favor early. The judge pushed the prosecuting attorney to get a sense of his fervor in seeking a victory. The prosecuting attorney sent the appropriate signals, which allowed the judge to enforce extra protection for Cindy. Cindy cried a lot during the trial. She used this as a special weapon, which was effective. When she cried, we all cried. I could see our witnesses cry in their seats. A few times, I even saw a few tears rolling down our judge's cheeks. The police officer, which Cindy lightly slapped, testified in court that she might have been confused and scared. The judge acquitted Cindy, after asking the victim or police officer how he felt this case should be judged. He recommended the judge acquitted Cindy. I could not relax until I heard the judge rule in Cindy's favor. I trembled at the thought that she could go to a correctional facility. The courtroom erupted in joy when the bailiff removed the cuffs from Cindy's wrists. That was a scary sight, watching them escort her around with her wrists and feet chained. Notwithstanding it was so ridiculous to think she was a danger to society. The police told me they did this to protect her. They thought that she might try to escape and run the risk of being a fugitive. We agreed that she was too precious to spend a life on the run.

Afterwards, it was time for Mitch's two cases to come before the judge. Originally, we had a massive offense planned to bury Mitch; however, with our victories and the community rushing to our side since everyone wanted to be on the winning side. The week before his trial was to begin; Saladus-naine visited Cindy once more. This night she also came to me in my dreams. She told me that Mitch would go to a correctional facility for five years, and be transferred to an adult jail when he turned eighteen. He would search for us when they released him for two years. Saladus-naine told us to leak to several friends we were going to Mexico. We were to escape to Canada instead. I asked her why we had to leave the United States. She told me this was necessary because of events that would manifest in the future. We would understand soon. I asked Saladus-naine how I could take Cindy and travel north providing for her during this voyage. Saladus-naine told me not to worry over such things, because we would be okay. We were to leave after returning to school for one week. I verified the details with Cindy in the morning, as she had the same dream as well. I felt great knowing something was on our side. Likewise, I felt confident that Cindy and I were destined to spend our lives with each other. Like all good things, we would have to face many bad times and challenges together. Marked Tree is changing, and it is easy to see how rigid and threatening these transformations could be. I was surprised to see how many people originally aligned on Mitch's side. It was so clear that Cindy had no intentions for Mitch. She daily testified that Mitch was performing a security function at her dad's request. Cindy actually began angrily to refute Mitch's claims.

There never was any consent to any relationship. Mitch had created a fantasy that he would not let go. His allies originally believed that Cindy would crumble, especially if I went to jail. When Cindy and I won our cases, Mitch's followers began to put the pieces together. He was not the victim, as everyone knew that Cindy was the victim.

The prosecutor went after Mitch in both cases emphasizing the misery that Cindy had suffered. In the verbal assault case, he painted Cindy as if she suffered from a real attack. No one would witness for Mitch, even as a character witness. Mitch could see that the tide has shifted, yet even in this situation, he testified in court Cindy had promised to marry him. The judge asked him if he had any witnesses to verify this. My heart stopped when he cited three witnesses. These witnesses refused to testify, forcing the court to subpoena them. The three denied ever hearing Cindy making these promises and testified that she continuously rejected his daily proposals. The judge gave him a five-year sentence. Saladus-naine recommended that I drop the second case, citing that if Mitch stood imprisoned too long, he would never forego his revenge, having his life destroyed. With scarcely five years, he would have a chance to rebuild his life and eventually marry beginning his family when Cindygate would be a memory. I agree, believing that if we beat Mitch while he was down, it could generate support for him. The key was to allow everyone to rebuild. Old friendships needed to rekindle. I had many concerns about the neutral people, in that too much gloating could come back on our faces. Playing the victim appeared to work fine for us. The one side effect was the great number of protesters, which had been hanging around us. We had no choice but to submit as we needed the support. I came to term with the fact, while we stay in Marked Tree the people would always exist between us. Saladus-naine was leading us away from this suffocation. Guilt plagued my heart as I felt selfish in trying to keep Cindy just for me. My greed was taking her away from those who, like me, also needed her. My love went much deeper, in that I was dedicated to Cindy's life, protection, and providing. I was the one she wanted to mold her soul with for our future. Notwithstanding it is so hard to share her, yet if I do not share her, I will lose her. Consequently, I would have to make myself strong enough to carry her, but also carry myself. If I am going to carry her, I must carry both of us, if I want to be part of this team.

This is the team for me. I decided to ask Lisa how I could learn to share Cindy. Lisa told me not to worry because if I got between her and Cindy, she would thump me. It is so amazing how an older sister can deal subsequently strongly with issues when it involves one of their brothers. Since I revealed that I needed her help, in sharing Cindy, there was no doubt she would mobilize the entire family to honor this request. My father and grandfather talked to me about how they had learned to share their wives with their children. I never realized how that each minute with me was a minute less for him with mom. I asked Cindy if I were crowding her. Strangely, she was feeling my withdrawal from her and suspected my love for her was decreasing. I asked her for the reason my love for her would decline. She believed the pressure from so many court cases and social pressures from our community were pulling me away. I told Cindy these pressures cemented our bond, because they gave me the feeling, we were working toward the same goal. This relationship was forcing me to adapt to the current phase in my life, a phase that was combining elements normal at my age, plus elements that many did not have to face until they were in their late twenties or early thirties. We had left, so many issues buried so we could battle Mitch, who launched his offense in every phase of our life. Even though he could not break the people in our church, he could force Cindy's parents and relatives from their churches and pressured the neighbors who lived surrounding our church. We would even end with herds of people following my family when we walked to church Sunday morning. It actually became so bad that my father brought his shotgun to protect us on our way to church. The police tried to arrest my father who, after forcing the police to surrender their weapons, then promised to shoot them if they ever played, their hypocrisy in front of his family once more. He was so angry the police could not see the hoards harassing us, yet were purely concerned with him trying to protect us. He recorded the incident and promised to play it at their funeral and for any investigation to determine their death benefits to their families. The police backed off, purchased replacement pistols and ordered the people never to interfere with our church visits.

Instead, they harassed the other members of our church, who stood loyal to us. I often wonder how we survived these psychotic tortures. Our comfort now lies in the different cultural values inside the correctional facilities. We mailed letters to several of the prisoners with a photo of Cindy, and her testimony that Mitch had tortured and raped her mind. Mitch soon lost his virginity, yet not to the gender; he preferred. So many sacrificed for our relationship, as if they believed it was their battle as well. I am accordingly thankful they adopted this union. We needed them so much, because there was no way we could carry this great burden alone. The horrifying thought one maniac could derail our town, occupying our attention diverting us from a sleeping giant who was growing tired of sleeping. Back in our home, I felt reborn sleeping in my bed with Cindy sandwiched between Lisa, Julia, and Roberta in the adjoining bed. I could hear their foolish hen clucking into the wee hours during the night. Somehow, these women were putting their world together, into a format they could process. I just shook my head, because in many ways they could make this work, in such ways that every other female in the world understood. It is the same as one-half the human race is alien. Because man sinned, his punishment was a woman. Men could not live with, or without them. I am just thankful I understand Cindy. Whenever she tells me something, it makes perfect sense. My father and grandfather revealed to me; they also understand my mother and grandmother. I understand them as well, so our brains must have a bloodline receiver, which can translate their jumbled brain transmissions into comprehensible bits of information. The lone thing that invalidates this theory is that Lisa and Roberta's minds are like mousetraps to me. One wrong move while traveling inside their mind, then the trap will snap and trouble will be inevitable. I did consider myself secure while my mind gobbled in conversations with them; especially knowing the most, they wanted from me was a competitive advantage. Overall, they were overprotective of me and tried extremely hard to communicate with me on my level. In a way, it would be great to bring them with us on our exodus. I plan to ask Saladus-naine if they can go with us. There would be too many dangers, bringing Julia and my younger brothers, since they would have to depend on us and that would create an extra burden. I recognize that Lisa and Roberta are industrious and will increase our chances of survival. Subsequently, I asked Cindy how she felt about Lisa and Roberta going with us. At first, she did not want to be responsible, but then agreed that if Marked Tree was going to have Mitch striking back, he would go after Lisa and Roberta because of their claim to have made our match. That night Cindy and I asked Saladus-naine if we could invite Lisa and Roberta. Saladus-naine agreed that four would be much better than just two. Furthermore, she pointed out to us that Lisa and Roberta would help foster our new relationship. This would make it easier for our father to care for those who we left behind in our family. With Saladus-naine's approval, we now would approach Lisa and Roberta. We ask them to join us in our evening walk. Before we were detained at the jail pending our court date, we routinely invited them on our evening walks. They were excited with the prospect of getting life back to normal as before Cindygate. After we ate our first family meal since school began, we drank a little coffee on our porch and began our walk.

Cindy explained to Lisa and Roberta about our dreams with Saladus-naine. I verified my dreams with them and confessed my request that they accompanied us on our journey. I further revealed that when Mitch was once more free, he would exact a revenge on them, especially when considering we were not available. They needed to go with us, as we would return specifically after Mitch died, or no longer wanted revenge. Lisa believes, they will be safe at most after Mitch's death, a theory that Cindy and I agree. Lisa and Roberta reveal that they have $5,000 saved for their future. They saved this money from working plus Roberta's special spending account. We agreed to leave on a Thursday night. Our parents were going to work on a farm this complete weekend, as one of their friends was having a baby, and they wanted to help them. Lisa told our grandparents that Cindy's parents wanted us to spend the weekend with them. They felt bad for the way they had abandoned Cindy and wanted to make things right. Our grandparents agreed, rejoicing in the rebirth of Cindy's relationship to her family. They have traditionally been close to Cindy's grandparents and wanted peace in our community. Everyone wanted the healing process to begin. We planned what to bring with us. At first, the girls wanted to bring tons of clothing, averaging seven bags each. This was too much. Saladus-naine, who now also appeared in Lisa and Roberta's dreams, told us just to bring one backpack each. We would be able to obtain supplies during our voyages. Too much luggage would take away our flexibility. Cindy complained about the one bag; therefore, Saladus-naine let them each takes a backpack and a large shoulder bag. Naturally, each asked me to bring various clothing for them; as a result, over one-half of my load belonged to these partners. We would take a bus to Memphis, and there we each would buy blanket tickets, which would allow us to go anywhere within a two-week period. The goal was to zigzag around the United States, forcing massive searches. Friday came and after school, we rushed to where we had hidden our bags, collected them, and rushed to the bus station. It was time to hit the road, for as Lisa claimed, an hour could mean up to an extra radius of fifty miles.

Chapter 02

Lee Johnson and removing isolation

Our hour of departure was approaching. Since most of the busses went to Memphis, we jumped on the first bus. We were heading for Saint Louis, therefore, could not take any busses north, as they went to Chicago, and then branched. Lisa believed fewer busses would be easier to track by the police. One other couple merely accompanied us on the bus to Memphis. Cindy knew them and got them to pledge their secrecy. They knew why we were leaving; acknowledging that all couples feared the return of Mitch to Marked Tree. They feared that Mitch might try to break them up as well. Our bus rolled south on highway 55. We were on the road for precisely twenty minutes when we noticed so many new homes. Roberta had traveled this road many times with her parents and revealed to us that these homes were not here just a few years earlier. Cindy's friend agreed with Roberta. We knew much money came into our area, yet nothing such as this. Maria, Cindy's friend, told us if we thought this was strange wait until we see who lives in these homes. I figured that she was talking about Mexicans, who we knew traditionally floated into our area, yet they came for farm work and would not be able to afford such lovely homes as these. There were so many trucks and people working on these homes. Maria said the houses were a rush job, as hotel rooms in Memphis were hard to find. Our bus passed a wide-open baseball field. My heart began to pound, a reaction I would have for the rest of my life. I found myself angry for another reason. Many people, who I could not accept as American, were camping in tents on this field. I claim they are not American in that they do not respect the sanctity of a baseball field. Even though I do not favor Chevy's, I respect baseball fields and am a glutton for apple-pie. Maria asks our bus driver if he knows what is happening. The bus driver told us the Memphis city administrators kept the bus drivers and taxi drivers updated so the public would realize what was happening and by it reduce anxiety resulting from a lack of knowledge. The bus driver tells us that an Asian company bought two abandoned factories, afterwards renovated them with the latest technology. They imported their labor from China. The company owned all the houses and allowed their employees to live in them freely. The company also provided their employees and their families' food.

The company paid its employees, fifty cents per hours, and donated to their relatives in China. This qualified them for tax credits and both state and federal social benefits. The company received federal and state tax credits. They also received local taxed, benefits. The Asian company transferred decaying dead factories into a manufacturing entity. The company received exemption from pollution controls. The plan believed the payroll taxes, sales taxes, and transportation revenues would provide a boom for the American economy. No one thought the Asian company would import their labor. They used the American political greed, and competition kept these projects secret. There was no one monitoring this throughout the United States. Political theory believed these employees would eventually want American products in their homes and families, if even clothing and food supplements. Amazingly, their food transpired on the farms they were buying. The bus driver tells us these operations were so massive that it was impossible to detect the details. It was like spotting a tree inside a thick forest.

Lisa asks the bus driver about any public reaction to this massive infiltration. He reports the area has no concerns, especially considering these people were self-contained and did not interact with the locals. These people were transported to and from work, had their own schools, temples, and markets. Considering they are renovating a dying area, most believed they could do no harm. It would be wonderful if they hired several native locals; however, the future will need maintenance and other random services. They were not bothering anyone, so there is no need to bother them. The bus driver said now is the time to share a little Christian hospitality. I asked Cindy what she thought about all this. Cindy reminds me that our enemy is one of our own, named Mitch. Understanding these people from other lands is gaining our property legally and fairly, we should have no concerns. Cindy cites that in Marked Tree, the sellers were searching for these buyers to bail them out. She believes the same is true in this area as well.

In a way, it is exciting to see so much renovation and booming activity. This is as giving a rebirth to a dead land. I am not comfortable with these people staying secluded, yet I can understand this not being comfortable around the Midwest population. If you are not one of them, you are outside forever. They do not welcome strangers. Lisa came with trouble adjusting, even though her mother is one of our natives. Our mother worked Lisa into our social circles. Roberta counted as a native in that both of her parents grew up here. She had minor adjustments, and took Lisa under her wings pulling Lisa with her into the county's accepted newcomers. I hope the new areas we explore are more receptive to strangers. Maria tells us not to worry because we will do fine. We have to be open to new ideas and ways of doing things. I tell Cindy this will be no problem for our team, because Lisa adjusted to our family, then Roberta followed suit. They each grabbed one of Cindy's arms and pulled her into our clan milking each step for her. I did not realize how much they had done for her, yet now am so appreciative. I confess to my women that I do not have the adjusting experience that they have. Lisa tells me that I helped each of them, extending my heart as a blanket to cover them. I agreed that we have that special relationship, as evidenced by this being we now. Cindy and I confessed that having Lisa and Roberta with us was the same as being alone. I do not change my talk with Cindy if Lisa or Roberta is beside her. Cindy does not even notice if they are beside me, even though she prefers they are beside me, so she does not have to tell them later. Cindy is dedicated to have no secrets from Lisa or Roberta. I work hard to share everything in my mind with them. Accordingly, I try to run any of my ideas pass Lisa and Roberta before asking Cindy. Cindy understands that I do not want to do something stupid that could hurt her. My experience is with family females, which do not need the same degree of tender loving care that a lover would expect or need.

As we get off the bus Lisa's uncle rushes to us, welcoming us to Memphis. It is hitting me now that I am away from home. Although our voyage is beginning, the separation anxiety is hitting me. Lisa could sense my nervousness, and my mother hen rushes to my side to comfort me. I ask her why I am responding so strange, as this moment belongs to Lisa and her Uncle Bill. Nevertheless, she is giving me the attention that should go to Uncle Bill. Cindy rushes to my side and tells Lisa her, and Roberta will take care of me. Roberta tells Lisa to go to her Uncle. Roberta tells me to think of this as a practice or test. Uncle Bill has a car that we pack tight. He asks us where we plan to go next. Lisa tells him we are going south to visit her father. Uncle Bill reminds Lisa that her father is in Saint Louis, and Saint Louis is four and a half hours by truck north of Memphis. I did not recognize who was correct until Cindy agreed with Uncle Bill. Cindy was successful in academics, and once she confirmed what Uncle Bill told us, we accepted it as gospel. We stop at a fast-food restaurant and grab a bucket of chicken, and a few side dishes. This meal is not as good as my mother's chicken, rolls, coleslaw, mashed potatoes, and gravy. Uncle Bill added a little mac and cheese for us. Lisa could live off mac and cheese, which meant Roberta, had to force a handful of chicken down Lisa. Cindy explained to Lisa that we did not realize when we would eat again; therefore, we had to fill ourselves when we had an opportunity. We ate like pigs. Uncle Bill informs us that a megabus for Saint Louis will pull out around midnight. He gave each of us a small bag packed with canned meat and jerky. This would keep our protein levels with a solid source of steady energy. Uncle Bill invites us to sit around his table and study the various maps. He reveals to us that so many changes have taken place. He is a member of a radio club and talks regularly with truck drivers. Transportation is one field the Asians have not challenged. We sit around the table in amazement that so much money is pouring into our area.

Cindy asks why we must be suspicious because something foreign wants what we do not want and is willing to pay us more than we would receive from someone who knows the true value. She challenges us to name who are the awful ones and good ones in this situation. Cindy believes that we are the bad ones, in that we are accepting more than we should for what we consider as useless. If the foreigners can find another use for our unwanted things, what is the harm? Roberta warns us not to fear what we do not know. Lisa tells us that our trip may be our chance to learn more about our new neighbors. Uncle Bill reports that all his friends have tried to speak with the few Asians that mingle in public. They tend to be private and work hard to avoid contact. Cindy asks Uncle Bill if the people had been receptive to them. Cindy claims these foreigners have different customs and habits. Uncle Bill believes that if they do want to be bothered, then why bother them. I tend to agree, as we have been the victim of Mitch and appreciate what it is like to desire independence. We looked at his maps and planned our trip to Canada. We decided to split into two groups and sit a few seats apart on the bus and separate at the food and rest stops. Uncle Bill gave us the Mennonite outfits and me a fake beard. We selected the Mennonite style in that they are permitted to do many more activities that are social. It was a brilliant idea, in that we would be able to slip through most roadblocks. We knew that each mile we departed; we were expanding the search area. If the police received the information, we gave our friends to give them; they would be searching the southern states, while we worked our way northwest. Uncle Bill also gave us extra money and promised to call Lisa's father, so he could go to the bank Saturday morning and get more cash for us. We wanted to do everything by cash so that we would not leave any data trails behind us. Uncle Bill also gave us two pistols. Lisa and Cindy took the pistols and strapped them to one of their legs under their long dresses. We would simply avoid metal detectors.

Midnight came, and we got on the megabus to Saint Louis. Lisa had been to Saint Louis many times, as she would visit her dad at least once a month. Her father always came to Marked Tree and took her back to Saint Louis. He is overprotective of his daughter. At first, Lisa feared he would not allow her on this trip. He finally agreed, especially when he discovered Cindy, Roberta, and myself would be with them. Consequently, he ran away once during his high school days. He believes this experience will add particular depth to their social skills, allowing them to think beyond Marked Tree. I did not realize what to expect from Mister Theodore Jones, Lisa's father. My mother always spoke ill of the man; therefore, I am sure I realize every bad thing that he ever did. She complained so much about him, that my father made a rule that his name or actions would not be the topic of any discussion in our home. Lisa talked with her mother about her father in private. She told me that our mother spoke calmly about her father when they were isolated. We kept this our secret, agreeing it was a technique; she was using to dilute any jealousy on our father's part. Either way, I realize the way men tend to react around other men. Lisa's father will bless, Lisa, Roberta, and Cindy while blaming this entire idea on me. I asked Lisa about this. All three of these girls swore they would protect me. Their protection gave me the security I needed. Even though these women are small females going up against Lisa's father, whom I knew was big and strong; I knew he was no match for them. Even I tremble when they gang up on me. After all, I have given my entire life following them. My heart exists owned by Cindy, which fills me with fear. This is why I have my half-sister and cousin with me, as I recognize the sole defense against one woman is to have two for my protection. Deep down, I realize they would never openly go against Cindy, unless she broke one of their unwritten womanly rules. These female rules are a double-edged sword, in that they can protect, yet also condemn. I learned early in life to confess guilt and plead ignorance when facing these female wrongs. This saved me from many punishments at the hands of my mother and grandmother. I wonder if their mission is to womanize men.

This megabus has many people on it. Even though it is crowded, we are the sole Americans, as the remaining is Asian. One skinny, yet cute Asian woman sits beside Roberta, leaving Lisa alone in her row across the aisle. I am sitting with Cindy behind Roberta and the Asian woman. Roberta is the most outgoing in our group and causally begins a conversation. Roberta will not accept a non-reply, and will repeat the question until she gets an answer. The trembling young woman finally answers her name is Li Jing. Each of us introduces ourselves to her. Roberta tells her we wanted to be her friends and asked her where she was going. She tells us that she does not grasp where she is going, in that her father banned her from his family because she spoke to a white man in a store. Cindy teases her by saying she does not have to speak to me and then warns her that I am really a bad man who has taken them prisoners. Li Jing grabs Roberta's hand and pulls her to the front of the bus telling the driver that I have kidnapped these innocent white girls. Lisa and Cindy rush up to the driver explaining that they merely teased Li Jing. I stay in my seat as three Asian men have knives pointed at my neck. The bus driver stops the bus and looks at our school identification cards asking why everyone has a different surname. Our sole defense is that we all attend the same school. Finally, all three start kissing me, and screaming they love me. I am too scared to object to Lisa and Roberta's kisses. I believe that they are enjoying my inability to object. I concentrate on the sweet warmth of Cindy's lips pressing against my cheek. The bus driver finally accepted our strange sense of humor. Nevertheless, our challenges on this bus were not finished.

We had to reacquire our seats. Li Jing was afraid to sit beside Roberta and the remainder of the gang. Cindy sat beside Li Jing and asked her to sit beside Roberta, so she could sit beside me. Cindy told Li Jing that she planned to spend the rest of her life with me and raise our family. Lisa and Roberta began to plead with Li Jing. Li Jing asked them why we wanted her so much, as there were so many other Asians on this bus. I told Li Jing we wanted her as a friend because I too tired of having sex with white girls. Li Jing smiles at me and warn we will not catch her in any more tricks, and for revenge, she will sit with us. I joke with her by wondering what she would do if she liked us. Nevertheless, we resumed our original seats. Li Jing began opening to us and told her story. Her parents sold her, so they could feed the remainder of her family. They gave her two choices; one was to work as a prostitute in Beijing, or work as a slave in the United States. Cindy asks how her father can be in China and Memphis, at the same time. Li Jing explains that her real father is still in China. The one in America she called father is really her owner and master. She must serve him obeying his every command. Lisa asks her if this includes sex. Li Jing explains that a master is too great to have sex with his servants. Servants are for work, and making money. Servants are considered lower than dogs. Li Jing explains that she awakes each morning at four A.M. Afterwards, they strip her, and she appears before the master. He will explain her production for the previous day and the punishment scale if she was under her quota. Li Jing explains that each day she averaged three swings of the whip or belt. The belt is for temporary decreases in productivity. Li Jing tells us that several of the elders get as many as twenty whacks a day. They beat them each day until they can work no more and die. Afterwards, they feed them to the hogs or dogs. The hogs get the men, and dogs get the women. After her whipping, she puts on her clothes, eats one bowl of rice, and begins work by five A.M. They give her another bowl of rice at three in the afternoon, and rice with vegetables at eight P.M., and make her walk to her bed. She sleeps in a room with twenty other young women. We looked at each other in shock as she told us her story.

Cindy asks her how she could go to a store in the afternoon; she talked to the white man. Li Jing explains it was Sunday afternoon, and even though they work every day, they take turns going to the market to purchase special items for the master's wife. This was her day. The reality was the man was talking to his wife, who was standing behind Li Jing. The spy who accused her waited until she returned to her prison, or living area before telling her master. From his angle, it looked as if she was talking to the man. Since they were not at the store, she had no defense. If she denied this charge, they would beat her to death until she confessed. Therefore, she pleads guilty. The master reported this situation to his immediate leader. This leader declared her a traitor to her people and demanded they send her to die in the wilderness. Her bus ticket is to Saint Louis, where a Chinese gang will meet her and take her into the forest for the wolves to eat. Roberta told her we would save her. Lisa told her we would make her a member of our family, and she would travel with us. Cindy promises that we will feed her, and she will eat what we eat. I told Li Jing that I would protect her as I defend the other women in our family. Lisa tells Li Jing, she had better discovered how to fight because her brother is weaker than a woman is when fighting. Cindy disagrees with Lisa and tells Li Jing that she is so safe now, because her lover is stronger than ten men are. Li Jing asks if it was true these Americans have no morals when it comes to sex, and if she must be my lover for this protection. Roberta explains to Li Jing that I belong to Cindy, and if she is caught having sex with me, Cindy will fight her. I wink at Li Jing and wink, telling her the trick is that we cannot survive if caught. Lisa and Roberta slap me and order that I behave.

Cindy explains that we are country or rural Americans and have different values and morals. There is no uniform code to whom is moral and who is not. It does correlate closely with religion. Li Jing asks us if we are Christian and explained she is a Buddhist. We confess our Christianity. Li Jing reveals she has heard many bad things about Christians. Cindy relaxes her by agreeing she has also heard many dreadful things about Christians. Cindy explains to us that she does not want our relationship to turn hostile over religious issues. The important thing for us now is Li Jing. Li Jing asks us why we want to help her; she is merely a worthless seed in an ocean of seeds and does not deserve the right to live. Lisa kisses her on the cheek and reports to Li Jing that she is extremely important to us and to the world. Li Jing confesses she is afraid that her life is now in the hands of curious people. Cindy agrees that we may be odd, and that our goal is to make her strange as well. I tell Li Jing that all life is important, and that we are so thankful she trusts us with her future. Li Jing explains that trust has nothing to do with this; she is merely postponing her death. Lisa tells Li Jing that she will live and die with us. Roberta asks Li Jing if she wants a modern name for her fresh life as part of our family. Li Jing asks us to pick her new name. We debated names for almost one hour until Cindy asked about Lee Johnson. We agreed on this name and hugged the newest member of our family. This filled us with happiness. We felt a transformation flowing in our souls, as we did not have the same fear of the foreigners as we previously held. Our fear now was for her safety and care. Roberta and Lisa will not let, go of her hands on this bus. Lisa tells us Lee is flesh, just as we are. She could sense her pulse. We enjoy how our skin tones just about match. The small difference in the eyes soon becomes unnoticed. Cindy is the singular one in our group with blond hair. Lee's hair blends close with Lisa and Roberta's hair colors. The main differences in appearance, we will nullify with a permanent. Lee tells us that her master's wife got a permanent at a salon, and it costs more money than she makes in a year. Lisa explains that we will get a box kit and do her hair at her father's house.

Our small interracial group is bonding accordingly fast. Lee's greatest gift to us is her acceptance. We understand this is so hard for her, yet she is forcing herself to surrender to us. This is a fearful process for her. Lee continues to tell us how Americans are lazy, foolish, take drugs, spend money that is not theirs, steal from one another, and kill for sport. We confess that to start work at five A.M. and finish at eight P.M.; therefore, by those standards we are slothful. Cindy explains that if she had to describe Americans to someone who did not recognize them, she would give an evaluation much similar. I ask her how we could explain Mitch Anderson to Lee. Lee wants to be aware of what this Mitch means. I explain the rigid rule we have concerning boys and girls. Cindy declares Lee that she told Mitch thousands of times that she did not want to have a relationship with him. Lee was so happy that Mitch was in prison, telling us that she is lucky there is a Mitch. Lee explains, because of Mitch, she could meet us. Lee confesses this the greatest thing ever to happen in her life. We start crying. Lee asks us if she said something bad. Lisa tells her that we are not used to such deep devotion. Lee continues by asking us if we are her master. Lisa asks her if this includes me. Lee shocks us by saying these men should own all women, and that she would rather me own her than a stranger. I kiss Lee on her cheek and tell her she will never find a kinder master then me. Cindy, Lisa, and Roberta explain to Lee that she is free, and if any chains are in our relationship, it will be the chains of love. We realize it is important to Lee that she has a master. Roberta notifies Lee that with great honor, we will be her masters. Cindy tells Lee she is so special she gets four masters. Lee's face begins to shine, emitting the warmth that floods into our hearts. The people on the bus are shunning us, which is nothing new, except they recognize Lee as being with us now. Lee tells us she does not mind the shunning, in that her people reject each other for fear that they may do something wrong and be beaten.

Our bus pulls into Saint Louis. We marvel at how fast our trip went. Lisa spots her father and rushes to him. We follow Lisa with Cindy and Roberta pulling Lee's arms. She is scared and trembling. We form a circle Lisa's father. He at once looks at Lee and tells us she is not welcomed. Lisa tells her father that Lee is our blood sister now, and if he rejects her, we leave. Lisa hugs Lee and leads us in another place from her father. We get five steps away from her father when he calls us back and welcomes Lee. Lee is even more terrified than she initially was. Cindy declares to me that she cannot believe how cruel our society is to outsiders. It is no wonder they keep to themselves. Lisa reveals to her father that we must stop by a fabric store and a general store. Lisa is going to make Lee a Mennonite outfit, plus give her a perm and dye her hair to a strawberry blond. We will have all wear sunglasses. She is confident with these adjustments; no one will recognize Lee is Asian. Lisa calls a special meeting to introduce the new Lee. She looks so wonderful and proud. She confesses to us that she wants to appear just as we look. I explain to Lee that we trust she is beautiful in the way God, or whomever, she believes, created her. Cindy, Roberta, and Lisa immediately agree. Cindy explains that we are simply making these changes so others will not hurt her for being our friend. Her well-being is so important to us. Lisa discloses that she has made a prominent decision that will be Earth shattering to us. We must go to our bedroom for her to reveal this decision. Her father's house has simply two bedrooms. He took the bed out of the second room and placed blankets on the floor. Lisa has declared, because she is the eldest now declares that for our voyage, Cindy and I are married. Cindy looks at Lisa and asks how this can be justified for our Lord. Roberta informs us that if we declare our love for one another, Lisa has the power to declare us married, as our acting parent. She can give us one another. Lisa makes us promise to love each other forever. We agree and become married. Not quite the way I envisioned it; however, Roberta tells us that all we have to say when we return was that a minister in a small church married us. A married certificate did not mean anything to us, as no one got them, considering the government had no right to say we were married.

Lee now declares that we must follow a special ceremony to be her master. Cindy asks Lee to explain. Lee tells us that she must surrender all to us and be humbled. She begins by removing her clothing. Lisa rushes with a towel to cover Lee. Cindy puts her hands over my eyes. Lee tells us she cannot serve masters who refuse to take her honor. Lisa removes the towel as Cindy, Roberta, and she examines Lee's body. To their horror, they see her back and buttocks plastered with scars. Cindy begins to cry, keeping her hands on my eyes. Lee tells Cindy that she cannot travel with me if I do not see her shame. Lee is serious, causing Roberta easily to pull Cindy's hands off my eyes. I cannot believe Lee's body, and how true; she is what a woman should come across as looking. I do not really know; in that, Lee is the first naked woman I have seen. Cindy teases me by saying this will let me see what she will be showing me tonight, as this is our wedding night. Lee slowly turns around for me showing me her mutilated back. She is so beautiful in the front, yet a victim of such cruelty. I immediately fell to my knees, crying. My mind was falling apart on me. I asked Lisa, who in the world could hurt another person this much. I begged Lee to tell me who did this. Lee explains that she is one of the lucky ones. The others, especially the elders are beaten much worse. Many have scars everywhere except on their faces. These masters enjoy hurting others; nevertheless, want to be portrayed as Saints in public. I promised Lee that if I ever get my hands on her master, I would tear him to pieces. Lee had not purely removed her clothes but also pulled us into her heart. We were so deep into Lee that her naked body was clothed with our love. All my life I longed to see a nude woman, yet today I will see two and be willing to die for them. Life is confusing me.

Lee is not finished with us yet. She throws another humbling curveball at us. Lee reminds us that for her to become our property, we still have one more ceremony, so she can prove her loyalty and give us her honor. Lisa tells her as long as it is not intercourse, as our religion will not allow this. Lee asks why we are the unique Americans who do not want to rape and abuse strangers. Cindy explains to Lee that we are not the lone ones who have morals, and even if we were now that we love her, we cannot hurt her. Lee explains that she must kiss our feet and wash them. She has a pan with water in it that she brought to the room when she came. We did not think anything about it, figuring it was part of her culture, and we want to act normal when she does things that are important for her. She washes Lisa's feet first and then kisses them. Lisa is crying through the entire process. Lee thanks her for giving the special honor that she can serve her. Lisa is the bravest among us. Roberta goes next. She tries to get out of it. Lee is serious about doing this and tells Roberta this is her tradition, and if we do not take her as our servant, she will have to go back to her master and die. Roberta sits in the seat crying just as Cindy, and I did during our turns. While I was sitting in my seat with a nude Asian washing my feet the powerful eyes of my female escorts glaring at me. Lee feels this tension as well and declares to the other young women in our group that if they cannot trust her with me, we can never be a group. Cindy tells Lee that we trust her, just that they do not trust me. Lee stands up in front of me, after that asks Lisa, Roberta, and Cindy, and then asks if they understand the importance of her nudity in front of me. She tells them there is no longer a mystery under her dress. With the secret and mystery revealed, lust could not get a grip on us. Lee tells us that now she can serve us with honor and dignity.

We stare at each stunned by our new bond with Lee. Cindy asks Lee if all should be unclothed in our group. Lee tells her this will not work, as a brother should never see his sister and cousin nude. A man must protect the mystery of the women in his care. I was relieved when Lee spared me this disgrace. I do not want to make Lisa and Roberta human; they are my Saints, and I want always to have them walk with honor. Lee smiles at me while I continue to scan her body. She asks me if I had seen an unclothed woman previously. Lisa tells her that I am the first one. Lee looked at me and apologized for not having a wonderful body. I told her that everything looked like it is where it is supposed to be. Lee looks at Cindy and tells me that I have a, much greater delicacy in store later this night. She also pleads that I will forgive her for her underdevelopment. Roberta tells Lee not to worry, the difference is so minute that no other woman will ever replace the glory of being the first living memory that her cousin will carry with him until his death. I tell Lee she will always be the honorable and divine angel who was the pioneer who taught me how different, yet the same that we truly are. Cindy tells Lee not to sell herself short, because every woman in our group wishes; they had the courage that she has. Lee tells us this was not the intent; the goal was to prove how much she truly wants to be our lifetime servant. Lee explains this is her debt because without us, she would have no future or life. I tell Lee that we have a future and life now, because of her. Lisa warns Lee that I am trying to keep her talking so she will stay nude longer. Lee asks why this would be a problem or concern. I agree with Lee, while Roberta and Cindy offer Lee, one of the nightgowns and help her dawn it. This dawn led to the darkness in my heart instead of the light of another day; however, I knew this was the right thing to do. I comment how beautiful Lee looks in Cindy's nightgown. Cindy winks at me and tells me to hold on for just a few more hours. I told her there was no rush, since I understand what to expect.

Lisa tells me that I have barely seen the icing on the cake, and that I will enjoy the cake much better. I examine the four of them shaking their heads yes and then asked why every woman, no matter from where on the Earth knows this, yet I do not. I did not worry so much because all the women from Marked Tree knew things that no boy knew. Nevertheless, for a foreign woman from the other side of the world to realize this as well greatly puzzled me. Lee comforts me by telling me that Cindy will enlighten me tonight. I asked why all the women knew this when they were single, but a boy must get married before learning this. Lisa winks at me and explains that someone has to teach the boys, because, if the boys knew this before getting married, they would not want to go to work. Therefore, I ask what is it about being married that will make the husband go to work. Cindy smiles and reports the wife makes him go to work. Cindy looks at me and asks me if I plan to get a job someday. I ask what would happen if I say no. Roberta tells me to keep the memories of Lee in my mind, for they will have to hold me for the remainder of my life. I glance at Lisa and ask if she is part of this slavish plot. Lisa tells me all women are part of this rule, and that every woman will believe this bad thing about me. I confess to them that I will get a job for one reason, and that is to have time away from them. Lee begins laughing and tells me that is the same reason that her father and uncles went to work. I humbly submit this as the fate of man. Cindy asks me if this is the fate of man, then why, so many rush for this fate. I confess to her because it is the foolishness and curse of man. Cindy asks me if I want her as my curse. I smile and tell her absolutely. Lisa smiles at Lee and tells her that Roberta, and they have trained their little boy as well. I tell them this deal does not appear to give justice to men. Lisa claims that I will change my story after tonight. Lee adds that I should remember what I do for pleasure, would give the woman nine months of suffering, if she is blessed, and both a lifetime of joy.

I must be careful with my expressions now, as everything Lee tells me seems to balance things. As one side of her represents God's gift to men, and the other side represents the evil in men. Cindy bails me out by confessing to Lee how much she values her view of the world. Lisa and Roberta confirmed this at once. I breathed a sigh of relief, confessing how I feared being the single one hypnotized by everything Lee tells us. Lisa reveals this is because our servant speaks to us from within our hearts. Lee declares that she is exhausted. I alert the gang that I am tired as well. Lisa laughs with Cindy as Roberta tells me I will not be sleeping this time. Cindy confesses that she will let me have a little rest, but just a little. I ask Lee what they are saying. Lee winks at me, and reveals she cannot say anything, because of the code of women. I am puzzled and ask my gang if this is going to hurt. Lisa tells me that I will lay down in the bed as a boy and leave the bed as a man. The four of them smile at me shaking their heads yes. Lisa tells me not to be afraid, and just to do what Cindy tells me to do. Roberta, Lisa, and Lee take their blankets to the living room. I ask Lee why they are leaving me alone with Cindy. Lee tells me this is my honeymoon, the night where the love of angels will guide you into your manhood. If Lee claims I will survive, then I shall. Lisa closes and locks my door. Cindy stands in front of me and loosens her dress. She removes all her clothes and asks me if I like what I see. I confess to her that I see a perfect angel and ask her where she hid her wings. Even though she looks so much better than Lee, something inside me cries for Lee when I examine Cindy. I confess this to Cindy. Cindy tells me that she understands. Lee is a part of all of us. When I massage Cindy's back, I see Lee's scars and appreciate how lucky we are. Cindy made me a man this night, and entered deep into my soul. We are soul mates. Lee tells us she can sense the great love in our hearts.

We finally wake up Sunday morning. The Friday night megabus and our introduction with Lisa's father, plus Lee's ritual and my conversion into a man wore us out. We sat at the table planning our bus route to Canada. Lee alerts us to an unexpected danger that we will meet on the bus. Now that we have given the punishers an extra day to set up their search, they are looking for her. Interaction with Americans stands forbidden, and cohabitation is punishable by death. Cindy asks why they did not say anything when we were on the bus. Lee responds that they did not do anything because it was public, and they do not want any problems with the bus company. When we exited the bus, our gang ran to Lisa's truck. They needed to organize themselves first and most likely are searching Mennonite areas presently. Lee explains that we will not be safe on any public transportation. The Chinese enforcers will search for them, and execute us. Lisa's father offers his car and tells us, while we drive sensible it should be okay, as it is just four years old. He explains his truck is all he needs, and when we return, to give him back the car and take a megabus to Memphis. Cindy tells us to be rid of the Mennonite clothes and put on our school clothes. They will donate selected of their extra clothes to Lee. Lee must wear a baseball cap and sunglasses. Her red dyed hair, which the young women cut to be our regular length, will not reveal her. We will, always, keep Lee seated in the middle of the back seat with one of us at each of her sides. Lee asks if we are guarding her and promise not to escape. Lisa tells Lee we are protecting her, as anyone who tries to hurt her will have to go through us. Lee, with tears flowing down her cheeks, asks if we truly want to provide and protect her and to tell us why. Cindy advises Lee these are a few of those strange situations, when loose spirits spinning into unknown orbits combine themselves. Our spirits or unconsciousness pulled us together into a new family. Lee professes this is the greatest gift of her life, to have masters who love her. I tell Lee we truly love her, because no one else has given so much of herself to us.

Roberta tells us we need to hit the road and get many miles in today before everyone discover we are missing. Lisa's father packs several blankets, a tent, and a camper's grill. We find a gas station about one mile from the house of Lisa's father, filled up and began our trip to Kansas City. The idea of traveling by car was great. We would keep a low profile, until we were close to the Rocky Mountains. We plan to hide in the mountains for a short period until we get into Canada. Lee will be our eyes and ears explaining everything to us. Lisa would not allow me to sit with Cindy, explaining we can eat, clean, and sleep together; however, when we are on the road I am to ride shotgun. She wants the fact there is a male in this group, because four unprotected women to create too many temptations. Lisa believes that if the attackers do not discover a male is among us until they are raiding us, it will be equally important to late. I agree, and promise to make myself visible. We will begin with Lisa driving and Cindy behind the driver, Lee in the middle, and Roberta behind me. I worried the cars from behind us would see a redhead, blonde-haired woman, and a brown-haired woman. This could be an invitation for trouble. Lisa agreed with me and told our backseat divas to wear their baseball caps and sunglasses. Lee warns us the Chinese Mafia will do everything possible to kill her. I think of Lee, nude, on her knees washing my feet, which causes a fire to burn inside me wishing; I could protect and provide for her a wonderful future. It scares me to think how such a force can be producing, and supporting slavery right beneath our noses. This is so shocking that so many foreigners are bought and placed here and exist invisible among us. So many events manifested themselves in such a manner that a car of four women and one man can have a psychotic Mitch and Chinese Mafia chasing them. Lisa reminds us the power of our love will propel us above the hurdles that soon will try to trip us. I am accordingly extremely fortunate that Cindy and I have a great love, and hope our journeys will find love for Roberta, Lisa, and Lee, even though I think we want to have Lee's heart we understand she deserves to have a family someday. This is a challenge we have before us, to include this open interstate as we roll through this empty flat land.

Lee explains there are many basic safety precautions we must take. Many are simple habits such as, whenever we see two gas stations or stores, never select the one that is the closest. Her people believe the second one will have the better prices and wasting money simply because of slothfulness was American. The mafia will be watching the immediate places. I ask Lee to explain what makes this mafia so terrifying. She explains that they are the worse prisoners from China. The government brought them here to reduce the costs of their prisons. Lisa asks how they can keep control of them here. Lee reveals that they have the prisoner police force that his harsher on them than they are on those they hunt. Lee continues that they take the dead bodies and grind their flesh for the American Chinese restaurants. Roberta begins to vomit as Lisa tells us we will not be eating at Chinese restaurants. Lee discloses that no one she knows eats in any restaurant that is not strictly by a relative from the homeland. The Americans place too much emphasis on the taste, which might be coated with sugar. Her people enjoy eating the food without special taste pleasing deceivers. Food is for life, not life for food. Roberta tells Lee she is safe because they do not comprehend how to cook, so we do not have to worry about good taste for a long time. I stare at Cindy and complain how she told me she could cook. Lisa tells me all women declare this to their men this, so they can get them as their husbands, because man's lust begins with love; however, always ends with hunger. Lee adds that her race controls their men through their stomach. Never feed the man great food, for he will want better tomorrow. She continues by saying the wife must keep her man slightly hungry, so he will rush home. I glance at Cindy and ask her if she is going to treat me like this. Cindy kisses me on my cheek and tells me she will feed me five times each day and spoil me every minute. Lisa asks what she will do if I get fat. Cindy says that she wants me plump so no other women will want me. I tell Cindy no matter how fat I get Lee will still love me. Lee quickly adds, forever and incessantly while I stay her master.

I wink at Cindy, glance at Lee, and declare that I must reveal a great secret to this gang. After seeing Lee and Cindy nude, I consequently am hypnotized by Lee that I want to have Lee as my wife and throw Cindy away in the nearest dump area. Cindy winks at Lisa and Roberta; therefore, we are all in harmony now. Lisa confesses that she understands why, and that even she can never compete with Lee. Lee tells us she is confused because Cindy's body is the perfect body of a woman, she has no fat, entirely muscles and large breasts. I tell Lee her breasts are perfect for me, in that I can use one hand on each and have twice the pleasure, while with Cindy, I have to use both hands on each one and even at that they are still wobbly while the other breast bounces everywhere. It is so hard on me. Lee volunteers to help me with Cindy's breasts. Roberta tells her that we do not allow two women with one man for sex. Lee qualifies this by reminding us that she is our slave and can never be joyful if one of her masters is suffering. I repeat to Lee that my love for her is too strong, and that I will, at no time, be happy if she is not mine and needed her to help me dig the hole to bury Cindy. Roberta volunteers to help me. I tell Roberta that I am accordingly much safer with Lee protecting me. Lisa discloses how we believe Lee protected us. Roberta asks Lee is she is really a God that has come down from the heavens to save us. Lee screams that she is our slave, and if we do not keep her as our slave, she will leave us. Cindy begs Lee to tell me that I must stay married to her. Lee does as Cindy's asks. I beg Lee to let me have her instead. Lee begins crying that she loves Cindy so much, and if we kill Cindy, she will be sad the remainder of her life. Lee drops to her knees and begs me to spare Cindy her life. I stare at Lisa and ask if I should spare Cindy's life, even though her breasts are not as small as Lee's. Roberta defends Cindy by saying that maybe we can find a doctor, who will make Cindy's breasts smaller. Cindy promises that she will do anything to keep me.

I scratch my head, pretending that I am tormented with a stressing decision. I ask Lee if she is sure that we should allow Cindy to live with us. Lee promises if we do this, that she will serve us twice as hard. I examine Cindy and say, I will allow her to live purely because Lee begged me. Cindy rushes to Lee thanking her for saving her life. Lee begins to tremble as sadness overcomes her. Lisa and Roberta take her hands and confess that we were teasing her. Cindy and I kiss Lee's cheeks affirming we were taunting her.

Lee begins crying, which makes us all ashamed. Lee asks us why we would deceive her in such a terrible and cruel manner. I tell Lee she should have known we would never kill Cindy, especially just for having large breasts. Lee shocks us by confessing she simply knows Americans love to kill, and will kill for any reason. She also informs us the Americans are not loyal to their spouses and will search for any reason to take a new sexual partner. I ask her how she knows all these things. Lee tells me she saw it for real at the movies and the movies never show lies. Lisa tells us that in China, the government controls the media and uses it as a source of information. Notwithstanding when they see the American movies, they accept this as acting documentaries. I apologize to Lee; nevertheless, tell her that I do truly love her as we do. Roberta promises that we will wait until she knows us much better before we play any more jokes. We were simply trying to have fun on such a boring flat road trip.

I change the subject by complaining about so many cornfields, miles and miles of corn. Lee reveals that her people will keep the cornfields, because grain is precious in foreign trade. The hungry will pay anything for food. The Americans are not using their business skills in allowing the grain to be sold cheaply and pay high costs for the goods they want. Take the grain away, and when they are starving take what you want. The Americans were so greedy, in that they supported others to do their filthy work, thus protecting their helpful big brother image. They do their dirty work in the dark and smile in the light. They kill the fathers and feed the widows. I focus on Lee and confess to her; I understand nothing about foreign affairs. Lee reveals to us that these traits are what give the Chinese their advantage. They take the small things, one by one. Lee is confused why no one has put this together. All appear the other way, believing they have taken advantage of a foolish foreigner. The sad thing is that if they worked together and share, they could all prosper. Nonetheless, they become simple prey. Lee warns that standing alone makes it too easy for others to cause your fall. Lisa asks if we are wrong for escaping. Lee responds the reason for the separation is as well important. We departed because of the danger, created by a weak justice system that fails to protect the innocent. Her people have a system; they compare the accused. The evidence she has heard against Mitch, when laid out in their system would require Mitch beaten to death. Roberta wants to understand why their system is so harsh. Lee explains that Mitch has proven he is defective and cannot control his social responsibility; hence, he will be a danger to the innocent. The government must protect the innocent and property of the masters. Lee tells us that if a master even perceives a peasant is a threat; they will execute him at once. The wisdom of the masters can see actions before they happen, thereby saving victims from suffering. The evidence of law is the words of the masters. Sometimes, if the restaurants need more meat, they will execute old people whose production are low. Lee explains this is harsh, yet it keeps everyone in their place and maintains order so the masses will have food and a place to rest when not working. Lee adds that our group is special because our power comes from our hearts, and we are not selfish, as we have promised to provide for her. She believes that we were playing our game to make her stronger. I reveal to Lee, we are so comfortable with her that we want to enjoy the gift of her friendship.

Cindy kisses me on the cheek and Lisa whispers in my other ear that once I see a naked girl, apparently I will do anything to get in those pants once more. Lee responds by telling us this is good, because most men try to conquer more women, rather than enjoying that, which already given to them. Roberta asks Cindy what she would do if she saw Lee, and I naked together. Cindy kisses Lee on the cheek and replies she would be happy because I would be in the hands of someone we love. Lee compares the American style has the women jealous of each, which destroys their happiness. Her people have a simple rule, that when they catch one who is married, having sex with another, they execute that person. If both are married, they are executed. Single people caught having sex have a large X cut into each cheek. They will never be able to marry, because any who marry with them must go to prison. They must remain within the clan because of the scars on their face. Lee also adds that they overlook sex between masters and servants, as the master owns the servant and may do as he or she wishes. Servants are the property for production and any form of pleasure. Lee begs us to understand she must be our property and if a male master wants her to submit, she must obey. I tell Lee not to worry, because my morals forbid it. I reveal to Lee the truth is that I want to so much, yet my love for her forbids this sort of behavior. Cindy reaffirms that she does not care nor will ever worry about this. She jokes that it could give her a little time to relax. I ask Cindy why she would want someone else to share in her marriage rights. Cindy professes that she is not asking for help, just merely saying that if Lee and solely Lee were the one helping she would consider it a blessing.

Lisa explains to Lee that she has the place of honor in her new family. We are approaching Kansas City and Lisa pulls over because she wants me to drive while we get gas and gobble fast food. Lee asks us if the black screen, in the middle of our dash, has a GPS on it. I tell her that I can figure out the streets and get us back on the interstate. Lee explains the GPS can tell us where the gas stations and restaurants are located. This way, we can use backstreets and go to where we want with minimal visibility. Roberta asks Lee how we do this. I pull our car over, and we start playing with the GPS. Sure enough, we found an economical gas station and a few Wendis. We wanted to have a little chili for the road, and a few baked potatoes since Lisa did not like soggy French fries. We take the side streets and purchase the best deal with the gas. The GPS leads us to a perfect exit, and soon we were on the road once more. Roberta asked why we were on the main interstate and not on the state highways. Everyone soon will be looking on the interstates. Lisa told us our car would not stop until late tonight, since we could now find gas stations, we would try to make it to the mountains. We would exit 70 at Elseworth and take 56 to Dodge City. They had to slip pass the logic of American searchers and the logic of the Chinese Mafia. Lisa believes today's miles are critical. Once they were on 56, she believed they would be under the radar. The Americans and Chinese would search the interstate assuming the runaways would try to go to Mexico on easiest and fastest routes. The state department was already filing the request, these foolish runaways sent back to the United States. Therefore, the bulk of recapture efforts would be with the Mexican government. Lee told us not to relax, because this will give the Chinese Mafia more freedom. Roberta notices a vehicle that looks similar to ours sitting in a parking lot of a bar. She tells me to park beside it and for Cindy and Lisa go to the entrance of the bar and if any men come out to start fighting a rip each other's shirt showing a little bra. Roberta tells me to exchange the front plates while she swaps the back plates and for Lee to help one of us if we run into a jam. We each grab screwdrivers and an adjustable wrench. We have Lee start dropping ours, while Roberta and I take the ones of the other vehicle.

Off go the other plates, while Lee starts putting ours on the back and front. She is merely to get the screws started, as we will do the final tightening if possible. The priority is getting ours secure. Once we secured ours, I rushed to the front and did the final tightening, while Roberta secured the back. We had Lee doing our watch out and once finished drove our car to the front and picked up Lisa and Cindy. I told them how disappointed that I was because I wanted to see Lisa's bra. Lisa reports to our gang, I have already seen her bras. She caught me peeking in her dresser drawer many times, nevertheless, kept it quiet because she did not want the town to recognize her brother is a pervert. Cindy slaps me as I tell everyone Lisa is lying. Lisa denies lying. I pull the car off the road and refuse to continue until she tells the truth. Lisa at once confesses that she was teasing me. Cindy apologizes for not believing me. I walk away from her saying she should have known it was not true. Lee tells me she knew it was not real. Roberta asks her how she knew, and Lee explains, because I was so amazed when I stare at her nude body, she could sense I saw something for the first time. Lisa brags; this was the solitary reason she made this joke, because she thought we knew her younger special most loved brother was a Saint. She rushes and gives me a hug and then tells us if her pervert brother wanted to see her bras, she would have brought them to my room and given them to me, with herself as a willing sacrifice. Roberta jumps in by adding; I would have brought my bras as well. Cindy complains that everyone is making her appear bad, while, in fact, she is the lone one to have surrendered her bras to me. Lisa and Roberta escort Cindy to me, while Lee intervenes and begs me to forgive poor innocent Cindy. Lee reminds me that she has already begged for Cindy's life today, and that should have given her a little time for a truce. We laugh, while I confess that if Lee wants me to forgive Cindy, I will. Lisa and Roberta, thank Lee for saving Cindy once more, while Cindy kisses her cheek blessing her. I forgive Cindy, glare at Lisa and Roberta, and tell them to lay out their bras. Lisa tells me that will happen when pigs fly.

Lee looks over at the field beside our road and asks why the pigs are flying. We almost break our necks looking at the field, while Lee begins to laugh. She got us good on this one, so I tell her since she is the winner; we must kiss her one hundred times. We kiss and tickle her, causing her to laugh hysterically. I can experience our joy pouring from deep inside her as Lee's excitement is feeding our souls. I finally tell my lunatic nuts that we need to get back on the road before someone has the police put us in a crazy house. I inform Roberta that it is her turn to drive. She will be must better on these rural highways, considering grandpa gave her intense driving lessons, telling her he did not want to lose her in an accident as well. I often find myself believing the pieces to our puzzle have a purpose. I understand that at the end, all things will be known. As I focus on the gang, I belong; I experience no desire to see the end, but just to travel the road that leads toward this summation of love that waits at the final gate. I believe, we have made it pass the dry lands, or least the flat dry lands. Lisa tells us we will continue until late night, keeping an eye out for any state parks. Lisa wants us to live in the forest for a few days, while the search parties exhaust themselves of the energy and hope that accompany a fresh adventure. Within three days, Lisa believes they would dwindle or shift their search for the big cities. We understand the Chinese Mafia will search all places, and like to follow the American search, so they can limit their visibility. Once we are caught, if they see a Chinese among us, they will rush in and claim her. Our government will surrender Lee to them, not wanting to ruffle any feathers.

We trust Lee's assessment; and ask her to notify us if we are doing anything that could put her in danger. I tell her not to be shy in these matters, because just like the rest of our world, we do not understand their rules and methods. Lee informs us that we are strange masters, in that between Lisa, Roberta, and my Cindy, her back, arms, and legs have been massaged this entire trip. I think, we hope to take much of the pain from those horrifying scars that plague her back. Logic tells us this will not help, nevertheless; our hearts want to try. Lee is extremely special to us, as we think; she is one in a billion. Lee reports there is nothing unique about her, all servants are like dirt and not worthy of this sort of folly. They are simply material for production. Cindy argues to Lee that she is the material for our hearts, and she is our folly. If it is foolish for us to give our emotions to her, then we wish to be known as the mountains of foolishness. Roberta notifies me that she sees a part entrance ahead. We enter the road and to our joy see, there are no pay gates. We are not worried about the funds; we just do not want a paper trail. Lisa believes that with most children in school and the weather, this time of the year is out of the camping season. This means more privacy for us. We follow the road to a parking lot that is close to a pleasant lake. At least, it looks pleasant at night. We do not see any lights on, thereby suggesting there are no homes or villages near us. We get out of our vehicle, lock it, and put our bags along the side of the parking lot and each stretch out on the grass. The grass is just high enough to offer a little cushion when we laid on top of it. We lay there for about one hour; afterwards, Lisa told us we needed to find a place to put up a tent. Lee asked if she was afraid of men finding us. Lisa said that was not the first danger, in that Roberta could fight them. She was afraid of snakes and wolves. Lee began to tremble, telling us about her fear of snakes. She believed that they were evil dragons, which had not arms or legs.

Lisa reveals to Lee that I am our defender against snakes. She elaborates that when I take my shoes off the stink paralyzes the snakes. Lee rolls over beside me; her legs wrap my right leg, and arm ties my right arm. Cindy secures my left side, a side she has held fast since we declared our relationship. Cindy takes one of her hands and pets Lee's hair. Subsequently, I whisper into Cindy's ear for her not to get Lee too excited, considering I am the lone one with the equipment to quench certain thirsts. Lisa returns informing us she found a pleasant place for us to put up our tent. We jump on our feet, grab our equipment, and follow Lisa down into the trees before us. I always marvel Mother Nature when I am walking through a forest. The trees are crowded, yet through their tiny branches find a small hole in the sky to feed on the sunlight that travels pass the clouds. These sunlight feeders take advantage of all possible angles the light can pass through the sky. I love hearing the birds chippering, and insects playing their songs. The amazement of a squirrel dancing through the branches or a rabbit crawling into his hole is just but a few of the lives that survives here no matter what season is on them. The majesty of the moonlight that showers through the leaves testifies the sky is the source of all power for life. I can hear each footstep of the angels that are with me in our journey to find our resting place. Something about all this darkness enables danger to join our group as if also a member. My girls are staying near me, although they do not realize I am staying so close behind Lisa that if she stopped, I would trip over her. I have confessed to Lisa so many times how she is my hero. She refuses to accept what I tell her, and instead commits herself to follow me. She is leading now, because our sleeping place is more of a motherly activity. Roberta always watches our rear. She has excellent vision and hearing. Nothing will catch from behind us. Cindy and Lee have me sandwiched in the middle, as if I am the heart of our small moving band.

We pitch our tent, and take our positions. Lee, still terrified of snakes lies on my right, so tight that I can hear her heart beating. Cindy has my left side. Although the three of us should take the space of three, we are barely occupying the space of two. There will be no movement for me tonight, as my angels have me nailed to the position they want. Lisa has us sleeping with our feet to the tent's entrance and her at our head and Roberta at our feet. Lisa desires the area around Roberta to be free from our respiratory noises such as breathing and snoring. By doing this, Roberta can hear any outside noises easier and thus alert us of any possible impending danger. Lee wakes us up twice with screams from her bad dreams. Cindy and I calm Lee back down at once and comfort her as she returns to sleep. Lee has been through the rough times. I am still puzzled that she stepped into the unknown and gave herself to us. Even though she is the servant, we take what she says as gospel and struggle to get anything she must have. Her cries immediately wake all four of us as we rush to her aid. We instantaneously wipe any of her tears. Her tears are like burning flames for us. I also compare them as a swarm of bees attacking. A tear on her cheek hurts as real as a bee stinging me repeatedly. Lee asks for nothing solely for her. She has requested that we do certain things so her culture can allow her to give more to us. I believe Lee as filled any empty spaces emotionally we may have expected from leaving home. Perhaps, she is our new home. We passed many busses on the interstate packed with Asians. Within just a few days, we can see a great change in the population not reported on any news. This trip would have ended quickly without Lee with us. She takes away our ignorance of these new neighbors, as they can be neighbors because we understand them so much better. The thought that we could, or for that matter, many Americans will hate these people, who are treated as property solely for production. The sad thing is many American do not realize many of these people are already in them. They have unknowingly eaten their flesh, believing it to be animal flesh disguised under sauces and spices.

I fear that these innocent victims, similar to Lee, may someday die in battles against the Americans. It is so easy to think we are the greatest peace lovers; nevertheless, gluttony, greed, and lust were exact the high price taking away the freedom of our righteousness. Both sides, at the people level, want to love and share, it is at the master level where the concern for production overrides the dignity of life. It is easy for us to see this in Lee's world, although we have not seen, we are looking through Lee's eyes. I can see how our American culture exists in a similar format. Our master is money, a master that we foolishly think that with credit cards we can control. Our production is our greed and gluttony. This forced us to produce to satisfy our cravings. This craving takes away our independence, making us the slaves of what we have or want. I am one of the lucky ones, in that our father and mother teach saving and sacrificing to satisfy our needs. We so often felt isolated as the other children came to school with their new cell phones, and other electronic gizmos. I learned long ago the newer things these kids have; someone comes up with something just a little better, and the wave washes the things they could not live without back into the sea, leaving them on the beach burning for the next wave to bring in what is in style now. We are fortunate in that our country social network has certain flexibility, yet I realize that the denser urban areas, the peer pressure is nothing less than burning swords. This addiction will aid our enemies, who just as Lee, comprehend life as work, eat, sleep, and hope your punishments will not be so severe that you will not be able to work, eat, and sleep the next day. Just these few days with Lee have taught us how to understand the words from the eyes. Lee's eyes talk to us. Even though before I cherished an opportunity to be one with the Chinese, now that we have Lee to protect, anyone, be it American or Chinese, who attempts to harm her will be the object of my offensive actions.

The next day produced the greatest bonding our gang could have ever hoped for in one million years, and surprisingly this one did not originate with Lee. Our veritable leader, our sacred mother, Lisa slammed the ball on this field well over the centerfield wall. She taught us that we could write our own laws and create authentic right from true wrong. We had already learned, how wicked could torment sincere love, and try to destroy the truth by covering it with lies. We knew the faith of the heart would open wells so deep in the water of love that we would never need another well or thirst again when we discovered our Lee. Lee made herself ours by giving herself first. Now, it was time for Lisa to guide us into the nearby sea, which was, would the destiny of the river we flowed. Lisa complained about how filthy we were, and we must clean ourselves before the dirt sank into our souls. We had a large peaceful lake before us, as she distributed the five bars of soap, she had. I wanted my angels bathing close to our tent, so I began to walk down the shoreline and figured to walk around the bend a short way from us and sink into the bay apart from their view. As I walked away, Lisa ordered me back asking where I planned to wash. I told her that I respected their privacy and honor. Lisa told me that I was part of our group and would do what we did as a family. I confessed that I forgot to bring any swimsuits. She smiles and tells me we forgot the suits. I ask her how we can bathe as a group without our suits. Lisa smiles at me and explains that I have already seen two of the four, and if I can be foolish enough to think there will be that much difference in two more, especially since we are the ones from the equivalent blood. I then realize that they are the same, nevertheless; I am the different one.

I stare at Lisa and say that even though I will not see much different, if I were to catch a sneak peek, three of the four of them would see something new. Lisa and Roberta tell me not to believe them so perfect, after all they had the two largest football players, and you do not keep the big players like that in your game unless you let them score several points. I then ask about our precious Lee. Cindy tells me it is not fair to expect others to share if we do not share. Before I can wink, the four of them are nude in front of me, staring me down, as if I were a pervert or something. I ask myself who is the odd person here. Is it the one that is on display, or the ones who were putting me on display? I ask Cindy why we cannot go to wash together. Cindy explains that we must stay jointly, so Lee can receive the protection, we promised her. Cindy knows my weak spot, and shoots her arrows without mercy. I glance at Lee and ask her how she feels about this. She asks me why Americans do not bathe together, because to wash separate would be a waste of so much clean water. We should clean our bodies not by creating dirt for our world. All who waste will invariably be wanting for more. Lee explains the servants never bathe alone and always in large groups. This is nothing new for her. Lisa laughs and claims the truth of my real apprehension is that I do not want Cindy to realize her misfortune in having me as a mate. I told her I feared no such thing. Although not the most blessed of men, as known from my gym showers, nevertheless, I recognize I am not on the side of misfortune. We were trembling, questioning our dignity and honor dealing with issues, which for us borderline on our sanity of civilization, merely to discover the uncharted territory, we venture traveled by more than who do not. Our separation or preservation were nothing more than an excuse to waste and squander our worldly resources simply to hide something that everyone has. I asked Lisa if she had discussed this with Lee. She denied any collaboration with Lee, citing this as her belief. Consequently, she asked me if I were going to obey her, or must she have to cast me from our gang.

I glare at them and plead that I should not have to surrender myself in this evil manner. Lee asks me why I consider this dirty, when, in fact, it is to remove the dirt. We soil ourselves together; therefore, why would we not clean in conjunction? Lee tells me I must trust her in this fearful event, just as she trusted me. We must be as one to make sure everyone remains safe. This is so hard to do; I had no trouble striping for Cindy, as it was my duty as a husband. I was not too shy about Lee, especially since she is a different race, and I deeply trust her. It is my half-sister and cousin, because their disapproval, or if they make fun of me. An image of me will be in their minds as a source of humiliation the remaining days of my future miserable life. Cindy and Lee begin to remove my clothes, while Lisa and Roberta remove theirs. It seemed as I simply blinked my eyes, and I had four women staring at me, while I was scanning them. I was so proud to have a half-sister and cousin with such wonderful bodies. I told them about the pride they gave me. Likewise, I told them how I had seen their true beauty. A part of me hoped this would create a little sympathy. Lee scanned me once more and told Cindy she was an especially lucky woman to have such a wonderful husband. Roberta and Lisa smile and tell Cindy that she should not have expected anything less from her kin. Cindy confesses this was one reason she is so proud to be my wife. I felt as if hundred tons lifted from me. My special family girls were treating me like a human being and not an object to tease or torture. Lee was a cement and now things felt so great. No mystery on concealment, we can bear all and still have the protection of our bond. I trust all of them. Now when I hold them, I will realize I am in their hearts. We stand united at this moment in time. We finished scrubbing ourselves and decided to take a hike through the beautiful hills and small shallow streams that flow over the rocks. There existed a vast colorful array of leaves, which painted the surrounding land. Lisa informs us that fall must come earlier with more intensity here. Our hands have formed a human chain since we left the lake. Something is so different now, and this thing is stronger than all of us were. It is a blanket the not simply covers our outside; it covers deep in our insides. Lisa pulled the rabbit out of the hat on this one. Lee proved that she is for real, and she knew we are genuine as well. We have all shared as Lee shared. Lisa brags how we are now a gang of many cultures. Little we knew that everything was transforming, and about to change as fast as we had. We belong to one another. Our human chains were ready to continue our life-revolutionizing voyage.

Chapter 03

Journey into another domain

We packed in our car and began to travel over the highway once more. The reloading was quick, as we hummed a special unknown tune together. Lee began the hum; nevertheless, it flowed from our mouths as one. Our radio was playing the news about our escape. I thought it was strange that so much attention was devoted to our story, since so many runaways each day. Lee explains the Chinese Mafia is putting the pressure on our hunt. Lisa gets off 70 at Salina, altering our original route. She planned to take 50 north pass Scipio Lake; continue north to Scipio and afterwards 15 north. We continue to Nephi, and then hang in the East Tintic or Gilson Mountains until we can formulate our exit to Canada. We notice many vehicles driven by Asians, thereby Lee begs us to get back on 70 through the remainder of the night. Nighttime will be too dangerous on the small roads Lee warns. Lee explains that Canada will not be an absolute sanctuary, especially as, so many there depend on the sale of their shale oil to China. I explain to

Lee that she was lucky not to discern my dad when one of our foolish presidents refused to pipe the Canadian oil to the American manufacturers, who needed this oil to keep their costs mildly competitive on the world market. This was another of the things that led to the decay of American Manufacturing. Lee reminds me that we cannot always blame the president, especially since the people choose them. Stupid people who elect foolish leaders do not deserve to live in comfort. Lisa tells me to develop another plan, or have alternate plans, as we will make our final selection when morning arrives. We agree with Lee on this issue. We make it around Denver while the traffic is flowing fast. After Denver, and as the sun comes up, we move slower, now we have gone around Denver, as Roberta wants us to make sure no one is following us. In Idaho Springs, we take 40 north to Grandby. We are in the mountains now, as we seldom can see more than a few hundred feet around us. This is excellent for our low visibility. Lee warns it is also good for the Mafia. Either way, I argue the number of side roads is so great that it will take a little time for them to track them. Another advantage is the number of side roads that branch off the side roads. It would be like finding a minnow that left a river and traveled upstream. Lee kisses my cheek and tells me, thanks for using my mind. After that, she thanks each of our other clan members.

As we move along, Cindy notifies us that she is hungry. We agree that the little breakfast would be fine. Since we are in the mountains, Roberta takes a handful of bread, begins to make several sandwiches, and gives us each soda as we eat in our car. This gives us much energy. Lisa begins a song that we join. Our smiles are about as wide as our car as we go merrily on our way. I happen to catch a truck approaching quickly behind us as I see in my passenger side mirror. I glance at Lisa and tell her we might have company behind us; therefore, we need to find a driveway to pull off this road. Cindy turns around to see the truck and screams at Lisa that it is getting too close. I tell Cindy to pass up our shotgun and two slugs. Just as she passes it to me, the truck rams us hard. Lisa almost loses control of our car; nevertheless, she yanks the car back on the road. The truck rams us once again. Lisa swerves in such a way that she can swing back into the truck ramming its front wheel. This truck swoops around, and prepares for another ram. Roberta warns the two men to have guns and appear angry. I put the two slugs in my shotgun, and asked Lisa to slow down and drive closer to the side of this road. I tell Cindy to close my door after I roll out and for Lisa to swing back later to find me. We are all too terrified to argue, and I fling my door open and exit before my women tried to talk me out of this. I hit the ground and almost lose my shotgun. Fortunately, I can use it to stop me and position myself as the attacking truck is passing me. I appreciate whatever I do must be done without hesitation. I glimpse up, see the gas tank from under the truck, and at once fire my two barrels. I get a direct hit, which is not new for me. My father raised me with a rifle in one hand and a knife in my other hand. The truck explodes at once. Human body and truck parts mixed, begin flying all around me. I start to run down this road, hoping Lisa has stopped. I figure that she did not see the explosion, with all these turns. To my surprise as I run around the first turn, our car is waiting for me. All four of my angels leap from our car and come running to me. I yell for them to get back into our vehicle. I do not see any danger; I just want to be safe with my little angels. They elect not to argue with me on this and do as I ask. When I get to our car, four more trucks ascend on us, two trucks from the front and two from behind us. I yell for Cindy to give me several more slugs.

Eight men come running out of the trucks surrounding our car. I realize that with just two shots, even if I could reload in a flash I cannot get eight shots off in time. Likewise, I do not want many bullets flying around my angels. I put my shotgun down and wave at these men. One of them begins yelling that I did a wonderful job and asked if there is anything, they can do to help us. We start by pleading that they take me and not hurt these innocent women. One of the men asks why they would want to hurt any of us. They stand around our car and seem not to have any desire to harm us. I ask them who they are. They tell me this is their home area; they are trying to defend from outsiders. Lisa tells them we are not from this area. One man tells us they realize who we are, or at least who four of us are. Another one from the group continues by telling us that we are the four runaways from Arkansas. I ask them if they are going to turn us in to the police. An elderly man from the group tells us the people from this area emphatically turn in Chinese, and because we have no Chinese in our group, they will help us escape. Lee smiles, as she stays hidden behind her blue sunglasses. One of the boys asks her what her name is. Lee remains quiet, as Cindy rushes to her side and tells him that her name is Lee Johnson, and she is her younger sister. A gang beat her five years ago and since then does not speak to those she does not know. I took her jacket off and lifted the back of her shirt. These men looked so sad and told Lee that they would not let anything happen to her while she was here. Lisa pulled her shirt down, and Roberta puts her jacket back on her. One of the elders commented that she was without question our little sister the way we care for her. I tell them my young Lee has been through too much in her adolescent life. Each of us shook our heads agreeing. The amazing aspect of this was that I lifted Lee's shirt up and showed her body to these men, who had merely one reservation; she must not be Chinese. I believed her scars would boggle their minds as it did. I felt twelve Americans find themselves smitten by Lee surround her. We do not understand these men well enough yet to share Lee's identity. The way we hover over her had convinced these strangers that she is part of us. We do it so automatically, almost as if she has been with us our entire lives. It feels to me like she has, strangely, I am experiencing difficulty in believing it has merely been one weekend.

Peter was their leader. I asked Peter why they were so happy to see us. Peter told me they saw me destroy the truck from their lookout point on the top of the hill. They hated the two foreigners in this truck and daily tried to kill them, yet they continued to evade them. Peter said everyone in this area testified there were no Chinese in this area, yet these two troublemakers followed everyone they could while stalking whomever they could. Although they never hurt anyone, they did make everyone uneasy. I asked Peter why they stalked so many people. He said that they were trying to buy land in the mountains for a company called Building a New America. No one would sell them the land because Asians completely staffed the company. They were covering up a lie, since Americans should build a New America. The company sent hundreds of trucks into this area to harass the citizens. The Sheriff avoided them, as also did all the law enforcement. The law even stopped their search for stills.

Cindy asks Peter what a still is. Peter tells her it makes Mountain tea. Lisa tells Peter she loves tea. The men in the group begin to laugh and promise Lisa they will let her drink all the tea she desires. I realize what a still makes, so I tell Lisa the tea is too strong for her. She at once begins to argue with me. I then whisper in her ear, they are talking about moonshine. Her face turns red. I tell the boys these women are as pure as angels are. Peter tells them to sit on the nearby hill, and that they will be safe. He looks at his gang and tells them to treat these women as if they were his daughters. The boys gather wood and begin cooking eggs and country ham. They have truckloads of food with them. Peter smiles and tells me we are lucky, because they were on the way to the market to do select trading.

Peter and I walk over to the fire and seat ourselves. Peter looks at Lisa and I. He tells us that we are not safe driving our car because the police discovered her late father gave her this car. Lisa tells Peter that her father would never betray her. One of the men informs us the paper told her father the Chinese this before his accident. Lisa begs them to tell her more. They tell us that Lisa's father was working on top of a building and accidentally fell, and during the drop, his body bounced off many things, because, when the police found him, he was covered in bruises. Peter explains everyone in the mountains knows foreigners own the American government. No one trusted any government official in this area. They would shoot them on sight. I ask why the government has not called in the military. Peter tells her the area is too large for the American government to attack, and the mountain people are equally important powerful in these mountains. The challenging issue is paying tax. While they pay taxes, the government stays away. Roberta agrees that while they fill their pockets with our hard-earned money, they merely search for other places to fill their pockets with more money. Greed and the need to take all they can is their law. Peter continues with his warning how the Chinese are increasing their aggressive actions against the mountain people. He continues by expressing his disbelief in why; so many are searching for us.

Peter continues by pleading to support us in every manner that he can. He tells us that if the American and Chinese forces want us, then the mountain people will hide and defend us. Peter tells us to grab our belongings and spread out among our trucks, and we will take us to the market. Lisa asks if Lee can travel with her. Peter agrees without reservation. He tells us that one of his men will drive our car to the market. They will take it to a country car ship that will paint it another color and put it in a high mountain seldom traveled area. We understand our vehicle is no longer safe, and that travel on it could result in our deaths. Our enemies may wish that we perished. We do not understand why they cannot let one, which they did not want to go free. They have established a by no means interaction barrier between the Chinese and Americans. They must continue to search for, and kill Lee, so all servants will recognize they have no chance of escaping. I am so sorry for Lee, as she knows death could be around every bend and in danger every minute of each day. I realize that she has placed her life in our trust. I admire her trust, as even now we are traveling with men who clarified that if they encountered a Chinese person, they would execute at once. We consider it strange riding split among four trucks. We travel to a town called Grandby. Here, they take us to a country hardware store. Peter whispers something into one of the store clerks, who immediately leaves the store. A chill runs down my back with worry they may have detected Lee. Lisa shares in my concern. I recognize this by the puzzled expression in her eyes. Peter sends another truck away after whispering instructions to two of his men. This second departure surprisingly gave me a sense of calm. I believed that Peter was executing a mystery plan not directed at Lee. Common sense dictates that they should have no reason to suspect Lee as being Chinese. Many times, I fear we worry too much about Lee as she has so little control over those who wish her demise.

Lee came crying to me, telling us she just heard on the radio reports of Chinese servants found tortured. The Chinese ambassador is blaming the Americans. Lee advised me the Chinese are executing their servants to gain advantage in search restrictions. They will submit endless lists against those they who have property they wish to steal as a form of harassment. Once inside their homes, they can harass and torture at will, planting evidence and filing false charges. The secrecy of their actions hides their intentions and nullifies any alarm, permitting them to destroy them one by one. So many things are happening behind closed doors, except for the things that should be occurring. Young people seldom marry, waiting for many years later to marry. The middle-aged couples are bearing fewer children, and adoption of Chinese children has skyrocketed. The Chinese government pays for prospective parents travel to China, formalize the international adoption once the couple selects the child. They return to the United States with the paperwork to gain the child's citizenship with the ease of a mechanical part on an assembly line. Lisa reports her amazement at the magnitude the Chinese are filtering into the United States. They control of the elected officials, law enforcement, manufacturing, and middle-class families through their children. These children attend private schools and remain under constant security. Their concern for the welfare of the children is founded, as the tensions between the races continue to escalate. The change is small in each area, yet the number of areas is large. Those who monitor each area are unconcerned because many detect no change. One such example, three times a week one channel reports of an abduction by emphasizing a different name and limited occurrences. Each listener hears merely the few incidences, ignoring the names. When the names exist as recorded in a list, and the different days totaled the summation is terrifying and incomprehensible. With such a vast choice of distinctive areas of invasion or infiltration, the dilution almost stands as invisible.

We tend to deal with the overall situation in limited spurts, as it quickly depresses us. Roberta reminds us we are not in a position to settle our nation's problems, notwithstanding; we fear that too many share the same restrictions. Nevertheless, we must figure how to survive the short term. We are in the hands of a group of mountain people we do not recognize in the mountains, with no transportation or place to stay. At least when we had a car, we could travel at night and sleep in our vehicle if we needed. My comfort now lay in the calm style that Peter was directing the people the surrounded us. My comfort was not as devoted as my angels. These women have more qualifying concerns, before they give their trust and make themselves dependent. This is a basic male, female interaction process. I realize this balance will help keep us in the middle of the road, which is better than driving into a ditch. Peter asks Lisa and me to follow him in this store. He advises us that in the mountains, we will need to pack what we need to survive on our backs, and we will need weapons, knives, axes, and ammunition. He also recommends that we buy extreme cold-weather clothing, and be prepared to survive over long periods in subzero weather. Peter explains that new fashions offer lighter weight and more temperature protection. We will need climbing rope and extra traction footwear. We selected our equipment, to include a pistol, with holster, rifle, ax, and knife. Afterwards, we put on our cold-weather clothing, backpacks, and stood in a line in front of the store. Lisa had a compass, and I, a map. I asked Peter if he recommended a path for us to travel. Peter requested, we wait a few minutes, as he had a surprise for us. Within a few minutes, animal trucks arrived while certain men began to escort, seven saddled horses to us. Peter reveals the horses are his trade for our car. The horses will give us speed and mobility in the mountains. We can stay hidden for years. Peter tells us he will send Pedro and Phillip with our group to show us a cabin tucked in a valley higher in the mountains.

Cindy thanks Peter, as we prepare to begin our journey into the Never Summer Mountains. Phillip explains that we are too late in the season to travel to Canada. The winter would starve and freeze us, if we by a miracle could travel through the snow. The cabin is one day's ride from the station, which means that we could travel back to Grandby for special supplies or a deadly medical need. We ride through the rich green grass. Pedro explains we are fortunate this cabin is still available. An elderly couple lived in it until they died. Their last will gave the cabin and four-hundred acres to the local church, which Peter is the minister. Phillip discloses the church received about one thousand requests to sell, all from Asians. The requests came from unending phone calls to all the members in the church. It got to a point where everyone canceled their landlines and switched to cell phones. Then the hundreds of written requests flooded the area. These buyers knew everyone's phone numbers and addresses. Their final attack was disrupting the church services. They stood in front of the church entrance requiring the members to push their way into the church. Then they packed the seats, leaving no open seats requiring many in the congregation to stand. The congregation took this harassment for the Sunday morning service. Peter announced a special service Sunday evening. When the congregation returned that evening, they equipped themselves with axes and pistols. Peter was surprised when he saw seventeen law enforcement officials mixed with the Chinese. Peter warned the law enforcement officials to get off the church's property, or they would die with the Chinese. Approximately fifty of the trespassers went to their vehicles, leaving three law enforcement officials and eight Chinese still at the entrance. Naturally, the congregation used their cell phones to video record the morning service and the evening warning by Peter. Peter announced that he would count to ten and any who remained they would shoot. No one moved, therefore, the congregation opened fire, aiming for their legs. Down the trespassers went as the congregation entered their church with no Chinese. One of the law enforcement officials entered the church attempting to arrest the congregation. Peter warned them that he would send the cell phone videos to the press. The trespassers immediately left the area.

That was the beginning of their war. The Chinese killed six Americans in their homes the next day. Pedro explains that was the last time an Asian set foot on any mountain territory, as they mobilized lookouts, roadblocks, and attack dogs. Lisa asked Pedro how the dogs identified Asians. Pedro explains the dogs usually hold anyone whom; they do not realize until their masters tell them to let the strangers pass. Cindy rides close to Lee on her left side and Roberta at her right side. Pedro warns them the path will be too small for them to ride tree deep and promises they will help protect blue eyes. They call her blue eyes because of her sapphire sunglasses. At least by calling her blue eyes, it shifts any Asian identifiers. We are getting comfortable with our horses. Pedro reports our cabin has a stable attacked enabling us to feed and care for our horses during periods of bad weather. Pedro also reveals they have one month of firewood already chopped and will help them split enough for five months. The elderly couple lived on this small farm for fifty-one years. They built a wooden fence around their large pasture. Our horses will have plenty of fenced-in pasture to graze. They cleared many trees, creating open space where the horses can detect predators. The immediate geographical features permit this valley to be a place for easy protection. We were getting excited the more

Pedro told us about this place. This sanctuary had three wells; one was in the house, which meant the availability water even during the Arctic blasts. Entry into this valley was limited to a small path, which sloped slowly down the south side. Three sides were almost cliffs, dropping virtually forty feet. The remaining side was where the elders built their fence, so they could enjoy many more acres of pasture. We could not ride our horses on the minute entrance trail and instead would need to walk in front guiding our horses down the path.

We began to search for a place to camp for the night, since this was a two-day journey and Phillip warns that travel in the night throughout the mountains is deadly. Phillip and Pedro sleep in one tent, and my gang slept in the other tent. We asked Lee to sleep on her belly with her face down in her pillow. We placed a dark shirt over her head, as a precaution if Phillip or Pedro entered our tent. Our gang discussed many possible situations in which we would have to protect Lee's privacy. We fall asleep in our tent enjoyed the peaceful night with the occasional wolf howl or insect singing. This advance into a chilly cloudless night with a full moon and many sparkling stars. The wind dies down to an almost still extremely feathery breeze. The sole noise is my light snore, which Cindy pinches my nose repeatedly. She finally gives up when I stop snoring, and Roberta begins to snore. Lee usually snores, yet not when she is sleeping on her belly. We discovered Lee snores when she fell asleep in our car. Roberta and Lee become easily embarrassed when we tease them about their snoring. We never tease them in front of others, as this is our private personal privilege. With merely three hours before dawn, snake entered our tent first crawling over Roberta, who by nature is a light sleeper. Consequently, as she awoke and regained her senses, her fear of snakes made her scream in hysteria. As we awoke and began to free ourselves from this long snake, we found ourselves grabbing and throwing the snake throughout our tent. Roberta caught the snake and tossed it, unintentionally, directly at me. As I fell back, I spun myself in hysteria throwing the snake straight up bouncing it from the top of our tent. Fortunately, Roberta and I were the lone ones still in the tent. The snake landed back on me, nevertheless, this time I spun it around tossing it into the back of the tent. By now,

Pedro rushed into the tent leaping on the snake and cut its head off with his knife.

My stunned angels continued to scream as they lay in the group before our tent. Cindy reveals the snake is dead, as Pedro sliced it. This was the first time I saw my angels glorify another, yet as I looked at the snake, I knew Pedro deserved this honor. I stared at Cindy and told her I no longer belonged with them and would soon depart. I went to my horse until I heard Pedro scream aloud to claim he found a Chinese woman and for Phillip to help him capture her. I pulled my pistol and placed it against Pedro's head telling him if he said one more word, I would kill him. My angels gave Lee her sunglasses as we dressed her. Phillip came running. I told him to freeze in place and for Lisa to tie him. I ordered Roberta to tie Pedro. We completed their capture by tying them to a tree beside our camp next to the ropes that held our horses. I figure the racket they make will keep any snakes from our horses for the remainder of the night. I finished the night alone in my tent, while my angels slept in Pedro's empty tent. Likewise, morning came quickly, when my angels packed Pedro's tent and started cooking our breakfast. Lisa and I brought Pedro and Phillip to our campfire. Pedro struggled to get free from his rope while screaming obscenities to Lee. He cursed us as well, in how we could betray our people by serving a Chinese. He believed that we were Lee's hostages, and she was using us to get a foothold in the mountains. Lisa slapped Pedro attempting to bring him back to his senses. Phillip reveals to Lee that if his hands were free, he would stone her so to break every bone in her body, and then cut every muscle to produce a slow agonizing death. Lee puts her head down and begins to cry. Cindy and Roberta rushed to her wiping her tears and kissing her head. Lisa rushed to her back massaging it and promising that we would continue to love and protect her. Pedro asks Lisa how she can love such a lowlife angel of Satan. He spits toward Lee, while Lisa blocks it with her hand.

Phillip asks us why we are protecting Lee. He promises to free us from this Chinese monster, and everyone will protect us. Pedro begs for his freedom, so he may help save us as well. I tell Pedro that Lee is filled with our love from her smallest toe to all the hair on her head. Phillip declares Lee has been bewitching for us. Lisa asks Pedro to tell us what Lee did to them. Pedro declares Lee is Chinese, and all the Chinese want to own the mountain and destroy its inhabitants. The Chinese work differently in the secluded mountains, and then they operate in areas where the people are connected. Isolation appears to be a magnet in this perceived takeover. Phillip and Pedro continue to argue that Lee is a sea of evil. They continue to ramble until Lisa starts slapping them ordering they stop talking. I ask Lisa why we have our cold-weather suits on, and Phillip is wearing normal clothes. Lisa tells us to remove our cold-weather suits and tie them to our saddles. Afterwards, Lisa lines up with Roberta, Lee, and Cindy. The girls take Lee's arms holding them extended out and tell her to wiggle her fingers. Then each of the remaining young women wiggled their fingers. I ask Pedro to explain what just happened. Pedro laughs while replying the young women wiggled their fingers. Lisa clarifies that four human beings obeyed the command to wiggle their fingers. Lisa orders Pedro to examine their hands, face, and body while trying to understand their hearts. Notwithstanding I ask Phillip to tell me the things that are the same among the women before them. He leans toward the flirty side as he describes their bodies. Lisa teases him for talking so close to the line. Cindy asks them how they can hate Lee. Phillip replies because Lee is Chinese. I took at as a good sign that they added her name to her identity. Lisa caught this quick and began to talk directly about Lee. Lisa teases the boys by squeezing Lee's breasts describing them as firm and warm. Pedro and Phillip stare at Lisa's hands, as they stand stunned. Lisa then squeezes Cindy's breasts and reports how they are also firm and warm. Cindy asks her which ones she prefers. Lisa replies that she agrees with me, that Lee's are so much easier to handle. Phillip agrees with Lisa. Pedro disagrees, reporting that he likes the larger challenges.

I then ask Lee to drop upon her knees and begin crying as if in pain. Next, Lisa tells her to stand up and laugh. I tell her to remove her shirt, hoping the girls found a bra for her. Fortunately, they found one for her. When she took her shirt off, Pedro and Phillip smiled. Phillip tells me he is impressed both with the view and at how Lee follows our orders. Lisa tells Lee to kiss Cindy's shoes. Cindy tells Lee to kiss Lisa on the lips. Afterwards, Cindy smiles at Lisa and reports that revenge is sweet. Pedro asks Lee why she obeys us. Lee returns to her knees and tells them we are her masters. Phillip asks her to repeat what she just said. Lee answers that she is their servant. Lisa tells Pedro that they will die and kill so they may keep her protected and loved. I report to Phillip and Pedro that I love Lee so much that Cindy and I allow her to sleep with us when she asks. Roberta adds that we love Lee with our hearts, and thereafter she gave up her world, so she could serve us. Pedro wants to understand more about what Lee lost in her relationship with us. We tell them the Chinese Mafia is searching the United States for her with instructions to torture and kill on sight. Phillip looks at Lee, clarifies the Chinese wanted her dead, and asks why they want her life. I tell them when Lee rejected them and accepted us; she broke their strict rule about servants remaining the property of their masters until they die from their beatings and starvation from not meeting their production needs. Phillip asks about the production requirements. I explain that if the servant does not meet his quota, the master will beat them, starve them, and eventually have them ground into hamburger for the American fast-food restaurants. Pedro asks why they fall below production levels. Lee tells him that work begins at 5 A.M., and they end at 8 P.M., most times working on just a few bowls of cheap rice. Pedro discloses he knows nothing about the Chinese servants.

Lisa tells him most of the Chinese in the United States is enslaved prisoners. These masters keep their servants hidden. Phillip looks at Lee and confesses he had no idea that this situation existed. Lee explains this occurs for two reasons. The first reason is that they keep extreme tight control over their servants, as they sleep, eat, work, and clean in a group. There is no private time nor freedom. The remaining reason is that the Americans do not care, ignore, or even brutally hate them. The four of us rushed Lee pushing her flat on her back, forcing the ground to stop her. Subsequently, we started kissing and tickling her. Lee was laughing, causing all of us to laugh, especially as Lee was struggling to escape. Pedro and Phillip began to laugh watching this. Phillip confesses how he never realized the Chinese were really people. I tell them all the humans in the world love, hate, hurt, cry, and get hungry. Pedro reveals he remembers his father making the same argument once when he was a child. They were squatting in a shack when the landowner discovered them. The landowner told them they were lower than his dogs and slaughtered his father and younger sisters. He and his mother hid on the floor and crawled through sewers during their quest for freedom. Even during this horrifying experience, his mother made him promise never to forget these people are more, the same than different. I asked Pedro why he forgot this about Lee. Pedro answers with ease this is because she was not Mexican. Lisa questions Pedro if his mother was solely speaking of Mexicans, who were invading the United States. Phillip, now angry, wants Pedro to tell him why Mexicans are different from the Chinese. Phillip accuses Pedro of shifting our concerns to the Chinese, thereby allowing the Mexicans to walk in unnoticed. Cindy reveals to Phillip that this was not Pedro's intention because he was too limited in his mind to recognize anything different among the non-Mexicans. The hate in his heart will never tolerate others.

Lee tells Phillip the Chinese masters think the same way. When hate is your master, you can never again see others. It is sad when hate blinds you. I start kissing Lee's left cheek, while Cindy smooches her right cheek, Lisa left hand, and Roberta Lee's right hand. Pedro asks why we are doing this to Lee. He further declares us hypocrites by pleasuring ourselves with Lee's flesh. Cindy tells Pedro the hate of his eyes has taken the fresh blood from his heart. Lee moans how well their love feels pouring down her body. I reveal to Pedro that we love Lee as if she were a part of us, as she genuinely is. Lisa puts Phillip's hands on her heart, much to his delight, and then declares he is truly feeling her blood filled with her love for Lee. Phillip boldly declares that what he feels is pure. I walk over to Phillip and tell him that if he must betray someone whom, we love, and love us this much; I will give him the chance. I cut his ropes and hand him my knife. Phillip looks into Lisa's eyes and after that Lee's eyes. He then looks at me, hands me my knife, and tells me that Lee's blood will not be on his hands. Phillip walks over to the campfire and tells us the smell of eggs and bacon frying was all the torture he can withstand. Lisa invites himself to eat his fill and when finished, she would cook more. Phillip gobbles his late breakfast without hesitation. Lisa volunteers to prepare seconds. Phillip tells her he is full and not to worry. Phillip asks to speak to me privately. He informs me that Pedro will lie or do anything to get favor with Peter. Pedro has too much hate in him to pass up a chance to satisfy Peter. Phillip warns me that Pedro must be executed. I tell Pedro that we have not evolved enough to kill based on what someone might do. Phillip takes my knife, walks over to Pedro, and stabs him in his chest. Pedro cried out for Phillip to explain why he is killing him. Phillip answers because he has lost the ability to love and hate. Uncontrolled hate is too dangerous to remain free. Pedro pleads that he is not the danger, but Lee is the danger. Phillip argues nothing can kill someone who is loved such as Lee. Love finds a way to survive, while hate finds a way to kill.

Pedro spoke no longer. Phillip tells us that we must rush to our cabin as he pulls Pedro under the bushes. I ask him how he plans to explain Pedro to Peter. Phillip tells me he has a plan and grabs a few bear claws from his saddle and begins scratching Pedro's skin with deep cuts. He asked me lightly to push the area around his heart to force the blood through the wounds. Phillip reveals that Peter can read bodies and tell how they died. He will tell Peter he found Pedro after attacked by a bear and shot him to save him from such painful misery. Cindy asks Phillip how he knew he could trust us. Phillip tells us true love covers the body with a glow that his mother taught him how to see. The gleam flows through the air into the lungs of those who can feel. It fills your soul with a deep peace and warmth. Phillip conveys that he felt this peace and warmth when he looked at Lee and felt Lisa's heart. Lisa asks Phillip how he knew he was not feeling her love for him. Phillip explains the warmth was not the same as a lover's warmth. Lee asks Phillip if he can teach her how to experience this love, because it can perfectly be food from the heavens. Phillip smiles at Lee and replies he would be honored to share whatever he can do with Lee. We pack our horses; make sure Pedro's body is secure for Phillip to retrieve on his return trip. Lee appears jollier in this portion of our ride. Phillip bounces among each of us singing and playing each moment of our day. He shoots three rabbits for our lunch, and helps us gather various fruits. Our mood has not been this relaxed since our departure. The air feels wonderful as it releases a comfortable breeze that cools our faces. The sunrays send white arrows through the peaceful darkness of the forest. Our trail goes up the side of the sloping hills to the top, follows the ridges for a short time, and subsequently slowly swoops down passing through the opulent valleys then up to the neighboring ridge. This rising and the transparent effect of uplifting us and once on top of the adjacent ridge enjoy the view overlooking the enormous forest below us.

This view from the top feels as if looking down from the sky. The leaves are beginning to change into a rainbow of colors. I can completely read the sign of the times. This beautiful cover is the peace before the battle. Winter will paint this wonderful landscape white, with tree trunks absent their leaves. The lone thing that blocks our view is the occasional clouds. The strange tissue about these clouds is we are looking down instead of up at them. Most of these clouds are thinned now the midday sun has burned and thereby cleared. The winter most likely will be harsher on us in these mountains, nevertheless; the beauty of this far outweighs any hardships. I am enjoying the serenity provided through this trek on our horses. The steady stride of our horses carries us to our new home. Phillip is enjoying special attention from Lisa and Roberta. They have him between them on this trail, which is wide enough now for them talk while they venture to our temporary haven. Cindy, Lee, and I enjoy this refreshing competition for attention. I ask Lee why she is not enjoying Phillip's charms. Lee explains a victory for her would bring a life of danger. She is telling us Phillip cannot have a relationship with a Chinese woman. This area would not tolerate it. Cindy voices her disappointment with such racism and the way it inhibits people from following their hearts. We are not implying Lisa, and Roberta is not worthy partners for Phillip. Our disappointment is that Lee cannot compete. Actually, Lee is proving our love for Americans, and willingness to sacrifice for others for the harmonious welfare of all who surround her. She accepts this almost as if she believes this suffering is justified. I can read Lee's face even as she tries to hide her sugarcoated misery. Cindy and I grab hold of Lee's hands while I tell Lee she is the angel of our eyes. I am astounded that Lisa and Roberta are listening and watching us. Roberta and Lisa yell back confessing their love for Lee. Phillip pledges his loyalty and love for Lee. Lee reveals to Phillip if he loves her, he must protect himself first, thereby protecting her friend.

We continue to find ourselves amazed by the depth of Lee's philosophy. I recognized Lee is simply a part of our puzzle, and even though an important segment, we must keep any adjoining piece connected. This means we must maintain the world around us to support Lee. Even though everything appears to concentrate on Lee, I believe this occurs because we kept everything focused on her. She is the chick that is just emerging from her egg, and we are the chickens fighting off the wolves. Cindy claims that Lee gives us something to fight for, or a purpose. When she follows us, we believe ourselves to be leaders. Her honesty reminds us of our lies; the hate of those around us reminds us of our former hate. Consequently, having less hate provides us the opening for more love. Even though we have a few miles and days into our adventure, the road is going up for us presently. When we fall, the reason is to rise once more. These mountains remind me of life. It is not until one is on top the valleys appear. When viewed from the top, the valleys show their true barriers, which is nothing more than small descends either toward a greater height or toward a sea. The astonishing quality of the sea is now the surface is flat, yet the floor of the sea reflects the valleys and mountains or another world appearing as an opposite, yet so much is the same. Water kills those who live above it, as air kills those who go below the flat line of the sea. The line divides, attempting to forbid crossing, yet the airplanes travel the skies, and submarines break the laws of the dark mysterious world that thrives unseen. It validates these lines do not form impenetrable walls. Life above and life below an ageless border, which needs no guards, nevertheless, holds the promise of death for those who trespass. As in both realms, life exists by consuming death. The strong take from the week, the large engulfs the small. This circle cannot be broken, and as with a wheel continues to spin knowing where it has been and where it will venture.

We continue along another ridge, the number I do recognize as I gave it my mind. Instead, I fall helpless to the awesome beauty that the land holds. Their beauty exists magnified by the spiritual charm unleashed by Cindy, Lisa, Roberta, and Lee. The wind fluffs their hair and carries the heavenly harmony of their voices. These vessels created by God hold the magnificence of humanity. They purr, as kittens, yet roar like lions, appear as doves, nevertheless, strike as eagles. Warmth fills my heart knowing these precious bundles of love will wrap warm blankets around themselves as they rest before our fireplace in the cabin Peter has temporarily granted us. Our travel on this new ridge was different from the previous ridges. This time, as we did not follow the path that dropped to the valley below, yet flowed into a fork in the path, one dropping to the valley's floor while the other continued. I questioned Phillip about the destination of the ridge top path. He discloses this path goes to our cabin and continues into Canada. He smiles at Lisa and tells her their winter home is merely one hour before us. Phillip's words came true, as almost one hour before us; we encountered another fork in the path. This time Phillip has instructed me to descend into our valley. My angels and I freeze in absolute shock as we stare into this wonderful cradle for our winter life. I see the wooden fence created by the previous owner. Although no fence will control predators, they will keep our horses in our pasture. We must fight the pillagers as they attempt to feed from the beasts, which serve us. My father taught me many methods in protecting our beasts, as, both cattle and horses provided the foundation for our survival. I remember my anger that one animal would kill another simply to feed on its flesh, until one day, Lisa asked me to inspect my plate for each meal that day. That evening, she had me read the list to her, speaking solely of the meat. I ate bacon for breakfast, hamburgers for lunch and chicken for dinner. I ate from a pig beginning my day, cow in the middle and bird to finish this date. It comes as a shock when recognizing how I am also a creature that feeds from the flesh of another living creature.

Lee argues how humanity feeds not solely on flesh, but also on love, and how we value blood as a sign of life and not drink it, while the beasts consume it without regard or warning. Lee warns the love of blood is the desire for death. My minister warned how the Bible forbids drinking blood, except as wine for our Lord's blood during communion. I am confident we will have much time to explore our thoughts during the lazy cold days of the mountain winter. Now, we have a new joy to explore. Our cabin looks rather large from this descending path. I remember how Phillip told us the stables occupied the western wing of this cabin. We always wanted horses, nevertheless, living in a small-town provides no stable or pasture for these peaceful obedient beasts. I believe my four angels will give them plenty of attention this winter. We will need our horses as companions as we sink into the loneliness of winter as we battle our cabin fever. The sun begins to abandon us giving way to darkness as we close the gate, which will prevent our horses from using this path to escape from our pasture. Phillip leads us to our cabin, which rests comfortably under a group of trees. Phillip tells us the trees provide shade when needed and relief from the vicious winds when they sweep through the mountains. We remove our gear, saddles, and bridals from our horses and store them in our cabin. Our horses quickly begin eating the high grass that circles our cabin. I realize that we must cut the lofty grass away from our cabin and store it in the ceiling above our stable. We will not cut the grass around our cabin, as we wish for our horses to graze closely and easy to protect. Our cabin has one large room, with a loft over the back half of our home opposite the fireplace. Our first night, Phillip, and I will sleep in the loft as my angels will sleep in front of the fireplace. Naturally, they can use the fireplace to cook our breakfast, which will bring Phillip, and I out of our loft in the morning.

The next morning, Phillip departs our peaceful valley, bringing sadness to Lisa and Roberta. We spend the day cutting grass and gathering nuts, berries, roots, and wild herbs. I knew that we had much work ahead of us as we prepare for winter. Phillip and another three men brought us flour, sugar, salt, rice, and dried beans. Lisa gave Peter over $2,000 for a three-month supply of grains, extra blankets and their delivery throughout the mountain winter months. Peter also sold me a variety of traps that I will use to offer our clan with meat this winter. Lee watches us work, and without reservation labors beside us. We do not ask Lee to perform any task. She bounces among us helping each throughout the day. I notice how Lee searches for any who are falling behind or appear to need help and rush to their side. Our evening entertainment is a few hours listening to the radio. The Chinese massive investments seemed to either decreased or become skillfully surreptitious. Lee argues their operations are clandestine and merely expanding the strongholds; they have established. Lisa thinks the radio believes the public has lost concern over the speculation that has run its course. It is like warning people about a fire that at no time came. The secrecy of their operations, which even I must attest never to have witnessed, but merely aware of this through the insight provided by Lee, is remarkable. We need simply to worry about any passing strangers rather than the Chinese setting up a foothold in these mountains as the mountaineers stand united against their entry. Our cabin has no windows, and always we keep three boards preventing our door from being pushed inward. We nailed our saddle towels over the door entrance; if someone opens the door, Lee will stay protected. We agreed that while in the house, we will wear no shirts. This is naturally to my great benefit, and considered within the private rights of a clan. This justifies our need for security within our house, wishing to conceal our partial nudity.

Inside the cabin, we did not wear sunglasses, although we kept them in every corner. Roberta asked me one day why I walk around each day with such a great smile, especially since Cindy, and I am active during the late hours during the night, when they think, we are asleep. I ask Roberta why she must pretend to sleep when a married couple is coupling. Roberta's face becomes red as Lisa and Lee voice their disapproval. Lee tells Roberta that a matrimonial pair should be respected enough to be awarded the reverence of their privacy. Lee tells me to be of good cheer, for I am living in this cabin as all men dream they could exist. I tell Lee such is natural to me, to such a degree that I give no attention now to it. My love for Lee, Roberta, and Lisa is, as I love myself, thus, their chests are as mine, for they are mine in that my heart lives within them. Lisa rushes to my side and confesses why she would ever hide herself from her greatest protector. Cindy laughs and warns that we may be spoiling our protector. Roberta argues that Cindy merely promotes this so her husband can see how blessed he is. Lee agrees that I truly have the finest one. Subsequently, Cindy tells us the greatest that she has is the love, loyalty, and sacrificing she enjoys from this wonderful family. I smile and confess how magnificent it is to live among such a splendid group of angels. Lisa declares that we are bewitched sheep living among a wolf. I smile and tell her it is her turn to sharpen my fangs. Roberta enlightens us to the true reason Lisa has all walking topless in our cabin, since she wants to make sure I keep the fire burning high. If our cabin were to become cold, we would all need to wear our shirts. Lee confesses that she is amazed at how hard I work to keep the wood stacked. I tell them that freezing is an unyielding burden to bear during the empty cold of winter. Cindy kisses me as my angels confess they would desire no other to share their cabin. Lee argues the warmth of our hearts will keep our cabin from freezing. I tell her the fireplace increases the warmth of the heart as it also chases the cold from our cabin.

One night a visitor from before returned to us. In Cindy and my dream, came forth once more Saladus-naine into our minds. I was shocked to see how Saladus-naine changed her wardrobe to match that of my angels. I asked her what happened to the shirt she always wore previously. Saladus-naine declares because of the shame of being different was greater than the privilege to watch me blush as I do before my angels each day. I report to Saladus-naine that I do not blush before them as I do before her. I also tell her I did not understand that someone so old could still be firm. Saladus-naine tells me to watch my words, or I will enjoy the highest mountain on Earth handing upside down from a tree overlooking a great cliff. Cindy argues that she will tie Saladus-naine beside me and see which one cries the loudest. I apologize to Saladus-naine and tell her I hope she stays this bold or bolder as I am sure daring would make sure a blush on my face that she would treasure for many years. Cindy challenges Saladus-naine, citing her fear would be that once I beheld this sight, I would no longer want the angels I now have. Saladus-naine laughs and tells us that flattery will get us everywhere with her. Saladus-naine welcomes us to our winter cabin and reveals that our country cabin will be safe for us this coming winter. She tells us that we shall have three visitors during the winter months who will ask to enter our cabin. The day before these visits, she will place a flower in front of the door. The next-day Lee may not leave the loft. We will cover her with blankets and hay. While she keeps her sunglasses on, while outside, and all wear their hats so Lee does not odd by being the sole one to wear a hat. Saladus-naine warns that we must exercise much during this winter season because next year we will meet many challenges in our journey to Canada. Cindy and I are so relieved to hear Saladus-naine speak about our trip to Canada, as it leads us to believe we shall survive this winter. She honors us on the unity we have, as this will be a great weapon as we venture on our journey. Our pronounced mission will entail; we learn more about each. She gives one final warning before her departure; telling us that one among us was a traitor and that we must decide what is best for all when solving this terrible event. Saladus-naine gives Cindy and I, a hug and kiss and promises to watch over us. Our dream ends while we wake up for the beginning of the greater unity.

Cindy and I awake and begin preparing our breakfast by boiling water for our oats. We boil more water for our coffee. We have plenty to get us through the winter, especially with our resupplies, the next one just before Thanksgiving, and the final one during the first week of spring. No one can cross these mountains in the bitterness of winter, except the Chinese Mafia, who continues to search for Lee, sparing no cost. They are giving extra attention to the Rocky Mountains, since they have no strongholds. The sole benefit that they perceive the mountains offer on their behalf is their great hate of the Chinese. The Mafia loses seven warriors during the winter, two by weather, and five with gunshots. I admire the way they slip through these mountains, when, if spotted, they will need to fight to survive. We pray each day that they would cease this horrific search. My angels wake up and fold our blankets converting our one bedroom back into our living room. We had a table and chairs, which the previous owners ate their meals. We put the table and chairs in our front yard, as we enjoy eating outside at least once each day if possible. We spend much time sitting around while telling stories. We ask Lee to tell us more about her life. She tells us about the ship ride to the United States. They packed them into a storage container for a two-week journey across the Pacific. They had a small container of water for around forty people. The horrible aspect was how they disposed of their bodily waste. They could not let it leak out, as the smell would alert customs that human cargo was aboard this ship. The group selected one corner in the unit as a restroom. The stink leaves them with stomachs queasy. Lee reports this sickness overwhelmed any fear of their capture by the Americans. In fact, she prayed that either death or the Americans would take her away from the pain and misery that was in everyone's eyes. They had something deep within them, which would not allow them to die. Their destiny stood already laid out for them, with no pursuit of happiness. Everyone understood that they were properties used for production. The sole reason that they received food was the physiological requirement; they be fed. The masters gave them the least amount of food to prevent death. The servants accepted this destiny as it has been like this for thousands of years. The sole thing to change was the work they performed. The current production required skills, which the masters eagerly beat into the servants. The assignments are segmented into simple and repetitious. They believe this keep the production moving quicker as each part of the process performed with the least amount of thinking.

Lisa reveals our hayfield days. We would stack the hay throughout the entire day. The farmers paid us little money; however, it was the lone way to earn the money. Our parents made each of us save this money, a practice we agreed. We wanted extra money available if of a family hardship. This gave the work a purpose and us an opportunity to believe as if we were contributing to our family and therefore, a greater sense of belonging. We never worried about the excessive heat, nor did I worry about missing any baseball, because all the young people worked in the hayfields during the three annual cuts. We each had our farms we worked with a wagon crew. The work was strenuous, and we gave this no concern. The greatest motivator was how our father allowed us to use our savings to buy the gifts we wanted to give for Christmas. We will miss this so much this year, as I always enjoyed the expression on my mother, Fred, Don, Julia, and my grandparent's faces. Our home was filled with holiday cheer, as the miracle of our souls, because somehow we got each other exactly what they wanted. We were the masters at working secretly through mystery for this one great annual event of love and giving. We rejoiced in knowing that all our family had many of their dreams unfolding before them. We sang our Christmas songs and practiced our parts in the annual Church's Christmas play. Each class at school also had an exceptional activity. Holidays were extremely special in Marked Tree. Thanksgiving and Easter were the other pronounced family events. Thanksgiving was our harvest festival, and we spared no food on this great holiday. The school actually closed their kitchen for two weeks after Thanksgiving as all the students brought their lunches, as turkey salad was in all the lunch bags.

Easter was the other great family holiday, as we feasted with our extended families joined for a Sunday afternoon feast. Lee reveals the servants never have holidays. These are days when the work much harder, rewarded with the scraps from the masters, once their dogs completely eat to their fill. The servants rejoiced when watching the dogs devour the leftovers. Occasionally, a dog will reject the scrapings when the master selects the fattest among the servants and feed them alive to their dog. They share merely fifteen minutes of crying while holding hands as they share the grief and misery created by their birth. Servants are not permitted to marry. The master selects the men and women who will mate. They use the strongest men for mating. They watch these men and women when caged together. If they do not consummate by morning the one who prevented the action will be beaten. The female will remain until she becomes pregnant. Babies are the properties for the masters, as they understand their servants will not begin families because of the misery of their existences. They collect the babies who will be raised by the masters, as they realize the mothers will attempt to kill them and spare these babies from a life of pain and misery. Cindy asks Lee to chase these painful memories from the soul, for all have evil and murder in their histories, for not to have this would mean they would have died long before in our histories. I tell Lee that we had a great-grandmother that was Quapaw Indian. She passed many tales of our ancestors how they were massacred and tortured. They took their food, and next their lands. She told how they merely hungered for blood as their greed and lust never found satisfaction. Lee argues the Indians were occupying the American lands, as the Kings of Europe had given these territories. Cindy argues how is it just for a King to give away land, which is not his. Lee asks how this land is not the Kings since they discovered it. I ask Lee how the Kings could discover a land where the Indians already lived. Lee's smiles and answers with ease saying the Kings owned the land because they were the masters.

I study Cindy as we shake our heads in astonishment. I whisper in Cindy's ear that there is no arguing. Lee has been conditioned through years of imprisoning indoctrination. She cannot conceive the Indians actually owning the land. We are fortunate she has concerned over the contemporary takeover in the United States. The difficulty is Cindy, and I agree to current infiltration is legal and simply playing off the willingness of Americans to misrepresent in their sales activities. Suddenly, Americans believed they were used car salespersons. They also jumped on the do not ask, do not tell wagon. They kept quiet, selling their land knowing the schools were below standards, and the public services were declining. To justify their deceit, they cited the Chinese would need their private schools until they improved their English. They also believed that the decline in public services would be justified, as the Chinese received special tax benefits, therefore, if you do not pay, why you should receive. Either way, one considers this; the Chinese were operating within the law. They established their footholds and worked long and hard to connect them. The issue that concerned me presently is the way they reacted to the refusal. The way they are actually fighting with these mountain people is wrong. These current landowners have the mountain spirit, which justifies executing whatever is required, to hold on to their homes. The unity in their defiance is a two-way sword for us, as one-way cuts in our favor giving independence, yet their search and desire to harm Lee create the other painful cut. We are fortunate enough that Lee trusts us to the extent; she will try to stay free, even though every part of herself is pleading that, she surrenders. It is almost as if she is programmed in such a manner that if she is not suffering and in misery, she has no right to exist.

The second of many debates with Lee began with Lisa telling her the Indians owned America, and the European Kings had no right to settle in their colonies. Lisa asks why the original settlers traded or purchased the lands from the Indians. Lee surprises us by arguing the foreigners purchased the land, so they could establish footholds they could reinforce when they began their offensive campaigns. Lisa argues that China would never dare to use their military against the United States. Lee contends that China has the greatest military, considering every critical military weapon is either completely manufactured in China, or had vital parts manufactured in China. The United States is merely an assembly point, which even this step is shifting to Chinese owned companies in the United

States. Lee further contends that if it is a technical chip or circuit card, it is made in China. The American government supports and funds the Chinese government exploitation of the Chinese cheap, yet highly skilled labor. Many American and international companies operating in China would be nationalized, such as Bowing and GE. Merely a fool would believe that during a war, China would permit fighter jets to be constructed in China and shipped to the United States for offensive use against them. Freeze shipment of the small parts, and many tactical systems would become useless without repair parts. Lee also contends that China can use the technologies of all nations exploiting the cheap labor to their benefit. Lee cites that for each jeep, airplane, or ship the Chinese lose in America, they can reproduce another one hundred. The Chinese government could mobilize a 250 million person military force, supplemented by their revolutionary use of women. Ever since China industrialized itself and become leaders in the technological areas the government has learned the great benefits of using women. The requirements for women are harsher than they are for men. Eligible women are selected, and offered a position within the prestigious technological areas. These women must have all reproductive organs removed to accept one of these positions. Once removed, they dedicate their lives to their position and preserve their skills to the highest position level. The government fears that if these women have children, they would love their children more than they love the government. These women work, study, and must also serve as sexual partners for any of the men within the unit or group if they so wish. The government believes this will prevent the men from temptation from outside technology thieves.

Lisa motions for Lee to stop as she poses an important question. Lisa asks Lee how she knows all these things, because in the United States, such information is considered top secret, and the government goes to great lengths to prevent its release to the public. Lee explains this to be the difference between a government that pretends to serve the people and a government that serves the people. She debates the Chinese government accepts responsibility for feeding the people, and they use all this power to accomplish this mission, as it is their undertaking. The needs of the people rule the government, and none may accumulate too great of a wealth because most wealth goes back to protect and support the masters, who must make sure their servants are producing. The American government protects the interests of the extremely wealthy, as most of the elected officials depend on this two percent to finance their elections. Lee marvels at the misconception that it is a government elected by the people. Nevertheless, those who gain the power must give it to the few wealthy who control the nation in secret. There is no security for all, as many starve or have no homes. The masses work, and pay greater taxes using credit cards with outrageous interest rates to survive. The people believe in a free press, which must struggle against the secrecy and power of a corrupted government. Lee tells us she no longer desires to speak about the American government and reminds us the Chinese government has absolute control and power over all the people. They share all knowledge as they expect all will work to make sure their mission is successful. This is proven by the great fear they have in the possibility that she may share this common knowledge with outsiders. This is the same as blood leaking from the veins in a body. The more blood that leaks, the closer to death the body approaches. Lee reports that when all the people have the same mission, there is no need for secrecy. The indoctrination begins early in life and is reinforced by their complete and absolute environment. Even to voice any disagreement or concern is an offense punishable by execution. Actions are controlled through harnessing thoughts before they become actions.

Roberta changes the course of this debate by arguing that our safety is in danger through our continued association with Lee. We can never trust any Asian, especially now that we realize how they are networked through social bonded mental indoctrination. She continues to argue the cognitive chains lie connected to posts and will always be bound. All their eyes report to the same brain, a union that can singly lead to one result, which is our death. Roberta asks Lee what will happen to us if she were caught. Lee confesses the Chinese Mafia will execute all they can verify who had contact with her. They will spare none. Roberta asks me if I truly love Cindy. I glare at her in bewilderment requesting she explained why she would ask such a foolish question. Roberta questions, if Cindy existed tied to a rope hanging from a pronounced cliff, would I release this rope and watch her fall to her death. With great anger, I declared that I would jump over the cliff to save Cindy. Roberta argues that by having Lee with us, we are in constant mortal dangers. She continues by declaring the Chinese are everywhere, and that one small mistake on our part would lead to our deaths. Lee agrees with Roberta telling us that we must abandon her for our safety. Lee rises, and begins to put on her cold-weather clothes when Lisa asks her what she is doing. Lee confesses that she must depart for our safety, as no one has ever escaped from the Chinese Mafia, and it is foolish for her to believe she would be the initial. Lisa enlightens Lee there is always an original time, and that she will be the first of many. Lisa declares this our destiny. Cindy and I agree, telling Lee if we must die, we will die for something, rather than live for nothing. Roberta declares we are murderers and fools. We travel one road to death and face terrifying torture at the hands of the Chinese Mafia. Lee verifies their Mafia has torture techniques fine-tuned through the ages.

I walk over to Lee and begin to remove her cold-weather outfit. Lisa asks me if this is really the time for me to undress Lee. I confess that one more moment without seeing Lee topless would be a torture far worse than the Chinese Mafia. Lee looks started at me and asked if I am serious. Cindy laughs and confesses to Lee that she was the one suffering this torture and pleaded that I save her. Lee asks Cindy if such a want is natural. Lisa explains to Lee that certain women simply cannot control their need for great beauty. Lee laughs at us, revealing the sole thing she knows is the Americans who rescued her are strange. I explain to Roberta that she may leave us if she so desires. Roberta tells us that she will not leave or betray those of her blood. We hold our hands, knowing before this winter is over, we will learn so much more about our hearts, which overflow with love. I enjoy the comfort that Lee understands us accordingly considerably better. These offered a rich source of joy we can pray will flow before us on the rough road that are in front of us.

Chapter 04

Holders of the Truth

My parents returned home late Sunday night greeted by our grandparents with the disturbing news that many of their children were missing. They did not discover their absence until the hour of return Sunday night. We were often away from home over the weekends, especially as many of our friends live far into the country on their farms. On departing Friday night, we would not return until the Sunday night service. The churches in town held two services on Sunday; the town's people attended the morning while the farmers attended the late-afternoon service. They had much labor in their farms, several of which needed work daily, such as feeding their livestock. These people dedicated the remainder of their Sundays to family and church. Knowing that most of the rural attended church Sunday evenings, those who lived in Marked Tree expected their children home, so they could clean and prepare for their schooling. Sunday evening came and our grandparents awaited for Lisa, Roberta and I, nevertheless; we did not return. Our parents arrived shortly after we were expected, and the frantic search began. My father rode swiftly by horseback to the farm he believed we spent the weekend. Accordingly, these people denied we stayed with them. Consequently, my father knew of just one-way to discover where we stayed. He would question us at school Monday morning. This gave us critical extra time. My father questioned our friends and classmates. The school rushed our minister to comfort our father. He was losing her mind overwhelmed at the thought of losing so many of his household. Protecting and providing for the family was a value we held in the core our values. Our father believed his failure to protect us had placed us in danger. The school and police took him back to our home after the doctors declared solely our mother could revive him. Our grandparents and mother were harsh on our father on his return. My mother did not want to leave our family this weekend as her maternal instincts forced her to plead with our father to stay home this weekend. My father gave her no mind, as this was normal before time; they were to spend time away from their children. Fred, acting for our father, reminds our mother that she even pleads our father not leave for short trips to Memphis. Our mother agrees with Fred, but then reminds him that it is the father's responsibility to understand all things and when her warnings are real and when they are a woman's foolish ravings. Fred, having always failed in his arguments with his sisters considered this as no different and simply shook his head in wonder. His friends and he often talked about the mystery of the minds of women.

Fred and Don often depended on our father and me for counsel when the women in our family were behaving strangely. With our father ill and I gone, Fred was now alone and defenseless. The lone weapon that he had was the maternal bond with our mother. Although he knew they were not in physical dangers, it is the mental arsenals they unleash, which bring men to their bewilderment and defeat. Either way, Fred and Don so far withstood many such invasions through our mother, Julia, Lisa, Roberta, and Grandma Cathy. Fred knew that while his father was overburdened, he must comfort our mother. Fred reminded our mother how hard our father worked for his family and all the wonderful things he did to prove his deep love and loyalty to us.

He reminded her of the times he fought to protect us and how industrious, he was in making sure we were continuously fed, protected, and received any needed medical care. Fred argued the power and fortitude of our family depended on how united we remained during these times of great trials. We must believe that we shall someday come together once more. Fred reminded our mother that we needed our father to survive, and by destroying him now, would me the doom of her remaining children. Our mother and grandparents faced another great burden. Our customs place great shame on families who cannot control their children. To have children run away from home is notwithstanding a greater disgrace. This implies, these children existed not loved, provided for, wanted, or even worse protected. The community would shun the parents in all places except in the church. Our people believed the church was holy ground and while in church, all would behave as the scriptures.

The churches believed most of the Chinese were Hindu or Buddha and therefore, feared they would attempt to interrupt the family services. Although this fear was mythical, it was accepted to the extent the churches required any person believed to come from or represent China to undergo security checks and religious indoctrination. Other Asians simply had to prove they were not from China. The Catholic Church appended additional safeguards, believing Chinese was vulnerable to demonic influence. Many believed the church understood China's access to great wealth and was merely awaiting a financial offer for admission that met their expectations. The stores would continue to sell basic things; however, they would refuse luxury items claiming negligent parents needed to keep focused on their responsibilities instead of pleasure. The store clerks with everyone else in the community refused to speak with the shunned people. My father would not be disturbed much; as he spent most of his workday inside the trucks, he drove while making his deliveries. Considering how vital this network was to trade in our community, no one would attempt to obstruct his work. Our grandparents also found themselves shunned. Many held them accountable, especially since they lived so near and if the parents were gone, expected, as they did, them to stay in our house. The senior social groups they were members of at once expelled them. Our grandfather spent his days riding around the county looking for any clue about our whereabouts. Monday evening was extremely quiet in our house, especially as Fred, Don, and Julia had long days at school. The other children either shied away from them or bombarded them with questions. Marked Tree never had so many runaways at once. Concern arose over Cindy, and I because we were unmarried. The lone thing, which prevented a total community lynch mob, was the fact we were chaperoned by Lisa and Roberta. Accordingly, both were over sixteen and female, therefore, considered qualified adults. It was important to everyone Cindy's reputation stood protected.

Marked Tree encountered another surprise beginning on Tuesday, the first week after our runaways. The Chinese began an extensive search throughout all Poinsett County looking for clues, trying to determine our destination. They charged that we had kidnapped a defenseless Chinese girl and were holding her demanding a ransom. Our community stood divided in their response to this charge. Most believed us innocent in that our customs avoided Asians, as we had no desire to anger or associate with them. We welcomed their money when selling our land and farms to them. They were buyers, or as we believed fools with too much money. Our people would liberate them from their excess money and move to another larger city. The Chinese initially were paying well above market value. They notified all the realtors that those who sold this year would receive double market value. Those who will sell next year would receive seventy-five percent market value. November saw a mad rush to sell farms. This helped defuse the social shunning of our family, especially as people existed self-occupied with packing and preparing for a new beginning in a fresh place living by modern rules. The former community bonds now stood eroded. Many claimed our runaway woke up a sleeping desire in our area to live elsewhere. The awareness of tempting criminal activities emerged as many now forced to entertain the possibility that certain among them would become criminals in their new homes. This was possible because the social support system would no longer be available to reinforce our value practices. The cities were changing quickly as initially housing prices began to soar. The Chinese began building one-hundred plus story apartments with twenty housing units on each floor. They built these in the slum areas in the cities. They gave people who sold their farms coupons that would provide five years of free rent. Their ability to construct these gigantic structures was unprecedented as with their ability to house many of the sellers with new homes throughout the United States. If a family insisted on a specific area, the waiting time stood extended; however, most simply wanted, what they considered as a small fortune in the sale of their property and the five-years free rent, they grabbed the next available unit, regardless of where it was located.

The pace of the integration was increasing, not simply in Marked Tree but throughout the United States. The quantity of capital investments was overwhelming. The way these investors treated their new property presented a mystery. They disassembled old houses of no value, with anything of the recycled value delivered to their proper collection stations. Special house moving companies braced, homes they wanted to save, and relocated them to fresh locations forming new towns. They disassembled the other buildings on these farms as well, and massive modern structures built. Titanic storage facilities were appearing as an organized state of the art distribution centers. The American government labeled this as Building a New America for Arkansas. The state varied with the location, always being the state where the structures existed. This was to build both national and local pride and to shift attention from foreign investors. The politicians wanted it to appear as if they were creating this new infrastructure for the United States. The American Engineers and Scientists warned this rebuilding was vital as the roads and especially public water and sewage on the brink of complete collapse. When considering the cost of rebuilding the old, or simply creating modern cities with an up-to-date distribution network connected to a hungrier world, the fresh plan was more in line with global concerns and needs. No one nation was completely self-sufficient as all depended on each another in this new world. The politicians painted this as joining the new Earth and continued to warn about the environmental dangers created by outdated technology. The Chinese built massive solar panels guaranteeing a renewable ecofriendly energy consuming, manufacturing infrastructure. People found themselves indoctrinated that if they stood against this modernization, they were actually destroying the Earth. The Chinese began to recruit volunteers for these projects, asking Americans to give back much of what they took. They were careful to use volunteers to keep the financial greed separate from this rebuilding, and to paint large American companies as the monsters trying to destroy the Earth. The Chinese were prudent to provide many of their servants on these projects. This painted China as the nation that truly cared, especially as the servants removed in character to the image they created. We care, so why do not you care blared through so many advertisements throughout the American media. Who could deny this when since the Chinese volunteers working beside native volunteers?

Many people believed China was the salvation of America. Skeptics reassured everyone that China coexisted too heavily invested in America to allow such a valuable trading partner to fail. The media continually reported and emphasized the decay of America and the impregnable corruption in the government. The nation's support for the military began to determinate. This was a slow continue process, which was many years in the works. Constant economic pressures from all levels of government forced continual budget cuts. The foolishness throughout the government forced the politicians to spend tax revenues; they knew America could never repay. Each government official remained in office by giving their district more than they paid in taxes. Traditionally, the system could handle a few of these exceptions; however, it could not withstand this as a standard way of business. Every vote came with a price tag for their districts, as the honest and sincere candidates seldom made it to the office and those who did, failed quickly. The interest on the deficit was more than what the government received in taxes, nevertheless, no politician would vote for any form of a tax increase. The federal government shifted all they could back to the states and even forced states to pay more for any national activities in these states. One such example was the constant threat to relocate military installations. States began to tax more, including no longer permitting federal tax exemptions. The states stopped supporting education and law enforcement, forcing the counties to bear the complete burden. The counties raised property taxes, phone fees, and satellite taxes and local Internet fees. These fees were such that many removed their phones and satellite on the TVs and vehicles. The property taxes increased by almost four times while the counties removed any exemptions from churches. They argued that the separation of state and church did not apply to local governments. They also threatened if the churches did not pay these taxes, the people would. The people could not risk an increase and therefore, voted for the counties' rights to tax churches.

The increase in property taxes proved too much for many of the poor and the elderly, who as a result lost their properties. The counties, hungry for more revenues immediately seized the properties in default of their taxes. This existed as motivated by the ready source of eager Chinese buyers. Those who refused to sell to the Chinese so no relief as the government at once sold them. To reduce the number of private sales to the Chinese government, counties levied an eighty-five percent property revenue received tax. The public did not receive this well as civic uprisings spread throughout the nation. These attacked, were concentrated, and met no resistance from law enforcement. The citizens collected the county commissioners, and burned them in front of the county courthouses. The media published this directly as the congress and the President, who published an executive order for immediate relief until the official, passed a nationwide revocation of this tax law. The judicial system straightaway supported the people by declaring such property revenue received tax as unconstitutional. The Chinese began passing out ten-free year licenses to the new apartments built in the large cities. The media promoted this as the Chinese giving these people a place to live in areas, which should offer much additional employment opportunities and access to a wider variety of educational facilities. Many viewed this as the American government casting people on the streets, many because of the lack of jobs, and the Chinese government offering to help the poor and elderly. The media used the work of the foreigners to offset the continuous failures that began in Washington.

Washington sold the future of American beginning as early as the 1990's. They all knew the future existed sold, yet they arranged to retire in foreign countries, they did not care. They did not realize that history would paint them as traitors. The Chinese who released all the records to the media after the transformation recorded this history. Select senators and congressional representatives were hunted down like Nazi leaders after the Second World War. They were safe, for the time being, as their exodus began in 2025, which was still five years in the future. This story simply mentions it now so all can rejoice in knowing many who destroyed America existed captured and revenged. The Chinese government was merely using the American government's interest payments on their debt to make these monumental purchases. They could take control of America at any time they wished, simply by calling in the government's debt. The reason China had not called in the debt was that while the U.S. remained independent, Washington received the blame for the economy. China waited until they had a strong foothold before consuming America. The Chinese put firm pressure on the government to disband all labor unions. Once more, the Chinese government was working hard to make the U.S. government appear like the bad people. The public stood divided over the disbanding of the labor unions, especially considering all government retirement programs; except for social security, they simply dissolved. The funds remained transferred to social security as the media were watching this down to the penny. The public supported this as taking from the rich and giving to the poor. Teacher salaries dropped below minimum wage. Minimum wage laws stood repealed as the government was struggling to keep American service and production enterprises. One hand helped while the other hand hurt. Labor costs were now the lowest that they had been in sixty years. This halted the new car, and new housing units to a fat nationwide zero. Although the wealthy could afford new cars, the factories could not justify production for potential few sales. Ironically, this did not have a significant impact on the Americans. Used car sales picked up the vacuum on the car lots. Other nations, such as Canada, Japan, Germany, South Korea, Italy felt the impact like a sledgehammer. Nevertheless, the greatest financial blow lay just before us.

The blow came when the Chinese released the full details of the American debt, which for exceeded the value of the economy. Any further decrease in the credit rating of the United States would bankrupt the Americans. The United Nations called an emergency session at the request of the Russians and European Union. The world had to decide which currency should become the world currency. The qualifier for this new standard was the strength of the candidate economy. The final show of hands was all nations, including the American representative who received bribes, voting for China. The Yuan was now the world currency standard. China had vast production activities worldwide, and dependence on trade; therefore, most nations had much to gain. They believed with the Yuan, as the world currency, China's ability to manufacture would be stronger. This enabled the third-world nations to concentrate on social programs and not invest in manufacturing activities. The Chinese could manufacture these products much cheaper than any other nation. Most industrial engineers submitted their inventions to Chinese manufacturers as no other production network had the startup facilities that could make these unknown things advancing modern technology. Another if not equally important reason was the confidence and trust in the Chinese security. All knew the Chinese would maintain their privacy, except for the reverse engineering, which was going to happen either way. At least this way, the Chinese paid the startup costs. These nations knew that with critical components dependent on Chinese production, there was little difference between one part and the complete item. The logic and economics were there. With all focusing on the benefits they received in this process, none considered the global impact of these endeavors. The Chinese stood ready to trade and clearly had the efficiency and resources to pass savings on to their customers while at the same item enhancing their quality of life. It was hard not to appreciate the benefits, as everyone agreed, if you shopped in America, the container would say, "Made in China," so why should not the remainder of the world enjoy these same benefits.

Life in my family was as a dog riding on a roller coaster. Even though the town's people were still reserved for their inability to keep their children home, many found themselves confused trying to understand the new challenges that they were facing. The world was different, yet even the churches were proclaiming the Chinese as the best hope for an American future. The churches appreciated the social efforts that existed financed by the Asians as other Asian nations were exploring investment opportunities in the United States. Stiff opposition by the Chinese Mafia, who launched an aggressive campaign, put a serious damper on the other Asian investors who hoped to ride the wave of Chinese success. The Asian communication networks made the investment adjustments leaving the playing field staffed solely by the Chinese. Back in Marked Tree, social arguments were supporting the Chinese, especially as they were housing the poor, providing grains from their new Midwest farms. The Chinese donated twenty-five percent of the grain and all food products from their vast fields to the food pantries established by the Red Cross. The twenty-five percent was actually much more, in that these new mega farms far outweigh what these lands previously produced. Advanced land fertilization combined with genetic enhanced generated bumper crops. Another amazing feature was the increase in Chinese medicine as many of the herbs and special items such as deer antlers were available in the North American continent. The media were quick to promote this new source of medical care, for a wide range of general health problems. This was an alternative source of critical medical care, which was rarely available now, as the unemployed had no medical insurance, and the reduction in wages accompanied with a depletion of medical insurance. Medical insurance companies were going out of business and closing their doors. Government insurance programs carried the load and with financial cutbacks, left empty hospital beds, and all foreign doctors returned to their native countries. The public accepted more responsibility in their health prevention practices. The media overemphasized this because public concern declared a great danger in pandemics and plagues. The Americans were not aware of the massive accumulation of Chinese servants on American soil, therefore the Chinese worried much more over the dangers of plagues; as such, a killer would damage a vital link in their production resources.

The failure in Washington resulted in reckless administrations for the previous thirty years. Our nation now had, what many believed as the greatest President in our modern history. Nevertheless, this was too much too late. History would show her as the final President, and although she had previously governed the largest state, the resources she controlled were as a drop of water in a giant sea. The sole saving grain of hope lay in the world not able to predict her actions, as she spoke hard, yet with ration knowing her bark had no bite. She represented motherhood to the mothers in this nation, although mothers were not losing their sons on battlefields, they were losing the ground on which they walked, and the pride that once guided these fathers and husbands as they provided for their families. They placed the blame on the fathers who had deceived the masses for their own glory and coffers. They claimed, eat, drink, and be merry, for tomorrow will not come. Nevertheless, tomorrow came as they hid behind a skirt in the Oval Office hoping for mercy. The President exhausted most of her effort attempting to define the true impact and eagerly searched for possible solutions. She spoke of the United States being a loaded ship sinking in the middle of the Atlantic Ocean. She needed to find a way to unload the ship and make immediate repairs as the water entering was greater than the water removed. She tasked the financial experts and military specialists to develop all possible scenarios.

She established this secret group of the greatest minds as her advisors. The President commissioned the Central Intelligence Agency and the Federal Bureau of Investigations as their number-one priority a review of all major campaign contributions, and the receiving candidate favors rendered in Washington. The President, to ease the friction against these releases had her investigation published in the media. She informed the public the release and investigation were voluntary and exposure essential in these final days of America. The country's condition was so weak now that she won her election without any great promises as most conventional contributors wanted to create an appearance of genuinely trustworthiness. There was no pronounced gain in political power currently. The oval seat burned with fire and considered the seat of foolishness by the world. The world, who no longer received their free funding at the American taxpayers' debt suffered the withdrawal pains and found themselves burdened with the fear of paying their individual ways, such as their nation's citizens paying their own taxes. Naturally, when American foreign aid ceased so did support for American interests abroad. The serious need to cut federal funding forced the President to recall her military stationed in foreign lands. Americans welcomed bringing their boys home, claiming the world had the Chinese to abuse now.

The President permitted all who returned to separate or retire, if eligible, from active-duty. She soon elected to disband ninety percent of the active-duty force, deciding to revamp the American warrior philosophy to be solely defensive. Any nation that attacked the United States would receive a complete counter nuclear strike. The strikes would continue against that nation or group of nations until their ability to launch offensive actions no longer existed. The United States would not occupy any conquered lands, or place American in defeated nations for security purposes. The United States published this 'destroy the striker' defensive strategy to the United Nations. Any who attacked the United States would pay severely. The President ceased all weapon developments, considering no complete system could be assembled on American soil without imports from China. The American nuclear arsenal was the deterrent defensive weapon.

The President closed all American ports for imports. The ports stood dedicated solely to export American products. The President received a group of Chinese officials. Following a short thirty-minute meeting, all ports remained open for Chinese imports. The Chinese agreed to use their naval forces to prevent other nations from smuggling imports into the United States. The President justified these imports citing the Chinese needed to resupply and support most of the American Manufacturing needs. Special arguments supported the massive building of public housing as the Chinese construction depended on steel and raw material, coupled with building materials, from China. The public supported this; as the media pleaded, Americans solely purchase Chinese or American products and no other imports. The Chinese collected many imports in the merchant inventories, and sent back to their country of origin for a trade credit. The Chinese enforced this procedure, applying the funds against the American debt. The American government gave tax credits for the actual cost of the returned imports to the proper vendors. China also provided trade credit points for Chinese's products purchased. These points were given to a local government official who submitted them the state collection points and then to Washington and finally to Beijing for the debt credit. These points barely offset the interest increase in the debt since the Yuan replaced the dollar as the world currency, thereby degrading the American credit rating. Solid pressures were guiding government officials as all accepted the time for sacrifice was at hand. Americans tightened their budgets. Those who frolicked in luxurious activities remained targeted for public rage. The media began publishing personal financial information on the wealthiest two percent of the Americans. This group remained blamed for influencing lawmakers to engage in reckless activities, which led to the unbearable deficit. The Chinese wanted this last powerful, wealthy group, as it contradicted much of the communist philosophy. The Chinese officials pressed the American government to freeze this huge financial power and apply it toward the federal deficient.

The public demanded transparency for those who ensued labeled as greedy wealthy. Those who owned large manufacturing interests surrendered this to the federal government for the people's benefit. The media fine-tuned the public miraculously discovering causes for the American decline. The Chinese Mafia was providing the media these opportunity targets, and thereby controlling the people. The public needed to identify causes for the dismal state of affairs. Nullifying these sources proved to provide the release value needed to serve as a source of hope. Hollywood, Nashville, and other creative centers for musicians and actors disbanded their projects. TV and radio stations concentrated on the news, and Chinese created English media, which portrayed a fresh America rebuilding herself. No one hid the fact that rough times were ahead. The people were conditioned that honor lies solely in keeping our promises and paying their nation's deft. The public elected the leaders who created this disaster, and gave over to the pursuit of pleasure and listened to promises they knew were too good to be true. Just because one walks with their eyes closed, they cannot profess blindness. The churches supported sharing the blame, citing so many examples where leaders were followed because of the manner; they fed the lusts of the public. The media reported countless stories as they targeted areas, which knew their treatment far outweighed that which was fair and equitable. These people knew their benefits were at the harsh expense of others, yet claimed they received because of their wisdom in playing the political game. The glamorous schools with class sized around a dozen students in areas surrounded by outdated schools with standard class sizes close to one-hundred students were prime examples. The power of the media in identifying these injustices, coupled with the federal and states no longer supplementing their activities lay the foundation for certain immediate equalization.

The President survived her latest challenge working in unison with the Chinese. She stood before the media recalling how one who wore a beard eight-score bloody years before declared no state could separate from the union. Ten states declared their independence. The President prepared for the second civil war. The Chinese declared before the United Nations that any state could become independent, once it had paid its legally bound part of the nation's debt. China declared that each state was liable for ten percent of the national debt. They justified the fivefold increase by citing the remaining states would suffer from the betrayal of the rebellious states and thus would have increased defensive and social expenses, for if the fifty united, could not pay their expenses, how the ten separate, could and merely forty united that could carry the weight made by the once united fifty. The world studied the elegant reports the Chinese presented, which clearly supported their position. China's secret purpose in preserving the union was to keep the American credit rating from dropping further as a too great of a decrease would place this excessive debt borne by the Chinese as worthless paper and place the Yuan in jeopardy as a world currency. The world supported the Chinese proclamation, rallying around another important purpose, which was the fear of the American nuclear arsenal spread among weaker separated governments. If any among the ten detached states became power hungry, they could fall prey to the temptations offered by lust and greed. A small state could desire to regain former glory at any cost, having less to lose and so much to gain. The President received the official revocation from each of the ten states, which attempted to vacate the union. She restored the union without the bloodshed of another civil war, one of which the nation could not win causing all to fall in defeat. She postponed the demise of the United States discovering the people and the world followed their new leader. She asked the Chinese representatives if they could afford to buy the world as the Americans had once tried. The Chinese Mafia explained to her that these hungry people lowered the price of their loyalty to what can reduce their hunger. Solely those whose bellies transpired filled daily will feed both their hate and lust. She sat down in the Oval Office shaking her head, realizing this new dragon breathed a fire that no ocean could squelch.

The Chinese Mafia, working through the Department of Justice imprisoned the governors and legislators belonging to the ten treason states. These legislators faced public execution under treason laws, with the complete support of the media who portrayed this as love for America and these treasons motivated by their private thirst for power at the expense of a dying America. They portrayed this as murderers enlarging a hole in the bottom of a ship, which is sinking. Everyone must remain dedicated to the future of the United States or be labeled as a traitor. The media, which now completely owned by the Chinese, believed the public's loyalty, needed constant motivation and inspiration. This Mafia covered the doors to their offices and vehicles with the flag of the United States. They covered the rest of their walls with pictures of former presidents. The media continued to present these people as the saviors of America and holders of great mercy. The Mafia caught all servants who had attempted to seek their freedom, most with the American public's support. All caught, they portrayed as rebels attempting to seek and kill innocent Americans and initiate a rebellion. The Holders of the Truth, or Chinese Mafia surrendered these escapees to the American courts, agreeing that they must be executed in public. The hypocrisy remained in disguise as the monster of American self-conceit rejoiced at the misfortune of these innocent servants. The executions coexisted televised and reported on all radio stations. Lee shook with terror as all stations reported the final rebel had joined with American children from Marked Tree, Arkansas. Our fortune lay in Peter declaring TVs as Chinese's tools to mislead Americans, and forbid both TVs and newspapers from the mountains. Peter could not control radios, as even we listened, nevertheless, to our benefit, radios shared merely words and not images. Our mountain exclusion and solidarity kept us from the public's eyes, even though many search parties crossed our mountain farm, never able to identify us, as I now boasted a beard. The pressure of the nation's wrath was breathing around us as the public celebrated to torture and death of each Chinese servant. Americans perceived themselves as, once more, the masters of the world, as even the Chinese fell before them. These illusions of grandeur ended as quickly as they arose. The terrifying revelation was how much anger and brutality the Americans harbored as sickening. They hungered for the opportunity to lead another Chinese to torture, and a miserable death, even filled their prayers at night. The Holders of the Truth concealed the legalized slavery that chained the Chinese servants. The masters kept these servants out of the public eye. Accordingly, the security increased to such an extent that underground tunnels connected the titanic apartment complexes with the miserable secured sweet shops and incinerators used to cremate the bodies of those who died under the horrifying work conditions. Those Americans who attempted to document this insanity transpired captured, executed, and cremated in the factories they were investigating. The outside of these structures ensued not maintained as all windows that broke boarded. Since no cars parked in the lots, most believed jobs were unavailable and with the structures looking so poor, none desired to explore these places. If work was available, the majority believed the work was for illegals or bums and would not lower themselves to this level. All products manufactured in these factories legally bore the label as Made in the USA. They made products for store brands, such as Wal-greens and Wal Mart, by it guaranteeing distribution and offering these retailers lower prices.

Those who lived in Poinsett County were constantly under investigation by the FBI, CIA, and the Holders of the Truth. Their hunger for the prosecution of Lee and us was forcing them into starvation. They studied every part of our lives, capture, and executed Uncle Bill. They captured Theodore Jones, Lisa's father hiding in Mexico. The extent of their search was comprehensive. Mexico provided the freedom from the restrictions of visible morality the United States imposed. Theodore stayed in the remote desert areas in Mexico. His mistake was the use of his cell phone, which revealed his location. We saw a movie where cell phone batteries could serve as GPSs. Our family, as most in Poinsett County, never could afford cell phones. Personally, we believed them to be cancer sticks such as cigarettes. Our minister revealed this great secret to us, embedding a resolution never to smoke or talk on cell phones, which we considered the same. Theodore, living in Saint Louis modernized his philosophy with a cell phone as part of his need to communicate. The Holders of the Truth surrounded his home, and bombarded it with smoke. Theodore had two Mexicans with him. The Mafia captured the three people, hung them forfeiting torture because of the limited time not risking any more chance of exposure than needed. They quickly buried them. Considering Theodore led a private life, the Mafia depended on the call log of his cell phone. Each contact was interrogated, and most secretly executed. This comprehensive cleanup executed as if invisible escaped detection from the public. The Mafia could not find our escape vehicle, as we had altered the license number, thus eluding all video surveillance. Our vehicle was a common style and color, consequently creating an extensive workload on law enforcement.

A new group emerged throughout the United States, solely by a common purpose. Many believed us as innocent and created tales of our rescue. Accordingly, extremely few knew our situation, these storytellers created tales, which elevated us to modern-day Robin Hoods. The tales reported how we lived in churches and in caves, walking America during the hours of darkness. One reported that we found Big Foot and traveled with him. An additional story reported that we escaped by ship to South America. Even so, another claimed we burned our vehicle in Saint Louis and dumped it in the Mississippi River. The story we enjoyed the most reported that Chinese smuggled us into China and with facial surgery, transformed into Asians. The media, in fear of missing a true story, reported these tales on the radio. The saving aspect in these tales is that it sparked the public in rushing to report seeing us. One day, we were in Florida, the next day in Maine, ensuing day in California, followed by Washington. The Mafia completely investigated each lead. The rate these stories appeared soon left the Mafia with a three-year backlog. We found ourselves amazed at how this new support group could coordinate their efforts. They passed all information personally and by word, except story submissions to the media. Nothing was committed in writing. The group dedicated themselves to the fictional aspect of our escape adventure. They added stories of feeding children in orphanages and us visiting hospitals comforting the injured. One more story reported that Lee (Li Jing) left our group and escaped to Taiwan. This separation broke our hearts as we divided with Lisa and Roberta going to the West Coast then Cindy and I were going to Florida. This story claimed the Chinese tried unsuccessfully to kidnap Li Jing, each time saved by the police. America was hungry for a new hero.

The difficulty lay in whom, the hero would fight, as the Chinese remained respected for their heroic humanitarian deeds, as within a few short years over seven million Americans lived in Chinese rent-free homes. These Goliath structures materialized within weeks, completed, and ready for residents. A new twenty-first century world was lifting itself out of the decay and emptiness of disappointing social experiment that failed to survive three centuries. Another marvelous aspect was the modern factory that appeared beside these housing complexes. Many complimented the Building a New America for the foresight in their planning. The United States failed in understanding these happy people needed jobs to support their families. This housing connected the livelihood, allowing the families to stay in these homes. Too many people lived in these homes because their government did not protect their jobs as they watched these jobs go overseas. A miracle was unfolding in front of people who had lost all hope. Someone cared for the regular or average American. Even though they did not recognize us, the legends they created came to life. They identified the enemy as any who sought to harm us. Therefore, the media blamed the American law enforcement and the Holders of the Truth seeking solely to protect and save us. Lee warned us those who believe they are helping would share their secrets freely. When the heart believes it loves, the blind eyes will see angels, where devils hide. We accepted Lee's warnings as food for the wise as our actual survival depended on her. We did not appreciate the true dangers, which surrounded us as well as Lee. She was from that world. Lee ran from dragons her entire life, staying barely one foot in front of its burning fire. Lee was the umbrella, which kept the rain from soaking us. The hypocrisy of American politicians led to backroom secret deals where they received the glory for the new rent-free housing in exchange for tax-exempt status of the goods produced by the construction company's factories. Even in the decay of America, the spirits of her leaders were still addicted to lust, greed, and blood.

Building a New America announced the erection of four mega-apartment structures between Marked Tree and Memphis, with four modern grain-processing factories near the Mississippi River. Millions of these housing structures rose throughout an unknown America. The Chinese owned the companies that extracted and converted the raw materials into steel, cement, and other resources needed. Old towns and villages stood dissected, and materials recycled. The Building a New America devoted itself to rebuild the United States with the plan of maximum efficiency as a paramount foundation for the modern Earth where all would have food, clothes and the chance to earn a life providing for their families. The American continent offered a strategic setting for worldwide distribution, and was centrally located for planet wide defensive and offensive operations. A portion of the Chinese lived on American soil now, which lessened the population burden on their Asian lands. This portion was subdued from the American populace because the Chinese government felt it was not strategically viable for the current time. They also thought that the smuggling of people into the United States would cause many to question their motives. Americans were willing to receive, yet no way willing to give. They would fear the poor impoverished slaves China had dying in these camouflage factories may reduce, even if by a small portion, the totality of benefits the Chinese were bestowing on them. The Chinese servants understood the American vices such as greed, lust, and hunger for power. This provided one effective tool by which the masters used to maintain unquestionable obedience from their human property. Lee explained the four of us terrified the Asians on our bus. This was one reason why no one questioned us for taking Lee with us. They were afraid that we would unleash a deadly curse or plague on them. These Chinese counted Lee as lost to death with no hope for a future, simply to suffer miserable endless tortures. The idea a servant would trade her master for Americans was beyond their conception. The Mafia instructed the servants residing in America to understand the Americans could hypnotize them into betraying their masters. When they witnessed this demonic enslavement, everyone must fight to save them. This remained an effective tool to prevent escaping when in a group. The exoduses now occurred when alone, with no witnesses. The Mafia killed any who helped another getaway. Therefore, all escapes transpired individually planned and secretly.

The American economy was weak, as businesses were not producing at earlier levels, causing tax revenues to plummet. The Federal government could not receive any additional loans to finance government operations. They disbanded the active-duty military except for a small skeleton crew. National parks remained closed. All federal funding for roads, bridges, and education ceased. Every person who remained witnessed their salaries reduced by seventy percent. This still fell short of the needed cuts. Congress passed an emergency bill, which demanded the instantaneous execution of all prisoners who held lifetime sentences. They also authorized, the immediate release of all nonviolent offenses, such as drug possession and sale, was set free as well. Congress received reports that sex-related criminals would commit crimes once more when released. Based on these reports, they ordered the execution of all sex-related offenders. Within days, all fifty states followed suit. Mental institutions were closed, with those who had sponsors released to their sponsors. Those with no sponsor befell execution. The government's argument was the boat was too heavy, and if several not tossed into the sea, all would sink. The Mafia approved this tactic as this prevented the burden of execution from being born in the Chinese. China was solely interested in Americans who could produce; all others would lose their lives, following the same policies they currently employed with their servants. The media began to support the policy of senior execution. They claimed that any who could not care for themselves should be free to live in the heavens. The government accepted this as it would reduce social security payments and medical costs. The major revolutionary amendment decriminalized all drugs. The law also authorized execution for any American who was addicted to drugs. The victim would be placed in prison and if he or she displayed signs of addiction, they would receive their punishment.

The release of the non-violate criminals brought a deadly curse back into Marked Tree. Mitch Anderson's father agreed to sponsor him, bringing him back to his hometown. Mitch was angry and voiced his desire for revenge. He went through town harassing all who testified against him in the trials. Mitch cut car tires, broke bedroom windows, and throw tomatoes on students on their way to school. Mitch assembled a sizable gang from the few who remained in Poinsett County. While recruiting his fighters, he became aware of the magnitude of farms, which were sold. His unstable mind was as a head covered with matches crawling through striking pads. The instability began itself when Mitch saw the farm buildings disassembled, fences removed, super-sized farms created, and construction equipment working the soil. The Chinese maximized the available food producing lands. Roads that did not lead to a current resident were plowed. Considering the season was moving toward cold, they planted winter wheat. Trees covered the land and steep rocky hillsides they reserved for another need in the food chain. These areas were fenced and reserved for raising livestock. Extensive thought was devoted to the planning and maximizing this land, as they believed future food needs would require this to prevent worldwide starvation. Mitch could not accept that Poinsett County was facing modernization. Rational residents welcomed this. Unfortunately, Mitch was not realistic. He led his gang to the local Mafia center to a three A.M. raid. Mitch claimed he was searching for any documents that could be used as evidence for illegal activities. His true search was for updated information on capturing Cindy. He found the complete file, and took possession of it. Mitch ordered all the gang to wear head masks and plain black pants and shirts. Regrettably, four among this wore panty hoses over their face, a mistake they would later regret.

Mitch ordered that every file had its contents spread throughout this building. He hoped this would postpone or even prevent discovery of the file he took. This gang departed from the building as everyone went a different direction if someone was watching. Something, rather than someone, was watching. The complete break-in occurred recorded in thirty-two motion detector activated high-definition security cameras. They converted the images to 3-d by combining the angles of the cameras, which could cross-link and identify everyone. Even with this advance, they were merely able to recreate six of the thieves. Working with Poinsett County Sheriff office, they tried to seize these six. Mitch, along with many others in his gang recovered documents, which detailed the methods the Mafia used to obtain information. After discussing this as a group, everyone agreed that when the police came to apprehend them, they would commit suicide, most by hanging themselves. The six identified received calls the sheriff was going to bring them in for questioning. These gang members hung themselves at once. The Mafia discovered instantaneously that Cindy's file was missing. They suspected someone in our family organized and executed the break-in. They swarmed around our home and took videos of everyone's heads. They transferred this video to the computer through their cell phones. The computer offered one partial match with Fred's head. Accordingly, the Mafia completely trashed our house, looking for any possible evidence of contact with us, or the documents, which ensued stolen. They found nothing. The deputy, who accompanied the Holders of the Truth, arrested Fred and held him in jail, until his trial the next day. Our father asked if he could attend this trial. That night the Mafia put Fred in their torture chambers, first removing his clothes and burning his back, stomach area, arms and legs. They burned every part they could cover with clothes, so this horrible abuse would not be detected. After the burning, they threatened to beat him with a whip, which would cause horrid pain. He could escape further torture if he signed the six documents in front of him and pledged to plead guilty the next morning in court. To make sure his plea, they showed Fred, the document where he confessed his father organized this break-in.

The Holders of the Truth promised to destroy this document after Fred gave his plea. Fred signed the confession of his crime, and admitted to kill three Chinese. This was to make sure his trial went fast and Fred would be executed, as Marked Tree would fear Chinese's revenge on their area. Fred also signed confessions claiming three of his friends were accomplices. Fred did not recognize any of these three, as they were the people, the Mafia believed coconspirators. The Holders of the Truth met with the sheriff asking for sole jurisdiction over these three. Having no public funds to incarcerate these boys, the sheriff agreed, actually thanking them for not holding this against his county. Like all government employees, he wanted the fringe benefits the Chinese offered. The deputies apprehended the three, just one of which was a part of Mitch's gang, took them to their execution food-processing center, and ground their bodies mixing their minced flesh with beef. They sent these modified hamburgers to the collection center for this area for distribution to the fast-food chains. Our father and Mitch watched Fred confesses to the break-in, before the court was emptied before reading the murder confessions and sentencing immediate execution. The judge declared this as a national-security issue and separate from the break-in charge. Our father and Mitch re-entered the court as the judge read Fred's confession and ordered that he be surrendered to the Holders of the Truth, with a seventy-five year sentence in China. The deputies rushed Fred out of the court, never to be seen again.

Mitch knew Fred was not a part of his gang and that these invaders could force any confession they desired. Mitch won favor with our father for the support he gave Fred. Our father invited Mitch to our home where in our basement, they engaged in one of our father's debates. Our father was still in a state of shock over the submission by our law officials, and how quickly they surrendered him. Our government for personal financial gain betrayed us. When the betrayal is against unseen and unknown people, it lacks the personal criminal element. This situation had the personal element; it was directed against Fred in front of our father. They surrendered an innocent citizen to these foreigners who delivered money combined with promises. Mitch apologized to all in our family over his inability to cope with the loss of Cindy. He confessed that his love for her was uncontrollable, and he believed the sole reason Cindy gave herself to me was that she sought to destroy him. Mitch asked my parents to explain Cindy's surprise instantaneous love for me. My mother remained disappointed that Cindy took three of her children who now were wanted for kidnapping a Chinese woman. She believed Cindy entertained too great of an influence over us as if the ability to hypnotize and control us as one would control puppets. Mitch's theory provided many answers for the questions that tormented my mother. Someone needed to take the blame; especially with the ease, they imprisoned Fred. My parents realized three more of their children were doomed once the invaders captured them. The question that puzzled the debate was how this could happen in the United States. The media sold Americans this was proof of our superiority. We had the great minds and knew how to conduct business much better than any other people in the world could. The Chinese were paying double market value for property that most dreamed of gaining their independence and move to a part in the country that offered more opportunities. The question my father and Mitch now debated was the true value of the farms sold. Individual farms had little value, yet combined, and reorganized; the new total would easily justify the investment. Mitch discovered these when recruiting people for his gang. He could not reveal to my father how he discovered this; therefore, he explained it with a simplified example.

Mitch asked my parents to visualize a large field with red bricks and various people collecting the bricks by hand and carrying them to a place just above on a hill. Once collected they bring master builders who build a beautiful, priceless castle like a mansion worth millions. The bricks that lay on the ground were worthless, nevertheless, they gave the landowners fifty cents each. Considering the landowners pled with so much and could not afford to have the bricks disposed. They believed heavens blessed them with an opportunity to make a little money and regain use of their property. Our mothers asked why those who were attempting to deceive by selling actual junk can be considered victims. She also questioned why these buyers would be expected to explain the purpose and potential profits and their brilliant plan. Mitch argued this was a moral issue dealing with the basis of right and wrong. My father disagreed, citing the complete foundation for capitalism rested on the wise using their money to create profits, and in this situation both the buyers and sellers both benefiting. Large corporations do not release their secrets for their new market revolutionizing products. They have extensive research and development expenses that must be recouped before entering the profit areas. Society wins with a technological advancement while the company, which took the risk awarded as permitted with the current cultural norms. My mother reminds Mitch these investors are giving between five and ten-years-free rent and considering they paid double market value is an act of pure social continuousness. The true vice in this scenario is the invisible negated, corrupt value system of the

Americans. My mother cannot comprehend why we think it is justified when making victims of others, yet when others create a profit from our greed and lust, and leave our deals without suffering a loss, we consider betrayed. Mitch lowers the argument closer by claiming the big difference is that we do not comprehend where these ends. When he adds Fred's execution into the equation, the boundaries of cultural acceptance and morality erode. My mother, who surprisingly sounds like an advocate for the Holders of the Truth, asks Mitch if we have created this warlike environment and created enemies from those who were operating within the rules for the game, which we created.

Mitch accused my mother of siding with our enemy. My mother asks when we defined them as the enemy. Accordingly, my father informs his wife when they took away their son. This was when they crossed the line. They falsely accused, an innocent child and used lies to further their mysterious agenda. Knowingly forcing false confessions crossed the lines of potential trust and morality. Exacting such a fierce punishment on an innocent child strongly suggests they are either hiding something or sending a deadly message warning Americans to take the backseat on this ride. The admission of guilt is established by the secrecy of their operations. They could have released more information without harming their operations considering they cripple community businesses in the areas they reduce the populace, and then purchase this land for pennies on the dollar. There was no great concern considering these establishments had no income producing potential except for the reclaimed land growing future crops, which would need almost three decades to break even. They agreed the bottom line was their mysterious thirst for violence as a retribution implied goals, which were not in accordance with Building a New America or Holders of the Truth. Before any finalized, analysis could be formed, more information was needed.

Mitch asked my parents how more information was obtainable, considering Fred died because others believed this need existed. My parents confessed to Mitch this presented a challenge it might be too late to overcome. The power of the media if redirected toward them would be deadly. The media were reforming America as all saluted our soldiers who returned home never to roam overseas again. Too many families suffered through holidays and special events as their loved one sat in an unthankful nation that desired merely to exploit them, without regard to the helpless lamb that they had at within their selfish grips. They could not fight America personally, so they were waiting until the United States sent a military force to do their fighting, and those who did not die, they exploited becoming giants around the minute American soldier they had within their grip. The media publish thousands of such stories as the Chinese intelligence could pull the deepest secrets concerning third-world former American policies. These nations no longer considered abusing Americans as the easy ticket to advance their agendas. The Chinese held the tickets now, and they never gave anything, unless they received payments first. A casual review of the way these nations treated the United States, clearly justified their precautious agenda. The little nations would have to earn their greatness the same way that all the great nations in history had done before. The Chinese were wise enough to realize that showering with gifts merely leaves them hungry for richer diets. When the offerings ceased so did any trace of loyalty. The direct response was an immediate raid on all American embassies. Americans found themselves taken in public and tortured. The President without delay launched, air strikes against all the world capitals, with the support of the Chinese intelligence and military. The Chinese believed that changes in the foreign governments would create enough confusion, providing an excellent opportunity to stabilize these new governments' positioning the objective infiltrations in strategic places. The public or even advanced intelligence organizations could not comprehend or understand the complexity of their operations. Working with the American government, they played the role of compliant subservient partner. Most nations recognized China was attempting to gain experience in the role of the world peacemaker, and were merely cooperating with the United States during this transition. Either way, China voiced their disapproval in attacking embassies, which way a disgrace to world civilization. If China was going to lead, embassies had to be recognized as safe havens, at any cost. Therefore, China got a show of force, and the United States received the blame.

Americans called for all citizens who lived outside their borders to return to the homeland or renounce their citizenship. China was active in the recall, although the role, they played was behind the scenes. The United States wanted its citizens where they could protect them, whereas China wanted them consolidated in one place. This concentration would prove beneficial by reducing the opportunities for Americans worldwide to conduct terrorist activities. The United States closed embassies in all countries, except Asia, Russia, and the Middle East, southeastern Asia and the British Commonwealth. The United States immigration control traced most illegal immigrants and assigned them to the new Chinese or Building a New America plantation. They were officially the properties of these food production companies. On paper, they were listed a contractual employee. These illegals had chips planted inside them; therefore, if they escaped, recapture would be quick. Those who returned to Mexico were secretly executed. This new legal form of slavery authorized these people to be treated exactly as the Chinese treated their servants. These slaves soon learned life was different now; they were beaten, and all freedoms denied. The Chinese decided to build an advanced subversive transportation network using many of the existing below ground mines as a foundation. They would use these fresh Mexican slaves when they were not working in the orchards or other agriculture areas. China would use electrical transportation powered by underground electric generators placed in the flowing subterranean rivers.

The Holders of the Truth additionally began installing a new technologically advanced air cleaning and oxygen generating system. Their research projected that current atmospheric conditions would deteriorate to level below what could sustain human life. The Chinese reduced manufacturing in their homeland while upgrading their facilities. Production in the United States by the Chinese servants kept the total Chinese production high enough to satisfy demands. The Chinese Mafia designed their production facilities to self-contain the air purification systems and thereby provide safe havens when the world's air could no longer sustain life. They had an extensive underground tunnel system created from the intensive subterranean mining activities available and upgraded air purification and oxygen generators. The total capacity stood at four million in China and projected capacity in the United States would reach three million, all Chinese. Seven million served as merely a small dent in the over one billion. This forced the communist party to create computer calculated lists of population skills and distribution for a balanced population to continue the human race after the air was clean enough once more to sustain human life. Those on this list were notified of their inclusion and the new duties they were bound. Secrecy was demanded, if the public discovered this salvation plan, worldwide chaos was inevitable. The selected, once they agreed to the terms received a chip next to their heart. If they disclosed this secret, the chip would execute them. Those who did not agree after notification were instantaneously executed. The government reassigned those in this group to join duty areas. This made it easier to control and limited contact with non-selectees.

Mitch sat puzzled with my parents as they tried to determine if any form of revenge or justice was possible for this terrifying turn of events. They vowed that a price would be exacted for Fred's imprisonment. Mitch agreed to think about this for a few days and return for a second meeting at that time. Mitch directly contacted each of his gang members and told them the gang was disbanded, and he planned to contact them personally of any future needs. He emphasized that no future contact by phone was safe and additional security would evolve once their available resources improved. He instructed them never to discuss any of the gang's activities, even to spouses and best friends. If he discovered one had told their secret, he would kill the person who released the secret and all those who receive it. Mitch warned them the Holders of the Truth would select neighborhood members at random, torture them, forcing false confessions, giving them a legal foundation with a free ticket for removing who they wanted. One of his gang members had a relative who worked for the Department of Corrections. This shocked cousin spoke about how people were brought in and led them down the dead man-walking hallway instantaneously. He furthered identified Fred as one of those took the one-way trip down the death corridor. He recognized Fred from their school days, as Fred often accompanied Cindy, Lisa, Roberta, Julie, Don, and I was walking to and from school. Mitch drilled his friend for as many details as possible. Mitch understood he could not ask the deputies or the Department of Corrections for fear the Holders of the Truth controlled all communications and especially any inquiries into likely criminal activities as defined by the American public. Mitch realized my parents needed told about this. Mitch went to my home, then after dinner told my parents the true fate of Fred and after that revealed his services. My mother and father broke down, insisting that my grandparents not receive this report. Mitch agreed and asked my father for instructions.

These murders under the cover of the law by a mysterious government were not a new phenomenon for Americans to suffer. The Chinese knew about the innumerable cases where the American government had stripped their citizens of any form of civilized rights and freedoms. There was a pretense of liberty being free; nonetheless, many from around the world learned this liberty was a sword that killed for profit and power. The Chinese began to leak reports, for sale by corrupt American government employees too eager to betray their political opponents. As one report saw the destruction of Republican, a new report the next day saw a Democrat fall out of grace. Many joked that D.C. was a bowling alley where the pins go down one at a time. The argument my father advanced to Mitch was the Chinese were doing nothing different from our government. The Chinese did not lie to their people; they simply conduct operations as normal under the system. They believe that if the people were supposed to know, the government would tell them. Obedience and the loyalty of one for all, compared to disobedience and the loyalty of none for all, or eastern philosophy versus western philosophy. The Chinese were loyal because to do so was good; the Americans were disloyal because to do so was good. The painful part of the betrayal Americans suffered was the disbelief that a just and honorable nation would abuse their citizens as such. The agonizing part currently was how the American government was surrendering their citizens to the highest bidders. America existed divided into three sections, namely, citizen, Democrat and Republican. My father told Mitch the Chinese had to suffer a little pain from what they had done to us. He also asked Mitch not to organize anything while in Marked Tree for fear; the Holders of the Truth would punish everyone in this county. Mitch agreed and gathered two friends and drove due north.

Chapter 05

Roberta's final tribulation

Lisa ventured over to the fireplace and tossed two more logs on our fire. We can hear a winter breeze brush pass our cabin. We have no glass windows; therefore, we cannot investigate outside our cabin. Two dogs roam around our cabin. They were hunting in our valley one day when Roberta offered a little of our meat and a few bones adding her country girl charm as she quickly turned them into loyal friends. Subsequently, Roberta supervised me as I dug a hole under one of our stable walls. Our stable has three stalls for the two horses we have. Roberta and Lisa converted the middle stall for our two dogs, Sunday and Easter. They sleep in their stable most of the night, except for their late night stroll through our valley. They take their extensive strolls during the days, sniffing the trees and snagging small game for us. They work well as a team when hunting and are eager to bring their catch back to us such as rabbits and prairie dogs. We eat the meat, and they eat the organs and other nonedible parts. The rabbit hides make excellent gloves as the raccoon hides make exceptional hats. The dangling coon tails aid in blending our appearances. Accordingly, the coons are too fierce for our dogs to handle one-on-one. When they spot one, our dogs come rushing back to us excited and jumping in circles. They usually alert me. Their mouths begin to water as I return with my rifle. I try to avoid my shotgun with the coons, as their hides make those wonderful hats, and my angels do not want a lot of little buckshot holes in their hats. These holes dampen the intended insulating purpose of these caps downgrading any cosmetic benefits offered by these natural hats. We have bonded with our two horses and two dogs. Phillip took our other horses back to Peter, promising to bring fresh horses in the spring. We kept two, in case of an emergency. All emergencies would be addressed to Peter, considering we could not chance exposure with any one else. Our animals follow us everywhere we walk in our valley begging us to pet them. It is almost as if our pets need our touch more than their food. Their milky eyes melt us, eliciting smiles that believe as if our faces are doubling in size. I just cannot seem to satisfy my urge to hug, pet, and play with these beasts of love. Considering, my angels are women these animals receive, lavish attention. Each day, I find myself talking to these animals exclusively when outside of our cabin. We agreed to remain spread out when not in our cabin, providing difficult targets for any hostile intruders.

Our dogs, as most canines bark at every little noise of movement, and twice as frantic when we are within their view. At night, when in the stable, they bark once and then return to their spot between the horses, where they consider safe. We can see how normal relationships are bonding in new patterns, such as dogs that hide behind horses, and Americans who hide with a Chinese servant. We hold each's hands when inside our cabin. None of us ventures far from our blazing fireplace. I ask Lisa if we should postpone our topless agenda until springtime. Lisa refuses, claiming that if we get cold, we should stay close to each other. She is unwavering concerning this. Lisa believes that we need this trust and confidence with each. She wants nothing to cover our hearts when we are in our cabin. Lee argues Lisa simply wants everyone to appreciate how much American women compare with Chinese women. I stood up positioning Lee between Cindy and I. Cindy,

Roberta, and Lisa lightly slap Lee on her faces, and confesses their greatest fear is I will run away with her and abandon them. I pull against Lee's hand and plead with her to leave with me now. She kisses me on my cheek and tells me that if I want her, I must be strong. Lee is not an easy pushover anymore. Cindy, Roberta, and Lisa begin laughing and tell me to stop acting like a small spoiled boy. I wink at them and tell them I will rejoice as a little man while they remain topless. Roberta cautions me to enjoy this while it lasts. I blow kisses at them and then confess that I pray this is the slowest winter that we have in our lives. Lisa informs me the season does not matter because she wants her younger brother to be the happiest young man alive today. I tell her the lone way that a teenage man could be happier than I would be one who has five sisters, one of which shares Lisa's wardrobe policy. My angels laughed at this one as each one attempted to tickle me. I confess that if I must die with any one, these angels would be the ones I would wish among to die. Lee confesses that we are the ones she desires amid to live. I disclose to our gang that I prefer Lee's longing.

We have no books, TV, or friends. Our radio merely reports the same watered-down economic woes and dissatisfaction with our government. Lisa prepared a schedule assigning the days and person to listen to the radio and share the news reports with the rest of us. We agreed this would provide us a chance to filter the hopelessness before informing the rest of us. Lee warned us it was extremely important to keep control over our minds because if you cannot control your mind, you cannot control anything. Lisa tried to offer us brainstorming sessions at least once each week. She reminds us that we must be prepared for unexpected contingencies. She did not like being astounded with surprises. Considering our world existed now packed with surprises, her nerves took a whipping each day. Even though we did not encounter much in our valley, there seemed to be the abundance of noises. Since we did not recognize the actual source of the various noises, we found ourselves in constant fear. Sunday and Easter were learning the relationships between the noises and their sources. They began to ignore noises they recognized. We found ourselves ignoring the noises we identified, which added various much needed stability to our lives. Cindy and I enjoyed an exploratory walk each day. Lisa instructed us to stay off the ridge, as she feared someone might spot us. Likewise, she told us not to walk through the wide opened pastures, as we needed to concentrate on our visibility. The more precautions we took that would make it difficult for our enemies to formulate a capture plan for us. Cindy and I tried to stay under trees and in forests. This worked well for us, especially when autumn hit and colored leaves covered the ground; we walked, close to the tree trunks. We walked slowly as our purpose was to talk. This valley seems to extract our thoughts out of minds, providing our words with peace and serenity. My relationship with Cindy has a development built on love, hope, and strength. We were fresh enough to enjoy risks and the excitement these gambles created.

Personalities, when combined, create a new soul. We fall under this same unification transformation. A part of me surrenders to a larger, more comprehensive and complete us. Roberta is our nervous Nellie. She worries about everything, and at times concentrates too much on the negative possible outcomes. She is convinced the Chinese will capture and execute us. Roberta believes compatible things should congregate, although she is open to fresh ideas and testing new parts for composition of an unknown completeness. In other words, she recognizes black and white as boundaries, yet these boundaries are not locked in stone. She believes that gray can darken to black or purified to white. Roberta professes the core of her belief system rests on information, as, when unused information is blended in with old information as new truth manifests itself. Roberta faced the death of her parents at a young age, which also destroyed her family and social life. Even though her father routinely visited, our grandparents and Roberta could play with her cousins. Roberta always enjoyed this time with us, as she knew it was temporary, and she could return home afterwards. She had her circle, with her family and friends. Nevertheless, she died with her parents, the sole difference being she began a fresh life with her relatives. From a lone child in the center of her world, to a face among the crowd, Roberta successfully found a home on her new road. She helped us tear down the walls, which circled her city. Roberta, unlike us, has seen her world fall apart and worked extra hard to make sure this never happens once more. I understand that she is extremely fond of Lee. She never thought of herself as better than she never thought to any other. We share this trait, since being farmers, there were few who would consider themselves below us. Roberta was eager to share this adventure with us, as she believed in her blood relatives. She considered herself as my brother and just as blood tight as Lisa, who is my half-sister. She developed this concept as reality because Lisa declared it.

Lisa and Roberta were closer than two sisters normally would be. Lisa told her siblings that we would treat Roberta as a sister, in that our mother was now her mother. We agreed with this, especially when Roberta followed Lisa's desire in having a strong football player as a boyfriend. This gave our small group specific muscle against any who tried to harass us. We would not have survived as long as we did our final semester in High School without their help in Cindygate. Lisa loved everyone in our family, and she gave herself to each of us. Lisa knew that I loved baseball; therefore, she planned carefully our summer activities, so we could maximize our baseball time. Lisa ran interference for us against our parents. She could make our parents laugh as she justified the stupidity of our naughtiness. Lisa always labeled our bad or questionable actions as noughties. Lisa and Roberta shared in caring for the children younger than them. Lisa kept a low profile among her classmates after Roberta arrived. She believed it as her heart's responsibility to devote as much time with Roberta as possible. Although they were one grade apart, they shared their lunch breaks and all their spare time. They even began to make the identical dress and notwithstanding included Julia, so all three looked the same. Lisa was serious about honesty. We promised never to tell each anything false. We had to make our word as the foundation for our relationships. With our word as gospel, we could function as a team. Lisa shared everything she had. She purposely placed her things with Julia and Roberta as a method to convince them the items of each were the items for all. Lisa always listened to our challenges and troublesome situations. She was the one who predicted our lives would be in danger when Mitch was released after his correctional sentence. Lisa knew that we had to pull together and live as one. She constantly was a softy for stray dogs and cats, for they often ended in our house and then funneled to grandmother's house. I repeatedly claimed Lisa was our leader as we incessantly followed her recommendations.

Cindy was the refreshing air, which blew life in our world we previously considered as perfect. We existed in harmony based on our perception of demands and desires. I at no time gave Cindy any mind as I wrote her off my list of possible spouse years earlier. She never hung out with my friends as I hung with the town kids who enjoyed baseball. Cindy belonged to the children of the large farms, a group that was rapidly decreasing. Surprisingly, the members of our family that knew the most about Cindy were Julia, Don, and Fred. They were watching us from the lower grades looking up at the heroes, or those they wanted to emulate someday. Julia believed Cindy to be the Cinderella. Cindy did not portray herself as better than any other person in Poinsett County did. She did not enjoy the way people always struggled to gain her friendship. Even her church offered her no sanctuary, wanting to use her popularity as a recruiting tool to gain a solid foothold into the new generation. Cindy soon discovered that most people looked at her as a source of gain and willing to use her to achieve this advancement. She continued to pull herself away from the others. Cindy wanted to be alone as much as possible. This created concern for her father, because he believed her depression would make her easier prey for the evil, which surrounded anything of perceived beauty. Therefore, her father commissioned Mitch to protect her to and from their private bus stop. Cindy revealed to her father, she had no romantic interest in Mitch, and she feared their classmates would place too much peer pressure on them to date. Cindy's father questioned Mitch explaining the guidelines of this assignment and the pay Mitch would receive. He wanted to make sure Mitch understood his escorting Cindy was a service for him, one in which he was being paid. Mitch guaranteed Cindy's father that he understood the limitations of this opportunity.

Cindy confessed to Mitch that she needed someone to talk about her family and friends' issues. She confided many of her challenges with Mitch in their slow walks to the bus and back to her house after school. Initially, she found comfort in this until the day Mitch gave her a compliment that she felt was not in the bounds of a normal friendship. Additionally, Mitch's casual goodbye kisses on Cindy's cheek prevailed elevated one day. Mitch shifted to her lips. The shock of such a sexual advance, considered reserved for married couples, puts Cindy in an immediate state of hostility. She screamed and began slapping him. Feeling mercy for Mitch, she did not tell her father, who would have executed Mitch that afternoon. Afterwards, Cindy never again spoke with Mitch. They marched to and from the bus each day, with Cindy walking behind Mitch. She refused to allow Mitch to glare at her body. Cindy had enough friends to hang around during school since she had no choice but to expand her network. Cindy made sure she spoke with as many boys as possible. She needed dates, to prevent Mitch from laying claims on her. Cindy began scanning possible mates. As a lone child, she wanted to belong to a large family. She had no wish to live on her family's farm, thus she desired someone who lived in Marked Tree. All in our county believed Marked Tree was a big town if not a little city. Few ever ventured to Memphis, therefore, had no concept of life in the large cities. When she saw the manner, in which we bonded after school, with all our laughter and silliness, she decided our family had something she needed. Cindy knew that I was in her grade and decided she would attempt to date me. She did not want to suffer from all the peer pressure at school; therefore, she waited until the summer break until making her move. Cindy met Julia during a play period, in which Cindy skipped a class to attend. Cindy asked Julia what her family did during the summer. Julia told her for most of our summer, they played baseball with George and his friends. This was when Cindy planned for her summer invasion of the baseball field. This was the time she had to perform in faith and have the confidence. She added acting as a helpless damsel would include to her invasion into the empire of George.

The unsung hero in our band sings the songs of Saladus-naine. She was the spirit that studied Cindy's and my spirit. She detected the potential that Mitch would turn psychotic if rejected by Cindy. Saladus-naine searched the hearts and options available for Cindy. One plan was to send her to a European nation; however, the time to gain the passports and visas would extend into the danger zone. Too many variables from now made forthcoming projection unfeasible in this zone. Saladus-naine could not risk this; therefore, she believed the best plan was to assimilate Cindy into a local family. Our family passed Saladus-naine's tests for compatibility, especially in our ability to love and willingly sacrifice for each. She appreciated our willingness to follow Lisa and her buffering skills in protecting us from our parents. Julia's intense devotion to Cindy calmed Saladus-naine's reservations about our family. Saladus-naine had one major constraint. She could not make people have affections for each other; therefore, she took a risk on me based on the emotions she plotted from Julia, Lisa, and Roberta, Fred, Don and myself. She used my sisters to project for Cindy, since she noted they held so many values in common, which were compatible with me. She took the risk and sent Cindy to the baseball field, making sure Lisa and Roberta were there. She knew that Cindy would be shy and unable to set up a relationship with me without the support of Lisa and Roberta, who were the big girls for the fifteen-year olds. This combination worked out great, as Cindy melted between Lisa, Roberta, and Julia as their huggable doll. Julia made the three older girls believe they are heroes. That was for security Cindy needed to jump in a lake even though she did not how to swim. She asked me for a life jacket, one of which I gave willingly with Saladus-naine as the life jacket.

Our escape took on a new persona with the incorporation of Lee into our traveling family. As a group, we were close to paranoia, having seen more Asians on our first bus than in our entire lives. This was strange in that we were the lone group to board the bus in Marked Tree, having argued with the ticket counter for one hour to board this bus. As we began to sit on the bus, the Chinese got up to open the surrounding seats. They wanted us in one area as much as we wanted to be together. Lee later explained that they were terrified of us, that we would take them somewhere and kill them for the money they possessed. Lee was tough to break; however, the warm eyes of Lisa, Roberta, and especially Cindy melted her resistance. We had no way of knowing that taking her meant the nation with the most people on Earth would seek revenge. Lee knew, at the same time; she was so confused in our words and promises and wanted to believe we were honest and kind. She never dreamed that we did not realize she was a servant, in that everyone believed all Americans were servants to the invisible masters who controlled their wealth. Chinese servants in their homeland owned their homes. They learned that in America, the hidden masters owned the homes, forcing those who lived in them to do all the maintenance work, pay taxes on these homes using money earned from wages, which were already taxed by at least two layers of government. They also knew that even if they paid all the money the invisible masters wanted that if they could not pay the excess taxes, the government levied, law enforcement would take the home from them. They were terrified when they learned that senior people with little money for medical expenses, food, or utilities had to pay these taxes first or end with no home to die in the streets. The Chinese pitied the Americans, especially since their government favored the rare, more than the majority. Minorities were the uncommon, and the majority had to surrender their property so the few could receive it. These minorities abused the government, since in China the government provided work and homes for the servants, as the masters understood that without their servants, their production would not increase the wealth of the nation.

Lee truly felt sorry for the way Americans suffered at the insulting hands of their government. We felt remorseful for Lee at the abusive hands of her government. Lisa tried to explain to us that Lee truly believed her nation cared for their people. We found ourselves intrigued by the range and depth of our debates. One day, while we thawed out our half-clothed bodies in front of our fireplace, which also served as our stove and indoor light. Lisa constantly fears candles since one of her friend's home burned down as she endlessly warned that candles burned more homes than any other hazard at the turn of the nineteenth and twentieth century. We used candles solely when Lisa was outside and put them out when she returned. Back to our debate, Lisa mentioned casually one day how the United States President was the most powerful man in the world. Lee began laughing while looking at us as if we were fools. Lisa asked Lee why she was laughing. Lee explained the most powerful person in the world was General Secretary of the Central Committee in China. She listed the first reason was he owned the United States debt. She furthered explained the invisible masters owned the President of the United States. He was just a puppet for the public to vent their frustrations. Lee explained that if anyone made fun of her General Secretary of the Central Committee, he or she at once vanished forever. Subsequently, any who made fun of the American President received praise and popularity. The more foolish that he made his leader appear, the greater, his reward. If the same group levied this foolishness against the invisible masters, they would vanish at once. Lee contends these people will not follow a leader they treat as a fool.

Lee adds the American President cannot guarantee work or housing for his citizens. Many are unemployed, simply because privately owned businesses want to maximize their profits rather than production. Lee reports the Chinese comprehend about the vast number of Americans who have no homes and who are starving. Consequently, the General Secretary of the Central Committee guarantees a career field for all, with occupations based on the individual's test scores. Therefore, those who want to be a scientist will review the fundamental skills needed and prepare themselves accordingly. Those who prepared themselves and displayed their abilities on the test, and if a position is projected to be available will receive the station. The labor and education parties work diligently trying to match the best candidates with the projected labor needs. Everyone works as everyone eats and has a place to call home. The profits from all production activities come about collected and redistributed to care for the population. Lee reveals the silent masters in the United States force the government to borrow money to finance their foolish business adventures. They do not worry about losing their money as they can pass their failures to the American public. Lee discloses that many Chinese reports claim that if the silent masters paid their share of the taxes, and were responsible for their losses, as is the public, there would be no American debt. We sit around Lee reasonably stunned at the logic underlying her arguments. Subsequently, we cannot argue on our behalf, as the possibility of a silent master could exist. We invariably knew there was a small group of Americans who held great wealth. Lee consistently divulged that no public official could afford his or her campaign costs. Even if they could, fear of great public campaigns levied against them for not voting as instructed force them to comply. Considering they are not free to vote their consciousness, they always accept the campaign contributions. The details of her explanations continue to leave us speechless.

Life would be grand if our lone worry was being speechless. Our initial disaster came in the first week of December, as the snow did not fall for three days. This temporary reprieve provided a small group of three men to advance through our mountain. They scouted our valley and became concerned with Lee's sunglasses. These men were meticulous and obsessed with detail. They kidnapped Roberta one day and tied her to a tree in their camp on the opposite side of the ridge. Fortunately, they had a campfire in front of her. These bounty hunters sensed that we were hiding something, as Roberta was shaky on her devotion to Lee, believing Lee would cause us all to suffer. They were convinced that Roberta would break down and was withholding something. Therefore, they continued to beat her with their fists and horsewhip. This produced no results. Next, they removed her clothing, and each one raped her. Roberta fought hard against them; nevertheless, they overpowered her and satisfied their wicked desires. Roberta refused to tell these men anything. She spoke no words during the twelve hours of torture on the first day. These three men, decided to wrap Roberta in blankets and continue their tortures and engage in more raping the next day. Considering they wrapped her in the darkness of the night, they failed properly to insulate her feet. Roberta was beaten to such an extent that she could not move her legs or arms, without great pain, throughout this night. She felt her feet beginning to freeze; nonetheless, Roberta did not want to ask these men to rewrap her feet for fear they would rape her once more. She was too tired, with the bitter freezing and her hunger to chance another battle to prevent their painful penetration. Shortly thereafter, her feet stopped hurting and became numb. Roberta noticed she was bleeding in too many places, most from the cuts on her skin from the knives these monsters unleashed on her. The cuts from the horsewhip added to the horrifying pain that burned over her body. Roberta held on to one powerful bit of pride, and this pride stemmed from her ability to give these devils no information, not even one word. She considered the bounty hunters as dangerous to all who were in her group and therefore the surrender of Lee would make no difference, for they would go after Cindy, Lisa, and me as well.

That night, since Roberta had not returned, Lisa became enraged. We discussed in detail our activities and noted that Roberta went off on her own during early morning. Roberta traditionally would sneak off to be alone reverting to her times as a solitary child. This would be the first time she went on a retreat since we moved to this valley. We surmised; she must have been scouting the area planning for her private adventure. Cindy complained claiming that since we are surviving in such a potentially dangerous environment, we should make sure these retreats coordinate with all in our group. We readily agreed, believing that surrendering individual independence would increase each person's chance of a victory from death. Lisa and I agreed to mount on our horses, procure our weapons and each took a dog, as I would fetch Sunday and Lisa would get Easter. We tied one pair of Roberta's socks around Sunday's neck, wrapped one of her bras around Easters neck, and had our dogs sleep with us around our fireplace. Notwithstanding, I found great difficulty in sleeping that dreadful night. Each time the wind brushed our cabin, my heart stopped as I looked at our door, hoping that Roberta would be passing through to our heartfelt hugs and cries of joy. When we awoke in the morning, a sense of reality hit each of our faces. Roberta had to be in trouble, because with the winter nights below freezing, she could not possibly survive. Our eyes transmitted this horrifying message to each as the fear of Roberta's demise paralyzed our mouths. Lisa pulled me off to the side and told me that Roberta's wandering on foot, combined with her setting up a campsite could be no more than three hours by horse if our dogs guided us directly to her; we may have a chance to prevent further physical damage. Cindy overheard our conversation and at once took Lee into her confidence. They instantaneously pleaded with Lisa to give the permission to help in our rescue. Our minds rested on a mission to rescue Roberta.

Adhering to the concept of a rescue, I requested Cindy and Lee to remain in our cabin, and begin preparing to provide care for Roberta's return. I also asked them to remain in the cabin, with our weapons ready for defense. On making sure their weapons were loaded and prepared for defense, Lisa and I went to the stables to get ready our horses for our day of discovery. As we jump in our saddles, Lee opened the cabin's door, out came Sunday, and Easter barking hysterically dashing through the open pastures rushing up the valley's back entrance toward the highlight that lay above us. Lisa and I instantaneously followed them, dodging the branches as we quickly passed them. I glanced at Lisa, whose face was now turning a glowing red from the wind as it burned over her skin. Afterwards, I saw the smoke from a campfire as it rose above the tree line. Sunday and Easter ran directly around this dying fire. I recognized it was going out, as the smoke was a darker black caused by the excessive smothering of black ash accumulating over the fire. We arrived at the campfire within ten minutes from leaving our cabin. When we glimpse on the ground below us, Sunday and Easter is licking Roberta's face. I notice one of Roberta's hands reaching out to pet Sunday. Our dogs would kill large packs of wolves for a loving stroke of our hand. Roberta was covered in blankets, nevertheless, for odd reason Sunday and Easter was pulling the blankets off her. Lisa and I at once jumped from our horses rushing to Roberta. I saw a few pieces of firewood lying beside the fire. I knew that we needed a little heat; therefore, I put a few more logs on this fire. Lisa screams to me that I need to get beside her now.

As I rush to Roberta, a few issues are blazing through my mind. The first issue is why there is enough wood to burn this campfire for at least another day, and with so much wood readily available, why Roberta let the campfire began to smother. The second issue is why she camped out within one hour of our cabin during such a cold mountain night. If she had the time and energy to get this wood and start a fire, she could have come back to our cabin. The last issue is why she stayed so close to her home. The lone issue that we debated was keeping Lee with us or releasing her. These concerns vanished as my eyes saw Roberta. Her face existed swollen; accordingly, Lisa pulled the blankets back over her body telling me I did not want to see this. I froze my poker face when looking at Roberta. There was no doubt that Lisa's panic and emotional release told Roberta she was in trouble. What Roberta needs from me is the hope of security. I plead with Roberta to tell me what happened. To my horror, she reveals that three men captured her, drag her out of our valley, and tortured her for information about us. Roberta boasted surrendering a partial smile revealing no remaining teeth that she told them nothing, clarifying she spoke no words. I expressed to Roberta that she should have given them little information. She should have allowed us to fight this battle. I disclosed that we fight together and reminded her how much that we loved her, and we would not leave her alone evermore. Roberta confessed she was surprised the men have left. I feared that they might have invaded our cabin, knowing they will not get in because Lee is no fool for any tricks or deceptions. Lisa tells me to help her get Roberta on her horse. We wrap the blankets around her and lay her on Lisa's saddle. Lisa sat with me in my saddle, back to back. We suspected a possible ambush; therefore, we were making sure no one could hit us in our backs. I considered three men that would beat on a High School girl and then rape her without mercy was not men but instead mice. Likewise, I knew the cat that was going to do a little hunting. We raced back to our cabin and put Roberta before our fireplace.

This was time for our family to drown in the river of love. Cindy removed Roberta's torn clothing. We placed her on warm blankets in front of the fire. Cindy told us to begin lightly massaging Roberta's body to determine what parts were frostbitten or broken bones. Lee did not like the way Roberta's feet felt waxy and hard. I noted the red, swollen blisters that looked extremely pale. For the first time, we saw what was in Lee's backpack as she emptied it on our dirt floor. She had small bags of herbs and roots she collected when we traveled and arrived here. I thought that she was assembling her collection of cooking spices. Lee had reformed these roots and herbs into special salves, which she immediately began rubbing on Roberta. Lisa helped Roberta drink a little water. Roberta began choking on this water as Lee pulled the water away from Roberta's mouth. We secured Roberta in our special chair so her feet could soak in the hot water from our fireplace. We knew to keep her feet in this hot water until the blisters began to regain her skin color. Cindy and Lisa began rubbing Lee's salves onto Roberta's body and confessing their love. I jumped to my feet and prepared to go hunting. Lee asked me where I was going. I told her it was time for particular country justice. She asked permission to join me. Lisa tells Lee we cannot risk another woman come about fed to sex perverts. Lee looks at me and reveals she grew up in the mountain farmlands of China. For a first time she declares she can become the ground, the wind, sun, or moon when hunting. Her confidence puts Lisa to ease as she looked at me and ordered that none of the three spared and not to place ourselves in any situation that would give them a chance to harm us. Lisa's orders were the same as the commands from our heart. Lee reports to Roberta that she knows of tortures that will create pain a hundredfold to what she endured. I looked at Lee and asked her what she needed. Lee reports the Earth will give us the tools to restore the balance in humanity they took from us.

Lee grabbed Roberta's rifle. Cindy asked her if she knew how to shoot this rifle. Lee looked at us and declared she never misses as she slides a few of our small knives into her pocket. I picked up the wonderful crossbow Peter gave me and put the arrows in the arrow bag strapped on my back. Naturally, I preferred to shoot with my rifle; however, with three of these monsters on the loose, I do not want to chance the noise from a shot alert the other two members of their cult. Lee and I advanced back to Roberta's torture plot. Sunday and Easter tagged with us. When we arrived, Lee instantaneously began studying the ground for footprints. Lee told me we were fortunate in that last night it snowed about an inch, and it has not begun to snow today. She verified there were three of them and that they were on foot and told me we must hurry before it starts to snow once more. Lee's eyes proved extraordinary as she could follow their tracks, report broken branches and scattered leaves. Lee wisely monitors the sky for bird movements. Lee comments as we cross a stream how lucky we are this stream remain, frozen. This provided her the footprints tracing where they crossed over the stream. Lee gets off her horse and then injects her finger into a footprint. She reports to me the rapers are just a thirty-minute walk ahead of us. Lee orders me to place an arrow in my crossbow, as we shall soon begin our revenge encounter. Lee reveals these men are following each other, which tells her they do not believe anyone is chasing them. We begin devoting our complete attention to the environment, which surrounded us. Consequently, Lee and I contacted our prey twenty-five minutes later. Lee got off her horse and motioned for me to get off mine. She motioned for

Sunday and Easter to return to her. She even gave each of our horses a hug on their heads and whispered in their ears. I asked Lee what she was doing. She reveals that she is ordering our horses to stay and our dogs to remain calm. Lee motions for me to give my attention to one of the men who is peeing on a tree.

Lee glows over the snow as quiet as a rabbit, rushing to flank this man from his side. I fire my first arrow, driving my arrow through one of his legs pinning him to the tree behind him. Lee rushes to this man, with her pocketknife in one hand and pulling this man's head backward with her remaining hand. She slid her knife into this man's mouth slicing his tongue in two dividing back to his vacant tonsils. Consequently, she takes her hand and pinches his nose closed. As he opens his mouth, Lee grabs the right side of his split tongue and pulls it out using her remaining hand to remove it. Afterwards, Lee pokes her pocketknife into each of this man's eyes completely blinding him. She motions for me to use the straps on his backpack to tie his arms around this tree. Once he is tied, she unzips his hand, pulls out his rape stick, and slices it in half in the same style as his tongue. I study this man's face and the excruciating pain that he now suffered. He would never again penetrate a female nor would words ever flow from his mouth or visions appear in the eyes. Lee looked at me and replied it was time for the next two to pay. I am still amazed at how smooth she destroyed this man's life, keeping him alive with pain I cannot even fathom. Lee looked at the footprints and told me the remaining two were three minutes ahead of us going up to the top of this ridge. It would be wiser if we proceeded at once to the top of the ridge, crossed over and waited for them to cross and attack them going downhill. We went over the ridge top, which had merely a small track for single file deer. Lee informed me this was another special break for us as we can check this path with excellent concealment. Lee placed her ear against the ground, froze, and then stood before me with a vital update. She shares with me these two men are beginning to tire, and walking in circles, hinting to her that they were preparing a campsite. Now would be the time to hit them because they will soon discover one is missing and be on alert.

Her eyes and ears scanned the hill that surrounded us. She points to a spot and tells me to reload my crossbow for another tree pin and then stands prepared for a possible rescue. Sure enough, monster number two walked in my strike zone, and my arrow got him sideways, driving through his legs pinning him to the tree. This time Lee remained in her position with her rifle braced. She allowed this monster to begin screaming for help. I asked her why we were allowing him to beg for aid. Lee questions me if it is wiser to search for our prey, or wait until the prey enters our trap, a place that we control. I asked Lee if we had this under control. She tells me to use my rifle this time, aiming for legs, as she will hit the arms. I ask her why she wants the arms. Lee discloses that she must hit certain parts of the arm so it does not bleed in excess and render them immobile. Such a shot is vital, and she knows this shot; she will not miss. I smile and agree, because I appreciate how much Lee loves Roberta, and she would risk nothing in this revenge. Her confidence is so powerful that I knew a bullet would be foolish to disobey her. Just as she predicted the last monster came running to rescue his partner. Lee shot twice, each shot in an arm. I popped each leg and down he went. She rode over to him and tied a rope around his chest, jumped back on her horse, and dragged this man to the tree in front of the second beast. Lee asked me to tie him to this tree, making sure each monster was facing each other. Once they were tied, Lee pulled out the monster's dick and partial tongue of our first victim and placed them on the ground between our two prisoners, explaining to them, what these were and promising them they soon would be making an equal contribution. Lee took the boots off these two beasts, explaining that Roberta's feet were frostbitten, and she wanted them fully to understand the joy experienced while your feet slow burn from freezing.

Lee explains the best tortures are long, and slow, nevertheless, fortune is not with us as the day is slipping away and a night in this forest could put us, and our animals, beside Roberta facing death. Lee stands between these beasts and explains they made their last mistake when they hurt her beloved sister. Both creatures continued to beg for mercy. Lee explains to me how wonderful it is to hear their begging. She then removes her hat and sunglasses informing these men they will never again speak or talk to anyone ever more.

Lee walks over to monster number two, unzips his pants, and removes his rape tool with her pocketknife. She walks toward monster number three and waves this tube of flesh in front of him laughing in amazement commenting how little this thing was and how disappointed Roberta must have been when he tickled her insides with it. Lee tosses this chunk of flesh beside the flesh freezing in the snow before them that was donated by beast number one. Lee pinches his cheek and complains how she hopes he has more to donate than the first two. Terror flushes his face as Lee gathers his donation adding it to the growing collection. Lee now apologizes to the men for having showed her disguise, telling them that while they can speak, she will never again be safe. They both promise at no time to tell any one about her. Lee tells them they proved their true character with her friend the previous night and asks me to hold beast number two's head while she ensures her future is once more secure. Lee slices this man's tongue down the middle and removes the left half, repeating the procedure on beast number three. I ask her why she cuts the tongue this way. Lee explains these offers the most pain and causes less bleeding; therefore, they live longer. Lee picks up a small stick and pokes it in their eyes, blinding both. She takes her pistol and shoots beast number two's arms, so he can use them no, more. She opens their coats, double checks; they are tied to their binding tree. Lee tells Sunday and Easter to bring our horses to us. Both dogs dash off like lightning flashing through the sky. Five minutes later, we have both horses and dogs with us. Lee asks me if I am ready to return to Roberta, as she puts her hat and sunglasses back on her head. I ask her why she took off her hat and sunglasses. Lee tells me that for torture to be served best, one must remove as much as possible to allow the Earth to feed their minds.

Lee confused me with this concept; nevertheless, somehow I believe what she just said had a rational basis, one of which was beyond me. I have learned so much more about the bestie I ever was accordingly lucky to have in my life. I asked Lee how she could get our animals to obey and understand her. Lee explains that when you love with your eyes and hearts, all things can understand your mind. I winked at her and confessed that I was one of those things as well. Lee tells me that I am a trained pervert and am merely kind to her, so I may enjoy the beauty of her breasts. I wink and confess that she knows my deepest secret mind. Link winks back to me and explains that I will never have to use any force, and that even if I beat her as Roberta was beaten, she would give me anything I desired. I held Lee's hand and remind her that if I were even to glance cross-eyed at her, Cindy and Lisa would torture me worse than she had tortured these beasts today. Lee chuckles and teases me about exaggerating so many things. I confess to Lee, one thing, I realize, without any doubt, that it is much better to be her friend than her enemy is. Lee reminds me that except for those who live in our cabin, the rest of our world wants her dead. Lee then opens the backpacks of these dying men and dumps them on the ground. She removes all contents in the side pockets and turns to me revealing these men are sexual predators as she lays out a collection of jewelry explaining these are their trophies. Lee saw one necklace she instantly recognized as Roberta's. I noticed that they had now wanted posters, thus began to rule out they were bounty hunters. Lee and I agree they must have been scouting our cabin, and after noticing four women decided to wait until one drifted into their ambush zones. What happened to Roberta could have happened to any of the women in our clan. I had certain peace of mind in that whenever I remember Roberta's rape, I will remember what happened to the three flesh sticks that penetrated her. I ask Lee if we should cut these men down before leaving. Lee claims the slow freezing will kill them before dawn, as they will not be wrapped in blankets or have a campfire burning in their campsite.

I recognize that I could never stop finding ways to praise Lee. I had always conceived her as a pacifist. Now, I recognize Lee is strong and strategic. Notwithstanding, Lee has consistently proven herself loyal to my family. Hence, I cannot imagine what would have happened to us if we did not have Lee with us. Before today, Lee's primary contribution was her vast knowledge of the new world evolving under the American's noses. I never imagined how deep her devotion and love for us. Lee is serious about making sure we are protected. She is a weapon that would save us in our future mountain life. I never thought of Lee as a mountain woman. Like most Americans, we picture Chinese as living in a factory in crowded cities. Lee explains this is true, because the young, like her, migrate to the cities when they are old enough. Lured by the dream of saving, adequate money to return to their homelands, they end in the factories. After a little time, they are trapped into becoming servants losing their freedom forever. Lee's relationship with our animals is such as; I have never before witnessed. They understand her mind and cherish her instructions. Lee emphasizes that are pets watched us in detail and naturally wanted to return to the stables. They were waiting for a signal for permission to take us back to the cabin. I will be spending more time with our dogs and horses, because I need their precious affection and devotion, the same as Lee gives us now. Speaking and promising loyalties are one thing; however, living and doing them is magnificent.

We wiggled our way through the forest, passed the stream, and zipped down the forest that protected our back pasture. I regained my eagerness for Roberta when our horses leaped over our rear fence. Every living thing in our mission wanted to get back in our cabin or stable. On returning, we guided our animals into the stable. Lee grabbed dried grass we had wrapped into three-foot rolls. I snatched one as well, figuring each horse could eat one. We unmounted our horses and gave Sunday and Easter each one bowl of dog food. We solely gave them dog food on special occasions, and scraps for their remaining meals. They earned their food, this day. Lee looked at me, as I could see from the expression in her eyes, she was scared to enter our cabin and receive an update on Roberta. I turned to Sunday and began to rub his fur, likewise; Lee rushed to Easter and began petting his fur. After a few minutes, I looked at Lee and asked her if she was okay. Lee, releasing a burst of courage suggests we should enter our cabin now. I knew it was foolish to deny my true feelings around Lee, so I acknowledge that I am somewhat afraid to face Lisa and Cindy. Lee confesses that she is also concerned; however, we should go inside, for even with the worst-case scenario, Lisa and Cindy would need our support. Best case, we should be celebrating the recovery of Roberta. Afterwards, I put my arm around Lee and told her these things would never be the same between us. She won a special place of honor in my heart now. I previously prided myself in my dedication to Lee's security, yet presently I consider my abilities may not match Lee's abilities. Lee could defend herself if alone, yet now I question if I could defend as well as her. I appreciate how great it is that Lee can defend herself, or at the minimum release havoc on those who trespass against her. The depth of my love for Lee is as deep as the deepest cave. Lee asks me if I would grant her a personal request. I at once shake my head signaling yes. Lee wants me to take the credit for Roberta's revenge because she believes Cindy and Lisa will believe much safer knowing the one man in this group will revenge any who would give them harm. She also fears that if they understand her full range of battle skills, they may redefine the limits of their relationships. I understand where Lee is coming from as I now have a new image of Lee. Fortunately, for Lee her behavior is more in tune with what I love in a woman, even though Cindy never exhibited these behaviors. I kiss Lee on her cheek and remind her that her every wish is my command.

Lee predicts that if Cindy and Lisa knew about convicting her loyalty, they would build an American wall around her, one longer than her Chinese wall. I confess to Lee that I totally understand her concern in this situation. Cindy and Lisa are traditional Midwestern country girls who work in their gardens, preserve vegetables and fruit, cook all the family meals, and support their menfolk that work in the fields. I reveal to Lee that if she were in danger, Cindy and Lisa would fight, even to the point of their death, in her defense. Lee confirms that she understands this, yet she would prefer to match their efforts after they reveal their true inner strength. I agree with Lee and compliment her on the intensity and accuracy of her analysis of Cindy and Lisa. I tell her I believe I am guilty taking credit for the distinguished work that she executed. Lee clarifies that she did not kill any of the three beasts. She merely prevented these defective creatures from repeating the same violations on other innocent women. Subsequently, Lee proclaims it will be the Earth kills these wicked monsters, if Mother Nature declares their works worthy of death, she will perform the execution. Lee claims her duty was to make sure they never rape, another woman, or violate their privacy by looking on the nudity of women who do not wish to share. Lastly, she took away their speech as a precaution for our security if Mother Nature decides their sins are not worthy of death. I ask Lee how she can believe that these men could have their lives spared. Lee reminds me that we do not understand the complete story and that in any manner we will be safe. She adds that even if they crawl back to our farm, Sunday and

Easter would tear them to pieces, leaving nothing, as all bones will be ground into powder. Once more, Lee has impressed me with the detailed planning in her strategic actions. I grasp that now it is time to accept responsibility. My confused unfocused mind has worked extra hard at avoiding our immediate task. Our avoidance is merely acknowledging our lack of faith that Roberta is recovering.

Lee tells me it is my time, and for me to follow her, citing that she needs me to protect her back. I wink at her and tell her not to worry since I will shield her. She thanks me claiming I am her hero. Lee is protecting my pride, as she knows I am scared to death to enter our cabin. She is taking the lead while feeding my male ego. Lee knocks on our door with our secret thump. Cindy opens our door and greets us. I ask Cindy if Roberta is recovering. One peek at Cindy, and I felt perfectly at ease, giving me the courage to ask anything. Lee pulls out a small handbag and proceeds toward Roberta, who is laying in front of our fireplace with Lisa holding her hand. Lee and I rush to Roberta while asking Lisa how she is doing. Lisa tells us in a joyful tone that Roberta is recovering rapidly, thanks to Lee's salves and herbs. Cindy joined us, as Lee, and I shifted our eyes to her, seeking verification of Lisa's comments. Cindy looks at Roberta to make sure she is not watching us, and then shifts her eyes to Lee and I and shakes her head, showing no. Lee and I shook our heads slightly acknowledging we comprehended Cindy's message. Lee asks Roberta how she is doing. Roberta tells us she believes tonight will be much better than last night. I make sure Roberta this night shall be especially different from her previous night. Roberta asks us if we found the men who did this to her. Lee tells her that we found them. Roberta begins to shake in absolute fear, asking us if we killed them. Lee tells Roberta that we are not murderers. Roberta warns us that these three beasts will come back and feast off any in our clan they select. Lee opens her small bag and dumps it on the floor beside Roberta. Lee then winks at Roberta and asks her if she has ever seen these flesh tubes. Roberta looks at this bloody mess and questions if this is what she thinks it is. Cindy looks at me with startled eyes while Lisa's eyes open wide. Lee glances at me. Up I stand and declare that anyone who sticks a part of them in one of my angels best, be prepared to pay my price.

Cindy thanks me for caring so much for our family. Lisa looks at the removed male body parts and asks me if this was truly necessary. Lee asks Lisa if she wants these devils to have another opportunity to violate more women who are the innocent. Lisa tells her that no other woman should have to suffer this. Cindy reports to our group how proud she is that her husband is this devoted to the women under his care. Lee looks at Roberta, Cindy, and Lisa and tells them her view and respect for American men is now higher than she ever believed possible. Lee tells them how proud, she was that I did not kill these men, but will leave the call to justice up to Mother Nature. Lisa asks me how I will distinguish Mother Nature's decision. I glance at Lee and ask her if she will explain this to our gang, in that it is so emotional for me to relive this. Lee provides comfort by patting me on my shoulder and promising to do this for me. Lee tells my angels that I will go back to the trees where we tied the violators tomorrow afternoon and verify if they are alive or dead. Lisa asks Lee what we will do if they are still living. Lee smiles and reveals that we will simply return the next day. Lee furthered questions Lisa about what she meant by we. Lisa declares that she will return with her brother so she can put this misery to rest and begin with her closure. I grab a washrag and dip in a pan of hot water, squeeze the excess water out, and then begin tending to Roberta's bruises. Sadly, she was bruised from head to foot.

Lisa reports that we are lucky in that most of Roberta's bones are not broken, except for a few ribs. This suggests that when they hit her, they either opened their hands or wore gloves. Lee boldly claims that they had to be wearing gloves because of the extreme freezing weather. Lisa takes me by my hand and asks me to go outside with her. We walk out the front door, whereas Lisa updates me on Roberta's condition. She believes Roberta's female parts are damaged beyond repair and bleeding internally. Her right eye will never see again, nor will she be able to use her hands.

Even though the bones in her hands were not broken, they were all cracked and blood veins smashed beyond repair. The muscles in her hands began to decompose when they began to thaw. Lisa believes two of Roberta's cracked ribs, punctured her lungs, and that she will die within a few days. Rivers of tears began to rush from my eyes. Lisa begins wiping my face with her scarf and then grips me with a tight hug. Lisa whispers in my ear that I must become a great actor revealing nothing to Roberta, which could scare her and endanger her possible recovery. I ask Lisa why she is concerned about Roberta's recuperation if she is so close to her death. Lisa tells me that she wants Roberta's final hours to be as comfortable as we can make it. Roberta has suffered enough pain. She needs her family to smooth the final minutes before crossing into the spiritual world. Lisa and I go inside, whereas Lisa asks Cindy to take Lee outside for fresh air. Roberta glances at me while she begins to cough. I definitely do not like the gurgling that accompanies her cough. I casually skim Lisa and ask her if she still has any cough drops. Lisa informs me that we will never have cough drops while I eat them like candy. Roberta asks Lisa to be nicer to me as we have to remember I am still their little brother. I stare at Lisa and tell her not to forget I am her younger brother. Lisa lightly slaps me, and then questions if I am still a little boy why do I get so excited every time I gaze at her breasts? Roberta tells us that our youthful brother smiles because Lisa's breasts reminded him of his adolescent toys. I reach over and kiss Roberta and then glimpse at them and confess that if I had toys like these to play with as a juvenile, I would have refused to age. Roberta releases a forced smile. Subsequently, I realize I was playing into Lisa's adult sex joke, which I am sure is not currently in Roberta's realm of funny subjects. Nevertheless, I rub my hand on Roberta's face and thank her for protecting me from Lisa. These pulls a smile across Roberta's face as I always complimented her for protecting me from my oldest sister.

This night was long and filled with Roberta's gargling. The gurgling sound of a pending death is mesmerizing as it scratches each fragile nerve and battles each hole filled thought, turning it into a tear producing factory. Roberta fought hard to minimize her painful moans and conceal the size of her agony. We could, solely with our total essence barely conceal, the anguish that was destroying our inner recesses. Roberta, who fought for each remaining moment of her life, survived the night. Early, the next morning Lisa and I prepared for the return to the revenge trees. With merely a step outside this morning, I realized we would not make this trip without help. We got three additional inches of snow during the night even though the snow now ceased. I confessed to Lisa that Lee was the tracker and with this new snow, I would not be able to find them without a massive search, which would place us in danger of mountain hunters of being capable of associating us with this revenge punishment. I was careful not to confess that murder was my true goal. Lisa agreed and went inside soliciting Lee as our tracker. Lee whispers to Lisa that we understand I am the better tracker. Lisa agrees contending that I most likely consider there is no more danger and wanted a little lone time with Cindy. Lisa appends that love consistently makes its slaves behave so strangely. They both entered the stable, where I was saddling our horses and asked me if I have their horses ready to travel. I laugh and complain I believe that they replaced me. Lisa laughs and contends that it is foolish to send a man for a job when the women would do so much better. I wink at Lee, knowing that her knowledge of our personalities has once more allowed her to influence us to do exactly what she desires.

Just as I opened the door to our cabin, I heard Lisa and Lee's horses running pass our home. Lee was guiding them toward the opposite cliff that we traveled yesterday. I understand that she intends to travel the open pasture close to our cliffs since the wind shall shuffle that snow as it swirls against the elevated terrain. She is going to cross over to the appropriate ridge once she is in the forest, after tying a few branches behind her horse, which will ruffle the snow weakening their horse prints. Lee has proven herself the master at keeping out of sight. We are fortunate she has these skills, in that our lives hinge on these gifts or skills. I must believe these are gifts, because, if they were mere common skills give me an even weightier fear. Consequently, if most of the servants had this ability and were still reluctant to escape, a much greater danger must be lurking around us. Now, as I ponder more on this subject, I realize that Lee consistently warned against the power of the Chinese Mafia, as she labeled them. We still did not comprehend of Fred's death and had no proof linking Roberta's capture to them. I wondered now if this Chinese Mafia had other avenues of influence. Any tale of a group of five in hiding, especially with four of them being young women, would attract the attention of sexual perverts, who did not want a bounty but instead wanted booty. I questioned why they stopped with Roberta and elected not to pursue my three remaining angels. Subsequently, I realize they would have returned throughout the remainder of this winter and plucked them one at a time. They must have recognized that as fugitives, we could not seek help from any form of law enforcement, nor could we afford the luxury of trusting unknown people. With these thoughts meandering through my mind, I realized Lee performed righteously with these three ogres. If they were to escape these mountains, they would bring back the abundance of bounty hunters.

What I thought that would be a day, now free from the freezing outside winds, turned into a clock with the slowest possible minute hand, which converted minutes into hours. Initially, I believed Cindy and me could enjoy a little marriage time together. Nevertheless, Cindy refused to leave Roberta's side, whispering to me that Roberta deserved our support during this trying period. We refused to acknowledge the impending fate of our Roberta, one who joined this family from the death of her parents. Roberta was the lone representative of our extended family, or the sole ambassador for the future of our clan beyond my parents. Roberta's death would represent the fatality of our initial belonging to expanded kinfolk. She molded into our family easily as all who were younger than she rested under her wings. Roberta and Lisa blended almost as if they were twins. They had a long tradition of holidays and summer vacations in each's company. Lisa always spent two weeks during the summer at Roberta's and Roberta stayed in our grandmother's house, with Lisa at her side. Strangely, this was the lone time that any child from our house spent at grandmother's house. Our mother did not allow us to stay overnight with our grandparents. She never gave us any particular reason. My father told us that she wanted to have her children in their beds when in Marked Tree. We always believed that she was afraid we would accidentally fall prey to grandma's sneaky questions. Lisa was now at Lee's side sneaking through the forests that covered the ridge, which surrounded our valley. Lee remembered the places to find the three she castrated yesterday. Lisa examined each man looking for evidence of a fatal shot, which would be lethal. The arrows and shots to the extremities hit bones, missing arteries. These wounds clotted quickly. Although not much blood was shed, just enough leaked out drastically reducing the heat in their bodies. Lisa complimented the modified tourniquet; we applied around the remaining part of their genitals. Lisa asked Lee if I had any reservations working with male genitals. Lee, who applied the tourniquets, told Lisa that I displayed great skill working on male genitals, as if I had much practice. Lisa tells Lee that they must keep this a secret; as such a thing, is considered taboo in American culture. Lee agrees that she will tell everyone that she did this, mainly to protect my image.

Once Lisa verified the three men were deceased, Lee led them back to our farm, with wide branches scrapping the ground behind them. Fortunately, it began snowing on their return trip. Cindy heard their horses gallop beside our cabin and alerted me. I rushed outside to unsaddle their horses and to make sure both returned. I was so glad to see both. I hugged each and ordered them to get into our cabin since I would feed and pat down our horses. Sunday and Easter were excited as if they knew those whom, they protected were together once more. Lee sends Lisa inside first. I was somewhat surprised that Lisa responded so positively to Lee's authoritative demand. Lee explains to me that Lisa wanted to grasp who successfully stopped the bleeding from our victim's genitals. Lee elucidates that she told Lisa I performed the surgeries, to protect our secret. Lee expounds that Lisa made her promise to keep this confidential, to prevent any abnormal cultural labels. I told Lee that she gave the correct account to Lisa, because I was the one who did not want her skills revealed, although I would now constantly wonder what Lisa thinks of me. Lee gave me a kiss and promised that she would constantly emphasize my manhood and promote the consensus that I did this surgery because of my great love for Roberta. Somehow, Lee's words comforted me since I knew she had a special way with people. She could embed her vision in any who surround her. Lisa waited for Lee and me to enter before giving Roberta our report. Lisa complimented me on my outstanding tracking skills, complaining how they could have returned hours earlier if I had tracked today. I ask Lisa why she did not help Lee with tracking in the present day, after all Lee did come from the large cities in China, and trapped in a slave factory while in America. Cindy criticizes Lisa for expected so much from Lee, citing that she could not find any more loyal than Lee at her side.

Roberta tells us that she believes Lee is the greatest gift God gave us. Roberta reminds us that these men never ask or spoke about Lee; they were savage rapists.

Lisa follows by telling Roberta these men will never rape or hurt anyone ever again, nor will they eat any more food on this Earth taking from the righteous. The country they grew up in changed so much, that all put, written laws above true justice. The invisible masters created foolish laws that protected their interests and greed, for if a poor man did what these gluttons did, that poor man would spend the remainder of his days as cheap labor in a prison, unknowingly producing more wealth for these disguised masters. Lee believes this hidden power is the cause of Roberta's misfortune. They promised these sadistic sociopaths their fill of lawlessness, with full immunity if not a reward from the law. I thanked Lee for simply revealing this to Cindy and me. If Lisa knew this, she would seek bloody revenge, and if Roberta learned of this, she could lose her desire to hang on to her life. Roberta told us that she could now rest at ease knowing those three men paid for their demonic exploits. She felt bad that they died on her behalf. Lee explains the spirit of our Earth punished them. The Earth gives perfect revenge when those who live on it break its primary law, which deals with fertilization rights. This was too complex for us to discuss; therefore, we took it at face value. The primary value was the comfort it would provide Roberta, knowing the death of her violators was answering to a higher law, and this justice law forced the penalty for their lives. Roberta began coughing again, this time scattering blood over her body. Cindy and I used our washrags to clean her bruised flesh. Her bruises were growing darker and harder. To touch her send chills up my spine. We had concerned ourselves so much with punishing those who wronged Roberta; we ignored the horrible ruin to her essence. Roberta's eyes were red and the pupils' large black. I pulled Lisa and Lee off to the side and asked them if they knew what caused this. Lisa shook her head no. Subsequently, Lee explains she has seen this many times in the elder or injured servants, as well as the disobedient servants. The eyes are the first to welcome death as the servant begins to prepare for the journey to the land of the dead.

Lisa asked Lee if this meant that Roberta was about to die. Lee replied that Roberta would die within a few hours. With this news, we surrounded Roberta comforting her with our words and songs. Roberta released a small smile and told us we belonged to the greatest family in the world. Next, Roberta revealed to us, one by one, that she loved us and thanked us for loving her. She spoke with Lee first, then Lisa, Cindy, and me last. I did not mind being last, because endmost was an honored position for us, and since she considered me as her brother, the man in her immediate world. I was consequently deep in her that she never expressed any reservation laying her completely nude with me washing and massaging her. Her body looked so hideous, thus no person appearing like this would want others to see their flesh. She trusted us, as her life existed breath by breath. She froze her eyes as her chest stopped expanding and contracting. Lee moved her ear to Roberta's mouth and gripped her arm where it met her hand. After a few minutes, Lee sat back up as our frozen bodies surrendered our eyes to her. Lee had tears flowing from both her eyes as she sat up straight. Consequently, she moved her hands to Roberta's eyes and pulled down Roberta's eyelids. I reached over and put a blanket over Roberta. I wanted her death to be with dignity and honor, just in case she was with other spirits looking down at her body. Roberta could float tall among them as they witnessed our love for her. Each grabbed a part of her body and held it testifying how deep our love was for her.

It is strange how the shock of a dead body freezes a mind. I sense her body growing cold and wonder how a life can depart from the body it was attached. Lisa asks how something so united can separate. Lee tells us her view of life after death differs from ours. Cindy explains that Roberta will hover around her body for a few days, and then the Lord will take her to heaven. She will have a wonderful mansion walking on streets of gold. Roberta will live with other righteous spirits in peace with many animals. Lee reveals that she believes no one dies, but his or her spirit reenters in another human. Her temple, believed when a human dies, they reenter into another human. This varied from the other temples in her city. Many were influenced by India, the others from the Middle East, while others from the southeast, especially Thailand and Cambodia. Lee explains that they had too many people to feed; therefore, to have cows existing and was not in the food chain.

Lee stares at Roberta and promises to remember the spirit of her eyes when meeting new people. Lee asks us if she should leave us and thus spare our lives. Lisa reports that we will be no securer without Lee, and if the truth was known, we are much safer with Lee in our family. Cindy repeats that it is impossible that Roberta is no more. Lisa informs Lee that she was heaven's gift to us, an advance payment for taking Roberta from us. Cindy expresses guilt for bringing Mitch into our lives and forcing us to flee for our lives. Lisa reminds Cindy that she and Roberta requested permission to join this travel adventure. Lisa looks at Lee and confesses that we would have suffered much more without her with us. We also would never have learned about the changes taking place in our world. Although we possessed no method to verify what she told us, her eyes constantly projected a deep belief in what she was reporting. Cindy asks us how we can survive without Roberta. Lisa tells us that Roberta would have expected us to carry on stronger. We must struggle together for those who yet live. Lisa and Cindy began to put on Roberta's clothes, and Lee collected makeup to paint Roberta's face. The important thing to decide now was where, and when to bury Roberta. Cindy explains the ground is too frozen to dig a grave, and thus we must wait until springtime. We will put her on the frozen ground and place our firewood over her high enough to prevent predators from eating a free meal. Lee believed that we should bury her in the place where her last two violators left this world. Lee said that Roberta's karma would have exact justice for eternity. Even though we did not believe this, we could not risk the possibility that it could be true. Roberta deserved this chance, and we would not cheat her from this possibility. We put Roberta's body in the loft of our stable for now. Lisa claimed this would allow it to freeze a little before we placed it under our firewood. This night we kept her beside us trying to forget she was gone. I hoped that such a night would never befall me again. I did not realize that this story was beginning to do.

Chapter 06

Declaration of Dependence

Silence filled our depressed cabin as the bitter days of January froze the mountains we lived. Roberta's frozen body rested under our firewood during the winter kept it stiff. We increased the days that we allowed Sunday, Easter and our two horses to warm in our cabin. These temporary visitors helped to fill the emptiness that Roberta's departure created. We debated naming our horses, nevertheless, finally agreed that chancing another death of a living love so dear to us was a risk too high to chance. Naturally, we loved Roberta more than our horses and never claimed both, as equal. This was more like chancing, adding the needle that broke the camel's back. We struggled quotidian to fight our cabin fever and justifying hope for another day throughout our lives. Lisa and Lee spent most of their time together, leaving Cindy and I, occupying each other. We established that we would never step outside alone and without a pistol. Our rifles were used for hunting, and pistols for defense. Lee told us the pistols were smaller and thus easier to use for neck and neck combat, followed closely by knives. Rifles were better for when the invaders tried to escape. Lee argued with us about shooting attackers in the back. She reassures us that when the thief raids once, they will return. Lee explains the best time to stop a crime when the target is prime. Her rhyme kept this concept fresh on our tongues. We had the death of Roberta as the testament that we did not live in a friendly sharing world. Lee furthered, contends that she does not want to search for trouble; however, when trouble chases us, we must fight or die. There is no choice for those who do not fight, for they will die. There is no guarantee that those who fight will win, as there is also no guarantee they will lose. Lee twists our minds by adding there is a guarantee those who do not fight will lose. We filled a few hours during each day refining our hand-to-hand combat. The truth was before us, in that we must accept our lives will be filled with more dangers once we leave the freezing Arctic of the Rocky Mountains. Lisa declared the next group of men who tried to rape us would get less at a higher price. We saw how a life could be taken and realized if we wished to survive; it would not be a free road. There were tolls on this road, and we needed to fill our purses so as not to become stranded against the side. My angels forced me to develop my fighting skills. They told me if one man was to have so much beauty among him, he had to pay a higher price to be worthy of such a great honor. As they spoke, they studied my face for any reactions. I smiled at them and declared this was a debt so high; I wondered if I ever could repay it. Subsequently, I declared that if any other men came around, they had better get their shirts on quickly. Lisa laughs and adds they would be more dangerous as a man might cherish what to do with what they were sharing. I remained calm as Cindy rescued me by declaring I knew what to do because she trained me excellently.

All our batteries drained; thereby we had no radio or flashlights. Lisa calculated our usage based on wall clocks, where batteries last forever. Radios and flashlights drain them quickly. Without our radios, we had no contact with the outside world, which we doubted existed. The snow accumulated to over one foot, and with the constant swirling winds in our valley shifted without meaning or mercy. The angle we looked at the ridges revealed, empty tree trunks drowning in a river of white. It is so hard to visualize this area will be green and warm within a few months. The sheer volume of this snow is amazing, notwithstanding we recognize subsequently that much of the world is covered now. Lee claims the quantity of water in the oceans, and the air in the sky is monumental quantities. She stands flabbergasted by the process, which the ocean evaporates into the air, and the air returns it as rain. A cycle that normally we declared impossible miraculously exists as the physical law. Lee tends to get us off into confusing subjects, nevertheless; we accept there is nothing else to do. Our walls try to depress us by standing dull and square, or more, of the logs stacked on log line; nonetheless, we identify what is on the other side. The wall is livable on the inside while freezing on the outside that faces the world. Except for the loss of Roberta, this January is going smooth. Our supplies are holding steady with less demand for them through Roberta's departure. Sunday and Easter provide another benefit for us. When they hear another animal, since no humans hike in the weather, both will bark in their stables. They have a special bark when detecting animals, which are loud and chaotic. Accordingly, I grab my crossbow, which I keep stored with an arrow loaded, and dash outside with my coat on the other hand. I can usually scan the situation and determine if I should shoot instantly, or put my coat on quickly and began tracking, with the final option of aborting the hunt and going back to my angels. The rabbits and squirrels could use our cabin in their escape.

Fortunately, I did receive a lucky day. As I rushed outside our door, out a twelve-point deer went pass me, and I got my first arrow in his rear leg. This was enough to prevent him from getting around our stacked firewood. I pulled out my pistol and shot him once in his head. He dropped at once, nevertheless, continued to wiggle fighting to hold on to his life. Without thinking, I grabbed my ax beside our woodpile where I split the wood, and with one stroke, chopped off his head. Accordingly, I drag the deer's body to the stall door, holding his legs up trying to drain his blood. I take his head, open our stable door, and toss it into the stable for Sunday and Easter to enjoy as an appetizer. Meanwhile, I went back to our cabin and put certain heavier clothing around me. Cindy wanted to figure out why I was going outside and exiting alone because we agreed always to have a partner. I told her that I was working on a surprise in the stables and should be okay. Using my knife, I removed most of the meat and his hide. Sunday and Easter cleaned up the leftovers as I went inside and called for my angels to help me. They came to the stables and helped carry this life-saving meat into our cabin. We enjoyed a diet heavy in meat when possible. This surprise guaranteed several special meals that could help us build up the protein in our bodies as we figured this year would give us come harsher challenges. Vegetation and fruits were impossible to find now in the mountains; thereby this meat could keep us alive and supplement our grains until springtime when we could return and trade with Peter. Lisa claims that Roberta gave us this deer. Lee agrees this could be possible, as she knew of many tales about the spirits helping their loved ones. Our ears now were tuned in for any noise hoping it was a part of Roberta returning to us.

Simple Midwest people such as we have difficulty in accepting a loss of a family member. We added a few in our lives and hoped to lose even less. Lee was our first true addition. She lived, ate, cried, and loved by us. She was deep in our minds, without question, as we also believed we were the fixture in hers. The stretched days could have felt longer, except for our boring stories and ritual singing. We must have learned over one-hundred of Lee's songs. Lee was so bored with sharing her songs she begged each day for us to teach her ours. Her hunger astonished me for our culture. She always complimented us on the essence of our philosophies yet could debate us on the fallacy of our implication. I asked to explain our fallacy. Lee reveals that nothing created by humanity will survive. Lisa boldly claims the United States has already fallen, in less than three centuries. Lee asks how the Roman Empire, Egypt, and China, which is lasting much longer, with China expanding and growing into the greatest Empire ever to exist. Cindy questions Lee on how China can do something that has never been done previously. Lee confesses that she does not recognize all the reasons, nevertheless; she knows the lone reason that they can survive is they make sure their people live. The pursuit of happiness must begin with the assurance of food and security. Most will worship any who will save them from starvation and harm. Lee elaborates that no Empire can survive when they first destroy the weakest among them. Lee warns us not to be foolish, and as we climb a ladder to elevate ourselves, never break the step from which you came, because, once you reach the top, the lone place, you can go is back to your beginning. Those with their heads too high in the sky are in danger of being hit by airplanes or tripping while stepping in the small hole. Lee also warns that at no time to cut the bottom out of a trash can, for when you do the trash will never follow the trashcan. They are no longer united. A house cannot stand on weak ground, when the foundation falls, so does all, which they built on it.

Cindy argues the family unit is the ladder that great lands are built. Lee agrees the family unit is critical in the foundation and complains how America has fallen so much on this task. She claims that American parents spoil and overprotect their children. Lee asks us what happens to a baby bird when it must leave the nest when its parents never taught it how. The baby bird will be trapped in its nest forever. In the wild nature, the parents work hard on preparing their newborns for the future so that they can survive. Lee reveals that most Americans of this generation are so attached to their portable devices; they forget their will to gain freedom in the future. They can depend on their parents, nevertheless; their parents will not survive forever. They will be an easy prey, as the future generations of the poor nations will defeat them. An authentic family will have parents who provide the rod of knowledge and love their children so much that they instill within them true values and responsibility. Lee reports that she saw various children badger their parents in a store demanding they purchase nonessential items. She also saw a group of eight teenagers walking to a movie theater. She witnessed them walk about three blocks as she tagged beside them on the sidewalk on the opposite side of the street. Lee, with tears flowing down her eyes, confirmed that at no time did these teenagers talk to each. Lee believes that when a person loses the ability to socialize and solely release emotions through electrical devices, they will never be able to love or have any other intense emotions. Not at any time will they be united and divided; they will fall.

Lee explains that in her culture, the parents rule their families. If children cause trouble or show disrespect at any time, the government takes them. The government sends them to a cultural awareness center where they stay until they are eighteen and receive their lifetime occupation. Most parents require their children to earn money for the things they want. Since most parents have low incomes, their child finds part-time work to purchase these extras, and out of love and respect helps their parents financially. The grandparents provide most of the childcare for their children because their fathers and mothers work for their master. Her government mandates the masters must make sure all the children of their servants receive childcare. The masters own all the children from their servants. The government mandates that if the master sells the servant, he or she must also keep the child with its mother. If the master can include the father in the transaction, he or she will receive a bonus from the government. Sometimes this is not practical; in the master, most times will use his strongest male to impregnate all his female servants. This will help to produce a better stock for him or her in the future. They may have solely one child per female servant. This is why most women have their reproductive organs removed. Any women who are part of a clan where they caught a woman with more than one child will have her reproductive organs removed. Lee continues by telling us; these reproducing laws no more than apply in her China homeland and do not apply to servants in the United States. Lee suspects the government wants additional citizens and has no space limitations in North America. There are a few other laws for the servants living in the United States such as total discipline. The servants understand that they must stay concealed until the Americans are more accepting. Lee is despite everything confused why these masters are produced in the United States and in constant danger of ensuing capture. Lee summarizes that China has the stronger family unit; their children are more satisfied and believe they are loved and a part of something greater. Her culture plans many community events where the children in their city or region can socialize. Lee discloses one of the greatest challenges she experienced from her move to the United States was leaving her multitude of friends. Her region successfully bonded their children.

Fortunately, for Lee, most of the servants in her group came from the same area and share identical friends. They have bonded accordingly, tight in America as they rotate a couple of rooms where most sleep together. Sleep for a servant is different from a free person, in these servants is so tired of their hard work and standard diet. When they sleep, they spend much time in deep sleep; therefore, they cannot hear any intruders. By sleeping together, someone in the group will hear the invader and wake the group up for their defense. Lee discloses their masters constantly warned them how Americans invade people's homes, rape, rob, beat, and sometimes murder them. They plastered the bulletin boards with newspaper and magazine stories of rape, robbery, and other crimes. They reported the truth; however, they exaggerated it. Lee tells how the grapevine always had horror stories going into everyone's mind. Sometimes they would peek out the windows and watch the Americans walk or drive pass them. They believed these people were empty inside and craving just luxuries. The multitudes crave solely luxury, and they do not care what expense it takes to obtain it. The Americans use so much oil for their cars and now that most nations have cars and building their infrastructure; nevertheless, the price of oil will go up subsequently high many nations will not be able to afford it. They need this for survival; the Americans want it for pleasure. Lee reveals that hardly any food is wasted; at the same time, Americans continually squander it. Lee explains her masters told his servants that if the Americans see them, they would kidnap them and demand too high a ransom. Even if they pay the ransom, these kidnappers would still kill them. The decay of the American family easily is seen from the outside. The key in preventing the decay of these families is for them to spend free time in conjunction and especially eat with each other. Chinese families always eat together, and even though they have little time from work, they spend most of it jointly.

I looked at Lisa as she begins to respond to Lee. She tells Lee that she can see how her viewpoint, or the philosophy of her master. Several elements are true. Many places exist in the United States that is not safe for the public and indeed, if you give the impression of being confused or lost, they will destroy you. Lee asks why the police do not clean these areas. Cindy tells her that many police officers are afraid to do their work, in that so many political organizations are looking for something to excite the public. Therefore, since they cannot enforce the law, they accept brides and make sure there is no interference for the highest bidders. The drug business is extremely profitable and funds an underground Mafia making it impossible to penetrate. Lee intensifies this is another great foolishness of the Americans. Most of the drugs they have marked as criminal, ones in which people can spend a lifetime in prison for possessing are legal in most of the other nations in the world. Coke, a popular soda was initially marketed with a drug, which is now illegal. She insists that many people in her country make large sums of money simply collecting certain plants and flowers that can create various drugs; they are legal in her home but illegal in America. No one in her home region misuses these drugs because they are aware of the great danger. Nevertheless, the American government makes it forbidden, which instantly creates the challenge and perception of pleasure and reward for taking it. Moreover, by making it illegal, they cause those who become addicted outlaws and criminals. This is a waste of government and total unnecessary confusion. Cindy looked at Lisa not knowing how to respond to this. Lisa agrees with Lee and tells her she is praying the American society will fix this wrong before so many more suffer. Lee continues her argument by adding that when a person loses faith in a law, these leads to them losing faith in all laws. When so many lose their devotion for their society, that culture will decay. This is a cancer, as it will spread until it destroys what it has entrapped. The bad apple in the bushel will spoil the bushel.

I ask Lee how she knows all these things. Lee confesses her master has a large collection of news media. They want them to recognize the dangers that surround them. Lisa confirms many times the innocents are unprotected from those who wish to steal and break the law taking advantage of any possible weakness. Their lives will never return to where they would be if they perceived society would have provided the protection. Cindy contends there would be no protection from Mitch when he regained his freedom. The current legal system provided more rights and privileges for those who intend to promote antisocial and self-satisfying agendas. Cindy begins to cry. Lee asks her to explain more. Lisa tells her that because one person decides he wants to take away Cindy's freedom from a pursuit of love with the one she selects Cindy must exist in fear for the remainder of her life. She must tremble because of her sense of morality as a victim of one who does not have the basic respect for the civil rights of others. Lee asks if Cindy led Mitch to think he had a right to elevate their relationship. Lisa reminds us the female or male in a courtship has a right to end that engagement before the marriage and request a divorce after the marriage. Cindy actually declared her love for me and moved into his home. She went to my church and declared to all her love for me, and her intention of marrying me. She never publicly declared an intention of establishing any form of a relationship with Mitch. Cindy claims that she at no time, even privately declared any emotions for Mitch. Considering there is no method to prove she never declared intentions for Mitch in secret, bears any weight. Anything established in private has no validity until confirmed in public. Lee explains that such a thing would not happen in her community, in that Mitch's parents would have commended her forget about Cindy, and that would have been it. If Mitch disregarded their orders, they would place her in a social correctional facility.

Cindy confesses Lee's system is much better and asks why her society would offer protection such as this. Lee answers that they must protect the mother's rights, especially considering the wives are the property of the husband and his family. The shame of a son married to a woman who loves another man. This could forever leave a doubt on who the true father was. The neighbors would privately ridicule their family and would live in shame. Cindy, Lisa, and I stand faced with another shocking challenge. Our complete world is coming down in shambles. Lee's world provided the minimum rights, yet the rights they had been guaranteed. In America, we had more rights; nevertheless, these rights were not protected. Lee contends most Asian nations stand socially shielded. They must understand the privilege to enjoy modern civilization requires responsibility. The punishment for social disobedience is isolation. If you cannot live with people, then you must live alone. Laws require obedience. The nation must believe their leaders pass these laws to protect them and create a safe environment, which makes production possible. These basic needs must always be satisfied. There can never be any uncertainty they exist, because, when the doubt abounds, everyone is walking on quicksand. Lee asks us if we believe the United States can protect their innocent citizens. Lisa explains whether they believed they were secure; she would be playing with Roberta in Marked Tree. Lee acknowledges that she understands. I comment to our group that life might be better if we had a strong honest government controlling our world. We were lucky in Marked Tree in that we could walk on the streets at night without any fear. Most crimes involving theft were solved immediately. Everyone pretty well knew what the neighbors owned. They purchased most high-value products in a group accompanied by their friends. We were extremely fortunate, as this has not been the case for over a century in many American communities.

Lisa thanks Lee for joining, accepting, and teaching us. Lee contends that she is not teaching anything special, but instead reporting on many of the differences between the eastern civilization and the western civilization. Lisa begs Lee to share more by explaining more about why these differences exist. Lee believes her nation, and so many other Asian nations had no choice but to establish rigid guidelines to control their citizens and provide an opportunity for them to survive. Lee supposes the type of government is not a factor; it is the ability of the government to provide and protect their people. She considers the democratic nations receive extra favors from the representative superpowers. Lisa argues the United States supports China in trade more than all the other Asian nations combined. Lee complains that although the United States trades heavily with China, they do not pay for them, but instead borrow from China. This forces the homeland to create more money, and in the end spread too thin. She believes communism is best for China because of a history of weak leaders, in which the masses starved. With so many people to oversee, China needed a strong central government. Once this central government got, control, they could move her nation in one direction. Everyone gladly worked hard because of the pride of being a part of something big. No one expects riches, and therefore, do not rob and cheat others to advance. They expect food and security, and will be mated and given a chance to reproduce and part of their family. Lee also adds that they have spiritual responsibility and benefits. If they work hard, they will get a better life, the next time they are born. If they do poorly, their ensuing life will be much more difficult. Cindy asks Lee what sort of life she will live next. Lee reports she will have a poor and difficult life the forthcoming round because she was so bad this life evidenced by her escaping from her master. He will be extremely angry about the spiritual world and demand they punish her severely. Cindy informs Lee that we are going to convert her to Christianity, so she can go to heaven with us. Lee agrees heaven would be so much better than she has in her future currently.

Accordingly, I tell Lee we will get her in church with us. Lee confesses that if we are in a church, she wants to join us. Lee claims that she needs us. I tell Lee not to worry because she will be with us. Cindy kisses Lee's cheek and asks her if being the different race worries her. Lee confesses that race always can play a role; you either ignore it, submit to it, or fight it. Lee continues by stating she enjoys her total submission to us. We are much better masters than her former one. Lee compliments us on sharing and caring with her. She believes that we sincerely care for her. The truth of our situation is Lee has turned into a boat, and we are in that boat on a river for the first time floating into the unknown. Lee reveals the Asians tend to blend easier with other races. Her people remained separated from all foreigners. They existed forbidding any contact with any one not in their master's group. This even included other Chinese; therefore, she did not speak with any Chinese on the bus, except for two from her group. Curiosity forced me to ask Lee why she was on that bus. It seemed strange that she would be with one other slave or servant on a bus away from Marked Tree. Lee reveals they were supposed to collect a few new servants their master had purchased. I ask Lisa if she noticed Lee's partner after leaving the bus. Lisa tells me that she wrapped her coat around Lee concealing her. Lee told her that if any saw her, they might use violence to retrieve her. Notwithstanding, Roberta helped conceal Lee as they rushed Lee away from the bus and to Lisa's waiting father. It was tense, yet Lisa decided to keep Cindy and me in the dark, so we would behave normally, because our public display of affection was highly visible.

I am now, for the first time, comprehending what Lee did, so she could join our family. She jumped into a storm, and she put out the solitary light in her room. She was a mermaid trapped on land. She crossed through an iron curtain. I ask Lee how she describes what happened in our Union. Lee believes that sometimes our unconsciousness takes over our consciousness. It is as if our spirits took control of our bodies. There just was not any mystery or learning time to develop our relationship. Lee reveals everything inside her believed she belonged to us and strangely had always been inside us. We were forever her spiritual masters. It felt like we had been her masters through many of her previous lives. Lee stares at us with a mountain of confidence, declaring she constantly was with us, and most likely will invariably be with us. We are one and will always be one. Cindy, who kisses Lee about one hundred times a day, as does Lisa and I, confirms she senses Lee deep inside her soul. Cindy tells us that she honestly feels as if Lee is a part of us. Lisa hopes that all her contact with other races is as rich as this one is. Lee argues this cannot qualify as a race relationship because we are not different people in distinct bodies. Conversely, we are the same person spread in separate bodies. Lisa agrees that she knew there was something special and wonderful between us. She confirms this is what she was trying to discover by mandating we remain topless when inside the cabin. She simply felt our shirts were feeding a separation that should not exist. I enlightened them; they were the most beautiful angels ever to exist. Lisa thanks Cindy for giving her and Lee this freedom around her husband. Cindy divulges that she sees no reason for concern, initially because Roberta and Lisa are my older sisters, and thus have a right to appear any way they wish around their younger brothers. Cindy says Lee is our love, and secretly she hopes Lee will bear our clan a child, and to do this; she must mate with her husband. Anything that can make me more relaxed with Lee is to her benefit. Lee questions if she is worthy of such an honor. I inform her that my wish is that she finds a mate, and they have a family. Lee declares this would be against everything in her being. She will emphatically mate with whom, I tell her. There is no such thing as love when it comes to create a family.

Lee elaborates that setting up a home and raising a family requires a strong man and his servant wife. She will obey him as his master. Lisa warns Lee never to talk like this around American woman, for they will hate and hurt her. Lee continues that if the wife does not obey the husband, who can expect their children to obey him. Lee reminds us the husband is the protector and provider. His greatest concern is that his wife and children do not starve and have a place to sleep. He will give all he has for his family, and what he gains is given to his wife, so she can make sure their family has the care they need. The wife has all the control of the finances. She manages this so her husband can concentrate on providing, and protecting. Lee repeats the wife and children belong to the father, absolutely; nevertheless, the father belongs to his family. This is a dependent circle. It is the lone way to make sure the children receive the best from their parents, and this culture moves on to the next generation. Cindy surprises us by saying she enjoys when I tell her to do things with courage and confidence. I tell them that if I do not perform as Cindy demands, Lisa will punish me. Lisa and Cindy, ask me when they have ever remotely questioned my manhood. Lisa assures me that one of their primary objectives has always been to develop my authority over them. I ask Lisa why she would want me to have authority over her. Lisa tells me since I am growing into a man; it must be this way. As in the Roberta case, there are those times when we need the muscle and courage of a man to survive. Lisa emphasizes that having a man in the group also can act as a deterrent. Lisa claims that Roberta's violator must have scouted us, and after discovering me, decided to wait for one and then sneak away from our farm. If I were not there, they may have come to the cabin and raped all four females. I ask them how just one of me could scare three men. Lisa tells me they most likely calculated I would get one of them. None of the three wanted to be the one. I ask Lisa how she is so confident that I will not take Cindy and leave. Lisa tells her there are many reasons, the first one since Cindy will not let me leave; the second is that she, as my older sister would not permit me to leave, the third reason is I would never leave Lee. Lisa then says the icing on the cake is obvious. Lisa smiles and asks me where their shirts are.

I ask my angels, why they make such a big deal over being topless. I remind them that after a few days, it should be obvious I have not simply seen them, but may have overseen them. This is the same as having candy everywhere. Soon the thrill of having candy is gone. This could progress into a dislike for candy to the degree of becoming sick when thinking of the candy. I was given the true account of what happened in our family. My mother left large bowls of candy in several rooms in our home. We eventually began to ignore it completely. None of us has any desire for candy. Lee tells me they have a hidden weapon. I ask Lee what this secret weapon is. She tells me it is Mother Nature, and she at no time shall free me from my longing for the female breasts. I smile at them and confess that I never want to make Mother Nature mad, so at least I will pretend I am still impressed. Cindy and Lee hit me claiming I will be more than impressed. I confess to them that Mother Nature blessed me with three of her best female creations. Lisa jumps and kisses me. I give her a charming tight hug and whisper in her ear that she is the best. I sense her body relaxes as if she just got a drink of water after a long journey in the desert. Lisa is not as stable and confident as she was with Roberta at her side. They fed off each other, for when one would waver, the other would stabilize her. Lisa was previously the superhero in my life. She was and still is my dreams come true. She made my summers so refreshing with the baseball games she organized and the work she managed so we could earn enough money for our Christmas gifts. I worshipped the ground she walked on, in fact; I still worship the ground she walks.

I decide that she may need to understand this. I am still holding Lisa's hand, accordingly; I pull her back in my arms. She has a surprised look. I hug her tight, gaze straight in her eyes, and tell her she is the greatest woman evermore in my life, and no one will ever be greater than she is. Cindy and Lee rush around us gripping us in their hug. Cindy informs Lisa that Lisa is, without any doubt, her older sister, and second mother. Cindy, as she repeatedly kisses Lisa's cheek with her tears flowing, pledges that she will never put any one above her. Lee begins kissing Lisa, on the other cheek and tells Lisa she is the greatest master that she has ever served and dedicates her life to Lisa to use as she wills. Lisa begins to cry and tells us she is not as great as we claim she is. Lisa becomes too weak to stand up, so we hold her. Cindy agrees with Lisa that she is not as great as we claim she is, but she is even greater. Lisa explains her unbearable fear that she may lead us, the wrong way and more disasters such as Roberta would fall on us. I tell Lisa there was nothing she could have done to prevent that. The nature of our world has no guarantees. Lee tells us that an airplane could crash into our cabin. We could catch a disease from passing animals.

Death is always just a few minutes away. It is most likely the closest adversary that we will ever have with us all our days of our lives. Fate is the master of whom survives and who suffers. Faith and trust are powerful forces that lend to leadership. Lee reassures Lisa; they have absolute faith and trust in her leadership. Even if they are on the wrong path, faith and trust can put them on the right path. The emptiness and the feeling, existing within the followers can alone be the reservoirs that if filled by the leader to create loyalty beyond questioning. Lee explains to Lisa that she fills this sense of lost and wonder, which was with us by removing the feeling of being on a path without guidance. No one cared what path we were traveling so long we were on the path with Lisa. I explain to Lisa, we are in this to the end, and with her in front of us. Lisa asks us how we can believe she knows so much, especially since we grew up together. Cindy responds by telling Lisa this is why we need her to survive.

Lee tells Lisa that her belief in Lisa's leadership skills happened in the short time they have been together. Lee further adds that she would have never risked her life with us unless it was for Lisa. Lisa looks at her gang and tells them that we will survive, yet now we must never trust any new people. I ask her about Peter. Lisa tells us Peter is trustworthy, for if he were not, he would have already betrayed us to retrieve his horses and not be obligated for his final supply shipment. Furthermore, when Phillip returned without Pedro, Peter would have come after us immediately, unless he trusted our character. Lee discloses this as one of many hundreds of reasons we must keep Lisa as our leader, and that she is so thankful for the way in which Lisa puts all the pieces in place. Cindy asks Lisa if she has any worries she has not revealed to us yet. Lisa explains that we must make sure not to go outside unless in pairs, and we should take one trip up to the ridge each day, just to get a sense for anything that does not appear normal. If we had done this when Roberta was with us, she may still be alive. Either way, we must believe more dangers lurched in our mystery hideout. Lisa also explains that we must exercise for at least two hours each day since when we return from our trip to Canada; we must believe those who hunt us will be less patient and under greater pressure, especially as the foreign servants will be wondering if an escape now is possible. When we leave this valley, we must be prepared to fight every inch of our path. Lisa asks Lee if she knows any fighting skills we can use for both our offense and defense. Lee tells us she will gladly share with us the knowledge she has.

Subsequently, we began to prepare a ten-week exercise program. We believed our hibernation; she would terminate at the end of this ten-week, and even if it did not, we would expand on the program we established. Lisa similarly wanted us to bring Sunday, and Easter inside a couple of hours each day. Lisa, likewise, believed the trip up the ridge each day would give our horses exercise, as we would be taking them for longer rides once springtime arrived. Lisa asked us if we sang for a few hours each day mixed with a little storytelling. Lisa warned that Lee would not be telling all the stories, because we have a responsibility share as much about America with Lee as possible, considering she gave up her world to join ours. I tell Lee the stories we tell her will not be representative of American culture; therefore, I share a few stories learned from news and true story movies. Lisa compliments me on this suggestion and explains to Lee that Cindy, and she will do the same. Moreover, I clarify to Lee many of the stories she has told us about Americans has elements of truth expounded by unfounded relevance and application. Lee claims the same can be said about what Americans believe about the Chinese. We agree with her, claiming the lone rightful way to discover the truth is through the people who live it. Lee agrees by claiming we have changed her perception of Americans. Cindy cautions Lee not to project the way we behave and believe as the standard for Americans, we are small-town Midwestern. Our difference from urban America was the same as the difference between day and night. We were different. Lee verifies this by adding that no groups of people are identical with all its members. This is the dynamic of humans over machines. People can be reprogrammed and serve with much more flexibility than machines. Lisa informs us this is amazing news coming from a citizen of the greatest machine-producing nation in the world. Lee also reminds us that China is as well the number-one people-producing nation in the world. We shake our heads in agreement. Lisa gives Lee a kiss on her cheek. Cindy and I rush on top of her, as Cindy kisses the other cheek, and I proceed to tickle her. The sound of someone laughing in our cabin is so refreshing and wonderful. I was almost convinced we would never again hear the laughing sound in our cabin.

I saw how this laughter was bringing something back to us that we lost with the death of Roberta. Accordingly, I ask Lisa if we should take a ride to the top of the ridge and if so, who should go. Lisa tells me that she wants me to go each day, with her and Cindy rotating as my partner. Lee asks if she can help with this duty. Lisa reminds Lee she is the person of interest, and we must keep her as invisible as possible. I remind Lee that we are all persons of interest. Lisa rebuts this may be true; however, a male and female couple departing from a cabin is normal, a male leaving a cabin with three females is the cause for concern for the legal citizens and an opportunity beyond aborting for criminals. Lisa tells me she will go with me the first day, so she can identify any avenues of concern. I agree and ask her to wait while I get our horses prepared. Lisa smiles and tells me this is one reason she wants me on each trip, because of the manner, I care for, and protect the women who share my life. Out into the cold, I go to prepare our horses. Lisa comes to our stable just before I am finished and calmed Sunday and Easter asking them if they want to go with us. Oddly, they act as if they understand her. I am beginning to wonder if I am the lone person that these dogs do not talk. I ask Lisa, who explains they are responding to her eyes. I thank her for this information and explain I was beginning to wonder if people could actually talk with dogs. Lisa clarifies these people may not be able to use expanded language with dogs; nevertheless, they can communicate with them. Lisa believes having these dogs with us will provide needed protection, if we require it. I ask her if we should bring our weapons. Lisa tells me bringing our weapons will not hurt anything, yet could protect us from intruders, and that we could get lucky with various unexpected game. I agree and rush back in our cabin grabbing our repeating rifles, pistols, and knives. The knives are for cleaning any game we capture since I prefer to clean them after the kill.

We dawn our weapons and begin our short scouting mission. Sunday and Easter are excited running in all directions. I ask Lisa if it was good to have dog prints over our land. Lisa smiles and explains, “Little brother, dog prints are an excellent deterrent for those who want to snoop around our property.” I smile at her and confess this is the reason we need her as our leader. She is consistently able to discover the benefits to new variables introduced to our surroundings. Sunday and Easter kept a tight watch on us, waiting for us to go up the road to the ridge. They rushed before us just in time as we began our ride up the path to the ridge. Up we went to the top as Lisa led me north first. We never traveled this far, yet Lisa wanted to do select snooping and exploration. I must confess it was wonderful to realize more about what surrounded us. Lisa was thrilled; we had no neighbors for a one-hour horse ride north. We knew the south was clear from our ride here. We finally turned around, and proceeded south for one hour from our ridge. This meant at least three more hours. I asked Lisa if this was our daily route. Lisa while laughing says this would be too much each day. She just wants to detect any possible entry points that would justify extra monitoring. When we reached the turnaround point and began to ride back to our cabin Lisa spotted a little movement three ridges west of us. She asks me if I see this movement. I focus my eyes, adjusting them for the medium freezing wind cuts across my face. Afterwards, I spot a man on a horse. I tell Lisa this man may be on the same path that we took, and if so I estimate, he will be here in less than one hour. Lisa explains that we will wait around the bend just ahead and watch the traveler to see what he or she is doing this deep in the mountains. Notwithstanding, I remind Lisa there was no snowfall yesterday and today; therefore, these were the lone two days that someone could travel.

The stranger stays true to our entry path, appearing on the second ridge from us, and then appearing on the next ridge. Lisa told me we should now hide on this path, one on each side. Soon the rider came to pass us. I was startled with whom; I saw. I looked over to Lisa, whose face also looked surprised. We charged out, rode up to the stranger, and told him to halt. He turned around, and shouted, "Lisa and George, how have you been?" I looked at him and asked Phillip what brought him back to our vacated land. Phillip tells us that so many things have changed now, and that Peter wants us to come back to Grandby, so he can prepare us for our new future. I noticed Phillip had a few bags of supplies with him. Lisa asks Phillip if we are to return with him to Grandby why he is bringing supplies. Phillip tells us it is foolish for all the returns.

Peter believed that Roberta, and I would be the best candidates to return. I informed Phillip that Roberta died as a result from being raped by three wild lunatics. Phillip wept. Lisa declares that she just discovered a secret admirer for Roberta. I tell Lisa this is not the subject to pester Phillip. Phillip confesses to us that he was indeed an admirer of Roberta. I ask Phillip not to talk about this around Cindy and Lee as we are just beginning to recover from this tragedy. Phillip asks if we recognize where they are. Lisa tells him, that by a strange stroke of karma, we discovered them frozen to death tied to select trees over on the next ridge. Phillip smiles confessing this is the best news that he has heard during his life, because, if they were not dead, he would track them to the ends of the Earth and torture them. I tell Phillip that Lee insured, they did not take to their deaths what they defiled Roberta. Phillip asks how she did this. Lisa tells him she sliced their male shaft and after that chopped it off, then removed their tongues and blinded them. Phillip tells us that if Peter discovers this, he will beg us for permission to adopt Lee. Lisa asks Phillip if we can agree that she extracted this justice. It will be more believable if we claim, Lisa performed these acts of justice, since she is the leader and strongest among the women.

I tell Phillip that it is amazing he noticed Lisa's leadership skills because we had a long debate trying to convince her. Phillip looks at Lisa and questions how she could ever doubt her natural leadership abilities. Phillip confesses that even he would easily follow her orders, notwithstanding into battle. Lisa asks Phillip, which head he is using for his thinking. I yell at Lisa to watch that sort of talk around me. Phillip appears shocked as I continue demanding Lisa apologizes. Lisa, realizing how offended her little brother is over, these remarks, asks me if she is ever permitted to have a life. I tell Lisa she is naturally entitled to a life, one I hope would be better than that of an alley cat. Phillip explains to Lisa, he would be proud to be included among her favorites and believed he was a part of our family since the first time they met. Lisa suggests that we should get back to the cabin, eat certain food, enjoy a little heat, and then hear this wonderful news. Lisa asks Phillip if he can stay with us tonight. I tell Phillip he must stay, to return late means he must spend two more nights in this freezing mountain. His endurance would weaken with each freezing night. Lisa looks at Phillip and tells him he will stay because the one thing she wants Grandby to remember them by is our hospitality. Phillip laughs and confesses he thought we might invite him and thus brought a variety of extra food for a long-awaited feast. I glanced at Lisa as a smile flooded our faces. Accordingly, I yell for Sunday and Easter as we begin our single file ride back to our cabin. Phillip explains to Sunday and Easter, he brought a few special bones for them. Sunday and Easter began jumping with excitement. I ask Phillip if he knows these dogs. He tells us they are his dogs, and he has raised them since they were pups. Lisa questions Phillip about his difficulty in lending his dogs and asks him if he misses them. Phillip confesses that he misses them, nonetheless, knew they would be in excellent care with us. We arrived back to our cabin, placed the three horses in our stables. Lisa invited Sunday and Easter into our cabin, where they would sleep tonight because their sleeping space would go to Phillip's horse.

We completely unmounted our horses and prepared to enter our cabin. Lisa gives our secret knock on our door, and Lee opens it with her robe covering her. Lisa reveals to Lee and Cindy; we have a special male guest and need to get appropriately dressed. Lee and Cindy put on their heavy winter shirts, and once they have their buttons buttoned; we begin to bring our supplies into our cabin. We unpack our fresh supplies and compliment Phillip on the way they have mixed with various new grains, such as oats, barley, and sugar. He could do this since we brought enough rice and noodles for the complete winter. Phillip brought us extra potatoes and vegetables. He brought five jars of home canned vegetables from his family's cellar. He brought certain red pepper, salt, and black pepper, with a few additional spices. Lee gave him a hug for the red pepper. Phillip confesses that he did not discern for sure if Lee enjoyed the red pepper, he was roaming the web for Asian diets. He apologized for not doing a deeper search; however, Peter was afraid that someone might be monitoring Asian web traffic. Lee tells Phillip she understands. Phillip joins us since everyone is involved with our cooking. Phillip reports, how impressed he is with our meat supply. Even Sunday and Easter are excited as scraps are passing their way this early in our preparation. Phillip gave them each one bone, which they have secured. He has more in his bag that he will give them before leaving. Phillip tells us they will be munching on their bones tonight while we try to sleep. We are excited causing a rush of positive and happy energy flooding our small cabin. Phillip shares general news with us, such as the style of the new cars and describes several modern styles of dresses he saw in a catalog. He was disappointed in the rifles that were currently on sale as the available selection was limited and required police authorization to order them.

We load our plates and sit down to eat around our fireplace. Phillip tells us that Peter is dedicated to their safety and survival. Lisa asks Phillip why Peter is giving us this special attention. Phillip tells us this is because he considers us as part of his family. Subsequently, Phillip surprises us by telling us everything they recognize about us. He continues by glancing to Lisa and asking if Lisa Jones misses her life on Locust Street in Marked Tree, Poinsett County in Arkansas. Lisa smiles at Phillip and asks if such a person was here what would happen to them. Phillip smiles and reveals such a person would enjoy extra supplies throughout the winter and emergency support from their mountain father. I remind Phillip the United States government wants this person. Phillip smiles and tells us he would not worry about that government. Phillip looks at Lee and brags how impressed he is with Li Jing's escape from the Chinese Mafia. I ask Phillip what he thinks should happen to the Li Jing, he is discussing. Phillip tells us he hopes she enjoys red pepper on her food. Lee asks Phillip if they can count on him not to report them and wants to see if Phillip is going to turn them in to the authorities. Phillip stares at us and asks how we can think he is here to surrender them to the bounty hunters. He continues by revealing the reason Peter sent one person, so we would not experience fear. This is also one reason he merely wants two to return to Grandby. I tell my angels that Phillip and Peter have always done us right, so I do not believe we have anything to worry about in this situation. Lee glances toward Phillip and declares her trust in him. Lee laughs, saying that if they do plan to capture them, they are going about it in the most inefficient way possible. Phillip smiles at us and asks if we enjoyed our dinner. Lisa thanks him for our great meal and his companionship. I suspect that Lee will be lonely tonight, not that she has ever done anything at night, except sleep. She is insecure and likes to be snuggle against someone. Cindy enlightens me not to worry because Sunday, and Easter will be glad to snuggle beside her.

Lisa asks Phillip when he is going to share the news he has for us. Phillip tells her he will in just one minute. He opens his backpack and pulls out a bottle of wine and a few plastic cups giving each one cup. Subsequently, he pours us each one-half a cup of wine. The wine goes down so smoothly. I did not realize how stiff my body was. I felt as if I had been walking on needles and holding my screams inside sharing a false smile with the world. Now that I am enjoying the wine flowing in my body, my smile is sincere. I notice Lisa, Lee, and Cindy is relaxing as well. This cup of wine was long overdue. Phillip tells us it is time for him to give us the latest news. He begins by telling us to forget the Pledge of Allegiance. It takes us a few minutes for this to settle in our minds. Lisa is the first to respond by asking Phillip what he means by forgetting the Pledge of Allegiance, as she believes he is talking metaphorically. I do not discern what to think. Lee asks which Pledge of Allegiance he is telling us to forget. Cindy, with her beautiful confused eyes, asks Phillip what he means. Phillip agrees to add a few more examples to his report. He starts by telling us the Constitution of the United States and Declaration of Independence are void documents that now merely represent a period in history. Lisa glares at Phillip and asks if he is telling us the United States is history. Phillip grins and tells us the United States of America now belongs to China, and all the leaders in Washington D.C. are in custody, or he should say, those who remained, which were, for the most part, were the staff and administrative clerks. I ask Phillip how this happened so fast. Lisa quickly asks Phillip if there were any battles and destruction. Cindy asks Phillip what changes have occurred with the citizens in their daily lives. Lee warns us that we must give Phillip time to answer our questions as she asks Phillip to commence at the beginning and tell us what happened.

Phillip tells us the decline of the United States began with the loss of the dollar as the world currency. When the Chinese Yuan took over as the world currency, China lowered their rate against the dollar it made the cost of American exports too high to compete in overseas markets. Because the United States agreed, their debt would be in the current Yuan rate, this new exchanged raised the American debt substantially. Lisa asks why the United States agreed to repay in Yuans instead of the dollars they received. Phillip reports that they bribed enough politicians to pass it, using the concept the United States could influence the dollar and pay on the debt when the exchange rate was favorable, especially since the dollar was the world standard then. When the Yuan became the world currency, China foreclosed on the debt, demanding we switch to the new world currency or repay immediately. The United States had no choice, especially considering China would not want dollars when their Yuans were accepted currency worldwide. The exchange rates were favorable to the dollar so the public and media painted it as advantageous for Americans. Accordingly, this story stood ignored. Soon the media began reporting on financial disasters in the American markets, especially when China refused to load any more money causing the United States to operate in a balanced budget. This caused panic in the federal government as the administrative agencies prepared to operate on a skeleton budget. The states were affected mildly by this national freeze since they received limited Union support. Naturally, most federal defense projects were canceled. This was not beneficial to China as they stole all the military secrets from the United States. Notwithstanding, unemployed skyrocketed and American production almost stopped. Lisa asks Phillip how so much happened consequently, fast. Phillip laughs and reveals that in a society based on information, it does not need to happen, computers simply need to project it, and the markets adapt instantaneously. Lee explains to Phillip that China owns and controls the American media. Phillip asks Lee how she can perceive this. Lee laughs and explains that when a government does not hide things from its citizens, and controls the tongues of its people, everyone can comprehend everything. Phillip agrees that he can see this coming to America.

Phillip continues by explaining that when the American government pulled its spending, and the private sector began to collapse; China put a motion before the United Nations to foreclose on the Americans. The United Nations granted their motion, and with the world's support, China foreclosed on the Americans. China ceased to import any military equipment in the United States. Subsequently, China dropped troops from their planes to protect the Chinese living in the United States. They had previously planted viruses that disabled much of the American military radar systems and networks. China notified the United Nations that it was merely protecting the seven million Chinese living in the United States. The media laid the framework, which gained the public's support for securing China's people. The media reported on the American imprisonment of the Japanese during World War Two. Considering no war was declared, the use of military force had not been established; the public felt no concern over these soldiers appearing with the masses of Chinese, who were appearing from their underground. The public was surprised by this surge of people who had survived in secret within the United States. Many felt sorry for the way these people had lived. Confusion mixed with feelings of guilt left many Americans regarding their government performed the human violations that they were supposed to be preventing. It was hard for any one to believe these people remained, hidden voluntarily. Lisa asks Phillip if he knows the truth. Phillip confesses to believing the American government was involved. Lee tells him the American government did not know because China put them here to work in their factories for production. Phillip smiles at me and reveals that Peter will love this true information. I ask Phillip if Lee should return with us. Phillip argues, taking Lee back would be too great of a risk, as the bad and evil always discover a way to make the righteous pay.

Phillip explains Lee is in the greatest danger, all though technically we face the same charges. China has pressed charges against Lee for violation of her servant contract and alleging we kidnapped Lee. I ask how they can indict Lee if they are charging us for kidnapping her. Philip revealed the media claimed that Lee could escape, especially over such a long period. Phillip reminds us this new government does not have to use the same evidence standards of the previous states. Lisa concurs that nothing has changed except the public image of whom is searching for us. At least, it is now done in the open, and everyone knows what is happening, whereas, too much was done in secret, allowing the wicked to take advantage of his or her vices. Cindy asks Lisa if she blames this practice for Roberta's death. Lisa summarizes that if may not have been the direct cause; notwithstanding, it contributed to it making it possible. Phillip explains that once Americans are completely indoctrinated and the Chinese security forces in position. Lee asks why it takes, time to position the Chinese security forces, knowing the Chinese Mafia is in full force currently. Phillip believes this is more of an administrative process. The Mafia is moving their equipment and resources from private to the public, with most of the resources going toward standardization of their public image. They want their community image to create comfort, much the same way as McDonald's image generates hunger. The media were creating a warm perception, gaining the public's full trust. People would volunteer information providing this fresh agency, an ability to serve and protect. The media broadcasts many of the new social and financial laws. The most popular law was the forgiveness of all home-mortgage loans as the contemporary government took ownership of all property. Our media reported the Building a New America negotiated with the communist party to allow the current residents to remain in their homes the remainder of their lives. The sole result was Americans no longer had to pay property tax. Insurance payments were direct credits against their annual taxes.

Lisa begs Phillip to tell her more about the passing of our baton. Phillip continues by verifying the Chinese government foreclosed on the American government, giving them a choice of war or surrender of all military forces. Congress held an emergency session as the house and the Senate agreed to surrender all property and rights as collateral against their debt. Peter told everyone that leastwise the politicians received their final bride. Amazingly, once the United States' surrender was received by recognized by the United Nations, the American media released detailed reports of bribes politicians in the United States received. Most could escape the United States much as the Nazi's evacuated Europe after World War Two. Those who were caught were publicly tortured, with the media not missing one-step. The new government agreed to pardon any who helped punish corrupt members of the former government. Cindy surprises us with a brilliant question asking about the state governments. Lisa compliments her by reasoning that if the federal government fell, then the states would collapse as well. China sent administrative groups to replace members of the executive branch. The legislative and judicial branches were dissolved. State national guards were disbanded. Police officers were given an opportunity to sign allegiance to their new government. Arrests would continue as unusual as the United States was under martial law. The media flooded the airways explaining any changes in public law. Most of the changes are business-related, although a few such as no more divorces, affected the public at large. China rescinded all American laws and rescinded all taxes, including social security. Initially, the public expressed concern until the media reported that their new government would provide for all seniors and disabled. They promised full employment as well.

The Building a New America organization became the power base during the transition. They used the media to publish the information they needed the people to know. Hollywood was put on hold until the martial law was lifted. The actors were used to play in educational shows explaining the new laws. They also visually showed what is expected from the public. The Chinese government nationalized all utility companies and assigned their current employees to permanent positions. Once assigned a position, it is a lifetime obligation. Lisa asks if there will be any changes in fashions, styles, or public education. Phillip tells us there will be slow transitional changes in what subjects are taught. The new working age for those who are assigned lifetime labor positions is thirteen. All students are given special exams when twelve. Based on their aptitudes and the projected personnel positions available, assigned an occupation. Subsequently, they will attend the school that will prepare them for their future occupation. Certain children will go to the school and live in the school's dorms. Cindy asks what happens if a student does not like their assignment. Phillip tells us the student can request the reconsideration and submit any special needs that can justify the switch. Students may also request to trade with other students while their test scores qualify them. They must also reveal the reasons for their requests. Phillip elaborates the media reports that our new government tries to understand the reasons and will adjust assignments if possible. Many times, they can agree on a compromise. Cindy asks Phillip if there are any other large changes. Phillip tells us all mental institutions and prisons were dissolved. The mental patients who are permanently disabled were to be executed. Merely those who can function in society were released to their families. Prisoners who were serving any sentence for violent crimes were executed. Most non-violent crimes and drug charges were pardoned. Any borderline cases were transferred to a national center for final judgment.

I tell Lisa this could mean that Mitch was released. Phillip sighs, then told us that Mitch was indeed free, and currently a great friend of our family. Cindy asks how they recognize this. Phillip explains that Peter has a few church members who moved to Marked Tree. Lisa asks Phillip if he has any other news concerning Mitch. Phillip tells him the Mitch is believed to be forming a group to help ensure justice for the poor. Phillip did not grasp much about Mitch, because few knew their activities, especially since all walls had ears. Phillip reports that even in the mountains, people worry about their walls, as everything in secret seams to end as a report for the Chinese Mafia. Lisa wonders how her stepfather could become friends with Mitch. Phillip explains rumors were floating that Mitch was going to avenge executing Fred. Lisa jumps and asks Phillip to explain what he meant by the execution of Fred. Phillip reports the newspapers accused Fred of invading a Chinese Mafia shop. A court found him guilty and judge sentenced him to immediate execution. Phillip also tells us that Fred was innocent, and Peter believes our father will help him. I tell Cindy that if our father goes against the Chinese Mafia, he will be a fugitive. Phillip tells us if he goes with Mitch, our entire family will be fugitives. Lee verifies this by explaining the family must pay for the crimes of each within that family. Lee is surprised my family is still out of prison. Phillip explains the new established government will not carry non-violent crimes forward. There was no evidence that Lee was restrained or any form of violence or threat of fear to deprive her of any civil freedom. Cindy reasons that if we were not in trouble, then this would make Lee the guilty one. Phillip divulges the Chinese did not want to broadcast Lee's successful mistake and even fear she could be martyred as a hero and unifying force that could unite the Chinese servants and Americans.

Lee questions Phillip why he classifies the Chinese, yet lumps the Americans as one. Phillip explains that all wealth was removed from individual Americans above $100,000 excluding the value of their home. Any home value over $150,000 will be split into condominiums. The total values of property, real state and personal, cannot exceed $200,000. They labeled this program as Giving the Poor, More Social Equalization Project. This project removed the wealth from the rich and gave it back to the poor. They also established acceptable lifestyles and segregation for occupations. All doctors were placed in certain living areas, lawyers stripped of all wealth and with all politicians placed in labor camps. These massive labor camps would work on remodeling current structures adapting to the modern needs of our new government. They would also work on building new roads and rebuilding the sewer systems. The American infrastructure was on the verge of collapse. The Chinese were extremely angry about this. Phillip explains that common sense reveals the Chinese got a bad deal with this deal. Unpretentiously, must they scramble for payment of the American debt; they must rebuild the infrastructure to prevent a total social collapse, with a widespread of starvation and disease. The Chinese are also liable for the American trade deficits with all the other nations in the world. Phillip further reveals the media declares the sole reason the Chinese did not abandon the United States was because of the strong influence of the Chinese-American citizens. The media have proven how corrupt public officials made promises they could not honor and concealed important environmental data from the public. Many communities would suffer drastically if immediate intervention were not activated. Lee is concerned with the greed, gluttony and lying that covered the old United States. She asks what the overwhelming number of churches was doing through this. Phillip tells Lee the churches naively believed what their leaders were swearing as truth.

Phillip elaborates that so many changes are occurring so fast. These new changes incorporate a loss of rights, yet at the same time guarantee survival and more equality. Every person is entitled to free health care. Phillip tells us that no more must we worry about medical costs, stripping our life savings in our golden years. Doctors and medical community work for the public and not for personal riches. The government will build ten modern healing universities. Within ten years, there will be more than double the new doctors present to practice medicine are. Quality medical care will now be available for all. Peter and many seniors are particularly optimistic about this new program. Lee asks me if Americans lose the wealth over medical care. I tell her that if they do not have insurance, they are in trouble. Lee asks why people do not have this financial umbrella. Lisa tells her that insurance is expensive, and most people can merely receive it through employment. Lee asks what would have to those people if they lost their job. Cindy tells her they lose their medical insurance. Lee tells us such a system is so inhumane. I tell her what is worse is the medical providers must accept the amount the insurance pays, therefore they allow these insurance companies to pay less, while wickedly charge those who have no insurance the full amount. These hospitals will destroy these victims' credit and hire collection agencies to harass them until they receive their unfair overcharge. Lee looks at Phillip and asks if it is possible to charge the rich less and the poor, more. Phillip lowers his head and nods it signifying yes. Lee looks at us and asks what sort of government would permit this. I examine Lisa and ask the same question. Lisa tells Lee that we did not realize any other way, nor did we grasp the secrecy. I tell Lee the sad thing is the secrecy appears to be motivated by financial incentives. Lee asks us if this is what we were willing to use as a basis for the world to model.

It hits me like a rock discovering that so much of the old America was based solely on financial benefits and not public survival. Phillip agrees that learning about the social injustices that provided the safeguards for the inhumane abuses of the economically impoverished. Lee tells us we suffered through indoctrination. She asked us what value is having rights, if your own culture takes everything, you have. Lee asks us if anything is of greater value than food, a home, domestic security, and medical care. How can one claim to be free when they must die from a medical condition when a cure is possible? Phillip explains to Lee that we truly believed our society was the utmost righteous ever in the world's history by giving the most freedoms to its people. Lee asks us if it is not true that we had to buy licenses to do such things as get married, drive a vehicle, or go hunting, and to go fishing.

We stare at her in confusion, wondering why she would ask such a foolish question. I tell her of course. Lee questions us on who we believe actually unite a man and woman in marriage. Cindy reveals to Lee that she believes God does; however, other groups believe in additional forces. Lee then tells us that in her homeland, the man and woman report their intent to marry, and afterwards submitting an application. Once the delegated authorities make their decision, the requesting couple discovers if they can marry or not. The overwhelming reason for denial is medical. There may be rare cases involving other remote reasons. The primary objective is to protect the woman, any future children, and the possible father as well. They check for any rare diseases, social or deadly diseases, and even the ability for each to contribute to their one reproduction. The people's government believes both the man, and the woman needs to realize if they cannot make a baby. Most couples simply adopt, or raise a criminal baby among their relatives. The government will permit this couple to adopt an illegal child. All people concerned, are given immunity. The government considers the baby was created to keep the family's blood in the future pool. Phillip congratulates Lee for knowing so much. Lee tells us soon we will understand everything. She tells us the number-one rule is to obey. Even in the former United States, the citizens had to conform to the laws. The primary difference is our new government will catch you. Now they have full control of the American environment and not have to function through the limitations of the former United States. It is difficult to conduct investigations when you have to work through lazy bureaucrats. Lee tells us that they were briefed on the poor, desk riding, bride taking, and racist, most times ignorant police crime investigators.

Cindy asks Lee if such a statement was appropriate, because she has seen numerous police, which behaved courageously. Lee agrees this could be true and that few statements can have no exceptions. She was more concerned with the brides and corruption. Phillip asks Lee how China can have no bribes or corruption. Lee clarifies that bribes, and corruption did not exist in China and now will eventually not exist in the former United States. Phillip informs us the new name for this territory is the American States of China. Lee repeats that we will all recognize the rules, and she wonders when they will be releasing the official identification cards. Phillip pulls his out and apologizes for forgetting this. He hands each of us one. Lisa asks him how he could accomplish this. Phillip tells us the Chinese gave Grandby extra freedom in issuing these cards because they recognized the somewhat erratic behavior, which is similar in history to many tribes in the Chinese mountains. They recognize that these people will slowly trickle in for supplies, and if they do not consider themselves threatened will comply with the laws of their new nation. I ask Lee if this is normal for our modern government. Lee tells us they can afford to be patient because time and space are on their side. They can pump a couple hundred divisions into these mountains and take full possession if they desired. Phillip asks her why they just do not release their power. Lee reaffirms; they do not have to, because they control the source of this river, therefore, there is no need to worry about what is on or along the river, because all things will go to the sea. Lee still had her Chinese servant identification card. She verified each of us had our true names on our cards because she said a false card is a capital offense.

I wake up in the morning and discover Lisa and Phillip sleeping under the same blanket. I imagined that they would want to be together; nevertheless, I suspected they would be too shy to bond. Love seems to find a way. I give Cindy a special kiss, then reach over, and give Lee a kiss. Cindy and I agree this is important because we have to treat Lee as a part of us. It is easy for me since I suppose as if a part of me lives in Lee. She made sure we bonded with her. We believe in the severity of the power in her heart. She required it even more than we did for an unknown reason. I tell Lee she had to have known China would absorb the United States. Lee tells us that if you fall in love with someone, these people are more important than the physical constraints around him or her. You must care about the person and forsake all other things. Lee tells us that when she is caught, they will persecute, torment, and humiliate her unmercifully. I ask her why she gave up so much to be with us. Lee tells us her heart could not release her. Initially, she felt us invade her soul. Lee loved the way we flowed into her heart and became hungry to belong to us. She needed to be our servant and give her life for us. Phillip asks us if he hears this right. I tell him that even though Lee tries to serve us, we work extra hard to serve her. Lee tells Phillip we are the greatest masters; she has ever attended, and she was to die with all knowing she was our servant. Phillip tells us that may raise a few eyebrows. Phillip tells us that Peter testified that he believed Lee was a great person worth the human investment. I tell Phillip we are Lee as Lee is us. Lisa jumps in by adding blood bounded us forever.

Phillip asks Lisa, who is returning with him for the meeting with Peter. Lisa tells him she, and I will be going with him first thing today. She wants to keep Cindy with Lee, and with me away, they should not have many distractions. Lisa tells me that Cindy is so much tougher and eager for responsibility. I explore Cindy and Lee and tell Lisa I recognize they will be fine. Cindy and Lee pack our bags and Phillip's tent. We load our horses and begin the two-day journey back to Grandby. I quickly discovered that Lisa and Phillip were riding together, and I was responsible for reconning because their heads were in the sky. Two hours into our journey, we stopped for a leg break. These breaks were usually to drink water, eat something light if hungry, and walk in front of our horses for a mile. It rested the horses and got our blood flowing again. I tell Lisa she should have felt kind last night, having snuggled up with Phillip under one blanket. Lisa asks me if I were warm while snuggled with Cindy. I looked at Lisa and asked her if she had feelings for Phillip. She stared at me and confessed with her heart that she loved Phillip. I glared at Phillip, knowing the answer, asked him if he loved Lisa. He smiles at me and tells me he loves Lisa with all his heart. I ask Phillip and Lisa if they want to be married. They both swear their desire to marry. I ask Phillip if Peter performed the ceremony; hopefully, while we are in Grandby. Phillip tells me Peter will carry out the ceremony and obtain the authorization. Lisa asks Phillip if it is dangerous running her name through the system. Phillip tells us the Peter will bury it inside a mountain. The law is specific against the name and does not recognize the social security numbers, yet our computers link everything by their social security number. Phillip says that we will simply transpose two numbers, and Lisa will be legally lost in the system. I ask them, while we continue to walk, if they are sure about their relationship.

I also wondered why they should belong together. Lisa explains that particular things are just natural and to go against them is like sailing against the wind. She wanted Phillip inside her, and she wanted to be inside him. She felt safe with him and wanted to be him because she was so lonely without him. I ask Lisa if she is sure Phillip is the one, seeing he is the solitary one that has or is in her life. Lisa reminds me that she did go to school and lived in Marked Tree. She remembers how she felt with her football player special friend and around any other male friends, and she has never had such an intense feeling of devotion or a want to belong to someone. Lisa explains that she now can understand how deep Lee's love is for us, and she discovered this mysterious love from Lee. Once she opened these parts in her heart, she began to acknowledge a part of her that belonged to Phillip. I ask Phillip about his part in their relationship and his understanding of their love. Phillip tells me that he almost had a heart attack the first time he saw Lisa. He was so afraid to talk directly to her, so he dropped hints to Roberta. Lisa explains that they figured out his shyness and wrongfully enjoyed pressuring poor Phillip as his innocence and devotion snuck deep inside Lisa burning a fire that she could extinguish. Phillip tells me every bit of his being emphatically wanted to hear her words and obey her. I ask Phillip if he is strong enough to lead Lisa. Phillip asks me why he should lead Lisa since we understand she is always going in the correct direction. Lisa interrupts by telling me that she will follow Phillip and make him the man he is. I ask Lisa what would happen if Phillip were going the wrong way. Lisa tells me she would first explain the alternatives and perceived shortfalls of each course and hope Phillip understands the dangers before him. If he is determined to go the wrong way, she will say goodbye and go the correct way, taking those, she is responsible with her. She looks at Phillip and tells him she will never risk Lee, Cindy, nor me for his ego or as a testament of her loyalty. Phillip agrees and reveals that is what he sees in this relationship, a hope for a better tomorrow and life of love. I explain to Phillip once it is discovered he is with us that he will then as well be an outlaw. Phillip tells me not to worry because we will simply need to find a solution.

I gawk at Phillip and agree there must be a solution, for totally a fool can stop searching. Phillip tells us that he will ask Peter, and he will never stop before finding a method of us to survive. No question, he will find our way. Lisa comments on how she is so envious for the faith we all have in Peter. Just to say he will help us brings immediate relief. Lisa looks at me and explains this is what she lacked when leading us. Even though we could see her victory, she could not see it. Phillip asks Lisa to explain how we recognize if Peter sees it or not. He may be creating or nursing the solution preying it to manifest in the way he suspected. Phillip argues that Peter has cared for people for over five decades. During this time, he learned from his mistakes. Phillip claims Peter has shared stories about his failure and what he should have done to respond correctly. Peter always claimed that if those who he trains never make that mistake, the cost of his original error is far less than the benefits the future generations gain. I ask Phillip what his plan is with his life with Lisa, will he stay with Peter or return to our cabin. Phillip confesses that he has no option but to plead with Cindy, Lee and I to live with us. He continues by claiming that Lisa would not be safe living in public because the possibility of discovery would be too great to risk. I tell Phillip he should never even question his place in our family. When he marries Lisa, he becomes my brother. Lisa reaches over and kisses me recapping to Phillip why she always claims she has the greatest brother ever to live. I tell Lisa to behave, I do not care that she is sleeping with Phillip; I just do not want her to continue being so mushy around me. Lisa claims there are specific things a proud older sister can never quit. Phillip winks at me and asks me if I have any ideas for various brother activities. I confess that I am so excited about having a brother to enjoy several boy activities and get a little breathing room from Lisa. Lisa slaps me and tells me I will never have any breathing room from her, even after she is married.

Fortunately, a few rabbits ran across our path as Phillip, and I shot all three. Lisa cleaned them, giving the non-meat parts to Sunday and Easter. Phillip and I started a large campfire. We erected our tent and gathered a handful of brush for our horses. Lisa filled two pans with snow, hoping to melt this into the water for our canteens and animals. We were fortunate that there was virtually no wind. Phillip tells us that the weather will be good for another ten days, with at least five of them predictable. One more day to Grandby, one day with Peter, two days back to our cabin and then the eye of the winder will begin to shift as the furry of January, and February will be on us. I ask Lisa if Phillip brings back a third horse, we may not have enough hay to feed all three for the remainder of the winter. Phillip winks at me and tells me he has the perfect solution. He will ride with Lisa on their honeymoon horse and bring back an ox packed with supplies. We start back on our journey early the next morning with the vision of a warm bed awaiting us this coming night. The beauty of these mountains in winter is breathtaking, although the breath, it seizes is chilled. The chilly air tastes pure as it almost feels like the air cleans the lungs exhaling any cold impurities back out of our body. The frozen vegetation appears to have no life, yet within a few months, this white frozen land will be a bubbling green, as most wildlife will be nursing their newborns. I have trouble conceptualizing that so much life is preparing to come forth. Consequently, I easy could hunt for days and catch no game this time of the year, nevertheless, within a few months; the same area will have new animals bouncing from almost every tree. This is nothing less than a miracle. Lisa glares over these pure bleached mountains and wonders if our first spring as part of a new empire will bring forth life once more. Phillip tells us not to worry because life has a habit of living.

As we ride toward Grandby, the weather continues to bless us. I resumed challenging Lisa's new love. I give her a warmhearted hug after asking Phillip if I can ride beside my sister for a few miles. Phillip eagerly obliges sensing I am trying to protect my sister from being hurt. Phillip appears to be a sensible person by telling me his love for Lisa forces him to want to be sure she is not hurt and entering a relationship; she will enjoy. I shook my head remembering that a few short days ago, Lisa, and I was riding for hours along our ridge and now our bunch of rag tags has changed into two married couples and our angel Lee. Four Native Americans serving a Chinese servant who claims she is serving us. She just means too much to us. I think that a conquering feat, such as this should render Lee's amnesty. Sometimes the frigidness of rules foreshadows common sense. I ask Lisa if she feels her, affections for Phillip compare with mother's compassion for our father. Lisa tells me she sees many similarities and believes it is worth the risk. Lisa explains that she believes she feels the way for Phillip as Cindy does for me. Our relationship has taught her so much about the intimacy between a man and a woman. Lisa claims that she lived through this process holding Cindy's hands. Lisa reports how she and Cindy discussed the final bonding and mental assimilation. I asked Lisa what she meant by mental assimilation. Lisa enlightens me this is when the woman searches her complete heart and soul and decides to dedicate or depart from her lover. Lovers change to companions for life, which resulted from her dedication through this spiritual accommodation. Lisa divulges this is a heritage passed down from mother to daughter in our Arkansas country tradition. I eyeball Phillip and confess to not knowing this process existed. Lisa tells me this is the mysterious way of brides. Phillip wonders if such a system exists in Grandby. Lisa discloses there is no way of knowing. Lisa tells us we are never to reveal this system. The important thing is that my wife explored this issue with her in detail. I asked when they had time. Lisa tells me her, and Cindy discussed this when cooking dinner. I ask Lisa if she had made up her mind that early in the evening.

Lisa confesses that she made up her mind while Phillip and I were talking on the way back. She was so impressed by how we got along with each other and decided he was the type of lifetime partner she needed. Being compatible with her family was the qualifying factor. I tell Lisa she needs to make the selection based on her needs and not ours. Lisa winks at me and professes that when she gave the ball to Phillip, he knew what to do with it. Lisa elaborates that she let down her walls for Phillip to enjoy and waited in full trust and faith what he would do. Lisa smiles at Phillip and asks him how he was so sturdy against subsequently too many temptations since she pushed him as hard as she could. Lisa winks at me and tells me she waved the candy all night, notwithstanding; Phillip stood strong, claiming he could do nothing until Peter married them. I glance at Phillip with the utmost respect and tell him he is a greater man than I am. Phillip explains Peter taught them the sole thing in life we truly have is our integrity. Integrity is a gift given at birth, and each day the world will try to take it away from you. Phillip claims that he could sleep with Lisa for one year, and Peter would never even think his actions were less than honorable and Lisa would emerge a virgin. I ask Lisa if she thinks I have integrity. Lisa tells me I have integrity and loyalty. Lisa explains the reason they all walk bare-breasted in our cabin is that they recognize I will not violate them, and that I will remain loyal by never placing them in shame and using this as a tool for our hearts. Phillip asks me if they go topless in our cabin. I tell him it is a Lisa law, and we obey her laws. Lisa tells Phillip this tradition will continue even after he joins us. Phillip asks me if I think Cindy should wear a shirt. I tell him Cindy will do as Lee, Lisa, and that once he and Lisa are married; he is Lisa as Lisa is he. It is just that simple. Phillip is the invisible half of Lisa, which is now taking form.

I line up beside Phillip and ask him why he loves Lisa. Phillip explains that she is so different from all the other girls he has seen. He could sense her courage and love. Phillip claims he could experience the bond in our group and wanted to be a part of our group. I tell him we were afraid and hiding behind Lisa. Lisa smiles and tells Phillip her life is our family. I tell Lisa that Cindy can take care of me. Lisa tells me she is responsible for Cindy, partially Lee, and me. Moreover, that responsibility begins with when she breathes the air they share and ends when she no longer lives. I ask Lisa to tell me why she believes she is responsible for us. Lisa tells me because she is the oldest and first child from our mother, she must step in and care for us if our mother may not. Lisa argues this is the code of their heritage. Lisa recounts grandma, and mother explained her responsibility. I tell Lisa grandpa, and our father gave me the same speech and made me promise to treat Roberta the same as Julia. Lisa chuckles and tells us she got the equivalent spill concerning Roberta. Grandma also spoke with Roberta to explain her role. Their primary concern was with Fred, Don, and Julia. Lisa tells us what she and Roberta did to Fred, Don, and Julia was irresponsible and now Fred is dead. Lisa swears that she, and Roberta planned to return before spring once they had Cindy, and I settled. She asks me if she had the right to trade them for Lee. I tell Lisa that grandma, grandpa, ma, and pa were there to protect Fred. Next, I tell Lisa the wise reason she helped us escape from Marked Tree was Mitch, who somehow has reentered our scene, until we realize what role, he played in this; we need to hold our position. Phillip tells us that Peter can get this information for us. Afterwards, Phillip reminds Lisa that she has him, and he will stand by her side helping her every way he can.

Phillip's mood becomes somber as he shares with Lisa that the choices we made during the past cannot be judged as good or bad based on the outcome, but instead must be based on the heart's intent and available information at that time. We cannot see the invisible before us; we must first attempt to make it visible and then plan our plan for the solution. While we keep love as our light, we will not walk in the dark. Lisa commends Phillip on such a view. Phillip gives the credit to Peter, who we will be speaking with shortly. I wish them the best of luck in their love and future. We recognize Cindy, and I will be beside them as our families' journey into the forthcoming as one. I can see that with Peter's wisdom available in Phillip and Lee's Chinese knowledge, we may have a chance to survive. I appreciate Lee will be excited having Phillip with us as they have gotten along so fine since the Pedro incident. Phillip is the hillbilly country as well, although he is in the hills' hillbilly, whereas we are west of the hills (Appalachian Mountains) hillbillies. Guess there is little difference between the foothills and hill on the higher plateaus, except for the elevation. Lee has that similar mountain spirit from her mountain homelands. These must be what holds us together, the reason our eyes twinkle in tune with our words. Phillip tells us the home, we will be staying in is now merely a few hours away. Lisa asks Phillip why we will not be staying close to Grandby. Phillip smiles and tells us it is not yet safe, with all the transitioning occurring so rapidly, it is hard to distinguish who the good people are and who the bad people are. Peter believes it is better to be safer than sorry. I tell Lisa it is not going to hurt us to abide by parental guidance. If anything, it will give us a little practice, in case we ever meet our parents once more. Lisa laughs at me and tells Phillip this came from the mind of her little brother. Phillip professes that it is sound advice, as he consistently listens to the words of all his elders. Lisa confirms her family respects elders as well. Phillip tells us to get ready, because we will have several elders to respect soon. The path widens into a wide white meadow with a farm before us.

Phillip guides us into the barn where we unmounted and give our horses' water and hay. Afterwards, Phillip knocks on the door, as Lisa, and I hide behind him. An aged couple opens the door and great Phillip, inviting us into their home. We step inside as the elderly woman asks for our coats. Phillip introduces us to Rickey and Tamera Cooper. Tamera tells us she has helped raise Phillip since he was born. Phillip explains that they are his aunt and uncle, and his cousin Larry, who is two years older, is working outside on something now. Tamera looks at me, then looks out on her porch and asks why the other young woman called Roberta is not with us. Phillip tells his aunt that Roberta is with Jesus now. Rickey explains to me that Larry will be heartbroken, because Phillip said Lisa and Roberta were among the two most beautiful that he had ever seen. Tamera chuckles and warns me there will have to be a showdown for whom gets Lisa. I glance at her and tell her Lisa is my sister, and no one competes for her as a prize. I ask for our coats, when Phillip rushes to my side explaining Tamera is merely joking. Tamera reaffirms she is joking and then clarifies no man marries here unless Peter gives him permission. I ask why Peter must give the permission. Tamera reports that Peter is the best in preparing a man to live up to the responsibility of raising his family. Once Peter approves it, everyone knows he will do whatever it takes to make this new family work. Tamera claims the lives of innocent children are at risk, so we need to protect our future generation as best we can. Lisa jumps in and adds that she is going to ask Peter if she can have Phillip. Tamera tells her she will have to plead a hard case, because, so many of the girls have tried to yet Peter denied them.

Lisa gives Phillip a stare of death preparing to slap him while yelling at him for having too many girlfriends. I argue with Lisa asking how she could believe all the other girls were blind and would not try to cash in on such a fine deal between those who were available to them. I remind her how on the farms around Marked Tree how the cows always surrendered to the strongest bull. Lisa tells me it is not fair. I tell Lisa she should be accordingly thankful that one so great found mercy in one so low. Lisa's face is burning now, when Phillip tells me not to make Lisa too angry, or she will chase us through the freezing mountain. I open my arms and tell Lisa not to worry; I still hold the down and the trodden, and those destined to fulfill their dreams as a spencer. Lisa grabs me by my hair and flings me to the floor. Tamera jumps and asks Lisa if she wants to help her with dinner. Lisa smiles and agrees to help. As Tamera heads for the kitchen, Lisa spins around, and hits me in my stomach. Then she trots along to the kitchen as if a perfect little angel informing Tamera how wonderful it is finally to have a kitchen with kitchenware, instead of the camping ware. Phillip came to help me stand up while we both laughed. Phillip agrees that Lisa can be a spunky one if she wants. I remind Phillip that Lisa is responding to a lifetime of brother-sister pranks. He thanks me for smoothing out Lisa current anger and forcing her to vent on me and not him. I tell Phillip it is important that she place a value in this relationship; the better, she believes the deal, the deeper forever she will feel. Afterwards, Phillip assures me that his intentions with Lisa are honorable. Subsequently, I express concern that Peter may deny the relationship, as the cow has now been branded, and the milk drank. Phillip explains that certain powers of persuasion from him on his behalf could help expedite his approval. I reassure Phillip; I will struggle hard on his behalf, especially since I do truly believe he will be great for our family. Phillip reminds me not to say anything about Lisa's topless in the cabin rule. That could present a great difficulty in convincing Peter the honor and decency behind our lifestyle. I ask Phillip if he believes this rule is not decent. Phillip tells me that as long as Lisa believes it is necessary; he believes it is. Phillip continues that sometimes the ways of women are strange. She may be keeping us out of the cookie jar by keeping the cookie jar open. I even confess to Phillip that these wonderful sights have, on more than one occasion fought my pending depression. I also notice that when I am starting to gain a few pounds, they mysteriously put less on my plate.

Tamera and Lisa bonded quickly in the kitchen as they prepared our dinner. It reminded me of the way in which Lisa and Roberta would help our mother. Rickey spent a little time with Phillip, and I was trying to think of arguments to support Phillip and Lisa's marriage. Larry soon arrived and helped us with this project. I asked Larry if he was truly supporting Phillip's quest for Lisa. Larry assures us that Phillip has been his sole brother throughout his life and unlike their mother, shares their fortunes and do not fight over them. Rickey assures me the men in this area would never treat women as property or as their livestock. The girls call us to the table where for the first time since running away from home, I had a home-cooked meal. I was surprised at the level of Lisa's style in this meal. Tamera tells us that she is always seeking new ideas for her cooking, as her family grows tired of the same taste constantly. Lisa tells us that for the true treat, we would need Lee as she has so many cheap, exotic alternatives. Tamera tells us they seldom talk about Lee, and when they do, they go into the basement, or garage for fear someone may have bugged their home. Although they have yet to find proof, certain matters were discovered that should not have been. Tamera adds no one will speak about personal things over the phone, especially not on the cell phone. They have so many cases where people talked of little things, like going to the store and leaving their house empty. When they returned, thieves stole from their homes. Rickey believes this will slow down or stop now the United States has fallen. In the past, the Chinese Mafia had to turn the other eye and allow certain criminals selected booty for their help.

Subsequently, we hear a knock on the door. Lisa and I freeze. Meanwhile, Larry goes to the door and tells us Peter has arrived. Peter comes to us, as Tamera brings him, a plate of food and asks him to have a seat with us at their table. Peter begins by verifying whether Phillip has told us the big news. We confirm understanding the fall of the United States. Peter tells us it may not be over quite so fast. The financial and infrastructure decay of the former states may be too much for China to manage. China has offered individual states to other nations; however, the federal debt allocation levied on top of the sale is equally important high for any one to take seriously. Larry adds that no other nation wants to have a state, surrounded by China, noting the security requirements would be too expensive. China is drastically attempting to settle the former states' debt and trade imbalances with the other nations in the world; considering China owns much of the nation, any loss occurred by absorbing the American debt reduces their holdings in these nations. The logical solution will be for America to manufacture products these nations will buy and slowly work down the trade deficient. Early projections estimate this could take twenty years. China has just proposed they will use American slave labor. Americans will not receive wages for their work, and those who refuse to work will be executed. The dilemma is that China must give up any profits from the raw materials and production costs of the items being given to these other nations. The Americans will still need to be fed, and housing provided so they can generate these products. Another problem arises in that most of the goods made by the Americans for this trade debt competed against the same supply that China can generate for a profit. Japan has requested a larger flow of oil from Alaska; however, Peter tells us he expects for the stage-one job assignments to begin to appear within the next few weeks. These assignments are to get the process started, and based on appeals and complaints they will work out a final solution.

All products will be rationed beginning next month. Peter has created various false people, shut-in, and set up a method to pass any possible inspections. He has generated three completely body burned and housebound disabled people. The police and hospital altered their records to establish this fatal house burning. Peter tells us that a house with three people in it did burn, and the victims were taken to the hospital. There were specific controversial elements, here, in which a young man from one family died beside a woman and her brother from another clan, who was and always will be at war. The details of this case were never released to the local media nor reported to any government agency. Peter altered his church books to show his church was feeding and caring for them. He will stock these supplies and have them smuggled to us. Peter tells us that he will be giving us an initial load of seeds. We are to plant as much along the ridges and in little meadows in our area. Subsequently, Peter tells us we must make it hard for small planes or helicopters to spot. Family gardens are to be registered with the government, and the crops yielded surrendered to the public for work credits. All planted seeds, and our new administration provided fertilizers. No one can work as a farmer without government approval. Many people who live on small farms will work in other occupations, while a farming company will farm their land. The administration wants to produce as much food as this land can consistently produce without destroying it. Grocery stores will no longer have shelves with tasty foods or frozen treats.

Meet will be standardized as well as dehydrated easy to prepare healthy food. Candy and sugary treats are solely for export. Most shelves will have grains, such as rice, wheat, flour, barley, and cereals. There will be bread and juice sections, eggs, milk, and other dairy products, with basic spices. The government has published the body weight and Body Mass Index (BMI) for all people based on sex and age. They plan completely to erase obesity within thirty years. They will give the public ten years to comply. Those who do not meet the requirement after ten years will be sent to intensive labor camps, where they will stay until they meet and safely exceed the government's guidelines. A few may spend the remainder of their lives there. The government is sterilizing all obese or mentally handicapped people. A couple may merely attempt to reproduce with government approval. All unauthorized children will belong to the government.

I stare at Peter and confess I picked these bad three months to hide from the public. It is a completely new world. This may be too much for us to understand. Peter tells us, that except for Lee, we will rotate occasionally to keep us on our toes and alert. I ask Peter how we will do this. Peter tells me a boy or girl will deliver various supplies and one of us will swap with them until the next supplies are sent. We will be receiving weekly supplies, because with the rate of current changes, any longer period could cause unwanted trouble. Peter has designed a special little electrical device that will perform like a telegraph. He will give us codes, such as three clicks mean return immediately; four clicks meant to hide; two clicks meant caution. He will send these clicks on the hour until we double click back that we have the message. He believes that they will never catch this one, as he has ten other receivers spaced out among the mountain farms. Next, Peter smiles and hands me a certificate. It is Cindy and my marriage certificate, and it is dated before the fall of the United States. Peter tells me it is recorded with the new administration, with the ceremony performed in Alaska. I ask Peter how he knows people in Alaska. He explains one of his former theology classmates did it for him. Peter hopes that once the modern administration has all the names loaded in their fresh massive database, they will believe we are living in Alaska, or ventured to Russia or Canada. Peter wants to get the searching out of former states, so he can mold our new identities.

Peter asks us how things are going in the cabin. I tell him about Roberta's rape and death. Peter cries and pats his heart as if he is having pain. He pulls himself with Larry and Phillip's assistance. Thereafter, Peter informs Rickey they must form a posy and clean up our mountains. I inform Peter that Lee, and I surrendered this matter to Mother Nature to exact the justice in this matter under Lee's customs and tradition. Thereafter, Lisa, and I returned the next day to verify Mother Nature's decision. Mother Nature did Roberta right. Peter tells us those men were lucky Mother Nature punished them, and that he did not get a chance at them. He would not have been tender like Lee. I smiled in agreement with Peter telling all these men were truly fortunate that a Chinese servant got to them first. Peter smiles and reports this turned out well in that with Lee controlling it; it will go recorded as a Chinese citizen enforcing the laws of their homeland, which will always override our laws even though it was before our defeat. I gawp at Lisa and tell her thanks once more for holding back and allowing Lee to protect us. Peter confesses the more he thinks about Lee, the greater that she becomes. It is the stories he tells the people around here about Lee that give hope we can work together and someday be a happy family. Lisa tells Peter our group loves Lee as if she were our heart and each would die gladly for her safe being, as she would cheerfully lay down her life for us. Tamera wipes her face with a clean rag and confesses to Peter that she truly believes these young people are telling the truth. Phillip reveals to Tamera that what he saw and felt being around her five days was nothing less than like being around an angel. He would joyfully marry her if not being in love with another. Peter looked at Phillip and promised to help him recover from Roberta. Lisa hits Phillip in the back, knocking him to the floor. Peter gives his confused stare to me as I tell him I do not believe we are talking about Roberta here.

Peter asks me to explain. I tell Peter that Roberta consistently talked about her desire that Phillip joins our family and never about a wish had she to marry him. She had another in mind. Peter looks at Lisa and asks her if Roberta told her, whom she thought that would make a great mate for Phillip. Lisa begins crying, falls to her knees, and confesses that she is the one Roberta always believed should be with Phillip. Peter looks at Phillip and asks him if he knows anything about this. Phillip falls to his knees beside Lisa and tells Peter that he not merely knows about this, yet begged Lisa for the honor of serving, loving, and providing for her the remainder of her days. Peter reminds Phillip that Lisa is an outlaw, and a life with her would be dangerous. Phillip looks at Peter and opens his heart explaining this is why it is so important to marry soon, with his permission, considering, he can never be at peace, unless he knows Lisa is safe. Peter turns his attention to me now and asks me, as the leader of our group what I think about inviting Phillip into our group, especially as he would currently be the leader. I acknowledge this a great thing, and that Lisa's happiness is what is of the most importance to me. I confess to having spent the previous two days questioning them, looking for a loophole. I tell Peter that Lisa and Phillip belong to each other, the same as Cindy and I. We accept the risks in our loves and depend on those in our clan to help us through the hard times. I believe Cindy, and I, with our children, will benefit by having such a fine role model as Phillip for their uncle. Any ways, it is easy to follow one who leads in love. Peter tells me to order him what to do in this matter. I fall to my knees, beside Phillip and Lisa, and beg that he allows them to marry and for their love to spring forth in our future generations as my nephews and nieces. Peter stands up and asks us to give him a few minutes to rest alone on the front porch. As he gets up and goes outside, Lisa goes to stand. I grab her hand and shake no suggesting that she stays down with us. A few minutes pass in silence. I almost am sorry for Rickey, Tamera, and Larry with all this drama unfolding in their home. They are frozen in their seats as well, waiting for the great decision.

Peter comes back in and asks all to join him at the table. He passes a marriage certificate to me. I am wondering if there was a mistake on the first one, he gave me thinking he may have been testing my love for Cindy. Such is not the case. Peter asks me to read the names of the certificate. I read the man's name as Phillip and the woman as Lisa Jones. I ask Peter if this means they are married. Peter confesses that he saw the love in their eyes when they first met. He was a little hesitant, in that he needed to identify if Phillip fitted into our family. He chuckles telling me after my convincing testimonial today, he had to accept that Lisa would be in great hands with Phillip. He looks at Lisa and tells her she could not have found better among the clans in this area. Lisa kisses Peter on his cheek acknowledging to have heard this same argument from others. Peter informs Phillip that they were married in Yukon, along the northern Alaskan border in a town called Old Crow on the Porcupine River about three weeks after Cindy's marriage. This is believable that this river is frozen this time of year provided an excellent road for speedy travel. I ask Peter if he is hinting we should head to the northern shores of our continent. Peter startles me by telling us we must stay in his territory. If we go on the move, we will be caught. Such a move would be suicidal. Once our world settles, we will explore the best options. I ask Peter if he can also make sure we keep Lee or if at least share custody of her. I can never be happy, unless I acknowledge Lee is in our arms feeding from our love. Peter tells me he completely understands and asks if we would consider allowing Lee to give speeches in the future to our mountain friends. Lisa tells Peter, while he can guarantee her safety. Tamera confesses to Lisa and eagerness to meet this precious person. Phillip asks Rickey if he plans to visit sometimes, if Peter approves it. Peter discloses that he believes this will be great in establishing a connection with the community. Subsequently, Peter tells us that he has several updates on Mitch, who is raiding the east as a mad man.

Chapter 07

The Johnsons and the Wangs

The climate in Marked Tree was markedly different from the remainder of America. The Chinese Mafia held Marked Tree guilty of Lee's betrayal of the homeland. The police; however, did not believe the Johnson family broke any laws; therefore, actually stood up in disagreement with the Mafia, filing numerous complaints with state officials. The authorities in Beijing did not like the public dissatisfaction that the Johnson case was brewing. These leaders could not risk the possibility of Fred becoming a martyr. Therefore, they went to St. Louis, rented a floor in a Hyatt Regency at the Arc hotel, and sent a special convoy to bring my family, including grandparents for a meeting. Beijing sent a few of the highest party members to the negotiations. These leaders convinced my parents; they had nothing to do with Fred's execution. This tragedy was at the hands of corrupt public officials who believed they would gain favor with the Chinese task force searching for Li Jing. They add that all documents are backup up on their computers and then sent to higher intelligence centers for inclusion in their master database. For a group of overanxious children burning and ransacking the local office should have only qualified to specific probation and curfew. One representative shows the directive that no administrative documents be maintained after submission to the document centers. It is nothing more than a fire hazard. They watched certain videos showing the offices burning papers. Next, they presented their official complaint on the unfair treatment of Fred by the United States Government. The Chinese treated our family as royalty, providing entertainment and distinguished meals. On the fourth day, my grandfather asked them why his family was receiving such special treatment. One of the leaders explained to Grandpa how nothing they could do would bring Fred back to us. They also explained that the United States was financially unstable and that soon they had to decide if they could save the American people or watch them destroy themselves. The United States could become easy prey for rogue governments. Dad asked the leaders, who were currently assembled in a small group, why they would have any concerns over the United States. The leaders guided our family into a presentation room and shared the data on their investments and holdings in the United States. They had so many millions of Chinese's citizens in the United States managing these assets. Those are too many people to relocate, therefore, must be protected against any harm. The leaders also present the data showing the massiveness of the American debt financed by China. These leaders explain that with the instability of the American Public, they truly do not Fred becoming a martyr for people to die and destroy in a rebellion. My father agreed this would not be good for Americans.

There was no denying the condition of our nation. Rough times were ahead. The leaders agreed to press no charges against us, if there is no evidence of harming Li Jing. They felt it was not fair to punish people who are caring for one of their citizens. My mother asks these leaders why her children would grant sanctuary to a young Chinese woman. One of the leaders explains it is the same thing when boys meet young women. The curiosity about something different at times can become a magnet bonding them. My mother tells the leaders that her children would never intentionally hurt or unlawful abuse another person, and if they requested this Li Jing to join them, they will make sure she ate first and received the best they can provide for her. The leaders confirm with my family that we are taking excellent care of Lee. They have pictures of them on store videos, which show that Lee is with us by choice and being cared for by all in our group. One leader laughs stating that we are grabbing and offering everything, we can get our hands on to her. They counted Li Jing saying no two hundred times in one store. The leaders show where they have taken full jurisdiction over this case. The way Li Jing has bonded with us has presented fresh concerns about the relationship model they originally projected in an interracial environment of the new America if China elects to fix it. One leader tells us they want to test models for compatibility; therefore, they want my family to move to a pleasant home in which nine Chinese will live with us. This unit must become self-supporting and establish their own household rules.

My mother was excited about this pilot program. My father discovered this house had a room for each resident. There was one large kitchen, five bathrooms all with showers, two sizeable family rooms. The leaders gathered all of us and took to this small farm. Grandpa asked to sit beside the eldest man from the Chinese and one high school girl for translation. Subsequently, they discussed their diets. Next, Grandpa discovered they ate much rice and since this farm could not produce the rice, they would have to receive it externally. Afterward, Grandpa asked the leaders how we could get the rice for our family. The leaders said that we could grow another crop and trade it for the rice. My father noticed a tractor and four cows in the barn, with two horses and four pigs. Fortunately, since this was autumn, the barn had plenty of grain and hay. My father took inventory of the animals, grain and decided we could get a crop of winter wheat planted. We joined in the family room, as Grandpa spoke first, with the teenage girl translating. He talked about the available stock, grain, seeds, and other supplies drawing them on the bulletin board. He asked for input from everyone on what we should do, grow, and trade at the market. He believes the three female cows with one bull, should be saved for breeding. Once we have the three calves, butcher one of the cows for meat, and sell the other two cows during summer when the market is advantageous. He wishes to do the same with the pigs, butchering the weaker piglets, and selling the mothers if they can make sure they keep the three females to one male ration, although, if an emergency arises, they can reduce the pig stock since one mother pig can reproduce a large litter. The sale of their winter wheat should give them money for utilities and rice. The fuel would be for heating, tractors, and trips to town. They had to cover the electric bills, telephone calls as well. He soon discovered the Chinese half wanted to make expensive calls to China and speak with their relatives. They agreed this was fair, and we would figure out a way to manage it. The Chinese elder, Wang Chang, promised to do all work; we were to assign them and obey everything we tell them to do. They pledged themselves as our servants. My father refused this and told our translator this was not satisfactory. He wanted to make this a join and equal project. Our high school translator whose name is Wang, Lien Hua explains these people have never made any decisions in their lives. They just recognize work, and following orders. The young man brags that once they have been through a process, they will be able to contribute greatly on fine-tuning it the second round, if we are willing to listen.

My father asks everyone to sit at our dinner table. He gives construction paper to Wang Huang and explains that everything he explains, he wants her to mark so she can review with her elders after the meeting. My father volunteered to run the tractor this day and start the two-day plowing and planting of the winter heat. Wang Deshi, the father of the children asked Lien Hua if my father allowed him to help, and maybe even give training on the tractor. My father agreed, and the two men headed to the field to start the farm work. My father asked Don and Lien Hua to assign chores equally among the children. The animals had to be fed, eggs collected; and work shed cleaned. My father tells them to check with their mothers to verify if they needed any help in the house. When all the work was finished, they could play and learn more about each. Don and Mei hung together, as Julia and Huang formed a group, Zhuo and Ju-Long formed the third group, as Lien Hua searched for chores to assign and checked with their mothers on any help they needed. Mom and Ng Da-Xia, the mother of the Chinese children worked with each other. This was a learning adventure as they struggled to communicate, using tablets, hand jesters, and charades. Grandpa and Grandma joined Wang Chang and Hsu Bao in the den where they drank tea and using tablets, hand gestures, and charades tried to determine a solid course of action for survival. Grandpa taught them the general dynamics of farming and Wang Chang quickly added our resources to plan an efficient plan of action.

The three couple gangs became so bonded they begged their mothers to allow them to camp in the living room. The mothers agreed. Lien Hua was the sole person with no partner; nevertheless, she was the middle woman who bounced between the young children and the adults. Wang Chang explains she is of the age where we should begin looking for a spouse for her. My mother asks if he wants a Chinese man or American man for her. Wang Chang explains that an American boy would be wonderful if we receive permission from the leaders. My father tells him to hold on, and he goes to the phone where he calls one of the leaders and explains they were wondering if they could entertain the idea of an American boy for Lien Hua. The leader responds by telling him he does not think an American boy would want her. He adds that if we can guarantee the American boy would treat her as a wife and not an animal it would be fine. The mixing of the races could produce children who can do great things. Since my father has the phone with a speaker phone, and we do not have Lien Hua translating because we do not want her to understand our matchmaking activities, my mother answers that we will provide Lien Hua the same parenting protection as we would do for Julia or Lisa. The leader asks to speak with Wang Chang. They speak in Chinese and discuss what happened our first week together. The leaders were so impressed; they asked my father if they could visit tomorrow. My father gives him an open-door invitation. These leaders visit this farm in midmorning witnessing the children doing their chores, our grandparents rearranging the basement, mothers working in the kitchen, and our fathers' fine-tuning the fields. Lien Hua greets the leaders and explains what everyone is doing. The leaders ask Lien Hua what her responsibilities are.

Lien Hua explains that she supervises the three groups of children on their chores; checks to see what the mothers and grandparents need and assign the children these tasks. Lien Hua also takes the lunch and water to their fathers working within the field. She is the official translator as well. The leaders compliment Lien Hua on her outstanding efforts and ability to keep everything flowing. They also tell Lien Hua the family called them the previous night asking them if she could date American boys. They ask Lien Hua if she would like to attend the Marked Tree high school. Lien Hua promises to do, as her elders believe she should do. Next, they ask Lien Hua if there is any one in this American family, she has any concerns. Lien Hua tells the leaders everyone is working hard to compromise and cooperate. Lien Hua tells them this short week has changed her mind so much about Americans, and she hopes to work alongside them and live among them, the remainder of her life. These leaders tell Lien Hua that not all Americans are like this Johnson family. Lien Hua reminds them the Wang family is not your ordinary Chinese family. The leaders return and speak with the grandparents who discuss the possibility of various projects. The leaders offered additional support and told them the self-sufficient rule was intended to cause integration. They have completely integrated and appeared to share the same dreams. Based on the early results from this project, they are going to recommend that China attempt to save the American population from starvation, genocide, and plunder from foreign rogue nations. The leaders demand Lien Hua keeps this plan secret. They do not inform Lien Hua; they have hidden cameras spread out in the house. The leaders want to know everything going on in this interracial home. My father calls for all to sit at our dining table and discuss any issues or problems they may have. The first complaint comes from Zhuo and Ju-Long. They are upset that they do not have any Americans to work with. My grandfather agrees this is not fair and suggests that we give them extra playing time supervised by the grandparents and a little special time with the mothers. This excites them as all agree this is proper. At least, they will have selected time with our mother, and the playing time through my grandparents with their grandparents to balance the activities. Our grandparents will teach them American children's games considering their English is sufficient will hear many old fairy tales. Grandpa claims that he wants them to experience the activities' other American children are enjoying, so when they meet they will have an idea what to expect.

Wang Chang began to grow suspicious of all this hospitality. He called Lien Hua and my grandfather for a personal discussion. Wang Chang's discussions with leaders created concern over a potential for mysterious intentions. Wang Chang told my grandfather, he was growing suspicious about the way the Johnson's were attempting to deceive his family just to gain favorable benefits for the United States. My grandfather denied any such intention, explaining he did not understand this when offered, a peaceful farm, with an opportunity to provide for his family in a secure environment. The Johnsons always got with other people, especially with so much Indian in their heritage. Grandfather continues by revealing they invariably wanted a farm and with this opportunity to live in such a wonderful home believed the price was fair. Gary adds the house is, consequently, specious and everyone seemed to get along so excellently, especially with everyone being such fine friends; he came to believe we would get much more accomplished by working together in harmony. Grandpa tells Wang Chang, he saw no reason to be suspicious because the Chinese owned this farm and there were plenty of room for everyone notwithstanding a Chinese family. Grandpa asks Wang Chang, who has the greater right to this house, his family, or a Chinese family. Wang Chang reminds Grandpa, we are in the United States. Grandpa argues the United States is a capitalistic nation and those who purchase property own it, while they continue to pay their property taxes.

Wang Chang questions what the property tax is. Grandpa explains that those who own property pay a tax for this property to the government each year. Wang Chang asks what happens when the people do not pay those taxes. Consequently, Grandpa tells them the government takes them home. Lien Hua asks where these people would live. Grandpa informs them, he does not know; these people must find a place to live. Lien Hua wonders where they will get and keep their food, or if they starve. Grandpa reports that he does not know. Wang Chang accuses Grandpa of lying. Grandpa calls my parents and grandma into the room and has Lien Hua verify Grandpa's report. When they verified what Grandpa told them they were shocked in disbelief. Grandpa asked what other systems were available, they explain their people's party owns the land, and once they provide housing for a family; they continue to live there while they continue in their assigned occupation and abide by the laws of public safety. Lien Hua tells Grandpa she could never live in a land that only gives freedom to take all those who give it all back and when they no more can surrender, cast them off to the side caring not what happens to its people once they no longer have value. Grandpa asked Wang Chang if he understood how living on a farm, owned by another, provided an incentive to enjoy a lifestyle his former means did not provide. Grandpa continues by asking Wang Chang if he can see the benefit of sharing such a wonderful home with a family, who has worked just as hard as we have to get along, not just to sit back, and enjoy the ride for while it lasted. Accordingly, why should the Johnsons be greedy and try to take more than they could alone, especially when so much further can be achieved by working together? Grandpa asks Wang Chang if he believes these leaders are going to base their entire decision on what happens between two families, when they have rivers of intelligence available to them. If they are looking for the bad in people, then they should search elsewhere, because, if we continue to live together, our children can benefit. Lien Hua confesses to understand the situation now.

Grandpa asks her to explain it to him, so that we may lay this to rest and continue to build on this foundation. Grandpa begins by asking if we do not think it strange how our families match almost to perfection; the at most difference being a young girl replaced Fred and Lisa by an adolescent boy, with Roberta and George are the exclusion. We can only assume that when our children ran away, they made the adjustments based on the current family composition, believing, adding two younger children would supplement to the family composition and provide the mothers more to bond within our integration process. Lien Hua tells my grandfather that she can understand why all here can benefit through our partnership, especially as they did not believe all the negative things the leaders told them about the American government and people. Grandpa clarifies that all governments pass false propaganda about the other governments to make sure their citizens will not revolt. We can treat each as people and let the governments play their games with their citizens. Thereafter, Grandpa asked Lien Hua if her grandfather understood this. Wang Chang told Lien Hua, he comprehended his message. Grandpa then requested an extended family meeting to make sure everyone knew what we were attempting to accomplish here. Lien Hua rounded everyone into the family dining room. When Lien Hua gave instructions, everyone listened because we depended on her to bridge the gap between us. Everyone loved and trusted her. When everyone was seated, Lien Hua sat in her chair at the head of the table with her Chinese grandfather to her left and our grandfather to her right. We believed that since everyone had to speak through Lien Hua for her translation, it served us best to have her at the head of our table. My mother began this chat today by stating that if Li Jing was to her children as Lien Hua is to us, she completely understood why they were so fond of her. My father reveals to Lien Hua that none of this would be possible if not for her translation and people skills, in removing any suspicion that can be buried in the words. Lien Hua tells us it is easy for her to do this, as she sees how everyone, but her, is working so hard. My family all stands up and tells her that she works harder than any among us do. When Lien Hua tells her family why we are standing, they as well stand up and begin clapping for her. Lien Hua tells us that her two brothers and sisters also help her. My family thanks them equally important.

Grandfather goes person by person on the Chinese side thanking them for their help. He thanks Wang Chang and Hsu Boa for the time they spend with him and Cathy is trying to plan how best to take advantage of this wonderful opportunity provided by the Chinese government. He stresses to our group that the Johnsons do not take to accept charity or want to be freeloaders. He believes that we can produce more here than the Chinese must pay for our care, and the excess can go back as a profit for those who believed in us. Wang Chang has Lien Hua explain that they also believe in working for their survival. My father tells Lien Hua that there are many Americans, who will accept a free ride. Moreover, he explains how ashamed we are with what has happened to our once proud nation. When the comfortable got easy, they wanted easier. When they got more, they wanted more. When they enjoyed the pleasure, they wanted more pleasure. When the politicians promised them more, they foolishly believed that they could give this to them, not caring whose suffering or exploitation it involved. Wang Chang tells us the Chinese have a long history, as did all nations in this world, of such behaviors. If it were possible today, they would try it. Fortunately, by having the people control all the wealth and share it so that all who work can raise their family and survive; the government needs merely to concern itself with the power. When the people are surviving with hope for a future, they willingly give this power. If the government takes their work from them, the government suffers in the production and thus fewer profits. One consolidated source of wealth for a nation is a powerful financial tool. This tool can hit with the power of an iron hammer, as compared to the spread of the wealth in the United States, as this force the multitudes to pay their debts. Grandpa confesses that when we sit back and see what is happening, it creates much heartache.

Grandpa Gary turns to Wang Deshi and thanks him for the great help in the field. He tells him that my father claims by the end of this winter wheat season Deshi will be good enough to handle to the corn crop. Grandpa tells this group that my father has wanted to work his own field his entire life. Knowing the crop you are working with will supply for those you love, provides a special dimension. Having a partner who can step in if bad luck comes our way is a wonderful advantage. My mother asks her husband if she can thank Ng Da-Xia. He nods his head yes. Francis, our mother walks over, gives Ng Da-Xia a kiss on her cheek, and then shakes her hands. Ng Da-Xia stands up as they hug. Everyone at the table cheers. These are the two current mothers and to see them bonding consolidates the umbrella of the mothers over all the children here. Any child knows that they can go up to either mother, and except for the language barrier, would have their challenge solved. My mother returns to her seat and blows another kiss to Ng Da-Xia. She returns the gesture. Consequently, my mother thanks Ng Da-Xia for wonderful help in the kitchen and with the housework. My mother has always favored Chinese food, nevertheless; the five Chinese children in this gang continually beg for hamburgers and pizza. Our mother makes pizza from scratch and uses her own sauce that she preserved during the summer. Our mother has a special potato slicer for French fries. She simply puts the potato in the unit's tray and lowers the handle as it pushes the potato through its checkerboard blade. Afterwards, she deep-fries them in our deep fryer. Unlike my grandmother that used animal fat for frying, my mother gets canola oil from the store. She tries not to deep fry that often; however, she always deep fries the French fries, because we told her, this was the sole way we would eat them. Both mothers try their best to accommodate for our family needs.

Don and Wang Mei surprise the family by asking if it is permissible for them to go steady. The two mothers give their approval before the fathers can respond. Seeing the mothers already blessed this, and to keep the peace, both fathers put their hands up to surrender. Julia and Wang Huang surprised the family by declaring they also were going steady. My grandfather proclaims this could be what the leaders truly wanted to explore. They could be wondering if not merely would the younger generation marry or mate outside their birth, race, but how would the family react to it. The elders agreed to let love take its natural course. They explained to the children that they should not feel pressured, in that we would do whatever it took to get them a compatible mate, having the qualities they desired. Grandpa tells the family that he feels all the children should be in school and it started not that long ago. He smiles and declares the grandparents will take the children to the school and get them registered. Grandpa asks Lien Hua if they have their birth certificates, shot records, and passports. Lien Hua reveals they do not know what papers they brought with them. The leaders put them in a briefcase, which no one has yet to open. Grandpa asks Lien Hua to bring the brief case to him. He opens it and inside finds the shot records, school transcripts, birth certificates, government school-visa approvals, and passports. He rejoices telling his counterparts everything is in order and soon the children will be in school during the days. Wang Chang asks how we will be able to take the children to school and bring them back. My grandfather tells him a yellow school bus will pick them up and drop them off to this farm. Wang Chang has confessed he always wondered about those yellow buses, which most times had children on them were doing. They believed that they took the children to the factories, or a farm to work. Wang Chang confesses the Chinese government put extensive training in their children so their English and social skills would make sure the success of this project. Grandpa smiles and says that having Lien Hua in the head seat and four of our children going steady, he would say the project is working fine. They will have to keep their eyes open for any American or Chinese boys and girls for the future mates for Lien Hua, Wang Zhuo, and Wang Ju-Long. Wang Chang disclosed to my grandfather whomever, he believed fit would be fine.

Grandpa argues with Wang Chang that such a chore is not acceptable. This is why the original doubt and suspicion arose. Naturally, they will not be able secretly to select a mate for Lien Hua because she is the translator; however, they can get away with it on the two fourteen year olds. The mothers rush the children the bathrooms to begin their deep scrubbing, as they label it. This means getting their necks, elbows, and behind their ears. Everyone must also brush his or her teeth. While the kids are bathing, the mothers rush to begin cleaning the clothes and shoes. Ng Da-Xia is so excited that her children will be going to a real American school beginning tomorrow. She claims they will no longer be hidden or underground. She asks our mother if the children might hurt them. My mother tells her they will be safe, as she will ask the principal to help protect them and make sure the other children understand these new children now live in Poinsett County. Francis adds that Don and Julia will be in the school and keeping an eye on them. We will declare the Wang children as being part of our family professing that we live in the same house. My mother does not anticipate any problems, especially since this house is so grand and new. The main task is to make sure they go to school clean and take their lunches with them. Grandpa declares that we have enough money for the children to buy their lunches at their school. Wang Chang cannot believe the school has a cafeteria that cooks food. Grandpa furthers, tells the families' children they will buy the lunch meals and stay away from the snack food line. Both mothers jump to confirm Grandpa's mandate.

My father calls the leaders and asks them if it is permissible for the Chinese children to attend the local American school. The leaders rejoice telling us this is wonderful. They then ask my father, how we will get the children to school and bring them home. Subsequently, my father tells him they only need transportation to the school the first day, because everyone, including adults, will help register the children. The leaders ask why the Chinese adults are also going to the registration. My father explains that he believes it is important for these children's parents and grandparents to understand what the school is like and communicates with the school officials, so they will have a feel for their children's education. The more at peace they are with the children being at school, the more productive that, they will be on the farm. They will have more of a vested feeling with this land, knowing their children are prepared to have a future here. The more productive phrase brought the leaders to an agreement, as they volunteered to take the family to the school on the initial day. They asked about the daily transport of the children. My father told him the school would pick them up and return them home. The leaders wanted to see why the school would do this. Accordingly, my father explains since it is American law the children attend the school our government provides transportation. The leaders asked if we needed any additional funding for this opportunity. My father told them we would make it work in our current budget. The leaders agreed to have two luxury vehicles at our house in the morning to take us to the school. With this, my father set out the seating arrangements. The four grandparents would be with Lien Hua, Don, Mei, in the first vehicle. The second vehicle would have the four parents with Julia and the remaining Chinese children. He stressed it was important that we always go in public, mixed with each other. This will show our devotion to a single family with shared values.

Wang Deshi wondered how the bus would recognize to stop at our house the first night. My father explained that Don and Julia would make sure they got off in the right place. Ng Da-Xia wanted to understand how Don and Julia could control the five Chinese children. My mother tells me they cannot; however, Lien Hua can. Ng Da-Xia is pleased with this answer, as she has complete confidence in her bugging daughter. When they arrive at the school and begin the registration process, with Julia and Huang assigned to the sixth grade. This is a K-12 school, thereby;

the children will be in the same cluster of buildings. The school's principal calls for the teacher to come to escort them back to her classroom. The teacher shakes everyone's hand and assures our Chinese counterparts that Huang will be safe. Julia and Huang go inside the classroom, find two seats beside each other midway back, and sit. The teacher collects certain books gives each one pen with paper. She tells them not to worry about their supplies since the principal will give the supplies list to their parents. The teacher asks them to introduce themselves. Julia begins by telling the class that Huang is her best friend forever, and they have just moved here from Arkansas. Their parents are farmers and that her older sister and brother are the famous outlaws that kidnapped Li Jing. This overwhelms the students in this class because they now feel special in having celebrated people in this class. They also believe that since Huang appears to be Chinese, they will not be harassed by the Chinese Mafia. Huang stands up and introduces himself. The teacher compliments him on his outstanding English, as she reports this will make it so much easier to teach him. Huang confesses not to know all the customs and courtesies and pleads that if he does anything to offend anyone, they tell him, and so he will not do it once more. The teacher asks Julia and Huang to tell her if we do something offensive also, because she believes it is extremely important for her students to understand more about foreigners.

Don and Mei were the next two to be assigned. They were placed in the seventh grade. The principal followed the same sequence as Don and Mei settled into the classroom comfortably. Don introduced Mei as his best friend forever, much to the disappointment of the boys in this class. The Wang family had beautiful daughters, as Lien Hua, Mei, and Zhuo was splitting images of their angelic mother. Initially, my father worried about this; however, my mother convinced him, they could defend themselves if they needed. She believed this farming area in Oklahoma had a code of honor. The mothers would work with the girls on the proper way to behave. They did not worry much about Mei, as Don would protect her, and Lien Hua was old enough at least to know how to cry for help. The primary worries were for Zhuo, because Ju-Long might not be able to detect the warning signs. The principal ensured our parents that he, and his assistant would work hard to monitor these children because they did not want an international crisis in this school. The media continued to promote the Chinese activities in America as American and trying to protect their investment. This protecting their investment release was to promote believably in these reports. The primary complaint was the mysterious segregation, because the Americans wanted to see Chinese living among them. The Johnson-Wang project was one of the more than two-thousand such ventures. This may sound like a massive project, yet considering there were over seven million Chinese secretly living in America, or living in closed communities; this was but a drop in a, much larger pond. Americans knew a change was on the horizon, and could merely hope this change would not be as harsh as the media showed them it could be. The media were instrumental in reporting how the Chinese are saving Americans from a downfall that could be the most drastic in the history of humanity. It somewhat resembles living along a river, knowing it has rained severely upstream and waiting for the flooding to begin. You do not want to lose what you have, so you stay hoping fortune will spare this pending disaster.

Wang Zhuo and Wang Ju-Long were next to be assigned. My father stresses on the principal these are the two we have the greatest concern, as we have no American family members to pair them. The principal explains that he will go to the eight-grade classroom and ask for a schoolmate volunteer for each. My father asks if he can also join with the children's father. He wants the student who protects Zhuo to know we loved her. The principal asks if we want a same-sex mate or an opposite sex mate. Lien Hua translates to her father who says he would prefer an opposite sex schoolmate. He believes this will aid in their social and cultural development. The principal agreed with their decision and promised to try hard to comply. They went to the classroom, as the principal introduced Zhuo and Ju-Long, explaining they were part of an American-Chinese family. The students saw my father standing beside Lien Hua, who is always with us for interpretation, even though Zhuo and Ju-Long could easily have translated. My father wanted her there so these students would know Zhuo, and Ju-Long had a high school student available for their defense. My father was relieved when the principal asked to have female volunteers to be Zhuo's schoolmate, and every girl came forward. The principal asked the teacher to make the selection. The teacher asked my father if it were okay if she had a different girl be his schoolmate, and after they made two complete rotations, he could render his final selection or continue with the rotation if he so desired. My father agreed this would be best, so long as he had the option to continue the rotation, because making a selection could break several hearts and create problems. The teacher agreed. Ju-Long was next to stand in front of the class. Every boy came running forward, fell to their knees, and began begging her to select them. The teacher suggested that we follow the same rotation for her, with one minor adjustment. If, at any time she decided she was not comfortable or safe with one boy, she could rotate to the boy of her choice.

My father felt comfortable with this setup; therefore, he thanked the teacher and asked that she notified him of any concerns or anything else we should do. The teacher explained that she would be sending surveys home for these children to rate their experience. She told my father that unless these children answer these questions honestly, she could not make the necessary adjustments. She explains to my father that you cannot add two Chinese children in a classroom without making any cultural adjustments. The outcome is worth the extra work, in that these children will have a Chinese friend in their lives, which will help them survive in our future that she believes will be greatly integrated with the Chinese. My father was extremely satisfied with this setup, as they just had one more place. Lien Hua told my parents she would be glad to stay with the adults and work. My mother tells Lien Hua these will be the two greatest years in her life for socialization. Even though we need her at home, we cannot take these years from her. Lien Hua this explains to her parents. My mother tells Lien Hua not to worry if the boys ask her out for dates, or to attend a school sports event, because we have plenty of younger children who can go along as chaperones. Lien Hua asks if this will cause the boys not to invite her. My mother tells her it will just turn away the bad ones. Moreover, she tells Lien Hua that her father never allowed one of his daughters to go on an unchaperoned date, nor have they ever allowed Lisa or Roberta to go out without one of their youthful siblings. That younger sibling invariably turned out to be me, as

Lisa and Roberta would always scare Fred, Don, and Julia. I tried to give Lisa and Roberta breathing room, and we unfailingly seemed to keep their big football, players' boyfriends out of the cookie jar. Lien Hua meets her fresh eleventh-grade class. She is not ready to socialize with the boys. Fortunately, the girls gobbled her up under their wing. Lien Hua is gorgeous, and apparently; high school girls confirm their beauty by the girls they hang out with at school. Lien Hua enrolled in the advanced courses, where the mighty jocks were extremely serious. Most of the boys had their large glasses and noses in their books.

This high school was different from most in the better-looking girls were enrolled in the advanced classes as well. The belief was the successful completion of these leading classes would lead to academic scholarships and a ticket to the big cities. They were not interested in the farm boys. This would play to Lien Hua's advantage in that she came from the big cities and was engrossed in a farm boy to work beside our fathers. Lien Hua shared many stories with these girls about life in the considerable cities, to include New York City and Chicago, two places where she received her English and American culture training. Lien Hua was nominated by all the eleventh-graders and seniors to be homecoming queen. She was crowned the night before the fall of the United States. My father claimed this was a fitting way to end the old and begin the new. Each day Lien Hua and her siblings came home; they filled the house with the great adventures of that day, while Don and Julia crashed on the couches dreading the next day. My father claimed this was why the considerable transition would have to come. Those who are challenged and willing to work harder should receive the blessings. He considered his children not to be spoiled by the modern world, yet even as great as they were, they were no match for the Chinese children in this home. Wang Deshi explains to my father that his children are not ordinary Chinese's children, and they have worked long and hard for this opportunity. Their dreams are unfolding in front of their eyes, a dream that would not have been possible if not for the kindness and the sharing love of the Johnson family.

Once Lien Hua was settled, the principal gave our elders a complete tour of the school. The Wangs were impressed with the cafeteria, the basketball court, gymnasium, and outside playing areas. They were also treated to a tour of a bus, so they could sense what their children would be taking to and from school. My father collected the supplies' list, and off; they went to the market. Fortunately, our mother had Lien Hua get her siblings' shoe size and clothing sizes. They had the limo drivers drive them east on 160. My grandfather discovered our farm was twenty-five miles east of Ulysses, Kansas. They traveled to the junction of 83 north and took it to Garden City. Here they traveled to 3101 East Kansas Avenue to a Walmart Super center. My father had a Walmart Discover card and decided to put it to use today. However, on the way, he discovered a Goodwill on 2005 East Schulman Avenue and took the gang in here first. He decided that we would do a mixture of new and used clothes, this way the children would appear to have these clothes already broken and ready for living. He was afraid that too many fresh clothes would make them stand out. This goodwill had a wide selection of clothing. My mother was more interested in pants and shirts, trying to assemble at least eight used sets and two unused sets for each child. My father got each child a new jacket, used jacket, large winter coat with gloves, long underwear, and boots. My mother collected the undergarments and bras for the girls. They remembered the school supplies, and found a few used calculators. He also splurged for three laptops and a printer, hoping they would be able to get Internet access for the children's homework. The Internet came easily, because the leaders set that up at my father's request. They rushed back to the farm to get this organized before their children returned. The mothers washed all the new clothes, ran them through the dryers, and got the clothing hung up before the children came home. My father asked as amazed Lien Hua to manage the three laptops for everyone's homework. Lien Hua's first project was to show her parents and grandparents how the Internet could bring the knowledge of great libraries to their children's fingertips. She also set up links to their Chinese hometown papers and news channels, so they could catch up on the news while the children were at school.

With the children in school throughout the day, Lien Hua set up several English-Chinese translators on the computer so the adults could communicate during the day. This proved to reinforce their bond, as they would plan their questions and allow the computer to share their minds. The leaders put a family TV in one of the family rooms and attached it to a large antenna that could transmit to their satellite dish. As the temperature's outside began to plummet, the family spent more time, as did the nation listening to the rapidly changing world situation. The Yuan was now the world currency, and the American credit rating dropped drastically. The United States government began to close down, as even the schools went on a two day a week schedule, assigning massive amounts of homework to the children. This forced the teachers to grade this work on their own time. Few challenged this, especially as all labor unions were dissolved at the national and state levels. With so many Americans unemployed, there were not enough dues paid to support these unions. Americans refused to have such a large union deduction, which cut into their grocery money. Inflation became out of control, because many had to survive from larger profit margins on fewer sales. No one bought cars or houses, as most cars were sold between people avoiding the pricey dealerships. My father asked the leaders for several rifles and pistols claiming it could merely be a matter of time before big-city gangs began to raid the farms. The leaders provided the Johnson-Wang family with the weapons, to include a few machine guns and plenty of ammunition.

My grandfather studied the geography around their farmhouse and selected rooms on the second floor, two on each side as defense rooms. They divided their equipment to these rooms and assigned an adult and child for each window. Each side would have on English and Chinese's adult, with a child for translation. This left Don to double with Mei and Julia to double with Huang. They would be the mobile messengers to relay messages to the four sides. Lien Hua would be in the middle of the house, monitoring the first floor and resupplies as needed. The family kept a reserve in the center of the second floor in case one side was hit extra hard and needed more. Don and Julia would be the reinforcements if needed and run the distribution of the central resupplies. My father made sure each of his Chinese counterparts got specific training on their weapons. Within a few short lessons, they appeared to adapt extremely well. The American climate began to shatter at its fringes. Inflation has driven the price of food and products so high that there were no sales. Food spoiled in grocery stores, as most people fought for the dumpsters. Department stores and major national retail chains closed their doors, laying off their employees. The big oil companies joined the cause driving up the price of a gallon of gas to twenty dollars, nevertheless, still experienced trouble meeting the demand. When the unemployment rate skyrocketed to fifty-five percent, and inflation was at seven hundred percent the world downgraded the American credit rating, which tacked on a gigantic increase in the interest for their foreign debt. China became intimidated now, never expecting this domino effect to tumble so fast. They did not have time to get their seven million people out, therefore, forced the Federal government to support deployment of Chinese's troops to protect Chinese's citizens and property. Chinese troops were deployed on our farm, as my father, Wang Deshi, and Lien Hua welcomed them and set up accommodations in the barn per the leaders' instructions. My father told the leaders he had no problems with these soldiers staying in the house, especially at night because of the freezing weather. They finally reached a compromise for half to stay in the basement and rotate with the other half. My mother and Ng Da-Xia monitored the soldiers to make sure no one became sick or was frost bitten. They made sure that hot green tea and soup were available to all who entered the basements.

My father was animated with the leaders these soldiers were protecting their lives and deserved their support. The leaders agreed and allowed the soldiers to mingle with us. They made sure the soldiers understood that any sexual crimes would be grounds for execution. These women were to be treated as gifts from the heavens. My grandmother joked that it had been a long time since she was thought of as a gift from heaven. My grandfather told her he never stopped believing she was a gift from heaven. After Lien Hua, translated this to her grandparents, Wang Chang told Hsu Bao that she was the greatest angel that he ever knew. My parents felt refreshed from these romantic gestures from the grandparents, yet also believed they needed to focus and Mr. Death, who was knocking at their door. China's General Secretary of the Central Committee decided that if America continued to decline, they would fall beyond a point to restore, thereby decided China would have to bail America to protect the huge American debt they held and the massive capital investments they had in the United States. They realized that if a rogue nation took over the United States, they could capitalize the United States, refuse to honor the debt and financial ruin China. China called an emergency meeting with the United Nations declaring they would go to nuclear war with any nation that deployed troops on American soil and requested permission to call in the American debt, before the interest made the debt greater than the combined value of American assets. The United Nations granted the permission. The Chinese Mafia bribed the house and Senate, giving them a chance to vote for surrender or chance an extended and miserable war against the world. The surrender was passed and signed by the president the same day. The president was an outsider to Washington and did not understand the corruption that existed. She did not accept a bribe to sign the surrender, claiming the surrender was in the best interests of humanity.

She was the sole politician who was granted immunity and given a secret safe haven for her and her family. When the surrender took effect, the Chinese government published a report that revealed all the brides they paid to the politicians and what action they demanded in return. The media published this as America went on a politician inquisition. Those they caught were executed in public. Those who slipped off to other countries were eventually returned by the Chinese Mafia and executed by the American Public. China now was sovereign over the former United States, yet instead of victory and plunder raids; they now had the massive task of bringing order to America. They needed to prevent the starving of 330 million people. The government froze the inflation rate and restored all prices to what they were two months earlier. They nationalized the oil companies, lowered the fuel prices back to normal. Next, China nationalized all property and assets in the states claiming they were payments against the outstanding debt. They allowed all current business owners and residential owners to maintain control of their assets. The businesses were ordered to recall all their employees and begin production. Those who did not have work were assigned work. Prisoners with lifetime sentences for crimes against property or people were at once executed. Nonviolent and white-collar crimes were pardoned. Mental institutions were closed, with those who could function in society spared, all others executed. Prostitutes were made properties of the state and initial to be used as comfort girls in the military. The American military was to be completely reorganized and integrated with Chinese's military to form a new American division defense system. The communist party had a credit for worktable and maximum wealth systems established. Employees could use these credits to purchase food and other supplies needed to survive. All tax systems and former debt were removed. Everyone started with a clean financial slate. The banks were nationalized and the Chinese fiscal experts assumed control.

Within one short month, food was pouring into the grocery stores and there was no unemployed. The media broadcast special shows, which explained the new laws and the responsibility that each member had with a socialist nation. All children would attend public schools, although the class loads were increased. The educational system of the former United States was producing children who could not compete in the modern world. The party even declared that all young people who did not go on to college would attend a special two-year upgrading program to develop their skills. Every student would take a national exam and based on the results of that exam be assigned a future occupation and receive a free education to prepare them for this field. All boys and girls would do two years of military service before university study. They would try to match a military equivalent skill to that person's future occupation. This was going to take time to work out the wrinkles, yet everyone figured that once things settled, the Americans would not starve, nor waste their lives in welfare lines. China believed the young people, both American and Chinese would work together to create the greatest empire ever to exist in history. Chinese scientists and philosophers had much influence on their socialist party. No one wanted to deny the argument that space travel was essential for the survival of the human race in the distant future. The first thing that needed to happen was the Earth's air and water needed to be cleaned. Many scientists even worried about the greenhouse effect. The important thing for this new union was to remove the greed and gluttony of individual profiteers, which should allow all to work for a better future. Another project was bringing out the seven million resident Chinese, so they could work under a similar structure as the Americans. The master-servant relationship was dissolved. They used this merely to keep total control until it was time to make their move. The move was now made; thus, absolute control was no longer needed.

The socialistic party understood their American-Chinese wanted to know more about the new home their government had relocated them. The socialist think tank believes that by providing its people a chance to integrate throughout the former states and blind in with the workforce, this would increase productivity at the end. They had the media prepare information for these citizens to consider. This excited their people, as their government volunteered to provide any training needed to work in a position their test scores qualified them. The Chinese party had one future goal, and that was a melting pot of productive citizens, regardless of race. Production and potential were the driving forces. They believed while that they kept everyone fed, employed, and passed certain extra benefits, such as a free cell phone for everyone. The trick to this was these cell phones had transmitters in them, which allowed the party to monitor their movements. The party elected solely to get involved in any action the threatened public safety. Such actions could have a negative effect on production. The party justified the emphasis on production to finance the hospitals and education. The result was no one held any wealth, including the leaders. All wealth was used to provide for the public. The rewards were the history books, which would bring glory to those who provided the best quality of life for the citizens. The other great benefit the Americans received immediately was the state provided medical care. No one had to pay for his or her medicinal care or any prescriptions. The party was shocked how the capitalistic model would allow people to die when medical treatment was available. Many Americans would now receive the care they needed, even though many had medical insurance, the insurance did not cover them for certain complex curative procedures.

The Chinese financial administrators were scrambling to build more hospitals and medical schools. They were disappointed in the manner the American Medical Association hindered the number of American Doctors, creating the shortfall that forced the nation to bring doctors from Asia, India and other nations. They released the documents that revealed how the Association had deprived the former states of American Doctors to the media. They also released reports how the super wealthy had financially drained America and stole from the public. Within hours, these people were publicly executed. The party felt comfortable knowing when the Americans discovered the injustices they went on an inquisition. Most of America, most who lived their lives well below the poverty level, and now saw a future rejoiced at the chance to make this new system work. China found itself faced with another giant hurdle, and that was the American infrastructure was in decay. Bridges needed built; roads rebuilt to standards, water and sewage systems modernized before disease and plague wiped out the continent. They decided to use the American military draftees for this social project. The media did a wonderful job in showing the public that this was their water, their sewage, and their roads that brought the food and fuel they needed to survive. My father agreed with the leaders this was without question fair. Without this work, we would not survive. Springtime came as warm weather began to wake nature up and shine on the new American States of China. The leaders informed my father approximately ninety-eight percent of the Americans were in tune with this modern system; however, two percent were rogue violent guerilla terrorists. My father asked the leaders if his children were involved in these activities. The leaders reveal our children, except for Roberta are living securely in the Never Summer Mountains. They additionally report that Lisa has married a fine son of a minister named Phillip and Cindy is married to George. They gave my father copies of the registered marriage certificates. My mother asks if they are living in Canada, which is not far from where these certificates were recorded. The leaders tell them to give that no mind, as various mountain people were trying to throw them a curve ball.

My father asks since these leaders know where their children are and there are no longer charges against them, would they bring them home. The leaders explain these children are safer in the mountains, as they have soldiers living in secret mountain tunnels protecting them. They also do not want to bring Li Jing out of hiding until the seven million current Chinese are settled among the Americans, once this happens; her great escape will mean nothing. They fear that American terrorists or Chinese dissenters could use this as a battle cry to disrupt the public saving campaigns. Any disruption could just result in innocent people suffering. My grandfather could find no fallacy in this argument and asked the leaders to keep him posted in any way this family can help. The leaders then reveal that they have camera spread throughout the house and ask for permission in using several of our integrated family events, with the other two thousand one hundred families to bear witness to how the Chinese and Americans can function in cooperation, and live happier lives in the process. My grandfather complains that their privacy was invaded. The leaders explain privacy is outdated, and that public safety overrides any rights to concealment. They explain these cameras were to protect both the Johnsons and the Wangs. They did not want any embarrassment for their people harming innocent Americans, nor did they want to chance any unknown accidents. Everyone's safety was important. The leaders also declared that any tapes capturing intimate or personal activities were erased. They respect this moral privacy. The leaders also report their homes have the same camera setup and surveillance. The additional sense of security eventually overrides the feeling of being spied on by an intelligence agency. They advise Grandpa that if he has a message, he must keep the secret; to take the person or people he is talking with, and take a walk in the field, covering his mouth when he speaks so the satellites cannot read his lips. Think nothing about doing this, as they all do it, a few more frequent than others do. A few things must remain secret.

Grandpa explained to our combined family about the cameras at a meeting at the dining table. The Wang's were surprised their Johnson counterparts did not know this. Grandpa then explained that it was impossible for such a large group as this not to have any arguments. Notwithstanding, he asked each member if they had any issues they wished to discuss. Everyone confessed to be content. Next, he asked the children how school was going. Lien Hua complained that all the students believed she had all the answers, and if they did what she said, they would be safe. Ju-Long and Mei also confirm this. They claim that any strange noise or even when a Chinese soldier walks by the students all rush behind them, believing they will be safe. One soldier even told the students, while they were kind to the Chinese citizens who attended this school, they would be protected. My father explains to Lien Hua, Ju-Long, Mei that so much has changed, and these friends, who adored them before the downfall of the United States, now need them for guidance. They look at you and know you are sympathetic to them, because you live with Americans, two of which are students in their school. You are the living manifestation of the global events unfolding in front of them. My mother recommends these girls explain that since they live with Americans, they are in the same boat and there is no need to worry. We believe things will work out, as long as we work hard to rebuild our former nation and provide for a greater future than we could have before dreamed. She tells these daughters to explain what they would do and hope whoever is judging the situation finds in their favor. It also would not hurt to tell them that if they get into trouble without an intent to disobey to ask the police to get them, so they could figure out how to remedy the situation. Lien Hua, Mei, Huang, Zhuo, and Ju-Long told this to their teachers and their friends. The teachers helped to explain these children were living as Americans and subject to the same rules as those around them, yet would gladly help anyone who was innocent. They will not help any who try to endanger their public safety. This reduced the stress these children were suffering, because they now felt safer, since their Chinese friends, were not worried.

My father warned the Johnson-Wang clan we had to be careful with each move we made, as many were watching us currently. Fortunately, the media began conducting street interviews trying to capture the mood of the nation. They also conducted mail surveys, which people could voice their concerns and worries. The socialist party believed information, and transparencies were the keys to community rest. They released detailed videos that revealed massive fleets delivering emergency supplies to the United States from Africa, Europe, and South America. They were instrumental in reporting riots in Europe and Africa because too much of their domestic goods were being exported to the former states, creating shortages in their nations. China elected to reduce their trade surplus with these nations, having yet to agree on absorption of the American trade deficit with these nations. The United Nations causally suggested China could honor these deficits. China refused, citing they were shouldering the world's responsibility in preventing the starvation of former states and a collapse of the world economy. Even though the Yuan was the world currency, the Americans still controlled the distribution networks and systems. If these fell, the world could drop into chaos. China did agree to pay pennies on the former dollars for these deficits, if they remained in dollars. They did not want this burden placed on their Yuan, nor did any of the other world trading exchanges. China refused to allow their trade surpluses to offset these trade deficits unless on a case-by-case basis. The party knew this had to be a slow conversion process, and they needed to determine what unfair trading policies lead to these deficits. These nations bribed American politicians to look the other way and slide their products into the American markets destroying the American domestic producers. China stood tall to convict these pirates, according to Chinese's law and vetoed every attempt of the United Nations to gain jurisdiction over these cases.

China soon discovered that they had two massive social problems to solve. Even though they did not enforce drug laws, because they considered western medicine inferior to Chinese's medicine, they believed the sales and distribution of these drugs could just be through official party outlets. They would stamp out all underground black markets. Their law stated that all items consumed by the public must be purchased through party public outlets. They activated former National guardsmen, and equipped them with packs of drug dogs and began a massive sweep of the ghettos, confiscating all drugs. They also enacted a social resettlement program, where seventy-five percent of the ghetto residents were relocated to the unknown titanic apartment complexes assembled beside new production centers. The party gave a three-day warning for all drugs to be surrendered to the public. After this grace period, any who were caught with drugs received a lifetime sentence to a public labor organization. They would be building bridges, roads, sewage systems, hospitals, universities, and community housing. Those Americans who believed the new party was as inefficient as the former states woke up to a shocking surprise. The ghettos were cleaned in one month. The Chinese Mafia discovered the supply networks and closed them, while disbanding the market. They also provided detoxification for those who wanted to break their old habit. These drugs were destroyed, as they were stored in public inventories and sold through party outlets, where they could be traded for credits earned through party work. China still had one humongous problem they had to consider, and this was the massive illegal immigration from Mexico.

The party held a series of debates on how to define this problem and determine if it could be integrated into their model for production purposes. The party production officials who managed the agricultural activities in these southern areas petitioned that this was a cheap source of labor, which could enhance the profit margin of this industry. The Chinese party officials finally decided the total social costs of having these illegals in their nation outweighed the profits. China sent a message to Mexico to call back their people, within two months, as those who stayed, would become the socialist property, and many executed through forced labor. The women would be made sterile, and then made permanent comfort women to the party. The children would be returned with enduring injuries. China immediately began securing the border. They used sonar equipment to detect tunnels and sealed them. China also declared a two-mile open zone, one mile on the American side and one mile on the Mexican side. Any authorized person caught in this zone would be executed on sight. Mexico tried to challenge the Chinese claiming they had no authority to implement these programs, and that war would result if one Mexican were executed. China understood that they had to show force to prevent any rogue nations challenging their claims to the former states. They launched seventy bombers and five hundred fighter planes, which bombed Mexico City, destroying over fifty percent of the city. They returned these bombers and loaded them with illegal immigrants, then flew over Durango dropping six thousand people, without parachutes in the city. The next morning these planes came from the south and dropped seven thousand people in Chiapas.

The party wanted to show that no place in Mexico was secure from the Chinese military. The next week witnessed a massive exodus of Mexicans from the former states. Apparently, their Mexican relatives who lived in Mexico warned their friends and family to get out of the Chinese states when possible. This exodus saw approximately eleven million Mexicans return to Mexico. The party was mixed in the degree of this exodus, realizing the loss of productivity from eleven million would cut into profits, yet also understood this loss would make the transition process go smoother and make it easier to feed the 316 million people that stayed within the borders. The party understood that they had the largest population field to resupply this American project, with well over 1,393,000,000. They needed the American population to move them ahead from India, who stood at merely 120,000,000 fewer. Plans called for bringing at least 700,000,000 to America in one of the greatest human migrations in anthropological history. Before this could happen, China knew they would have to defeat Canada, which would involve a war with Great Britain. China logged this as their projects for 2035-2050 duration. They would weaken Canada first by stopping all trade and disrupting their oil lines. Their game plan remained to make a surrender appear to be a great victory. The party knew that it would take the fifteen years to stabilize the American States of China. When the population fears starvation, they are compliant; however, once they begin eating once more and become comfortable with their surroundings, discontent and longing for the days of old begin to resurface. The parties' survival through these moral revolts would merely be guaranteed based on how deep their indoctrination was and how powerful their social compliance forces were. The party hated to rule with an iron hammer, as they believed this was detrimental to profitable production. Notwithstanding, too loose on a reign would seed open revolt. They depended on the media to report the massive investment that the Chinese people made in saving America and their right to receive their money back, plus a profit for the risk and hard work. Considering death would have been permanent and painful if they were left to starve and become slaves to the rogue nations, life in servitude and equally livable conditions was not too much to expect in return. The battle cry was America, repay your debt with grace, and honor.

The leaders asked our clan if they could give public appearances promoting peace and working together. They emphasized that no political statements were allowed, and they were to refer such questions back to the party. The emphasis here was to show working people living together and the struggles they shared. My father asked if several of our children's schoolmates could also join. Wang Zhuo selected her special friend Charles Benson whereas Wang Ju-Long selected his exceptional friend Lizzy Brown. Lien Hua found her circle of friends to vary from her younger siblings. Conforming to the style of her close study groups, which were female, she avoided contact with what she labeled as aggressive over possessing young immature boys. The boys found themselves seeking the favor of their homecoming queen and as such, struggled hard to get her attention; in the limited opportunities, she gave them. Lien Hua was continuously surrounded by the most popular eleventh-grade girls, even though she was eager to learn with all the students in her class. No matter which girl sat beside her, she enthusiastically struggled to make them comfortable. The advanced class eleventh-grade girls of Ulysses High School had a strict code against contact with boys. They only authorized public interaction was with the cheerleaders. Ulysses High School had twenty-six cheerleaders, six from the freshman class, and six from the sophomore class, seven from the eleventh-grade class, and seven of the senior class. Ironically, all seven of the junior class came from the advanced studies girls. Lien Hua could not join the cheerleaders because she was the reigning homecoming queen, a title held with great honor and prestige in the Ulysses community. Lien Hua asked her fellow female classmates she should bring with her on these public appearances. The girls recommended that they vote for the top two cheerleading classmates, and those two perform as her court on these tours. Lien Hua agreed this was the plan, as it gave all her friends a chance to be a part of the process. They elected Susie Masters and Janet Oakley. Lien Hua missed her younger siblings who were farmed out to Kepley Middle School, or Sullivan Elementary school. She found joy in that she could brief them on what to expect when someday they were promoted by Ulysses High School.

The leaders purchased a used recreational vehicle (RV) for the tour. My father did not want a new shiny one in that he wanted this to look like ordinary neighbors. RVs were popular in the Midwest, as families often had to travel distances on their former family vacations. My father attached a large U-Haul to the back, where they loaded folding tables, chairs, and bicycles for the children, so they could explore these new sights. The Grant County commissioners planned the locations for this three-day tour. The final day fell on a Monday, which was a school day. Notwithstanding they dedicated this day to Ulysses High School, Kepley Middle School, Sullivan Elementary School and Hickok Elementary School. This pleased the school's administration and gave my parents relief at least in knowing they get to meet the families of their children's classmates, and felt a closer bond with their local neighbors. The three days went smoothly. The children melted into the audiences with their friends and played throughout the days. The commissioners were kind enough to provide housing in the tour stops, knowing that we needed extra space for cleaning and sleeping. There were too many of us to sleep in the RV. Lien Hua, Susie Masters, and Janet Oakley were the highlight of each stop. She wore her homecoming gown and a crown as her court wore their cheerleading outfits. The confidence in knowing the community votes for the homecoming queen and that her classmates must have campaigned hard to get their parent's support opened the hearts for so many. They also knew about Susie and Janet, with their long history of academic excellence and high social ranking in the community.

Witnessing them with Lien Hua convinced everyone Grant County was fortunate to have this beautiful and smart young woman among them. The newspaper declared to one truism was Lien Hua, and her sisters' exceptional beauty. They even tossed in the little Julia was a blessing of beauty on the American behalf. The senior citizens questioned our four grandparents. They called Wang Ju-Long and Lizzy Brown to help them translate. The parents flocked around our four parents as they called Wang Zhuo and Charles Benson to translate. This left Don, Mei, Julia, and Huang to roam among the excited crowds and saw the migration of all the middle school and younger children flowing with them. The police department provided special protection for Lien and her court, as they found a stage to sit on and talk to the high school students accompanied by those who in their twenties. The leaders, who placed bugs on us, and gave us earphones, so they could help us with difficult questions, were surprised by the nature of the questions. The questions were everyday questions, like the sort of laundry detergent they used, and the favorite foods they enjoyed serving their children. Ng Da-Xia confesses she does not feed her children the healthy food that she wants to, and that instead she and Francis make pizza, French fries, and hamburgers. Ng Da-Xia asks the crowds of mothers whom flock around them if children ever grow tired of hamburgers and French fries. Ng Da-Xia shakes her head in shock confessing that Francis previously told her the same thing. One of the mothers asks why she continues to feed her children hamburgers. Ng Da-Xia explains her children tell her that is what everyone eats. She also enjoys the happy looks on their faces. Ng Da-Xia explains that she uses paper towels to press out the fat and then adds selected spices and Worcester sauce. Leastwise this way she removed as much of the bad as possible, toss on the pickles and onions and hope for the best. At least, they will not feel like outsiders. Ng Da-Xia asks how they made out on the meal line versus the snack line for the school's lunch. The mothers agree that they lost this battle as well. Ng Da-Xia thanks them for sharing this, as she believes her children are being honest with her.

Then seniors discussed their aliments with our grandfathers, although most questions focused on Wang Chang concerning any traditional secrets, he used for his routine medical abnormalities. Grandpa told us that night for the children to be careful when running outside, as he suspected there would be many holes dug in search of herbs and roots. Grandpa recommended these people go to the library and get online to order these supplements, as he did. He found numerous respectable herb and root retailers that had reasonable prices. My father and Wang Deshi received many general questions from the male farmers in the crowd. They were more concerned about the continuity of his operations and testing to ensure he was truly a farmer. My father knew much about farming. He confessed to the support and led the way his financial backers had given him in this project. He also cautioned that future projects would not receive the same lead way, because with so many, there had to be a form of control so everyone could succeed. When asked what he saw in the future, my father qualified that he was simply an ordinary Midwest farmer, yet what he saw was a chance to contribute to a brighter future for his family. Not having to worry whether our children will have work or be able to provide for their families was a great relief. The men folk accepted this as an unofficial vision. My father tells them we no longer can rule out hope, because hope is here. The leaders liked this answer and decided to begin the hope is here campaign. My parents and family could not believe how fast the first two days went and how everyone slept like rocks each night.

The final day shaped up with the High School as the clan prepared to go outside as Francis and Ng Da-Xia inspected behind everyone's ears. The children were so excited this day, as they would be able to share their academic activities with their parents. My parents even became excited with Julia and Don, because they did not want to lose any more children to school troubles. They began with the elementary schools, had lunch at Kepley Middle School, where the community discussions were in the cafeteria and gymnasium, because the school officials believed it was too cold to have the children outside. This worked out fine was the Johnson-Wang clan as they settled into their discussion groups. Ju-Long and Zhuo were the heroes here. The final stop was Ulysses High School. The leaders recommended the adults give a small speech first highlighting various topics they discussed the previous days. They believed this would cut down on the questions afterwards. My mother wanted to get their children home and in bed early, so they would be rested for school on Tuesday. The speeches went smoothly with just one more appearance possible. Lien Hua did not know if she was to speak or not, especially considering she was there daily. The students began chanting for Lien Hua. After a few minutes, my father pointed at her to go on stage and to take her court with her. Her friends worked hard for this cause the past few days and deserved a little special recognition today. Lien Hua, Susie Masters, and Janet Oakley go on the stage. Lien Hua thanks the student body for all the marvelous support that they have given to this cause. She confesses really to enjoying this school, the teachers, and so many wonderful friends.

Lien Hua tells them the story of her family. She spoke about raiders from another tribe burning down their village, which forced them to move to the city. They received permission to relocate from the region's party administrator, and when they arrived in the big city, gave their papers to the party leader, who assigned her family their jobs, a home, and advance credit to purchase blankets and food. Lien Hua explains in this city, the children work six hours, then attend school for four hours. If you fail a test, the teacher will give you two swings with a whip. Lien wore jeans and a sweater under her gown. She decided to surprise the people today. She had Susie and Janet help her remove her homecoming queen gown. The high school boys, now burning with heat, began whistling, cheering, and begging for more. She wore no bra today, as she felt the loose homecoming gown concealed any unexpected movements from her breasts. She felt herself lucky that her breasts were firm, and not as overwhelming as several of her friends were. She told her girlfriends that even though on the average Chinese breasts were smaller, their men never complained about them. Lien Hua believes this satisfies the men and reduces the risk of back pains later in life. She actually sold this concept so effective that many of her large breasted friends told her they wished they were made as she was. Her friends also confessed the boys in Ulysses High School had no complaints about Lien Hua's breasts. Lien Hua reminds her friends that they are dedicated to their celibacy until their university days, as they established before meeting her. Lien Hua pulled off her sweater keeping it on her breasts to prevent exposure. The whistling stopped, and the crowd became extremely shocked. Lien Hua had at least one-hundred scares on her back where she was beaten. Susie and Janet helped her return to the homecoming gown. One of the students asked whether they would be using this sort of punishment in the American-Chinese schools. Lien Hua assures them they will not do this, and that just a few places in China still do this. She was unlucky to be in one of those places. Lien Hua tells the crowd how happy she was the day her father came home and informed them they were being relocated to America.

When they arrived in America, the Chinese party leaders gave them aptitude tests. Fortunately, she, her two brothers, and two sisters did great on the tests. The leaders elected to put them in advanced English classes so make them fluent. They provided normal American lifestyle training to their parents, such as how to drink a beer and who the Kansas City Chiefs were. The audience applauded her on this one. The day came when the leaders told us we would share a home with the Johnson family and live fifteen miles east of Ulysses. We were so afraid they would beat us, and hate us. We had no rights, as the leaders said we must obey them. Lien Hua calls my father to the stage and gives him a big hug declaring her love for all the Johnsons. She thanks him for being so kind. My father looks out to the audience and asks if anyone could be unkind to such a gorgeous homecoming queen. My father reveals that he and the other seven adults have a meeting each day while the children are in school and brainstorm for ideas on how to make their families lives better. He recommends the other parents also do this, as simple things can sparkle the little hearts in our children. Lien Hua thanks the audience for sharing not only America with her, but their love and support. The crowd begins to clap, while my father hears a strange clack and throws Lisa and himself to the stage floor. Lisa, having to idea what is going on and believing she is falling by accident, grabs Janet, who tumbles with them. My father rolls around, keeping Janet and Lien Hua on the floor telling them to stay put. He looks over and sees Susie falling to the ground. The crowd stops clapping, allowing my father to hear two more shots. He sees one of the shots hit Susie in her head. Since my father is bugged, he alerts the leaders they are under gunfire and help is needed immediately. Next, my father is hit in this belly. The assembly is now fighting to leave the auditorium crowding through each entrance. My father tells Lien Hua and Janet to begin crawling for the curtains quickly. For what he claimed felt like an hour, they made it under the curtains. The local police forced everyone to stay in the grass outside the school. They will let no one enter. Afterwards, five Chinese soldiers who were patrolling outside the school rush into the auditorium to determine if the terrorist is still there.

Once they get the all clear, these soldiers tell the paramedics to get in here and rescue Susie. My father, Lien Hua, and Janet are surrounding Susie trying to control her bleeding. My father counts four shots in her. They rush Susie and my father to the hospital. Our family follows in the RV. The school contacts Susie's parents so they may go to the hospital. Meanwhile, the additional fifty soldiers parachute into the area and begin rounding up any people who left the assembly. The leaders had cameras set up outside the school, in case of a terrorist attack. They could identify those who left, went to their homes and brought them back. A few even got into their vehicles; therefore, they used helicopters to find them. They then could gain access to the data on our cameras and consolidate them into their 3d model. They searched this film for any gunshots. The films found the shooter, and rendered a photo identification of him. They matched this photo with their American database and identified the shooter and his cell phone locator activator. The leaders released the crowd, and were surprised how he could get to his vehicle and exit. They sent the police to apprehend the terrorist. He was surprised when the cops surrounded his house. Police work was no longer the confused and clumsy style of the former states. Modern advanced equipment would identify criminals and get them off the street immediately. The question was why he shot such a gorgeous cheerleader like Susie Masters. The leaders would not allow this gunman's name to be released. They claimed the days of glory for outlaws were deep in history. The gunman had just one warning. He claimed to be a member of a large gang, and they were going to execute those who mingle with Chinese. The Americans must stay with Americans. This puzzled the leaders. They knew that a military squad would remain on the Johnson-Wang farm. They would deploy another squad to roam among the three schools the children attended. Considering they were only going to school twice a week, they believed this to be feasible. This squad would roam aimlessly throughout Ulysses looking for anything unusual. They hoped this would keep the community calm, since this sort of shooting undermines their public security.

Lien Hua stood in the hallway with Susie's parents and Janet. Susie's mother tells Lien Hua that she should have checked in on her American father occasionally. Lien Hua visits him and our family for a few minutes each hour. Lien Hua felt so guilty that a friend was suffering because of her. My mother returned with Lien Hua to comfort Susie's mother and Janet. Susie's mother explains that she attended the elementary school assembly and the middle school meeting. Her children were complaining so she took them home. One of her friends had her cell phone and recorded Susie's stage activities. My mother asked her if anyone was watching her children now. She tells my mother, her sister, who saw Susie get shot is watching them. A few hours go by, and still no word from the doctors. The nurses continue to tell us she is in surgery. Then at eleven P.M., the doctors come out to speak with Susie's mother. Lien Hua is disturbed by the somber look on their faces. Janet reminds her they have been in surgery for over six hours. The doctor then officially informs us that Susie died. They tell how she fought hard, yet she had one shot in her heart and another in her lungs. The deadly shot was the one in her head. Even if they could have revived her, she would be in a coma or vegetable for the remainder of her life. My mother gripped Susie's mother in a tight hug and told her to let out the great pain. Susie's mother soon pulled herself together enough to go home. She called her house and asked her sister to invite their parents and the minister. She gave Lien Hua and Janet a big hug and told them they were welcome anytime. She also asked that if the school needed any paperwork from her would we bring it to her and return it to the school. Julia could do this as she had her license and a car. She told Lien Hua that in those days, she would take her home as well.

My mother told Lien Hua, she and Janet should stay close to her family and not go off exploring. Lien Hua and Janet sat in the waiting area across the hall from our father's room. Their cell phones began to ring just about nonstop. They knew one of them would have to release the news about Susie. Lien Hua wanted to wait until Susie's mother went home, so she could notify her family initially. Finally, after one hour, Janet answers her phone and tells one of their friend's Susie dead. She asks this friend to tell everyone else. Within about ten minutes, their phones stopped. Then their friends began to trickle in with extra food for our family. The hospital puts two folding tables in the hallway in front of our father's room. We sorted the food out on the table in invited all in our group to eat. Around midnight, the doctor released our father. As we were leaving the hospital, the leaders told us to get in front of a TV and go to Channel 5. We turned the TV in one of the patient's room and watched a special report. The report showed the mutilated remains of the gunman and explained how the Chinese Mafia had three more names members of this terrorist gang that wishes to kill innocent Americans. They also showed a report of

Susie's dead body and her mother crying when she got the news. Lien Hua told Janet the leaders got that clip from her camera, as she was watching the mothers cry. My father asks the leaders; through his pocket transmitter why they told the public, they knew of three more. The leader claims the gang does not know which three he reported; therefore, they are monitoring the three residences and their calls. They have also activated the cell phone's camera and recording microphone. They hope they will contact others in their organization and ask for guidance. Once they get a new name, they lock into their cell phone and expand their monitoring. The Mafia notices the first three are on the move thereby apprehended them. They put them in their sealed truck and take them to the torture chamber. The Mafia continues monitoring their calls, using these leads as new sources for their surveillance. Within three hours, they apprehended thirty-four confirmed terrorists in six states. By morning time, they had one-hundred and forty-two members, when they noticed the cell phone traffic stopped.

There was no way to make sure they got everyone in this gang, as they knew other gangs existed. Even though possibly a few of these individuals belonged to other gangs, they elected not to seek this information now and put a hammer on this case. They erected one-hundred and forty-two poles in an open field, afterwards tied these prisoners to them. Then they invited the media and gave them a copy of all the evidence, which with videos and phone transcripts was incriminating. They established a panel of three Chinese judges who examined the evidence and by the People's laws was convicted. This court hearing took about eight hours. During this time, the leaders invited Susan's mother to witness with Lien Hua and Janet. Most who watched the court were impressed by the quality of the evidence. It was precise and left no doubts. After the final hearing, the judge ordered their execution. The Mafia fired their machine guns along the poles putting at least ten shells into each body. Within a few minutes, the order was completely executed. The Mafia released to the public that they received their data from their satellites. Whatever the case may be; Americans learned one thing quickly. Crime was a thing lost in time. Their confidence in their security was growing. Nevertheless, there was that small group of troublemakers the Mafia still had to weed out.

Chapter 08

Massacres of the Innocents

Mitch was currently in a confused and angry condition. He could not believe Cindy had run away with me. Mitch was ample wise to recognize that Lisa and Roberta were old enough and had sufficient power in the family to conduct a marriage ceremony. By the code of their heritage, they would have to do this the first night, or Cindy would be forever disgraced in Marked Tree. Mitch developed his plan to win Cindy's hand, and it would involve my death. Mitch declared to his first gang that he would be the last face I saw on this Earth. His first gang barely survived one mission, a mission in which Mitch wanted to get particular information about where Cindy was hiding from the Chinese Mafia. He was not bright enough to realize if the Chinese Mafia knew where he was, they would have seized them. Their crime was in kidnapping Li Jing. They made serious mistakes, causing a few to be identified. Mitch was fortunate in the mental whacky he recruited, gave no names. He was broken hearted when Fred was executed, especially considering Fred was the lone one in the Johnson clan that feed him information. Mitch knew that if the Johnsons discovered he was the cause for Fred's death, they would never forgive nor accept them. Now, Mitch decided he would go to Saint Louis and bomb the Chinese headquarters for Missouri. He realized this would take extensive planning and absolute secrecy. He knew of several old, underground cave mines that his grandfather had the maps. He would set up a center underground and build his new gang one person at a time. He merely wanted four people in this group. Two would be responsible for gathering their supplies such as food, and certain chemicals. The fourth one would be his assault assistant. Everyone would work together to work out any glitches in his plan. He knew of two boys whose fathers owned stores. These boys would be essential. He went to speak with them personally and recruited them. Mitch clarified that everything had to be kept secret, as he believed it would be at least three more months before he got everything prepared. For the time being, they scouted through the deep underground cave mines, searching for air vents and climbing to the surface to establish an escape hole. Mitch stressed the Mafia could issue false charges and push them through court and six feet under the surface. These holes would give them a chance at escaping if they needed to get out of sight. His gang was established. He had George Plummer for assault. George came back to Marked Tree from three years in the Marine Corps. The food supplies duties fell on Larry Lingerman whose father owned the local grocery store and a fast-food restaurant. Larry explained that they throw away good food each day. He would tell them he had a few pet wolves, and he was feeding their den.

Mitch discovered a salt vein the crossed one of the tunnels, and he found a few tunnels that dropped down to where the air was freezing around them. They could store much food in these places. Larry recommended that they cook the meat first, then salt it and wrap it when they freeze it. This way, they can soak it in the water from a nearby underground stream and eat it. There would be no cooking in these mines, especially considering the smoke would seep out of the air vents and give away their positions. Mitch told his group, he was excited by the intensity of their planning. The final member was Jerry Glifford, whose father owned the hardware and grain outlets. His store could order any part that a farmer needed. Mitch knew he had to be careful that anything they ordered was normally in stock at the store. They had to set this up before the next inventory and make sure the list of shortages did not reveal any certain plans. They would tell everyone they were going to camp out on Mitch's farm, back by his pond. Ironically, he discovered an air vent from his mines close to the pond, so they could drop into their mines without causing many concerns. The boys purchased ammunition and arrows for their crossbows. Crossbows were the preferred weapons for Mitch. He believed that they were as deadly as a rifle; had no kick, easier to aim, and more importantly they did not make a noise. This would permit them to neutralize guards who were not near them. Mitch carefully sanded off any identifying information on the arrows, and then spray-painted them. The next big issue would be transportation. Mitch and his assault man believed motorcycles would give them greater flexibility, since they needed to move over country dirt roads and through forests. The planned escape route took them two weeks to establish. Mitch never went with George, as he at no time wanted them to be spotted together. Mitch learned the Chinese Mafia concentrated on small groups in their surveillance. They also knew to take a different route to Saint Louis. Four visits to Saint Louis were sufficient for forming his escape plan. He discovered a mine that ran under the city with an air vent to the park. He installed a rope system, whereas they could attack and drop their motorcycles.

Once inside, they had six miles of shafts that led them to an air vent alongside a network of country roads. Mitch studied this network, discovering how he could use it to get back to Memphis. Mitch explained to George, they could never take a chance of endangering the people in Poinsett County. Jerry and Larry were to stay in Marked Tree and monitor the police radios, providing Mitch with updated reports. Boring and tedious, Mitch knew firsthand how ugly this would get if they were caught. Mitch stored the chemicals he needed for this operation in his getaway mine. Mitch began studying books in the library, making sure not to sign them out or leave a paper trail. He was terrified to use the Internet. George accused him of being too precautious. Mitch was ahead of the public with this concern. He reported the documents he saw in the Marked Tree Mafia center had detailed reports concerning everything. He said there were boxes of telephone summaries and Internet surfing histories. Mitch said he was surprised at how powerful their search engines where these officials type in the word and, wherever this word emerges or someone spoke; in any call, it materializes before these investigators. They can add a few for search screens and ways they go to collect their victims. George and Mitch had another issue to solve. How would they attack this bustling center? Mitch noticed most of the traffic on the first floor was businesses and a constant flow of tourists who went there to collect souvenirs. This was Mitch's primary source of information, coupled with a few old sewage charts, which revealed the building's water setup. Mitch decided they would poison the water, and then poison the air through the heating system from the furnaces in the basement of this building. They smashed forty boxes of rat poisoning and placed it inside a miracle grow, style container screwing it into a drain style plug. This used the water pressure to blend the rat poison into the water, and spread it throughout the building. When the water container emptied, Mitch removed it to take with him. He spread dust over the pipes to remove any indications it was tampered. The harder that the Mafia searched for the source, the easier, it would be for him to get back undercover in Memphis. He did not have much time to wait, as their job started at five P.M.

The chemical gas, altered to include Nazi elements, was easy to plug into the furnace. He labeled the outside as air freshener, with fictitious company information. Mitch believed they would search for more advanced delivery methods. The chemicals blended with the intake air about twenty feet from the furnace. The blowers forced the air into the furnace where the heat bonded the gasses and lifted them into the ventilation system. These chemicals were odorless, thus once in a room would settle. After people began moving around, the chemicals would recharge and enter the resident's lungs, where within one hour they would experience illness and two hours begin to die. By this time, many were vomiting and going into convulsions over the morning tea and coffee. Emergency authorities had trouble identifying the cause, especially since the victim's varying medical conditions produced different results. Mitch had the gas installed, and water poisoned by seven A.M. They took the 'air freshener' container and stored it in another room in the maintenance section. They put on the business suits and walked into the business section, buying a Wall Street Journal and then walked along the street, where they got on the city subway. Here, they took the city park exit, went into a public restroom and listened to their portable radio. Their raid was not on the news yet. Accordingly, they changed into their exercise clothes, put on their backpacks and jogged into the forest near their mine air vent. They lie on the ground, dropping the backpacks in, while pretending to do sit-ups. George slid in first, and then Mitch, who pulled the drain cover back over this hole. They climbed down the rusty ladders to their motorcycles and quickly zipped out of Saint Louis. Once back on the surface, Mitch took escape route a, while George took escape route b. They secured their attack equipment in one of the side shafts in the mine approximately three miles inside the underground shaky path.

By nine A.M., they met at McDonalds for their breakfast and began chatting with their co-workers about the events of the previous weekend. Mitch and George watched the Saint Louis football game at the bar on Sunday, behaving like any red-blooded American, staying clear of any political debates. Mitch even made one comment that everyone in the bar remembered, at that was unless Saint Louis started playing better football, no foreigners would want to live in this area. In fact, a local police officer who was watching the game bought Mitch a beer. Mitch needed this, in that he wanted to stay as clear from the Mafia's radar as possible. Mitch and George left McDonalds and went to the laundry mat where they washed their clothes and watched the news alert on the public TV installed here. The news reported so far almost 7,000 Chinese were taken to the local hospitals. They were so overfilled now; they were taking them by helicopter to Memphis, Clarksville, and Little Rock. Once they stabilized a few, they took them to Indianapolis and Cincinnati. The public was shocked there were actually this many Chinese in this building, and the media had no way to conceal this. The Chinese explained this by claiming the massive increase in their American projects forced the financial backers to demand more extensive controls and safeguards. They downgraded this number by citing that 4,500 of these Chinese were women, and that for humane reasons, they had their families with them. It was not until three P.M. the police ordered an evacuation of the building. The number of hospitalized climbed to 10,000, of which 8,000 died in the first day. The Chinese hid another 3,000 in the basement, and took them out in body bags that night. This was the greatest attack on the Chinese on American soil in history.

The Chinese Mafia brought in the scientists the next week, with gas masks to determine the cause. They would not let them in earlier fearing this could be an unknown agent, which could spread as a virus or plague. By the end of the week, all the hospitals agreed this was not a biological attack. The confusing factors were the patients who drank water and breathed the air focusing on combining the symptoms. There were those cases in which the victims did not drink the water. A few delivery or messenger personnel solely drank the coffee or tea, and a few had hot chocolate, they made by mixing their packets with the hot water. The medical think tanks stumbled over this for most of the week, until the Federal Bureau of Investigation (FBI) arrived and began to sort this out. With so much time gone, the Chinese Mafia needed a miracle to solve this. They put their efforts into monitory public communication hoping the terrorists would brag knowing this to be the greatest massacre ever against the Chinese in America. Mitch, who confessed to George that he almost did not choose him for the assault position because of his name, forbids the four of us from ever talking about this. George asked what was wrong with his name. Mitch told him about me. That was in the past now, because Mitch had a taste of the big time. They had no idea this would be so successful. The killer was all the undocumented Chinese in the building who could merely leave when they were at the point of death. This did not apply to those lost in the basement. Many of the Chinese believed this was a sign one of their gods was angry with them. This concept spread through the servants like wildfire. The Mafia could not search for Mitch how they wanted, because they had to maintain control over the servants. Mitch also forbids his gang from talking with anyone who was a member of another gang, or planning a subversive action.

Larry complained that so many others were having the fun now, and they were hiding like cowards. Mitch reminds them that are raided will have killed more than all these others combined. He also described the way his three friends appeared after the Mafia had spent time with them. Mitch confessed he wanted another raid, yet this one would take more planning and be more dangerous. Small gangs from throughout the United States, most simply bored young people who were looking for a little excitement began their operations. Building homemade explosives became a popular pastime. The Mafia could match orders requesting certain combinations. They then studied the orders of these people of interest, monitored their phone calls, especially cell phones. They had special receivers installed throughout the United States that could provide one-hundred percent blanket coverage. The Mafia was also completing their giant database, which would contain all data, any person, or government agency had on all people. The Chinese had many expert hacking cells that could get into any network. They may run a search of a person; everything about the person appears, to include current bank statement balances, where they spent their money and exactly how much they spent on any items. A trip to Walmart, the data would show each item they purchased. They knew what brand of milk that person drank. They also had a detailed list of all phone calls made, the names of all relatives and their high school and college grades and courses taken. This would be the greatest single source of information ever assembled on Americans. The Chinese already had this on their citizens; therefore, adding the Americans was not that great of a chore. Mitch's precautions, plus decision not to buy their chemicals but to process them was an action that greatly reduced any chance of being caught.

As the minor attacks against the Chinese began to escalate, the Mafia forbids the media from reporting it. This turned out to be a two-edged sword, as the news now completely traveled by word-of-mouth. This caused the stories to grow, whereas an attack that injured one person turned into a ten-person massacre. The media did report the capture and punishment of these terrorists. This turned out to be questionable reporting in the crime they were being punished for was usually downgraded. The example would be a raid that slaughtered twelve Chinese would be reported as merely killing three Chinese and all females. The results were small attacks were exploding throughout the United States. Ten killed, was the largest Mitch ever heard on TV. Mitch had his eyes on Memphis since he found underground mines that took him to a park in downtown Memphis. Memphis had three minor attacks, thus the Mafia enhanced their security. The state permanently deployed extra National Guard in Memphis. Mitch argued with George; they had to wait for a while. He did not want to risk hurting a National Guardsman, claiming they were from our friends, or even could be a friend to a friend, or a distant cousin. Mitch says we are not at war with our comrades. George accepts this as fair and promises to remain low. Mitch continues to stress the Mafia is waiting for them to tell someone what they did. He accepted a growing sympathetic movement in America. This was being fueled by the sloppy work of the terrorists who were injuring innocent Americans during their attacks. One group planted a bomb in the wrong car on a train. This bomb killed fourteen and injured thirty-two Americans. This united the local Americans with the Mafia and FBI, in which they captured the gang of five within one week. They were executed in public by order of a regional judge. This was the surfacing of any problem in the United States. Americans were moving away from the sloppy and ineffective legal system, wanting a swifter, more ethical method to make sure effective justice.

The Chinese extensive video recording of many public events made this evidence gathering process easier. They found the video that showed the five planting the bomb. One group questioned the Mafia for not viewing this crime in real time and saving the victims. The Mafia clarified that based on the colossal quantity of recorded video it would be impossible to monitor it. Most of the video is stored in the massive data-storage facilities. The value comes through the ability to retrieve it after the fact. Video evidence is designed to protect the innocent. The media reports on the efforts this American-based security organization to protect innocent Americans. The media reemphasize the United States is not at war with the Chinese, and that all Chinese, who are on American soil, were invited by the federal and state governments. The stickler in these situations was how these administrative organizations did not share their data so a complete picture of the seven million who are here became visible. The facts were the government employees responsible for these programs were accepting bribes. The Mafia finally had enough videos of these employees accepting the bribes and stopped their payments using the media release of the videos as their bargaining chip. The General Secretary of the Central Committee decided to stop the massive immigration after Mitch's Saint Louis raid. He feared someone would get curious and discover this relocation. The end factors were these Chinese were enhancing American lifestyle by making less-expensive products secretly on American soil. The Mafia learned the American administrative procedures and capitalized on areas of overlapping authority. Here they could state that another governmental unit gave them the license to perform. There was no need to challenge these claims, because this would simply result in paying bribes to get the authorization, and then passing that cost back to the consumers. It was essential the American division be financially self-sufficient. The profits from production were used to purchase the farmlands and build the giant apartment complexes.

There was no actual abuse, and the major side effect was the loss of American productivity as many more factories closed their doors. The media were instrumentals in providing proof the stockholders of these factors did not invest in modernizing their equipment. Instead, they sucked the profits into their personal accounts and watched their factories fall into decay, and their employees in financial ruin. The Chinese Mafia began releasing information about Chinese's factories in America and proved that by protecting effective productivity, their factories were manufacturing, and the American factories could do the same. Labor costs needed reduced and compromises made by the stockholders who needed to focus on modernizing their production activities. The media did not get too deep into this, as it tended to get confusing and boring. The public simply desired summaries, such as seeing how these American-Chinese factories were saving them money at the market. This was a solid fact; the Chinese could make it better and cheaper, and they who have the lowest price won the sale. Ironically, the profits were buying farms and building apartments, which benefited Americans. Even Mitch experienced this transition as his father sold their farm and moved to Memphis. This provided Mitch a base in Memphis for his second great raid. According to George, it felt as years since their Saint Louis raid, nevertheless, it had merely been three months. A lot changed in these three months, as the United States fell into financial ruin with China as the lifeboat for the people. Mitch's views began to vary from the public's consensus. He argued the politicians that accepted the bribes from China were not the lone culpable ones in this process. China was also guilty in paying these politicians to act in ways that were detrimental to the American public. He summarized to his small force that China wanted this situation to occur, so they could take the United States from the Americans.

Once more, he warned his gang not to discuss political issues with the public. Mitch saw how the media favored the Mafia and how effective China was at eliminating their partners in these crimes. America blamed their former federal and state governments as the public hunted them in this national inquisition. When in his underground mine, Mitch could lay out how the Chinese stole America and made them slaves. Mitch kept his residential address in Marked Tree, with George, Larry, and Jerry. Jerry and Larry were assigned to their father's former businesses. The Chinese nationalized all property, nevertheless, let Larry and Jerry's fathers continue to run their businesses. They planned to install advanced computers for inventory control and improved the product placement and receiving docs. Mitch knew he would have to get the chemicals and food for his Memphis raid before they installed these computers. They had plenty of room in their mine. Mitch planned to hit two establishments this time, the new Chinese state division office and the Mafia's administrative center. This time they would wear their jogging clothes with their backpacks. Mitch would take Jerry and George would take Larry. He planned to release once again the gasses and poison at seven A.M., repack his backpack with a few blocks from the maintenance shops, go to the building's lobby, purchase a can of soda where the four would meet on a trial that connected the two buildings. At no time would they expose their face, wearing a toboggan that covered their heads. They also wrapped a blanket over their bellies so it appears they were heavy set. Once deep into the woods, they would drop into their air vent, erasing any footprints. Once in the mine, they would ride their motorcycles back to Market Tree, redress themselves, and get to work. They wanted to be at work when the news of their raid was released. Mitch led his group in several practice rides through the mines, because almost thirty miles underground was taxing, with solely the motorcycle's headlight. They quickly became comfortable with the escape route.

Mitch had one more change this time, in that he would release the rat poison into the water, while Jerry would release the chemicals into the furnace shafts. George and Larry would split their duties as well. Mitch believed this would prevent clumping, which could hold a chunk and dissolve slowly, reducing the sudden affect he wanted. Because of the secrecy of the Chinese party center and the Mafia's Memphis headquarters, Mitch could not obtain much data on who was working where in these buildings. Either way, he decided it was time for his big bang. They executed their plan. Things were going smoothly, when a Chinese maintenance man asked Mitch what he was doing. Mitch grabbed a block and smashed the man's head. Mitch and Jerry then placed the man back in the maintenance room and wiped any bloodstains by pouring, cleaning solvent on them. The gangs released their poisons and chemicals, slid into their air vent, rushed back to Marked Tree, and went to work. Mitch just about had a heart attack when Larry kept his soda can in his hand as he departed from the air vent. Mitch grabbed it and dropped it back into the mine. Larry wanted to realize why he did this. Mitch pointed out that this soda was not sold in Marked Tree, and that any who saw this would recognize he was in Memphis. Larry complimented Mitch on his precaution. Mitch once more warned his partners not to speak of this and to appear shocked when the news reports aired. They would begin hearing these reports on the radios and have to wait until their bosses guided them to a TV, if they believed this was an important event. Mitch told his gang not to worry so much, because it would be in the newspapers. Mitch suspected the victims would react quicker to this attack, as the chemicals in the air would create the alarm. He figured it would take time for the water poisons to create any panic. He hoped that many would take their hot liquid outside with them because of the spring chilly air.

This raid caught the buildings completely by surprise, especially the party center whose leader demanded his people stay put when he heard of the Mafia's raid. The thought of a double hit was behind his comprehension. Unfortunately, all fifteen thousand Chinese and Americans who worked in the party's center perished. It was not until 9:30 A.M. Memphis discovered this second hit, and this was because an American wife was angry because her husband would not answer his work phone. Three hundred and twenty-one Americans perished in this center as well. Most were maintenance and security personnel. Mitch was disappointed when he saw these reports air. George tried to ease Mitch by claiming these people were sympathizers. Mitch countered by the fact that we no longer chose where we worked, but worked where we were assigned, so we could receive our credits for food and such.

The Mafia center also experienced many deaths, although their leader accepted the shame and released his people after one hour. By this time, the poison was in their systems and just two-thousand out of the eleven thousand survived. There were no American casualties in this raid, because the Chinese did not allow Americans or media in their Mafia centers. This turned out to be the greatest and last terrorist attack on Chinese property. The nation was stunned especially since the videos did not detect anything abnormal. The maintenance stairs to the basements were beside the men's restroom in both buildings. The tapes revealed Mitch, Jerry, George, and Larry going down these halls to the restrooms. The Chinese were serious about certain privacy matters and forbid any video of men or women going into, or leaving restrooms. To inject the poisons and chemicals took scarcely five minutes; therefore, they returned to the food courts promptly. The Chinese laughed at George and Larry for getting sodas, and commented positively on Mitch and Jerry for purchasing juices. The videos showed them going down the path to the walking trail, which made sense to them.

The extensive monitoring removed any efforts to track who came back out of the forest. They knew this path went through the park, and therefore, many people would use it to get to their homes, so a return was not an issue. Mitch was wise in that they met with George deep inside the forest. The Mafia was reduced to try to match anyone who met with someone from the other building. Ironically, they found no connection. They expanded their study of these building's traffic for twenty-four hours from 8 A.M. Their crippled staff was coming up empty in this search. China brought twenty-four thousand replacements from their homeland, and assigned two military divisions to Memphis with one goal, and that was to catch this gang. The media televised all the American funerals; many prerecorded. The papers listed their names and reported their family information, such as the widows and fatherless children. The Chinese intensified their security to such a degree; Mitch declared another future attack would be impossible. They placed three painful nails into the Chinese board. Chinese began to install gas sensors in all their buildings, plus water sensors that would detect poisons in the water. Each water outlet had new water purifying and poison alarms installed. Each room also had additional air sensors installed. The American public became angered when the cost of all this equipment was prorated over three years, and a new terrorist recovery deduction came out of the American's weekly credits. These raids became a source of anger in American discussions. Mitch and Jerry could even feel the anger of their co-workers as they complained each week when they saw the deduction from their credit. Fortunately, by spreading it over three years, the weekly bite was not too severe. Nevertheless, no one went uninfected. The public agreed the Chinese administrators should be able to work without constant fear of a painful death. The Chinese also added more Americans to their operations. Even the Mafia added the American FBI, CIA, and Federal Marshals. They decided transparencies, was not an issue because China ruled the former states.

Mitch continued to have nightmares over the Americans he killed. The media continued to run reports on them and kept the public enraged. Because terrorist activities were so unpopular, raids ceased at once. The American public had no reservations in reporting these terrorist criminals. The popular belief was America finally had a direction and had no room on this road for those who wanted to return to the days of lies, crime, poverty, starving, and padding the pockets of the wealthy. The wealth of the American division was spread equally to all, with those who made greater contributions, such as doctors receiving a little more. Lawyers were now construction workers or janitors. They would not bleed the confused in the former deranged courts. The new system was much better, in that they spent extra time from the beginning, trying to obtain evidence of innocence or guilt. These Chinese criminal investigators prided themselves in never sending an innocent person to court. They did not believe in casting questions on a jury. If they could not prove with absolute evidence, the accused was guilty they released them. Therefore, when one went in front of the judge, as there were no juries because the party considered ordinary people were too emotional to evaluate the technical evidence. The judge always studied the case before taking his seat. He or she would give the accused to offer any other information they felt was related in this case. The judged then decided on this information and pronounced the sentence, which was standardized by the party. The prosecution always reviewed their evidence with the accused before going before the judge. There were no surprises, as their intense commitment truly to prosecute the guilty. The media educated the public on this method. Many agreed this system had many advantages, as they understood the community wealth paid judicial costs. All terms were punished by hard civic labor. The philosophy was not to let these people drain the public wealth, but to add to it.

One day, Mitch received a surprised visit from the Mafia. They found a coin at one of the food markets in the Chinese center with his print on it. Initially, Mitch believed his days had ended. The Mafia could not understand how a coin could make it from Marked Tree to Memphis and into one of these food courts. Mitch confessed to the Mafia his parents lived in Memphis, and that he spent many of his credits helping to support them. The Mafia was able quickly to verify his parents address and then concluded normal Memphis money exchanges moved the coin into the market. They told Mitch they even had coins that came from California and New York. Mitch asked them if the Chinese Administrators traveled to other cities in America, considering most Americans currently did not have permission to travel across America. Mitch, feeling confident, and a thousand tons of pressure lifted from his shoulders asked the Mafia if they had ever considered a rogue Chinese terrorist group could be responsible for these attacks. They asked him why he suggests this. Mitch told them he had no proof and this was based on his vivid imagination, as he always enjoyed mysteries. Consequently, Mitch tells them he cannot see an American killed over three-hundred other Americans. In his book, he considered such a person as a murderer. Mitch also questioned how Americans could have access to any materials used in these raids and be able to deploy them so effectively and be invisible. Subsequently, Mitch adds that solitary other Chinese could slip under their radar. The next argument Mitch advances is that all the cases they caught American terrorists were for a few murders and the Saint Louis and Memphis attacks each outnumbered all the other murders combined. Mitch continues by asking the Mafia if one large American group could outperform all the others combined, then why would not they share their secrets and attacks such as this appear across this nation. One of the Mafia agents tells Mitch he is advancing a solid argument.

Mitch threw the large American group conducting the Memphis and Saint Louis raids as a curveball so as not to create the appearance of knowing any of the case details. The papers or media never disclosed the group size. The Mafia believed it was a small group, and could surmise why Mitch, a country boy, would think this was a large group due to the massive number of murders. The Mafia agents ask Mitch if he is trying to blame the Chinese for these crimes due to his dissatisfaction in the new government. Mitch clarifies that he is not blaming the Chinese, but simply recognizing a possibility. He wants the deaths of the three hundred Americans avenged. Consequently, he also acknowledges the loss of so many thousands of innocent Chinese, yet believes China will avenge their deaths. Next, he reveals how the Johnsons, who are good friends of his, were living with a Chinese family, and that a former special friend was currently living with the runaway servant named Li Jing. Subsequently, Mitch confesses that he and his friends sit on benches in Memphis and watch the beautiful young Chinese women pass them. Mitch also reports he saw younger Chinese women walking the streets of Marked Tree. Mitch assures the agents that hating and hurting these angels is the last thing on his mind. The Mafia agents begin laughing and tell Mitch he has elegantly made his point. They ask Mitch if he knows of any peculiar people in Marked Tree. Mitch begins laughing and reports to them, everyone in Market Tree is weird. The Mafia agents shake their heads in agreement; as Mitch tells them, it might not be wise for them to enlighten the locals that they are strange. They agree this is great advice. In conclusion, they thank Mitch for his time and wish him considerable luck in his work for credits. Mitch thanks them and asks for permission to return to work.

When he returns to his work area, Jerry is almost passed out. Mitch gives him water and explains what happened. Mitch knows part of the Mafia's follow up will be checking to see if I shared this case with my co-workers. An innocent person would have no reservations in sharing this case. Mitch explains to everyone how understanding the Mafia is. He recommends that they always tell the truth when being questioned by them, because they are merely trying to make our lives safer, so we can earn more credits. Mitch knew it would just be a matter of time before George, Jerry, or Larry appeared before the Mafia. He had confidence in George and Jerry, although Larry worried him. Larry was constantly worried about something and nagging without end with his complaints. It was obvious he was coming apart at the seams. Mitch met with George secretly to plan a method to execute Larry. It had to look normal and like an accident. If it appeared as a murder, the Mafia would tear the town apart looking for the murderers. Mitch came up with a plan. They would all write goodbye letters to their family and friends and, save them, in case they had to make a fast escape. Mitch and George helped everyone with their letters, trying to make them look interesting and different. Mitch's argument was that if they appeared the same, the Mafia would be looking for them as a group; however, if they seemed distinctive, they would look in other places. He asked George to talk about his missing relatives in Canada; Jerry talked about wanting to live in California; Larry revealed his desire to live in Texas as a cowboy. Mitch talked about searching for Cindy in the eastern states. When they finished, Mitch collected the letters and placed them in a nearby side tunnel where he kept his crossbow. He came back out and when he was three feet from Larry, exposed his crossbow and shot Larry in his heart. George quickly sliced his neck with his knife to make sure Larry did not make any noise. Jerry put a rope around his neck and pulled him into one of the side tunnels where they placed him in a hole they previously dug and buried him. They made sure there was no blood on their clothes, and put dirt over the blood spills, fearing the smell of blood could attract several dangerous rodents.

Mitch and George snuck over to Larry's house, gathered several of his belongings, and placed the letter on Larry's bed. This was Wednesday night; notwithstanding, Larry's parents were at church. George and Jerry went back to their homes, while Mitch dropped Larry's bag into their air vent. Late that night, Mitch received a knock at his door. It was Larry's parents, and they asked Mitch if he saw Larry. Mitch told them he saw them earlier, but told him he had to leave early because he wanted to watch TV tonight. George and Jerry gave the same reports; nevertheless, Larry's parents went to the police. The police came to Mitch's house and asked him about Larry. Mitch told them he told Larry's parents that he wanted to watch TV. He loved nature shows so much; therefore, he could be looking for certain exotic butterflies or something along that line. The police explain that Larry left a goodbye letter and asked Mitch if Larry had discussed running away. Mitch explained that his parents were great friends with Larry's parents, especially since my father ran deliveries for them many years. Larry, as all his friends appreciate that if they are talking about running away, we will tell our parents. We live by this hillbilly code. Our parents give us too much simply to throw their sacrifices away. The police, being locals, understand this code and return to their station to plan their investigation. The facts there were no body and they had his runaway letter. Larry was seventeen years old and considered an adult by many. The police questioned everyone in town, as the media ran, pictures of him with his parent's phone number. Oddly, his parents received seven phone calls from people swearing; they saw him. The police researched these callers and concluded they truly believed that they spotted him. Larry became listed as a fugitive and now the Mafia was searching for him throughout the American states. This took much pressure off Mitch, who never wanted the police or Mafia snooping to close. He always feared the Mafia would stumble over evidence by accident.

Mitch's monsters from his past continued to haunt him. He found himself not able to justify all the innocent Chinese people he killed. Why did he believe them to be evil? Now he understood their social-cultural norms. They were working to generate wealth for the American division. Mitch believed in his heart the people he killed that would have preferred to die in China. They had lived all their days in an environment they felt was safe and secure, just to discover their intestines and lungs exploding and body shutting down. The terror and absolute inability to escape must have forced them to concede defeat. This invisible invader had no mercy or compassion. Watching their friends vomit, then drop to the floor in convulsions, and end their lives crying out in absolute agony. Mitch suspected another element to this trepidation was the not knowing, what they did wrong. These people had strong spiritual beliefs, which merged Buddha, Hindu, and various elements of Christianity and a few other faiths. They all believed these pleasant things would happen to honorable people. They also believed the bad things happened to greedy and lazy people. This was how they justified the terrible things, which transpired to the Americans. Then in the final seconds of their lives to have their bodies betray them and all the other honorable people, which surrounded them so quickly. Mitch's image of their astonishing shock of a world they believed in turning upside down the burned bridges these memories destroyed in his mind and tore down any foundation he built. Mitch foolishly began this American tragedy because of his belief that Fred was persecuted by the Chinese. He received a detailed envelope one day from my father who proved to him that the American police were responsible for this crime. My father also produced Chinese's court records when punished the judge and police officers involved in this crime charging them with treason against China by inciting dissension in the public.

Mitch sat on his porch and read each of these documents repeatedly marveling at the quality of the proof. Mitch could not believe they had yet to find him. To be on the safe side, he took his gangs back to the mines and made sure any possible evidence was buried deep in the side tunnels. He justified the motorcycles in the mine as a backup form of transportation during severe storms. They rehearsed their alibis repeatedly. Mitch made sure they never visited, these sites or ran inquires on the Internet. One evening Mitch walked to the Johnson houses on Locust Street and scrounged around their homes looking for anything that might have belonged to Cindy. He figured that since Cindy ran away earlier and did not take everything; her family would take just what they needed for their move to Kansas. He found several old photographs and a diary Cindy wrote during her elementary school days. Mitch believed this would help him understand Cindy's foundation better and give him certain ideas on winning her love. The photographs included a few school pictures. Mitch stared at them for countless hours each night, filling his dreams and thoughts with Cindy. The intensity of his love continued to grow, to such a degree that he petitioned the local party authorities for permission to search for her. They explained his request would be submitted up to their headquarters who had the jurisdiction for other American divisions. This party branch could merely authorize travel in Arkansas and Kansas. Mitch paid the required credits to submit this application and waited for a decision. After two weeks, the party summoned him to their offices and explained his request was denied because Cindy was currently wedded, and they would not approve anyone that tried to disrupt a marriage. Mitch refused to accept Cindy was married. The officials presented a copy of Cindy's marriage certificate. Mitch lost his discipline, began throwing things in this office at the administrators, and screaming out of control. The officials had no choice but to alert their security who arrested Mitch. They gave Mitch a shot to calm him, and then took him to a holding cell.

The Chinese did not favor jails except for a condition they believed to be temporary. The doctors who examined him believed he was suffering from an emotional overload. Mitch had an excellent production history; therefore, the party believed he could once more become a contributor to the public wealth. Even though Mitch was holding on by his teeth, he was still able to keep his famous raids a secret, much to the relief of George and Jerry, who never mentioned this when visiting Mitch. They knew that he was under constant observation now. They tried to talk about work issues and things their friends were doing. Mitch cried each night for Cindy. The Chinese party told him he would be wiser to get a Chinese wife and make a happy family. The motivating factor for Chinese who married non-asian Americans was they could have up to three children. Unfortunately, China would not give full citizenship to these children. Many viewed this as a method the Chinese were using to increase their non-citizen population. Citizenship did not produce many additional benefits, as the credit for work tables paid the same, and all were eligible for occupational training based on their exam scores. The Chinese citizens also had to do their two years of military service, and there was no voting for public officials in the central party made all the decisions. The media have compared the rights and privileges of each and discovered the noncitizens actually had added legal rights. China granted this provision to help in the transition process. Americans understood the need for more security credit deductions because of the Saint Louis and Memphis disasters. The Chinese population was still angry because their intelligence could not solve this mystery. This needed justice and confirmation the gods approved what China was doing in America.

The Mafia broadcast that they had an additional method to identify people other than DNA, and fingerprints. This new method, which would be operational with one-hundred percent coverage within two months, would use scalp and skeleton matching. Their current video recording could produce accurate X-rays, as these X-rays would be matched against their massive video database. The system had undergone debugging for the previous seven years in China, where it currently had every resident's data file functional. The American database was operational, with the last few months being dedicated to match a skeleton with everyone's master record. The Chinese new Tien-lung (protector of the skies and palaces of the Gods) hydro-based computer was approximately ten-thousand times faster than any other computer ever to exist with unlimited and instantaneous storage capacity. The Chinese took this system one-step further by backing up all their data in satellites, which rotated around the Earth. They were launching an average of one satellite each day for their advanced surveillance system. Their system was in place, as they were now setting up their blanket, umbrella for Canada and establishing their forward warning systems for Europe, Russia, Africa, and South America. Mitch did not worry so much about the Memphis raid since he made it a habit to jog with George and

Jerry through town. They would also jog in Memphis when visiting his parents. He constantly picked new routes to mix the courses. Mitch continually practiced excuses about why they never returned to the raided facilities. Their logical excuse was the fear of lung or digestive poisoning from any surrounding vegetation. Mitch continues to impress his gang members with his ability to remove the specific knowledge of this operation and function in the blind. He felt comfortable with this plan, and as he went to relax, his mind decided to take him on another Cindy ride.

Even Mitch confessed to George that this intensity of compulsion was not normal. George asked him if he had any interests in other women. Mitch argued the honor of his heritage forbids this. Jerry told Mitch to look around, because the old Marked Tree and America were in our history. We lived in a modern world now. Jerry warned Mitch that he must adapt to the new world and learn to survive by its rules and one such system that changed was the old mating rules. He was free to select fresh mates, and if they agreed, he could advance the relationship. If they do not agree, move on to other women. George bragged that he had already dated and kissed four different girls, two Americans and two Chinese. Mitch asked him which he preferred. George told Mitch the Chinese girls appeared to have more confidence, discipline and were actually skilled kissers. Jerry agrees completely, and adds the Chinese girls treat you with more respect, which is opposite what you would expect from an occupying force. Mitch asks Jerry how many women he has dated. Jerry tells him six, two Americans and the last four Chinese. Mitch asks Jerry why he has dated so many Chinese. Jerry confesses to be afraid to develop too deep of an emotional bond with one yet, because he does not realize how stable America will be. He does not want to take a sweet innocent girl and give her a life of misery. Once he feels more secure, he will take the plunge. Mitch commends Jerry on the responsibility he is taking in these relationships. Mitch also asks his friends why they never mentioned, this previously. George tells Mitch they suspected he liked boys instead of girls, having a bitter taste with women after Cindy. Mitch assures them, he is interested in dating women, yet needs a push to break the chains that tradition has on him. George jogs Mitch's memory about their school days, how their classmates could not wait for their parents to sell their farms; therefore, they could move to the big city and start modern lives. All the other students would envy them, claiming they wished they could start new. Mitch reminds George they are still living in Marked Tree. Jerry argues that Mitch's parents sold their farm, hence technically, he is living in Memphis, and the old social order and customs are history. George agrees by telling Mitch that we live in a new world, so simply a fool would die in the old world.

Mitch asks how he should talk with Chinese's girls. Jerry tells him simply to smile and act normal. Never assume they understand what you are saying. Remember, just the Mafia knows everything. The working people work just as we do, if not harder. Fortunately, the Chinese still filled most of the labor-intensive work to Chinese and American prisoners, believing the American public was not quite ready for this. Jerry warns that if you act like a monster, these women will think you are a monster. They are just as afraid of us as we are of them. Remember, we are the ones with blood on our hands. Jerry clarified the 'we' was all Americans. We were the people who lived such a high standard of living, while most of the world starved and suffered as slaves trying to feed our greed. Mitch confesses that if he knew, he would have demonstrated against it. Jerry reminds him the capitalist powers would have shut him down, just as they stopped the politicians trapping them in a jail cell tighter than that of many prisons. Mitch wonders why no one ever attacked these insanely wealthy powers. Jerry tells him they were invisible and extremely deadly, as they chewed up foreigners as we munch gum. George tells them they needed to count their blessings the Chinese understood whom the true criminals were in this financial battlefield. The wealthy foolishly believed the public would continue to allow them to exploit them as they fell into starvation and ruin. The Chinese party argues the people must have food and an opportunity to contribute to the shared wealth. Mitch confesses how the thought not owning any property was horrified until he saw this new system provided housing. This system also upgraded your housing when you got married and with each birth of a child, up to the maximum of three for any couple that had one non-asian partner.

Mitch begins crying once again, confessing a fear, he always had growing old alone. The loss of Cindy represented the loss of a hope for a future family. She took this from him. George could endure this no longer and argues with Mitch that Cindy took nothing from him, and she never gave him any reason to think she wanted a relationship, beyond that as defined by her father, with him. Jerry vents his frustration as well as explaining Cindy had to give up her hometown in fear that when he was released from his mental hospital, he would destroy her life. Mitch argues that he would never destroy her life. George tells Mitch that he would destroy her life, just as he wants to do now by searching for her. Mitch argues this is not true; he simply wants to find out if she is doing well. Jerry tells Mitch to awaken; Cindy is married, so she is her husband's responsibility. George agrees the one custom we must keep from the days of old is the sanctity of marriage. We have to support this if we want the same protection for our wives when we marry someday. Mitch argues Cindy should have told him she was going to marry and not have him find out about it from others. George tells Mitch Cindy had no such obligation. He remembers how she told him repeatedly that George Johnson was her intended. She told him kindly the first hundred times, and then she became hostile with her answers. George tells Mitch he made a fool out of himself through this childish embarrassing behavior. Mitch argues that Cindy made a fool out of him. Jerry rebuts by telling Mitch he cannot spend the remainder of his life blaming everything on Cindy, until he gets a grip on himself. He must accept this blame. Mitch accuses George and Jerry of taking Cindy's side against him. He believes that they also have romantic interests in Cindy. George shakes his head in disbelief claiming that Mitch planned the three greatest raids on the Chinese, and remains free, yet cannot handle the rejection of one small-town girl. Jerry tells Mitch he can see how beautiful the young Chinese girls who now live in Marked Tree are, and that he is a fool or blind not to notice this. Mitch begins to shake. George and Jerry can see that Mitch is getting ready to unleash his pent-up anger. Jerry tells Mitch to get this out as Mitch hits him in his nose and then pops George in his left eye. Jerry and George run out of the house trying to find any cover or concealment.

Mitch runs to his bed and opens a bottle of Jim Beam; he saved for celebrations. He drinks the bottle within a few hours and passes out. Sunday he was too depressed to get out of bed, except for using the toilet. Mitch recognizes Jerry and George are correct and innocent people have suffered because of his emotional imbalance. He also confesses that Cindy may have been the best-looking girl in their grade, but she was not the best looking at school. There were a couple of freshmen girls who were causing boys to walk into walls. Each day, Mitch fell deeper into his depression. After missing three straight days without contacting his occupational leader, the people's party sent soldiers to his house to apprehend him. They feared that he might have begun his search for Cindy without permission. To their surprise and relief, they found him in bed, too weak to respond to their orders. They contacted the emergency medical team that took him to the hospital. The doctors noted Mitch had no signs of hostility, so they concentrated on returning vital nutrients to his body. The Chinese public party questioned George and Jerry on their views about why Mitch was not adhering to the production standards. They told these officials that Mitch was still emotionally attached to Cindy and needed to have his confidence restored so he could learn how to court females. These administrators asked how Mitch could not understand how so far. Jerry explained the Arkansas law enforcement took him out of school and put him in a mental hospital. Then, he was recently released by the Chinese. His parents sold their farm and moved to Memphis, yet Mitch wanted to resume his life here in Marked Tree. They believed so much had changed that when he re-entered it was overwhelming. Jerry believes having a Chinese female friend could be the lifeboat to get him back on the river of production.

Jerry has already learned that when you spoke about something having a positive effect on production, the party administrators would give it an open review. They asked Jerry and George why they were so animated about matching Mitch with a Chinese girl. Jerry and George confessed to currently dating Chinese's girls. The central committee believed that Chinese-American marriages would help unify this new workforce and stabilize future programs. They actively recruited homeland males and females who expressed interest in American spouses. They underwent an extensive two-year English language program and shipped to the United States. Searching for an American spouse was an acceptable reason to request reassignment to another district. Chinese was the official language of the American states, with English as a second language. The party recognized the Americans needed translators when interacting with Chinese. All other languages, including Spanish, were outlawed in public. Anyone caught speaking another language in public would have credits deducted from the families pay. Speaking other languages on the phone or cell phone was discouraged, yet not punishable. The party justified this by claiming it helped the public to receive the benefits they should receive. The central committee enacted an amendment concerning citizenship. All adolescents who completed the K-12 party's indoctrination and social education program were given citizenship at graduation, regardless of race or heritage. These children would be fluent Chinese speakers. The media were offering Chinese language courses on public television in the hopes it would increase Chinese language speakers in the American division. Chinese was now the number-one secondary language taught in the world. This revealed how the world felt about an American recovery under rule by China. Chinese advanced technology combined with American resources would provide a partnership that would be hard to beat.

Mitch had a beating he needed to overcome if he were to survive and have a family in the future. The doctors explained to Mitch, they were going to offer him group therapies that they designed to help him develop a new set of coping skills. It was impossible to deny the vast improvement in medical care to everyone existing under the Chinese's rule. The party had other incentives, and those were healthy people produced more. Healthcare was a production component if they were to have a workforce. Any shortcuts or deprivations would cost them more in the end. Jerry, witnessing this form of social care, said for the first time in his life, he felt part of something and was part of him. The common argument by the media was that all wealth was the people's wealth and shared equally. The party occasionally offered bonus credits for specified occupations or activities. They had annual photography, painting, and poetry contests. The party decided to reopen the professional sports, with many revisions. Games would seldom be televised, although one football game each week and all the Super Bowls, and World Series of baseball and basketball, and the Stanley Cup. They were not extensively interested in hockey except from the standpoint that it was popular in Canada and would be an excellent productive motivator later for the Canadians when they joined as part of the American States. Attendance at all professional sports games was controlled by the people's party who issued the free tickets based on individual production performances. The people's party gave everyone a ticket for their birthday. The families submitted a joint attendance request, so they could celebrate their birthday game together on the same day. The general rule was those who worked harder and contributed extra received more of the public rewards. The reward for any information that led to the capture of the Saint Louis or Memphis raiders was five years of tickets to their favorite team in the region.

Mitch attended his first group meeting where they discussed coping skills. He returned to his new hospital room, which was carpeted, pictures, and books. They did not allow TVs; game consoles, or radios believing this promoted separation and introversion. The party recognized people needed people for effective production. Mitch picked up a book on Chinese's history as his new nurse walked into the room. Mitch almost had a heart attack, because she was so beautiful. She asked Mitch his name, when Mitch forgot his name. Accordingly, she tells Mitch it is rude for him not to talk to her. Mitch points to his nametag attached to his shirt. Therefore, she tells Mitch her name is Huang Yue, which means yellow moon. She laughs and asks Mitch if he ever saw a yellow moon. Mitch smiles and shakes his head no. Huang Yue gives Mitch a drink of water, massages his throat lightly and once more asks him to tell her his name. Mitch introduces himself, claiming Huang Yue has performed a miracle. Mitch tries to tell her he has always had trouble speaking with women. Huang Yue sits down beside his bed, takes a towel, wipes his face, and tells him she cannot believe one so handsome would have trouble talking with women. She accuses him of playing 'hard to give.' Mitch explains to her this is called 'hard to get,' and he never had enough opportunities to play this game. Huang Yue asks Mitch if he were interested in her life story. Mitch admits that his story is too boring to tell, so hers would be better. Huang Yue pulls out a map of her region in China and shows Mitch the town she was born in, the river; she bathed and caught fish, the hills she used to play, and the big city that she moved. She told Mitch the factory work hurt her back from having to bend all day. She begged her regional people's party for an occupational change. She wanted to be a nurse; thereby she studied nursing books at night for two years. She got a perfect score on the nursing entrance exam; therefore, the party sent her to nursing school. She passed both the Chinese nursing exam and the California state nursing exam, which is required now in China if a nurse desires to work in America.

Her father tried to sell her to a businessperson to be his wife. Huang Yue reports that she went to the people's party and asked to be assigned to America. Huang Yue tells Mitch that in China, she may have just one baby, but here she may have three if she marries an American. She confesses to be sad because all the American men believe her to be ugly. Mitch jumps out of bed and hugs her crying out that she is so beautiful. Huang Yue tells him she will purely believe this if he kisses her. Mitch immediately kisses her and when he finishes, he passes out on the bed. Huang Yue pushes the emergency button as the medical staff rushes in to verify the severity of his condition. They determine that he is okay. She asks for permission to sit beside him until he recovers. Her superiors grant this request, hoping they can soon add one more nurse to the married list. Mitch wakes up an hour later and rejoices when he sees Huang Yue sitting beside him. He was afraid their encounter was a dream. Huang Yue asks him if her kiss was so awful, it made him sick. Mitch assures her it was the greatest event in his life. She asks him if they kiss again, will he stay conscious. They kiss for almost one entire hour, when having to stop because of his room buzzer. Mitch asks her what does this mean. She tells him he has guests. Mitch asks her to bring him the food after these visitors leave, because for the first time in over a week, he is hungry. Huang Yue goes out to the waiting room and escorts George and Jerry back to Mitch's room, and then excuses herself, as she must get the cafeteria to prepare a special meal. Huang Yue reports Mitch's recovery and his appetite to the doctors, who decide to monitor his conversation looking for signs of recovery.

George asks Mitch, who is laying in his bed with a great smile, how he is doing. Mitch tells them he is feeling wonderful, except for being hungry and the hospital is working on that for him now. Mitch asks how work is going, and then promises to beg the hospital to let him go back to work the upcoming Monday. Jerry tells him this would be great, if he is ready. Mitch tells them about the group sessions they have and how he feels it is helping him. George asks him if he remembers what caused him to be here. Mitch shakes his head no. Jerry, wanting to make sure this recovery is solid fearing the multiple hospital visits could cause Mitch to lose his occupation, asks Mitch if the name Cindy means anything to him. Mitch denies having any special emotions for a Cindy. Mitch reminds them that Cindy is married, and that it would be wrong even to talk about such things. Jerry and George agree and ask Mitch if he has anyone new in his life. As he prepares to answer Huang Yue comes in the room with three sodas and demands to see who Cindy is. George, looking surprised, tells her Cindy was a friend from long ago. Mitch sits up as Huang Yue hands each one soda and gives Mitch a kiss telling George and Jerry that Mitch is hers. She excuses herself by revealing that she is going to the cafeteria to get her man a man's dinner. She asks George and Jerry if they also want any food. They tell her this night should be for her and Mitch. Subsequently, after she leaves the room, George and Jerry congratulated him on getting a female friend who is beautiful, but as a nurse gets extra credits in her weekly pay. For the first time in such a long time, Mitch feels free to love and begin his life afresh. The three sang a few songs, after which George and Jerry update him on work and Marked Tree news. The doctors are signing Mitch's recovery forms agreeing that since Huang Yue has made her claim, Mitch will be in great hands. George and Jerry offer to help Mitch and Huang Yue set up their home. Mitch asks how they can be so confident that such an angel would want to be with him. Jerry tells Mitch that Huang Yue has put her mark on him, and knowing this room is bugged; her authorities heard it. For Mitch to refuse her now would put her in great shame. She must have believed in Mitch to make such a solid claim. Mitch confesses that he would give both arms and legs to have Huang Yue in his life. George teases him by telling him to keep his arms and legs and give her his heart.

Mitch assures them that Huang Yue has his heart. He adds it is like being in heaven to have love in his life.

Subsequently, the alarms in the hospital sound as the intercom warned everyone to stay out of the common areas and go to their rooms preparing for an inspection. Mitch asks Jerry if he knows of such inspections. Jerry reveals once they had an inspection at his work, and it is merely routine. Next, they hear running in the hallways and finally a group of ten soldiers rush into their room holding them at gunpoint. The soldiers check them for weapons and then handcuff them. Accordingly, four-party leaders come into the room with the press and formally charge Mitch, Jerry, and George with the Saint Louis and both Memphis slaughters. The leaders move into the hall to lead their march out of the hospital. The crowds in front of them move forward planning the reform in the hospital's outside entrance. The soldiers sandwich themselves surrounding Mitch, Jerry, and George trying to protect them. Everyone, both Chinese and American in the hospital are screaming obscenities and demanding justice. Huang Yue rushes back to the floor to discover what the commotion concerned. When she discovered it, she threw a soda can that hit Mitch in the head and cursing him for deceiving her. She was the lone one permitted to throw an object, because the people believed that significant others suffered as much as the victims in a crime did. The people's party had to deploy an entire division to get Mitch, George, and Jerry safely to the party's headquarters in Memphis. Here, the prosecution presented their evidence to them. The deal breaker was the skeletal match of Mitch and George in both raids. They administered a three-dimensional scan on the three once more to get a one-hundred percent comparison. The comparison came back a faultless match with no error or chance of misidentification. Mitch knew they could not refute this evidence as they watched the videos reform their faces under their masks to a perfect match. The party did not want to understand how they committed these slaughters fearing others would copy them. They wanted this freak of murder program to die with them. The prosecution took them to court to stand in front of the judge.

The judge reviewed the evidence, trying to concentrate as hundreds of thousands of demonstrators was rioting outside the center. The party refused to disband the demonstrators believing the people had a right to express their anger at the massacre of so many innocents. The judge ordered all three stripped, given ten lashes, then tied to poles and slowly burned alive. The media covered the complete execution. The residents of Marked Tree were shocked and left in confusion, offering the single defense that Mitch was declared a mental danger to society by the United States, and released by the Chinese. This was strong enough for the media to clear Marked Tree of any wrongdoing. Cindy, Lisa, Lee, and I reemerged as the heroes that escaped from Mitch's evil. The Chinese now took credit for Lee claiming she must have sensed their dire situation. The party inspired the media to promote this idea, believing the nation needed much encouragement throughout this healing process. The central committee was relieved to see the degree of support for Mitch, George, and Jerry's executions. Everyone believed the murders of so many innocents, who most felt were working hard for a better future for American-Chinese. The police moved Mitch's parents into protective custody. The major effect of Mitch's raids was that it eliminated the terrorist cells in America, as the intensive search for Mitch exposed them. America once more had its sense of security, in knowing these no rogue governments were trying to undermine the new-shared public wealth they were struggling to build. The party was no longer under pressure of servants escaping, because all servants were released. The media began to petition for Li Jing's declaration of innocence. The party agreed that Li Jing's contributions in keeping the Johnson's away from Mitch could have, in reality, saved lives, believing that if Mitch had Cindy, he would have killed more to impress her. The other strong argument was that these Americans had not committed any acts against China during their time together.

Chapter 09

Repatriation

The mountain sang its quiet songs as the sun glowed on the icy snow, nevertheless, we did not notice. The intensity that Lisa and Phillip were kissing loosened Cindy. I decided now was just as good as any time; therefore, I reached again and wrapped my arms around Cindy and lifted her over to my saddle, seating her in front of me in my saddle. Cindy reaches over and grabs her horses bridle while retrieving the reigns. She secures the reins on my saddle horn. This is more of a precautionary measure for such things as snakes, which will put our horses in panic, and they run in any direction for their escape. We have been fortunate in gaining their confidence during this anxiety-filled situation. Now that her horse is secured, I lean over, lift her out of her seat, and sit her in front of me in my saddle. Subsequently, I rotate her around so she is facing me. This may have produced romantic excitement if it were any other time of the year except the eye of the dead of winter. Sure, there is not a power icy wind and oceans of snow, flooding our land, at least for a few more shaky days. Her eyes are the sources of my refreshing sunshine. We begin a series of kisses, fearing that our saliva could freeze us to each other. I can feel her frustration, as she is consequently, dedicated to our marriage, yet somehow we have never had any time to search deep in each other's heart. Any time that we begin a conversation in our cabin, either Lee or Lisa will jump in, and most times Lisa joins Cindy and Lee joins me. The argument always tends to move away from its original focus onto something that really has no great bearing on an issue, which needs solving for our immediate survival needs. One time, three months into our marriage, Cindy and I could ride our horses back into the pastures behind our cabin and up on the ridge where we found a small meadow. Behaving like two high school children behind the schoolhouse, we consummated our marriage. I hated that we had to do it like this; however, Cindy felt a deep sense of obligation to fulfill her perceived duty as a wife and grew hostile toward me for not taking advantage of this minute opportunity. I am one for absolute privacy, and do not even enjoy the thought of a bird watching me. She felt wonderful afterwards and struggled hard to make me suffer less. I tried to tell her it was not supposed to be like this. However, at that time, she told me that Roberta, Lisa, and Lee needed us as much as we needed each other. I finally understood what she meant when I closed Roberta's eyes for the last time. Love has no absolute method of manifestation. I consider myself fortunate to have a wife who was so dedicated to Roberta and Lisa. Now, with Lisa married and Roberta resting in peace, I believe Cindy may be testing our new waters. I can see from Lisa since then we started our return trip; she is not going to be as constrained as Cindy was. I wonder if she may be fighting for Cindy's freedom as much as for her. That evening, I take a short walk with Lisa while we gather more firewood. I ask Lisa how she is doing. She confesses not to understand how Cindy could control herself all this time in our cabin. I tell her that Cindy has always worshipped Lisa as much as she would a mother.

Lisa tells me she is now Phillip's wife, and that role will take over her role as an older sister. She looks me cold in my eye and tells me that she can no longer accept the risk for our security; this task placed too great a burden on her heart. Lisa stares me straight in my eye and challenges me to deny that Phillip would not be a finer protector than she can be. I explain to Lisa that Phillip will be a greater defender solely if he is protecting us through her love for him. I ask Lisa if she married Phillip for us or for herself. Lisa asks me if I have been watching them. I told her she was hotter than any cat I ever saw. Lisa smiles at me and tells me they need to hear much noise from my sleeping bag tonight. I ask her why. She reveals that Phillip is as conservative as I am. I tell her Cindy has waited long enough. Lisa pleads with me to make her proud of her little brother. This shatters my mind. I do not want my older sister, knowing these things, nor do I want to grasp these things about her. Lisa tells me not to worry, because they are not going to be listening to us. Lisa boldly tells me we are married now and have responsibilities to our spouses. I recognize that she is right, nevertheless, sometimes right just does not feel right. Phillip gets a radio message from Peter, who tells us a large storm is heading our way, and that we need to get on the path early tomorrow morning a hurry to our cabin. Cindy and Lisa appear disappointed, yet when our survival was at risk understood, we do what must be done to continue. Our women stand their ground tonight slapping us each time we snore. Phillip explains to me that many times the righteous must suffer at the hands of the wicked. He was slapped for that remark, and I was slapped for agreeing with him. I advise Phillip not to worry, when we get to our cabin, Lee will save us.

Cindy tells me that I cannot depend on Lee always to save me. Lisa argues with Cindy agreeing that Lee will never fail to save her baby brother. Lisa, on the other hand, looks at Phillip and tells him Lee may not save him. I notify Phillip that I will put in a special request for Lee to have mercy. Lisa changes the subject by telling us we need to get a jump on the path, because we did waste much time yesterday. Phillip informs us it is still too dark to ride our horses, so we will walk in front of them staying equally close to the inside hill as possible. Phillip volunteers to lead the way with the women following him and me at the rear protecting us from a rear ambush. I think this is the first time in my life; I am worried about being last. Any ways, we packed our gear rapidly, and had two hours of walking in by sunup. This was when Phillip told us to mount up and head for our home. He wanted us to keep the same formation, except he moved Cindy into the second position telling us today was not a day for any distractions. I would be strictly business. We made excellent time and around ten in the morning Phillip sent back word that if we kept our same pace, we should make it to our cabin late tonight, or early tomorrow morning. If we had to camp, we would be close enough in the morning to walk our horses home. We did not want to use the second option, out of mutual respect for our animals. The storm finally hit one hour before sundown. Phillip estimated that we were two hours by horseback, or four hours of walking from our cabin. The issue that worried him was identifying our ridge. I knew Lee would have the fire going high, since she chilled easily. I also knew Sunday, and Easter would be in the cabin with her. We still felt bad in leaving her alone, yet at the last minute, we decided to bring her to help with additional supplies. A big problem that we now would have is having three horses and one cow in our small stable. Phillip tells us the horses can be tied outside during the days and the stable doors open for them to come and go as they please at night. We would tie the cow in the stable stall furthest from the door. He also knew of a farm a few hours from us that we could leave two of the horses if we needed. We would decide this in February.

My idea was to bang on a pan when I began to feel we were within one-hour walk. Lisa and I explored this portion of our trail, and I knew the path went up, made a sharp half circle turn, went up a little more, dropped, and then flattened out. I knew of no other features such as this along the path. I also remember a patch of three trees that hung over this path before the sharp half circle. I passed this information up to Phillip, so we could be on the lookout. The plan was to begin banging on our pans once we started on the even path after the drop. I figured that we would be within twenty minutes of our cabin. Accordingly, Sunday and Easter, being trapped inside the cabin would begin barking. Their barking could cut through any snowstorm. After a few minutes on this flattened stretch, we would begin poking the side of the trail trying to detect any paths leading down into the valley below. We could also expect the smoke from our cabin to add a burned wood smell to the crisp mountain air. I knew that once our path started going up, we had gone too far. Fortunately, fate had mercy on us, as the smoke smell and dogs barking motivated the four of us to check for the side path. Phillip and Cindy missed it; however, Lisa found it, told me, and moved up to inform Cindy and Phillip to stop. I took my rod and verified our path's width, and began poking it to make sure it was safe. I did not remember any other paths along this ridge in this immediate area; nonetheless, to be safe I wanted to make sure this was secure. I guided my horse all the way down and walked over to our stable, put my horse inside, gave him selected dried grass, and headed back to the ridge. Once up, I told the gang, we were home and took the cow from Lisa and told everyone to follow me and to stay close to the inside wall. We made it down, packed our animals in the stable, and unloaded them. Lisa and Cindy went to our cabin door and started giving Lee our supplies.

Sunday and Easter came rushing outside to visit with Phillip and me. These dogs appear to favor men, and we can appreciate this. Thankfully, they also care and protect my angels. Lee is shocked when I tell her Lisa is wedded, and we have the official documents for my marriage. We also show her our identification cards. Lee looks at these documents and asks us where we got them. Phillip reveals that Peter received them for us. Lee noticed that box seventeen on our marriage certificates has a 9c code. I ask her if that means anything. Lee does not understand for sure, except nines are a code her government always used signaled they had additional information available, or that they were working with other authoritative organizations. With this, Lee confesses she does not recognize this exactly, since she has little contact with administrative documents. Easter and Sunday are scratching at our door, since our stable is packed tight. I take our shovel and dig the snow away from the front door by at least ten feet. We will check on the door every few hours to make sure we can open it. It would not be healthy for us to be trapped inside this cabin. Lee had a pleasant meal prepared for the hot blazing fire and us. Phillip and I bring in a few more days of firewood. It usually takes a couple of days for the wood to thaw so we can burn it. Once we get our wood loaded up, animals feed, and stable door locked, we head for our toasty cabin. We decided not to leave any animals out during this storm, since the snow is piling up quickly, which makes it extremely difficult for them to find winter brush. They will be better in the stables with at least one warm wall to draw a little of the heat from our cabin's logs. Lisa is concerned the wind will blow snow over our door. Phillip tells her we moved the snow we cleared to the backside of our cabin and pilled it against the wall, and then packed it with our shovels. This is to prevent the wind from striking these logs and to hold in the cabin's heat. He believes the snow that is against the warm logs will melt and then refreeze again providing us a thick coat of insulating ice. Lee compliments him on this knowledge. Phillip tells us this is common to all those who live in the freezing mountains.

After our dinner, we decided to unpack our new supplies, causing Lee to assume her position. We line up, each with a few objects, report to Lee, who tells us where to put it. The confused Phillip jumps behind me and asks if this is for real. I tell him that he does not want that job. I tried it and begged Lee to relieve me. I had to teach her how to ride a horse as my payment. Phillip asks how this can be so hard. He stands in front of Lee; she points to each item he has and tells him precisely where to put it and why it should go there. Phillip smiles at her and thanks her as he rushes to do exactly as she tells him. Lisa whispers back to Phillip the greatest help is Lee remembers where she told us to put it. This allows us to store more in a smaller area. Cindy tells him that Lee remembers it when we are doing something that could benefit from it. Lee asks Cindy to stop playing, because we have work to do. I tell Phillip that Lee is serious about how our home functions. Phillip smiles at me and confesses that maybe being ruled by the Chinese might not be as bad as he thought. Lisa tells him the one thing she knows is he will be ruled by one while living here. Lee smiles at Phillip and claims she has yet to meet an American she could not tame. Phillip laughs telling Lee the lone Americans she knows are here. Lee tells him this is because they love her and will not let her leave. Lisa, Cindy, and I agree that we love Lee too much and beg her to stay with us. Lisa asks Lee if she wants us to make Phillip sleep with our animals. Lee tells him we must let Phillip stay in our cabin, so he can see how forgiving she is. Phillip smiles and thanks her. Phillip confesses to me that living in the same cabin with Lee. I tell Phillip the day he moves away from Lee will be a sad day in his life. Phillip smiles at me and asks why such a day should come. I agree that such a day need not to come unless wanted.

That night Lisa and Phillip put their sleeping bags in the opposite corner from our fireplace. Lee put ours out as we always had done. Cindy and I realized Lee felt as she belongs to us. I smile at Cindy, go over to Lee, and ask her if she is going to help keep me warm tonight or Cindy? Lee asks us if she can keep both of us snug. I see that I fell into that one and there is no way to get out of it now. Cindy smiles, points for Lee to lie down beside her, and for me to drop to her other side. I smile and say, "Mommy, we have our baby with us." Cindy agrees, and we snuggle together. It is too cold to push anyone away tonight. Lee asks us since Lisa and Cindy, are now married and someday have their babies, will she be permitted to have children. I tell Lee we will help her every way we can. She will have her own family. Lee tells us she wants to be a part of our family. Cindy promises that she will enjoy having her own special husband. Lee wonders what she will do if no one wants to marry her, especially since we will have a criminal record that many will fear the new Chinese government will treat them poorly. What will she do if this was to happen, will we make her live a life with a barren womb? Cindy promises Lee that if she cannot find a husband, she will make me make her pregnant. Lee then asks Cindy if she will hate her baby. Cindy tells Lee she could never hate any baby unless it looks like me and then laughs. I tell Lee we would be miserable if we thought her loyalty and love for us would cause her to suffer. Cindy agrees with me and promises Lee that she is our bundle of love. She asks Lee how many married couples would let her sleep with them. I hate to tell Cindy that if the husbands were to decide, Lee would never sleep alone again. Cindy thinks about what the wives would say, I can rest assured that when they see how beautiful Lee is, Cindy would be sent scooting back to us. Lee is in our bed because we give her birth as her old life died. We saw her give up everything, and we felt her surrender everything for us. She would do anything for us, as I saw with Roberta's revenge. We each have a reason for loving Lee. I am not going to enlighten Cindy over my belief how husbands would respond, and instead will snuggle tight with Lee. I justify the sealed snuggle as my intent to get closer to Cindy. Cindy thanks me for trying to love her so much. Lee asks me to love Cindy a little less so she can breathe. We laugh, including Lee as I feel her soft body trickle, as best I can describe it.

Morning comes, and Phillip's walkie-talkie (WK) begins to clatter. Phillip answers it. Peter wanted to make sure we got here safe. He tells us he is worried about Lee not getting outside any and feels it would be good for her to go horseback riding today. Lee stands up, face shines, begins lightly to hop, and shakes her head yes. I get on this WK and tell him it might be hard to get her outside; however, I will find a way to bribe her. Peter thanks me for my hard work. I tell Lee we are going horse riding and ask Cindy if she wishes to go with us so all the horses get selected time outside in the fresh air. Cindy agrees to go for the horse's sake. Lee thanks Cindy for her sacrifice. We rush to the stable to mount the horses. Usually, I would do this, yet today Lee is so eager to get outside, and Cindy does not want to be outdone. I recommend that we walk our horses to exit path and once on the ridge ride for about one hour to an excellent lookout point. Cindy confesses that she never saw this point. I tell her I discovered it with Lisa when we searched what was ahead of us. Cindy gets excited, and I can see the enthusiasm flood through her. I tell them I will walk first, Lee second, so we will always have her safeguarded, and Cindy protecting our rear. Lee tells Cindy not to worry; she will be keeping an eye on her. This appears to calm Cindy. I tell them we must stay in a straight line close to our hilly side. Lee catches on fast and follows in my steps, as does Cindy. I take smaller steps, so they can stay in my steps. I can see that Lee needed this and marveled that Peter knew. We are fortunate this last snowstorm is deeper in the mountains. The disadvantage is it stays against the highest mountains longer as it tries slowly to work its way over dumping most of what it has.

Cindy and Lee become exited when we arrive at my special lookout. I never noticed before that it has a fascinating meadow on the opposite side, which is perfect for letting our horse graze a little. The brute wind blew most of the snow into the valleys below. I always bring a rope with me, so I will tie the rope from one tree to another and then tie each horse's bridle to it. This will allow them to find various brush packed under the thin frozen ice. I take my ax and whack a few cracks for them. Accordingly, I walk back to Lee and Cindy, who found them a large rock to sit on, where they enjoy a wonderful view. I ask them if I can join. They make an opening for me in the middle. Cindy and Lee lean forward to finish their conversation. I remember how impressed I was with this lookout when I first saw it; nevertheless, I am sitting here in astonishment. I not only see the ridge in front of me, but also see what feels like a world of raging high mountains that appear to keep rising in the heavens. They look so impassible from here. I understand that they would have to search for a long time to find a pass through it, and if they cannot, they would need to discover a path around it. Either way, they are not going over it. I get that we have a few towering peeks behind us, and we are fortunate Peter knew of the secret ridge allowed us to make it to our hidden valley. I tell Lee that when she lies back on the ground, she can take off her sunglasses. Cindy asks me if this is safe. I tell her that if anyone from above us can make that minute detection, he or she will find us any ways. Lee tells us not to worry, because the sun is too bright for her to open her eyes. I inform Cindy the sunshine is important for Lee's face. Cindy tells me the sun is significant for all our skin. I chuckle, and then reveal to Cindy the health gain from the sunshine would be offset from the severe flu that would follow. We laugh in agreement. I declare this much open space makes our cabin feel so small. Lee tells me not to worry; the warmth complements the lack of space. Lee shares with us that this view brings back many fond memories of her homeland. Although she was never in the giant mountains, she saw many pictures and read many stories about them.

We spend most of the day here, and then take our horses back to the cabin, where Phillip and Lisa have a pleasant meal awaiting us. Phillip tells us the latest news. The central committee has freed all servants in America and authorized them to go to other districts and train for new occupations. Phillip adds there are over seven million Chinese in this American division currently. This does not count the two million military being deployed to help the people in the transition process. Phillip asks Lee if she sees anything questionable in this. Lee confesses no one ever told them they would be set free here. They told her that they could marry Americans, and if they married an American, they may have three children. She remembers being promised an occupation, they were qualified. Notwithstanding, when they arrived here, they were shuffled into their hidden sweatshops and told the Americans were trying to find and destroy them. We had to remain concealed. Lee tells us the party must believe the states are secured if they are permitting the people to relocate and travel around this territory freely. I ask her how these people can roam around this land, where will they sleep, eat, and live when they arrive at their destination. Lee reports that they will take busses. The party will give those tickets for food, lodging, and busses. When they arrive at their approved destination, the party will retrieve and settle them into their new homes. Most will live in the giant apartment complexes, which currently have many Americans living in these. A party security measure is mixing Americans with Chinese. Phillip asks if they have mixed her with us for security. Lee tells him this security just works with qualified party members and not outlaws. She tells Phillip they will burn him alive. Phillip smiles at Lee and tells him it will be worth it while we keep her safe. Lee wishes him success in this task.

Lisa asks Lee why they believed Americans hated them. Lee explains this is because of the long history of racial tensions in the United States. They took everything from the native Indians and then massacred them. Lee asks how people can tell the world they believe in God, turn around, and murder Indian women and children. The party created many American western movies showing the savage murder of the Indians. Lee continues by describing the way Americans persecuted the Asians who came to America, forcing them to work dangerous jobs for such little money. They survived by staying secluded and accepting the harsh and unfair treatment from the Americans. Lee acknowledges the white Americans bought black slaves and worked them on painful plantations, with all manners of injustices inflicted on them. Not all men were created equal in the former United States. After their civil war, they freed the blacks, yet treated them as animals. The whites have always fought with the blacks and will never live in peace, except for now they are part of China. Phillip asks Lee how the Chinese will handle this. Lee tells us this nation will have Chinese and Non-Chinese. You are either Chinese or not Chinese. The highest qualifying factor is your production history, which reports your education, work history, family status, and any trouble with the party. This factor places you in an occupation. I ask Lee how important being married is. Lee claims it is extremely significant. Those who are working for their family produce more than those who are single do. Lee adds this does not mean you cannot have an occupation if you are not wedded, especially since most people obtain their occupational training before they marry. It will influence your promotions and relocations. Single people are transferred to open positions in other districts before married people are. The factor that controls all decisions is public wealth. This is why we do not own property. Even in the former states if you owned land and the government wanted it, they found a way to take it from you. They also made, you pay property tax on your perceived owned land. You did not own it; they did. They simply let you think you owned it, so they could take your money. Why not live in that house free and later if you want to move, you can submit your request to the party. If this move is possible and while you use your credits, you can move. We agree it is not fair to take public wealth for personal private desires.

Phillip asks Lee why these seven million Chinese are spreading out across this land. Lee reveals the Chinese have built many new factories in this country and are planning to open them. The qualified homeland citizens get first chance at these positions. Cindy asks Lee how we can become qualified. Lee tells her they will be translating the homeland qualification tests to English and examine the Americans. Those who pass will receive their occupation. Those who did not will be given the standard occupation exam and based on that will receive training for that work. Medical and other technical fields will be exempt from the test. Lisa asks Lee if the Chinese understand about American medications. Lee laughs and asks us if we realize where the important prescription drugs are made. Cindy tells us she always thought the pharmacist made these drugs. Lee tells Cindy the pharmacist merely puts the medication in a container and the instructions on the outside. They also give a large printout about this medication as most have the address where these pills were made, nevertheless, Americans throw these papers away. Cindy tells Lee reading those papers always gave her a headache and scared her from taking it. Phillip tells us he has never been to a doctor. His family has a remedy for just about anything. Lisa tells Lee that our mother and grandmother can cure almost anything. Lee confirms her mother, and grandmother can cure everything as well. Lee explains the good thing will be that all who can will have work and a chance to make their dreams come true. Lisa asks her what she thinks will happen to the blacks who live in the big cities. Lee reports the same thing will happen to all people, and the party will establish a minimum standard lifestyle. Those apartments that are not believed to be safe for people to live in will be destroyed, and modern homes built closer to the area's production centers. Lee advises us not to be surprised if new parks and public facilities emerge, where those old buildings were. The party is disappointed on how the United States let so many fine structures drop into ruin. We will clean it and rebuild.

Lee asks if we can sing a few songs and go to sleep. Lisa teases Lee that she just wants to sleep with her brother. Lee tells Lisa she wants to sleep with her brother every night for the rest of her life. Lisa, who is territorial, has a strange look on her face as she tells Lee this is good, since she knows Lee will protect her brother, and that means he will live longer. Cindy, who is patient, caring, understanding, and has never been jealous a day in her life explains to Lisa that Lee, will also protect her, and we will always fight to protect Lee. Phillip guides Lisa to their corner as Cindy makes a bold change in our sleeping order. She puts me in the middle. Lee asks Cindy why she did this and Cindy explains that she is scared when not sleeping next to her husband and this way we both can keep him with us. Lee smiles and tells Cindy if her husband makes one move to escape she will tackle him and bring him back. Cindy snuggles up to me resting her right elbow on my chest. I shake Lee a little and ask her if she wants to cuddle as well. Cindy tells Lee she will feel much better if she cozies up with her. Lee follows suit, except for holding Cindy's hands on my belly. Lee thanks Cindy for allowing her to sleep with them, and tells her it is okay if she wants to seduce her husband. Lee tells us so many couples had sex when sleeping in groups. They figured that if they did not do it then, they would never be able to do it. Cindy tells Lee she does not want to risk getting pregnant until she is in a stable environment. Lee tells Cindy she is too beautiful for the party to punish. They will allow her to live. Cindy asks Lee what she thinks the party will do to me.

Lee laughs and surmises that since I am so ugly, the party will tie a large stone to my feet and drop me into the river. I tell Lee this might hurt me. Lee laughs then get serious by telling us she does not realize what the party will do with us. They most likely will allow you to work. Lee tells us she is their point of interest.

The next morning Peter calls to inform us he received our personal identification cards. He did not receive one for Roberta, and our cards show a residence in Kansas and an occupation as a student. Peter asks Lee what this means. Lee asks him if he called the phone number on the cards. Peter tells her he does not see a phone number. Lee tells him to look at the photo identification. Below it will be a set of five numbers. Write them, and flip over to the back of the card and look at the last box and copy those five digits. That will be the number. They will be able to help us. Lee asks about the accuracy of the pictures. Peter tells us they are as if they were recent, except they do not have your windburns on your face. Lee tells him that is good; therefore, they must have been taken last summer when the mafia was setting up the national database. Peter wants to understand what data will go in this master database. Lee tells him they will eventually have all the data about that person in that person's database file. You can see how many credits he has saved; everywhere he spent his credits, every phone call he ever made not only the number but also the actual conversation. Everything will be linked and reached from one place anywhere in the world. Lee tells us to forget about a signal on your government cell phone. You will have one-hundred percent coverage everywhere, no matter the weather. I ask her how that can be. Lee tells us that when a signal is interfered with, it will go to another satellite and bounce it from other towers until that call goes through. Sometimes that can take up to two seconds. Peter tells Lee he has the cell phones in boxes here. A party technician is going to come to set them up for everyone. Peter tells us there is no fee for these phones, and everybody has been approved for their residence. Peter told us they asked him about the cabin in the woods our church owns. They claim that since there are no roads to it, it will be listed as recreational. Lee asks Peter what her occupation is. Peter tells her it is written in Chinese. Lee asks him slowly to describe the characters. Peter tells her it is one character and begins to describe it as Lee is drawing it on the ground. When finished, she tells us her occupation will also be a student. This is great news for Lee. Peter asks her what this mean. Lee tells us they will not judge or punish her.

She is excited about this news. This is as if we have a reborn Lee living with us. She is singing and dancing. I ask her what she will do now. Lee notifies us that she told her master that she wanted a higher occupation and to education to qualify for it. Peter calls back and tells us he spoke with a woman who is named Francis Johnson. He reports that a Chinese woman answered the phone first, and then when he spoke English, she called for an American woman to the phone. Peter began with his normal missionary recruiting message. He asked her how life is going and if the Chinese conversion is going for them. She asked Peter how it was going for him. Peter told her the free phone calls were helping him set up new branches in other areas. He asked her to describe her family. She told him they had three children run away, with two still alive, her son, who is married and her daughter. She explained the party offered her and a Chinese family, a large farm and an opportunity to share the largest house that they ever lived. Not only this, but the Chinese family also has grandparents who spend time with her husband's parents. Peter thanked her for her kindness and promised to call her when he established his branch in her area. Lisa became excited, knowing that her family was no longer in Marked Tree and in the possible grips of Mitch. Peter asks Lisa if she really believes Mitch is still a threat. Cindy tells Peter that she would put nothing beyond what Mitch would do. Although they are chatting Peter's radio stops ending their conversation. Cindy asks Phillip what happened. Phillip tells her Peter must have forgotten to charge his phone battery. We usually put in a new set of batteries every two days, just to be cautious since recharging is no option for us as there is no electricity in our area. Lisa and I felt relieved in knowing that our family was at least safe temporary. Cindy was so happy that they were living with another family. Lee tells us with this family being Chinese; they can obtain security from the Chinese party.

Lee had no way of knowing that Peter's phone was charged. Peter received a few unexpected visitors. A group of twenty party administrators rushed into Peter's home. They asked Peter to sit at their table, as the rounded the remaining family members into the living room, provided them certain snacks to eat while they watched the media on TV. The men played Peter the radio messages and asked Peter if he was willing to cooperate. Peter asked them why Lee's identification card listed her as a student. The administrators were impressed and asked him how he could interpret this. Peter told them he described the character to Lee, who told them what it meant. They ask if Lee is in good health. Peter assures them they are taking care of her to the best of their efforts and even yesterday; they took her horseback riding and sightseeing for most of the day. She could lie on her back, face the sun without her sunglasses. They praise Peter on the degree of his concern. Peter assures them that Lee is loved in this area and that the young kids with her care for her as if she were their own blood. These officials advise Peter; they believe him, and they have verified everything he told them. They have listed Lee as a student, because she will go to pre-occupational school with Lisa, Cindy, George, and Phillip. They congratulate him on Phillip and Cindy's marriage, although they believe Lee would have made a better wife. Peter tells them Lee is too devoted to Cindy and George and will not consider her life until theirs is stabilized. They confess to understand this. The leaders tell Peter it would be better if these kids staying closer to town where they can be protected, as they fear, rebels may try to harm them as a statement against our new government. Peter asks them if such a thing is possible. They told Peter that precisely a few days ago, they would never have thought anyone would kill three-hundred twenty-one blameless Americans just to slaughter innocent Chinese. These people had nothing to do with the American government's decision to surrender, and were here to help prevent mass starvation and chaos resulting from the fall of the American government.

Peter agrees that such cowardness was shameless. True rebels fighting for a just cause would have battles with the sword of justice. Peter claims this was the work of the devil. Peter informs the officials the mountain people will not offer sanctuary to anyone who claims to have been a part of this. The officials remind Peter that when a population believes their government cannot protect them; they will riot, loot, and destroy everything they can, especially if they can use a race card in the equation. This is why they want to promote stories and tales of positive race relations between the Chinese and Americans. They want to publish the adventures of Lee and the Johnsons. Somehow, there appears to be a force of love and bonding that sucks everyone who is around it into loyalty and devotion. Peter agrees that his little Lee is an angel from heaven. These men smile and report the way that even Peter claimed Lee, as he is so wonderful. This is spirit's bonding without regard to race. Peter looks at them strangely and asks them if Lee is Chinese. Peter's wife, who has slipped around the table beside them, tells them Lee is their daughter, so how can she be Chinese. One of the leaders asks them to explain why they believe with this many intensities. They tell these men that everyone knows Lee would die in a minute to protect her American friends and that her western brothers and sisters would die for her without question. They ask how these people understand this. Peter tells them it is written in their eyes, just as honesty is written in their eyes. Peter holds his wife's hands and tells them he will call these kids back. They will be here in a few days. The officials reveal that they will place several guards a few ridges back on each side to make sure they are safe. One of the men tells a member in his group to set up a house and to get three vehicles and their cards with credit, so they can set up their temporary home. He looks at Peter and tells him they will set up a two-week supply of food. Peter's wife informs them a few of the mothers will prepare the casseroles, pies, and country soups. The leaders smile and ask whether it will be okay for the media to visit these kids to get their story. Peter tells them if the kids approve it. The leaders remind them the media is an effective way to force the people to keep their promises. Peter agrees and promises to raise that argument with the kids.

The leaders provide, Peter with all the social documents these kids will need to reintegrate back into this new world. Peter asks them why they are setting them up here, and not taking them straight to Kansas to join with their family. They tell Peter this would not be wise until they can be sure Mitch is stabilized, in that they have reports he still may have emotions for her. Peter agrees this is smart. Peter calls Phillip on the radio and tells them they need to return to his farm as quickly as possible. He has information that a large fleet of planes and ground troops is going to clear this mountain. They will be searching for wood fireplaces first. He believes that they would have to go without heat for at least two weeks, which could be fatal. His area has already been cleared so they will be safe there. He will lead a crew to meet them. When they meet, he will set up warm tents heated by kerosene heaters for everyone and their animals at the Martin junction. Phillip knows where this is. They must continue until they find it. If the weather is bad, he will send roped guides to find them. Rope guides, plant special markers along the road with radio sensors that will help channel them back to camp. These are for whiteout conditions. They look outside and see a storm coming. Phillip tells them to load everything up tonight and have the horses packed. He also tells us to put out the best grain for these animals, so they can store up extra energy to fight this cold. They will leave about one hour before dawn. The first hour that they will walk, to get everyone loosened up, and then when the sun comes up, it is on the horses and on to the Martin junction. He also asks that our food be prepared and packed so we can eat and drink while still moving, so as not lose any time. Lisa asks whether they will rest. Phillip tells her they will rest when they are riding, and our horses will rest when we walk them. Phillip reminds us the conditions can change to be deadly within a flash during this time of the year, and a few minutes now could save hours later.

We understand the hazards this trip might be, yet also realize that no fireplace for a few weeks is out of the question. We must furthermore remember that even though we had no fireplace, the planes could have heat sensors, which would have picked up our livestock and us. Even the minimum this could trigger would be a humanitarian rescue. My bones adjust rather quickly, since I was outside yesterday with Cindy and Lee and on our five day (four outside) trip to Grandby. The sky is a dark overcast today, the somewhat overcast that could get nasty. Peter reports they have a medium storm that is passable. Phillip is leading our convoy riding our Oz. He believes that with its belly hanging lower it will clear snow making it easier for the horses to follow if a snow hit us. The Oz is not as easily scared as the horses, which adds to the stability of our animals. We brought Sunday and Easter with us. They are patrolling the surrounding areas. They are free spirited and adventurous dogs. We are confident about nothing or no one will sneak up on our sides. Bears are hibernating this time of the year, yet the wolves and mountain lions are still active. Cindy follows second; Lee is third, Lisa is fourth, and I am the rear guard. This means I see each time one of my angels goes to float against the edge and yell up for them to pull back to their right. They are attuned to my voice quickly and when I yell all three shifts. I am impressed with the way Phillip aligned this convey, so that the men are protecting the women. Phillip told me this was important in his culture, especially if a man does not protect his women, he will be shamed and even shunned. I had never given this much mind, because Roberta and Lisa were my overpowering heroes, which constantly rushed to my rescue.

When the sun came up, I noticed we made excellent time. It was wonderful to have such a jump so early in the day. We got on our animals, who appeared to enjoy the sunlight as well. Phillip sends back a message to wipe any snow off our boots and to wiggle our toes and fingers occasionally. He warns us against frostbite. He informs our women they can talk as much as they want because we have Sunday and Easter on our flanks. He figures the more they talk; the faster time will go for all of us. Phillip and I tend to enjoy listening to them chatter. We make it to noon when our first snowstorm hits. It is a total whiteout. Phillip runs a rope on the safe side connecting our animals and us. He advises us to walk on this protected side keeping one hand touching the hillside and the other keeping our animals on our side. These works excellent, especially considering the person in the front and behind can feel when the individual in the middle is drifting left and helps pull them back with the rope and verbal warnings. The snowstorm passes by in two hours, yet it did dump about eight new inches of snow. Now the wind will blow along this path shifting the snow. I can see why this path is so special, as the wind is coming from behind us and blowing directly along this path, pushing much of the snow into the valley below us. Phillip cheers us by revealing we are merely two hours by horse from Martin junction. We were moving steady through the storm and combined with the early start are still on track. It will be close to dark when we arrive there. We hope Peter will be there with the warm tent set up, and warm food. That is alone enough motivation to climb a cliff into the clouds. Lee begins one of her native songs, and we follow along with her. We have practiced this song many times. Therefore, we pretty well have it down pat. Phillip tries to follow with us and receives praise from Lisa for his efforts. He comments that it has a snappy rhythm that catches one by surprise. Lee tells him it is a tale about a family who moved from the mountains to a large city in hopes their dreams would come true. I tell Lee we will make her dreams come real.

Little did we realize the party was recording our conversations and became thrilled by the special bond they heard so much regarding. They decided to plan a national party parade for their entry into Grandby. This would be a few days henceforth, as they would give these kids a little time to settle with Peter, who would explain they had a church function in Grandby that wanted to meet them. It would be hard to refuse such an invitation considering the cabin they lived was owned by this church. For now, we simply hoped to the warm tent as we called it. Darkness fell, and once more; we ran our ropes and began walking beside our horses. Phillip told us he was beginning the final search. He asked Peter if they could flash a search light. Peter told him he would send up a flare. Phillip worried about the Chinese, while Peter told him, they were eating their dinner now, and it was safe. Up went the flare, and we saw it. Lisa always claimed this was the minute that she felt reunited with the outside world. Phillip tells Peter we will be there in twenty minutes. Peter tells him to take his time as they are setting up the tents. The snowstorm slowed them in the morning putting them a little behind schedule. We take our time noticing their bright lights from a small valley to our left. We eagerly rush in, hang up our jackets, and lay our gloves and hats beside the kerosene heaters. He had ten of them burning. A few of Peter's men cared for our animals as they rejoiced while receiving their grain and pat down their tired bodies. It always amazed me how animals can withstand such harsh weather, yet become excited when receiving heat. Peter has our meals heating on the stoves and provides us with rags and salves to regenerate our feet. The fresh pair of socks appears as early Christmas presents for me. Peter tells us we will begin tomorrow morning around six A.M., although he wishes, we could begin later; he knows we want to sleep in his warm house tomorrow night. We agree, eat, and snuggle in our sleeping bags. Lee jumps in Cindy and my sleeping bag. Peter asks about this and Lisa tells him Lee is our baby and sleeps wherever she wants. It is clear she is not budging without a fight, so Peter blesses them and slips off to the tent his gang is sleeping.

Five A.M. arrives; we eat, pack our daytime meals, as Peter does not approve stopping this time of the year in the mountains. Peter and half his gang lead the pack, while the other half follow in at the rear. Peter told the party to have the escorts tighten up because he feared they would suffer harm. He left meat scraps and dog food for them to feed Sunday and Easter. Once they feed them, they would be loyal. He would have his rear gang continue to plant food for them throughout the day. Sunday and Easter accepted these guards since they gave them their favorite dog food, meat, and called them by name. Our guard dogs sold us out for food. Peter put a handful of his special spices on the meat, which was a signal to the dogs that he was in favor of this union. Peter wanted his gang in the rear just in case the security forces blundered and became visible his gang would see them and not me or my angels. Phillip tried to join Peter in the front; however, Peter sent him back to Lisa telling him his place was beside his wife. Lisa agreed wholeheartedly on this when she hit Phillip for leaving her unprotected. Peter welcomes Phillip to married life. He reminds Phillip that anytime he sees him and his wife in public they are together. Phillip told him he always thought that was natural for them. Lisa tells Phillip that would be ordinary for us as well. Lee tells Lisa not to worry; she will make Phillip be a good husband. Peter laughs and informs Phillip he has no chance of escape now. Phillip looks at Lisa and asks Peter why he would want to escape. Lee smiles and reports the Phillip is getting the idea. Peter motions for our trek to continue. His mind is trying to process his experiences with Lee. What is so special about her that has bonded the Johnson clan and now evens a boy he helped raise? He knows Phillip and can see how in such a short time he is at total peace with Lee. A few short weeks ago, the Americans and Chinese were searching to execute her, yet now the Chinese want to parade her as a hero. Peter could see that Phillip will fight for Lee, no matter what cost.

Peter recognizes Cindy to be a woman whom so many men would fight to have. She has a lunatic named Mitch searching for her, and no matter what cost would try to capture her. Peter knows one thing, and that is Mitch will not be passed Lee when going for Cindy. Lee did not hide in Cindy's sleeping bag last night with Cindy and her husband. She leaped into it with full authority, the kind of mandate of belonging. That was where she belonged. Peter could only respect such executions of privilege. Peter could see this was going to be the Cinderella story of the new American states. Since it reduced the tensions between the races, he was for it. His former nation suffered enough from racism. Any fool could see how this new system was equalizing and leveling our wealth pumping it into a community's wealth. The media reported how much of the financing needed to save the American infrastructure was being provided by the public wealth of the homeland Chinese. He realized from the large shipments of fertilizer and seeds that were flowing into Grandby for distribution to the mountain farmers. A Cinderella story coming from these mountains would be instrumental in opening these mountains to the remainder of this nation. Peter knew these mountains needed opened because the remainder of this nation was moving ahead rapidly and could soon be so far in advance that they could never catch them. Peter prided himself as being critical and cautious. His former objection with the Chinese was they were taking America from America. This was no longer the case; China now owned and was responsible for the American people. They had two million troops in our former borders and complete control of the previous American military. They could save much money and completely execute these new legal slaves, yet instead they are trying to build a new unified productive society. Peter was relieved from the burden of so many fees, taxes, and regulations.

The caravan flows into Peter's farm that evening. Peter's men unload the supplies and then put the animals in his large barn. Peter's wife treats the gangs to a country-style dinner. She asks Phillip if his new family meets with the women at their church for lunch tomorrow. Lisa believes this will be exciting and a chance to show off Lee. Peter believes this will be better than their original plan of attending a service that evening. Peter plans to verify this later tonight. We meet the women for a special lunch at the church the next day. Lee marvels over the mountain traditional foods. Soon the media appears, scaring us as if feared this would lead to capture. Peter comes in and tells me we are safe and that America needs our story. We spoke about our ignorance of other cultures when we first met Lee. Accordingly, we explain how our original contact with Lee led us to believe she needed us, and we needed her. We could catch few sparkles in her eyes, which motivated us to continue. Lisa confesses that we had no idea that just by her speaking with us put her life in danger. When we discovered this, we decided that if she had to die, it would be over our dead bodies. When asked why she decided to trust the Johnsons, Lee reports her initial impression was these young people were insane, yet she believed they were honest and would never harm her. Lee continues as they lingered talking with her, the weaker she became to resist them and the more she had to be a part of them. The media ask Lee if she regrets her decision. Lee swears it was the greatest decision that she ever made. The media ask Lee if she is prepared to suffer the consequences for this relationship with her American partners. Lee tells them she hopes the people will solely punish her for bewitching these influential innocent American teenagers. Lisa and Cindy jump in front of her and declare they were the ones that kidnapped Lee and forced her to be their slave. Lee pushes through them declaring that Cindy and Lisa are lying. The media shifts the broadcast back to their station panel, which will now discuss this interview. I tell Peter that we need to make our escape quickly. Peter tells me to get the girls out front, and he will drive them out of this area.

We stream out front into a flood of people cheering us. I did not understand what to think about this. A group of Chinese men comes walking toward us. Lee tells us it is the party. They hold up certificates for the people and media to see. Lee tells us to stay put. The men come up to me, and one offers his hand to shake. We shake hands and he yells, "Welcome home, friends." Lisa passes out falling to the ground. Two of the men rush to revive her and once she is back on her feet; they present our citizenship papers, declaring we are the first people from the former United States to join Lee and become citizens and official members of the people's party. Lee will be the first Chinese servant to become a member of the party. I ask Lee what these papers mean. She tells us we are safe. She stands forward and announces to the media how thankful she is the party has shown so much mercy on them and hopes their works can prove productive enough to bring honor to these great leaders. These brought cheers from the crowd and the party's representatives rendering salutes to us. Peter tells us it is time to walk to our temporary home. Phillip stares at Peter with a shocked look and asks if he is telling the truth. Cindy asks him about our cabin. One of the party leaders tells us that party members do not live hidden in the mountains. Lee asks Peter to show us the way. Peter motions to the crowd that we are going to the party visitors' town house. Each town has living areas reserved for visiting party members. Lee explains that we can stay in these homes whenever in those towns. Lisa asks why we would be in those towns. Lee explains it is to our benefit to keep the peace between the people and the party. I tell Lee this sounded like unblemished advice and kissed her cheek. This kiss goes viral while causing the crowd to cheer. Lee, naturally swings around, wraps both arms around me, and kisses both of my cheeks. Accordingly, Cindy hugs both of us giving each of us a kiss. This was bobbled by the media as America's new Cinderella was flowing into every TV and cell phones making her debut as people of all races were rejoicing. Behind the scenes came congratulations from the central committee congratulating the Midwest party office for pulling this out of the graves that were recently covered in Saint Louis.

We walked to our new home and entered the front door with the party's representatives and Peter. We noticed a feast sitting on our dining room table. Peter guides us into the den where he passes out our identification cards, cards for our production credits, passports with visas, and official party member papers. The party spokesperson informs us that we may travel around the world if we so desire. Lisa tells them she would love to travel to Kansas when possible. The representative tells her that would not be safe until Mitch is stabilized. This is why they moved her family to Kansas. They want to keep us here now, because the mountain people are industrious in their defensive skills. Peter shakes his hand on this statement and tells us we will be safe, guaranteed. Everyone has a small catalog of pictures of Mitch with so many possible disguises. These images are on their cell phones. Mitch will never make it here, especially since he is under observation. Their primary concerns are his ability to disappear and then reappeared once more. Selected women knocked on our door and brought in various gorgeous dresses for my angels and suits for Phillip and me. They also brought in makeup and perfumes. Cindy and Lisa grab Lee and tell it is, time to play big girl. Phillip and I continue talking with Peter and the party's representative on what is ahead for us. I shake my head in disbelief that we are truly free and express my thanks for the gifts to our angels. Anytime they are happy we are excited. Peter reminds me that we are the sole former Americans who are truly free. I tell the spokesperson, we would have been happy just not to be executed. He laughs and agrees that most people prefer anything other than executions.

I ask him what he hoped to gain from this merciful act. The representative tells me he purely hoped for our honesty. He then asks me to turn on my cell phone. This first thing is envisioned is a site popping up from the media source showing Cindy and Lee kissing me. I forgot about this. They kissed me as I pulled out of our tight hugs. The man tells me these true human emotions can never be faked. They hope this will help create a safer and more productive nation so all may prosper. I tell him that I cannot perceive being with Cindy without Lee with us. I even feel naked without her now, yet am not worried because my Cindy with our leader Lisa puts me at total rest. Peter confesses not to understand it; nevertheless, he remains fascinated by it. I uncover to them; I held a precious scared trembling young Chinese's girl who told us her life now belonged to us. I could not, nor can we evermore, stop fighting to keep her life and love her for that great faith in us. No one ever had that much faith in us. It felt amazing to have someone believe in us; in fact, it felt so good we began to believe we could protect her just to discover she was the one who was saving us. I tell them that I believe with all my heart, we belong together forever. Parts of my speech hit the airways. I learned afterwards that Lee was one-year-older than us. This did not affect our class schedules as she took the same classes we took, even the ones she had already passed. Party members can take whatever classes they wish to take. Little did we know; we had created another great fan, one named

Wang Lien Hua, who was still living with our parents. When she saw us on TV, she fell to the floor crying and begging to go and stay with them, so she can spend a little time with them before they come home. My father calls an emergency family meeting with Wang Zhuo as the translator. He asked Lien Hua to wait outside the dining room. She, behaving as a western civilization child put a glass against the door, so she could eavesdrop. My father alleged that Lien Hua was stuck between the children and adults here and needed our sibling relationships. He thinks it is a sign of true family values that she would want to be familiar with Lisa, George, Cindy, and Lee. He believes that Lien Hua can help Lee to mold within our family and reduce the possible mystery and confusion from our children's family reunion.

Wang Chang asks about the interpretation and other coordination duties that Lien Hua performed. My father claims that we have four translators, and it is time we work harder to bridge our communication barriers. We cannot cheat Lien Hua from the niche in our family that belonged to her. The adults finally agreed, and ask Wang Zhuo to find Lien Hua. Lien Hua rushes to get free of the door, yet Wang Zhuo almost falls over her. She promises not to get her older sister in trouble and helps get her presentable to their elders. Lien Hua comes in, and her father tells her they will ask the leader's permission for her to join her brother and sister. My father's cell phone rings, confessing he was about to call them. He stops talking, as tears begin to fall from his eyes, and then asked how this could be. My father puts his phone down and tells us that several unknown terrorists just hit two centers in Memphis causing thousands to die. We got the same news in Grandby. I asked the representatives if they thought our videos caused this. They tell me that such an activity takes a long time to plan, especially when you perform it and escape being invisible. We later discovered that Mitch was concentrating so deep on this slaughter that he disregarded the news. The party asked Lee and me to make a speech, with Cindy at my side. We made the speech telling Americans this was murder. Lee and Cindy wore their silk dresses as I stayed in my mountain clothes. Cindy and I kissed Lee, which seemed to be popular, and then we raised her hands. I ask our audience to help keep America free from the slaughter of innocent people who are here helping us have a land to raise our children. Cindy claims the people who loved murdering large groups of people would grow tired of killing the Chinese and return, as they did in Saint Louis, killing Americans. Lee reminds us those who were slaughtered gave up their homelands to join the awesome task of preventing starvation and mass chaos. We did not want to see you lose your families, for parents to watch their neighbors slaughter their children and loot their homes. Lee cries how her people died because they worked for the good of others.

Lee asks American not to kill her, because she wants to work for a joint future where all will prosper and are equal. Cindy ended the message by begging America to punish those who kill in cold blood. Our message spread over America. When Mitch saw Cindy on TV, he once more began his obsession, yet realized if she was free and a party member he had to walk on his toes. He knew Cindy was a party member, because the media must disclose this with their facial images. This added to Lee's claim of working together so all may prosper. America saw an American girl who was a stockholder in not only America but also China. Cindy's party membership was one of the primary reasons the party would not approve Mitch's visit. A visit to a party member required a complete background check, which was now nothing more than a simple computer inquiry into the master database. This request also initiated surveillance over Mitch. They did not realize that they were watching their greatest enemy. We went to the funerals as China buried their dead in a national cemetery built in upper Texas. The Memphis victims joined the Saint Louis victims. The Americans were buried with the Chinese, which helped foster their 'we are one family' image. We cried that entire day, as images of Roberta flashed all day. We were shocked at the last grave we went to honor, who had a wonderful enclosed area. We told each other; whoever is buried here is special. Lisa looked into the casket and began to scream. The party had patched Roberta and brought her here to rest in peace. Phillip told them about Roberta and for them to bring her here to be buried. He was a party member so his order was executed. Phillip tells us the Roberta was awarded party membership, so she is buried in this section of honor. We walked around to the front of her marble double life-size statue had a face that was colored to portray her actual real-life face. We invite the press over and tell them the true story about Roberta and our revenge. Lisa and Cindy remain calm when Lee tells about the castration. Lee is filled with so much anger when telling this. It was so evil that three demons would degrade a teenage girl, such as this, and they deserved even harsher than she could deliver. The crowd and nation cheered her. This was a true test of the depth and devotion of the Johnsons as they were now labeled. The media painted this as how the Chinese will protect their friends.

This message was taking hold in a positive manner, trying to remove much of the distrust and replace it with teamwork. We lowered Roberta into the ground and asked for blankets, so we could rest here tonight. They tried to set up a tent. We asked them not to set up the tents as it might invade someone else's eternal space. They brought us several kerosene heaters as we huddled tightly. Lisa, Lee, and I did not sleep, but talked with Roberta all night. Cindy and Phillip fell into a deep slumber. As one of us would ask a question, the other would answer it, sometimes realistically and other times with comedy. When morning came, we were ready to head back home. We felt good that Roberta was buried among so many others who were innocent when they were slaughtered. She was buried as a citizen to a nation that did not exist at the time of her death. The public submitted so many requests for Lee, Cindy and me. Lisa and Phillip were given more time to develop their relationship. We soon discovered there would be another join us. I asked our party friends if our family could get citizenship status. They submitted our request to the central committee who believed this would be a great idea and approved it for both the Johnsons and the Wangs. The leaders came to my father's farmhouse the next morning and told them the pronounced news. The Wangs were surprised and honored. My father asked if Lien Hua could visit Lisa. The leader told us she could go wherever she wants when she wants. Lien Hua tells him she needs someone to take her to Grandby, as she rushed upstairs to grab her clothes. My mother calls Lisa and reports that her special Chinese daughter wanted to spend a little time with them and become a part of them. Lisa, Lee, and Cindy tell our mother, they cannot wait and ask about the kind of food she likes and things she wants to do.

My mother tells Lisa that she is a wonderful daughter, Cindy is a perfect daughter in law, and that Lee will be her angel daughter with Lien Hua. My mother asks when we are coming home and cries how she misses us. Cindy tells her they have concerns about Mitch. She will give him one year to recover and then had him imprisoned and come home. My mother understood, especially since she and my father were secretly fond of Mitch. Lee is so excited that a seventeen-year-old Chinese girl will be a sister. She tells us that in her homeland, it is considered a gift to have a sister. This is so rare in that all homes just have one child. Many parents are permitted to adopt another child if that child is from the community, and parents were died. Lee tells us she will have so many sisters now to include Julia. She did not about Mei and Ju-Long, who brought her great joy throughout the remainder of their days. Lien Hua arrived in Grandby the same time that we return from the funerals. She was so excited in meeting us. I laugh at Lisa and tell her I would be too shy to introduce myself. Lisa calls me a nut asking how a man who sleeps with two girls can be bashful. Lee tells Lisa that I am the bravest man in the whole world. Lien Hua asks me if I protect her. She is wearing an enchanting dress, with makeup and looking just as gorgeous as Lee. I look at her and complain about the heavens hating me because they made the two most beautiful Chinese girls my sister. Lisa hits me and asks what other things the heavens did. I tell Lien Hua and Lee the heavens also gave me the most beautiful American girl as a sister. Lisa smiles and pats me on my head telling this group we are so lucky to have George as a brother. I tried to move pass this and get to experience my new sister.

Lee taught us how special the love from a new family member. We were moving away from noticing our racial differences. It really was not that hard, because the smile was our family trademark and Lien Hua had our smile. I could feel our mother's influence on her. Lien Hua was so excited, and she declared her love for every one of us. Lee tells her Phillip is married, and she is not allowed to love him or Lisa will get angry. Lisa tells Lien Hua that Phillip is part of our family, and she may be devoted to him, just as she loves George. Lee winks at Lien Hua whose face is returning to its normal color. Our sleeping arrangements changed that night as Lee and Lien Hua now sleep together and talked all night. Lee was extremely tired the following day, having stayed up two nights in a row with limited naps yesterday. We decided to rest the next day. Lien Hua and Lee would lock on to Cindy and me during the day. Cindy and I enjoyed their companionship and became addicted to them. They gave us our nights, which was special. Later, Lee apologized for sleeping with us, telling us she did not realize this was incorrect. Cindy tells Lee this was not wrong because we could not let her sleep alone. Lien Hua tells Lee that if this is the situation, it is honorable. Lien Hua tells us she will protect Lee now. We added Lien Hua to Lee, Cindy, and me for our public speeches. She understood our plight. One afternoon, the TV ran a special nationwide report about how the gang, who murdered in Memphis and Saint Louis, was captured. I fell to the floor when I saw it was Mitch. We were so shocked. Cindy called the Marked Tree police and told the police to get them to prosecution and court immediately. I looked at Lien Hua and told her she may have to introduce me to our new brothers and sisters. The judgment and execution of Mitch and his gang were swift. We gained popularity as the ones who escaped the most evil murderer in our short history. On returning to Kansas, we received the neighboring farm. Our parents let us keep Lien Hua, who was now so complete. She transferred to our university and took the same classes. Lien Hua and Lee refused to marry and instead cared for our children. I always told Cindy and Lisa the saddest thing in our life now was no mates for Lien Hua and Lee. We would try to match them with men, yet they would order them to leave. The party used them to settle disputes between the Chinese with each other. The Chinese loved them believing them to be fighting for their future in a safe and secure environment with the former Americans.

Lee and Lien Hua did many great things for our union, as did the Wangs and Johnsons. I usually settled conspiracy allegations. Our family was given complete access to all government projects and plans. This was one-hundred percent transparent. They opened all the files in the Ministry of State Security and the National Administration for the Protection of State Secrets. This new master database automatically translates the Chinese to English. We would never release any intelligence that has the 'must stay top secret code.'

I simply tell the public if it had elements that could be harmful to our American security. The few things I found were immediately rescinded. The party would apologize and tell us the massive volume of information is sometimes difficult to maintain. I could see by the overall themes that a joint society where all work together and share the wealth. We saw so many projects appearing the plans called for undertaking years in advance. I asked to be notified before each project began ahead of time. Cindy, and either Wang Mei or Ju-Long, and I would go to make a big deal how the peoples' production was getting them extra public awards. This turned out to be a great motivator. That is what the Johnsons, Lee, and the Wangs did motivate, and help keep the peace. We prided ourselves in keeping the peace. Life was so much better for so many currently, and at the same time not as good for the former wealthy, who now worked with the masses. There were no homeless people or old people cast from their homes. I really cherished the fact the people from the third world nations were no longer terrified by the Eagle that flew no longer. All the fear that drove us from our world and love that moved us into these modern American States of China was now cherished memories. The party was transparent because there was nothing to hide. No longer were we walking around bragging about how you are free when your government bleeds you financially. We now share for the public good. My children will receive the education beside the children from non-party members. Previous segregation was dissolved. The lone difference is that party members wear a large red band around their left wrist. It is welded together and may never be removed. I recognize our foundation is getting strong enough for a future invasion of Canada, as they will someday share in the wealth of this mighty Empire.

Index

K

L

M

N

P

Q

S

T

U

W

Z

The other adventures in this exciting series

Prikhodko, Dream of Nagykanizsai
Search for Wise Wolf
Seven Wives of Siklósi
Passion of the Progenitor
Mempire, Born in Blood
Penance on Earth
Patmos Paradigm
Lord of New Venus
Tianshire, Life in the Light
Rachmanism in Ereshkigal
Sisterhood, Blood of our Blood
Salvation, Showers of Blood
Hell of the Harvey
Emsky Chronicles
Methuselah's Hidden Antediluvian Abridgment

Author Bio

James Hendershot, D.D. was born in Marietta. Ohio, finally settling in Caldwell, Ohio where he eventually graduated from high school. After graduating, he served four years in the Air Force and graduated, Magna Cum Laude, with three majors from the prestigious Marietta College. He then served until retirement in the US Army during which time he earned his Masters of Science degree from Central Michigan University in Public Administration, and his third degree in Computer Programing from Central Texas College.

His final degree was the honorary degree of Doctor of Divinity from Kingsway Bible College, which provided him with keen insight into the divine nature of man. After retiring from the US Army, he accepted a visiting professor position with Korea University in Seoul, South Korea. He later moved to a suburb outside Seattle to finish his lifelong search for Mempire and the goddess Lilith, only to find them in his fingers and not with his eyes. It is now time for Earth to learn about the great mysteries not only deep in our universe but also in the dimensions beyond sharing these magnanimities with you.